Luv Alwayz:

The Opposite Sex & Relationships

08

Luv Alwayz:

The ⊛ Opposite Sex & Relationships

Shonell Bacon & JDaniels

A

PUBLICATION

A STREBOR BOOKS INTERNATIONAL LLC PUBLICATION

DISTRIBUTED BY SIMON & SCHUSTER, INC.

Published by

S3I

Strebor Books International LLC
P.O. Box 10127
Silver Spring, MD 20914
http://www.streborbooks.com

ISBN 0-9711953-1-5

LCCN 2001091788

Distributed by Simon & Schuster, Inc.
1230 Avenue of the Americas
New York, NY 10020
1-800-223-2336

Cover Illustration: © *Andre Harris*
Typesetting and Interior Design: Industrial Fonts & Graphix

First printing November 2002
Manufactured and Printed in the United States
10 9 8 7 6 5 4 3 2 1

Dedications

Shonell Bacon

In my life, there has always been three people who seemed to know that I could write and would write and pushed me even when I began to doubt myself; my grandparents, Charles "Pop Pop" Bacon (1929-1998) and Audrey "G" Bacon (1931-1998), and my mother, Brenda Henson. If I never get praise from anyone else BUT them, I would still feel oh so blessed. Love you...here and up THERE.

JDaniels

This is dedicated to u mama:

When no one else believed, u did...
When there was no one who felt I would achieve, u did...
When no one else cared enough to press me forward, u did...
When no one else felt I was ahead of the rest, u believed all these things.
U luved me, u believed in me, u were my greatest fan.
U listened and smiled and clapped your hands with ever bit of poetry and prose I would pen.
U never got bored, u never got tired of reading my stories, of listening to my lyrics, music and songs, and u helped me never to lose the faith, u helped me to stay strong.
And thru all my struggles and pains, u knew I would find my way, and u knew that thru it all that one day I'd stand tall, *U KNEW*. And your luv molded me to who I am today, and so for that, till the earth's dying day mama, thank u, and Luvalwayz...

Acknowledgments

Shonell Bacon

Have to give another shout out to my mother for her love and support, as well as to family and friends who DID believe in me…it meant everything that you did. Thanks go out to the following people who assisted me personally in some point of my writing dream: Bonita Bennett, who gave my self-esteem and dream a boost with her praise of my tenacity and ability to be a good writer; my cousin Danyell, who's read just about everything I've written and has been a great lover and critic of it all; Aspiring African American Romance Writers Forum, Black Writers Alliance, Daily Diva, TimBookTu, Sisterfriends, Shades of Romance magazine, and my baby and literary love, The Nubian Chronicles. All of these online forums and communities have allowed me to express my love of writing and to not only interact with wonderfully talented writers, but to receive kudos for my writing. Much love goes out to my partner-in-crime, JDaniels. We met online, and through our online connection, literary magic was created…and we had a blast doing it! And to Tee of RAWSISTAZ, thank you profusely for reading LUVALWAYZ and using your critical eyes…it helped greatly! Love ya, Sis! Last, but not least, I want to thank Zane for believing in our work and helping us to achieve our literary dream…there will never be enough THANK YOUS to show you how much your advice has meant to us!

People can encourage you in different ways. They can encourage you by the traditional 'you can do it' way, or by the 'this is just a whim' way. I would like to thank them all. First of all, I would like to thank my immediate family, most whom have been just as hyped as I am about my goal of being a published writer, a goal I have had since forever. Those who know me most have been my cheerleaders from the start, I love you, and I thank you. (LOOKS LIKE WE MADE IT!) Special love to my spiritual sister and friend, **Cathy**…Te amo hermana, y abrazos! **Angel, Sean, Junnie, Tony**, I LOVE YOU!!! Love to my mom and my dad. **Dad,** your quiet praise for my efforts means more to me then you will ever know…I would like to give special thanks to some close online friends of mine who have been there for me through thick and thin, reading and being both my critics and my encouragers, both which was vital to me to get to this point. Shonie, you know that you were a main link in my growth as a writer, and it's been a pleasure working with you, ONE LUV sistah. Sharon (**Candygirl!**)**,** you have always been there for me, thanks and I love you. Virginia (***V***), you always believed, even when I didn't, and whether my novels or stories are good or bad, I know that with you, I have a fan forever. Warmth and love to the lady from the land down under! **Zane**! Thanks for your belief in us, and your support for us! Thanks to the supporters of *The Nubian Chronicles*, and the many writers and readers who pushed and encouraged the publishing of *Luvalwayz*. And last but not least, the people whose love and relationships have aided us in putting together an off da hook novel based on the undeniable love that flows in the veins of all African Americans. Those true characters, the real Chris and Tamaras, Joop and Shameikas, and Stephen and Deandras. We know you are out there, proving again and again, that for every broken relationship, for every negativity in some black relationships, there are the positive ones, the normality of falling in love, and building and having stable loving relationships. This is your story. ***Luvalwayz***

Luvalwayz...

By: JDaniels

Woman

One breath, one heart, one future planned one thought; we'll take a chance expanding on this love....
I hope, you see, that what you feel for me, is equal to my all consuming love... You see...
When the sun...cast its shining glow, and the stars'...twinkle gleams below, then we know we have found our way, and we know, it will always stay, we can say and have faith till the earth's dying day...Luvalwayz...

Man

No doubts, no fears, no wishing wells no tears, no misty clouds our hopes are very clear...
Believe, it's true, that what I feel for you, will last thru years until infinity... We'll be...
Like a child...with a spinning top, our sweet love...girl will never stop, yes we know, we have found our way, and we know, it will always stay, we can say and have faith till the earth's dying day...Luvalwayz...

Both

I was lost...now I've found my way (found my way), clicked

my heels...(boy/girl you're here to stay), there's no way, I will ever stray, we can say and have faith till the earth's dying day... Luvalwayz... Luvalwayz... Luvalwayz...

PART ☆ ONE:

Christopher & Tamara

Tamara. . .

Everything I learned about men, I've learned from my parents, Isabelle and Terrence Styles. They've been married for over thirty years, but they act like newlyweds. My dad often tells me about the first time he saw Mom. He was just starting out as a journalist and was covering a protest at the local university. That was all the information he was given...a protest, go and cover it. As he approached the Quad, the center of the campus, he heard the sweetest voice to ever grace his ears, my mother's. Heard her speak, strong and loudly, of the racial injustice that was taking place on *her* campus and what needed to be done to try and bring racial harmony. Upon reaching the Quad, he watched this tall beautiful creature speak fervently, igniting thunderous approval from the masses around her. At the end of her speech, he smiled and *knew* that this outspoken woman would be his.

Every time I hear that story, every time I see the love in my parents' eyes and know that they still love each other, I want that. I want what they have. It wasn't always easy for them, but with that foundation of love, it made it that much easier to get through the rough patches. I actually went out into the world, expecting to find some love like that, and I wound up falling flat on my face, time and time again.

Nowadays, we're all so *hard* on ourselves. You have sistahs

3

in one corner calling all the brothas dogs and womanizers and you have all the brothas on the other side calling us sistahs gold diggers, just wanting someone to give them cash for giving up the ass. You hear nothing about the good sistahs and brothas that do grace the Earth. Makes me wonder if there are any more out there. Besides me, that is.

I dunno, everyday, it gets harder and harder to find a good, decent man. I didn't say finnnnnne. I didn't say rich. I didn't say weak. I said good and decent. Someone who treats you as an equal. Someone who is your friend and your lover. Now, I'm not knocking the other things. I would be lying if I said a fine man didn't have me doing a double take, but looks fade. True love and admiration can last a lifetime. And that's what I want.

I'm so tired of meeting Mr. Wrong. Got a sistah thinking she's doing something wrong. I'm educated and I work very hard every day as an at-home web designer. I've been told that I have a sunny disposition. I can cook up a storm, I can sit back and wax intellectual with a man, or I can chill and watch a basketball game and actually know the haps of it. I don't think I'm ugly and I love to meet people. So why can't I meet someone that will treat me like the queen that I am?

Mm, mm, mm. This gets me hot. I don't think I'm weak in any way for saying I want a man...that I need one. He won't *complete* me, but to have someone that I can cry to, laugh with, talk to, play with, and then, after a long day, cuddle with and make love to until we both just fall asleep in exhaustion? WHEW...sign me up cuz I want some of that. Now, my relationships have been few and far between, but they have all been bad. Had one that actually tried to lay a hand on me and, after one time, he almost lost *his* life. The next man wasn't satisfied with just me. NO, he had two other women on the side, and when I finally found out — easy seeing that he and the trick were screwing in MY bed, in my apartment — I just politely threw them both out and rolled on, as I tried to heal my wounds, the wounds of getting kicked around by these damn men. My last relationship...excuse me while I laugh for a hot minute.

WHY? Please, someone, tell me why this man wined me, dined me, told me everything that my ears wanted to hear, bought me things, took me places, loved me till I came too many times to count, gave me keys to his car and his apartment? Oh, wait a minute. Did I tell y'all he didn't give me one important key? That would be the key to his five-bedroom house, the one that housed his wife of ten years, and his three children, ages three to nine. I can't even begin to tell y'all what that did to me. For a minute, I thought he was the one. I don't remember crying that much, *ever*. He took my heart, my smile, my tears, my trust, and my care for men. But most of all, he took away the thought I always had, that I was smart, smart enough not to get duped.

I don't know why, but it seems like every time I hear a tale like this, it's coming out the mouth of an intelligent, attractive black woman. I mean, what is going on? Are we so smart in our careers and achievements and compassion that we have lost our common sense? I dunno, but I do know that he left a very bitter taste in my mouth and it took over a year for me to approach or allow a man to approach me.

It was odd because I really wasn't trying to meet anyone after that first year. I was getting used to not having someone. Hanging with my girl, Shameika, reading, going places with friends, just hanging. But when this guy stepped up to me one day, I almost fell over myself to say hi. I was chilling in the park, lying on a blanket with my headset on and reading a book, when I felt a shadow looming over me. There stood a tall — about 6'2" — light-skinned brotha with a body that led to some heated thoughts. He looked down at me, smiling, and told me with his full suckable lips that he just came over to say hi. He had seen me a couple times here at the park while he was jogging and he had just gotten the courage to come and say hi and to tell me that I was the most beautiful woman he had seen in a while. Now if that ain't a line!!

But it hooked me in. That night, Chris and I went to a quiet restaurant for dinner and talked about so many things — sports, jobs, music, people we saw while we ate, any and everything. After dinner, we took a long walk along the lake adjacent to the park and just talked about whatever popped into our heads. I must admit, the brotha had it going on. He was taking time off work as a computer specialist to write. He was so animated as he talked about his writing that I was getting excited for him. He recited one of his poems to me and I was impressed. It was hard to look at him and hear him say he wasn't seeing anyone. Even through his slacks and jacket, I could see the tightness of his body and how attractive he was. His voice had one of those drippingly sexy tones and his eyes and smile just invited you in. As much as I was enjoying this, I had to keep in mind that he was probably doing this tomorrow night with another chick.

The evening, much too fast in my opinion, ended at my doorstep. He told me how much he enjoyed being with me and I replied likewise. He then gave me a kiss, a very soft, tempting kiss, and said goodnight. Left me on my doorstep with my eyes closed and my body warm. I didn't remember getting a kiss like that from anyone before, especially with them just leaving afterwards. I shook it off and laughed, walking into my apartment.

That was six months ago, and since then we have been each other's significant other. Not to say it's been happily ever after, because it has not been. I realized that he had many women before me and that, for the most part, it was all about sex. Fuck buddies or FBs is what he called them. Every time I saw one of his "friends" I immediately clinched inside, waiting for the shit to hit the fan. It never did, well hasn't, YET.

It's actually been pretty good, minus my slips into my favorite game — GUESS WHEN YOUR MAN WILL SCREW UP. We've been taking turns staying at each other's place and doing all those couple thangs. I'm trying really hard to open myself up. I told Chris about my last relationship, but left the other two out. Most men are afraid to hook up with a sistah who has emotional baggage, fearing that they will suffer the wrath. So, I figured I would keep the wrath inside of me and just try to imagine this thang between him and I as something that could last.

It's not the longest relationship I've been in, but it's the "realest" one, and to find someone like Chris, I just have to try not to mess it up with my thoughts and hope that he doesn't do anything to make me regret loving him. It just seems like whenever I start getting close to a man, and he starts throwing that love word up in things, or better yet, that IN love thang, things go downhill fast. I admit, I love Chris, more than he knows, but every time I utter those words, or hear him say them to me, my heart prepares for the day when I won't hear those words anymore.

Chris...

I guess everybody has it sooner or later. Some people seem to catch it prematurely and some are just plain late. Me, I think it happened just at the right time. I wasn't looking for her; I wasn't looking for anything, except maybe an agent. I had women I would date, but Tamara, everything changed when she came into my life. She wasn't just a date. She was a drawn out plan of action. For a while there, I didn't even know how to talk to her. I would get all nervous and shit. I was used to women coming on to me, giving me the play. I never had to do anything but sit and look pretty. Okay, I have to laugh at that one, but it's the truth! But when Tee came into my world, all that changed. She changed me and made me start thinking new thoughts of forever. I saw her, I wanted her, she was just too lovely...I swallowed my normal feelings of "no way am I giving a lady a chance to say get lost," and I approached her. And ever since then, I've been in a blissful zone. So happy that it's almost scary.

Before I met Tamara, I felt like I had been running game,

always looking for that new ass to hit, that new FB to call up for a fix. Of course, it was all on the DL. Women thought I was sweet and that's the way I liked it. It worked like a charm every time. It was the way I worked. My college roommate and I used to kick mad game, but I was the quiet, shy one, or so the ladies thought. But Stephen, also my frat brother, he was then and still is the in yo face type of brotha. Women never got confused about what he was after. We used to get a kick out of which of us could mack the most women, and which of our techniques worked better. Those were the fun days, but a man can change, you know? And I guess I did. This was my first; okay not my first relationship, but the first time I felt like settling down. I guess now at twenty-nine I'm ready for more, need more, maybe looking for that perfect union.

Tamara…well she spends a lot of time at my place, which is cool by me because basically I just love looking at her. She has this raw appeal about her and homegirl sassiness that is a complete turn on to me. And yet she's this good girl, you know what I mean? The type you marry. We started this romance, she dug me, I dug her, and nothing else really mattered except that fact. At least, that's what I thought…

I was working hard, trying to finish a tough chapter. I don't know where the mind freeze was coming from, but I just couldn't seem to get my thoughts together. I don't know if it was writer's block or not. All I knew was that nothing was coming out of my imagination, which was vital to me as a writer. So I got up early in the morning like I always did for writing sessions, and tried to make my thoughts fab together.

At first I didn't hear Tamara come into my computer room. Then I felt her, biting at the back of my neck, and then…well, you know, I was 'bout it 'bout it. She still had on her nightgown, so I grabbed her by the waist, sat her on my desk with her legs around my waist, dropped my pajama pants, and sunk deep inside her with one swift, forward thrust of my hips.

"Chris, you don't have on a condom," she moaned, "but, damn, you feel good..."

"Come on, Tamara. Just this once...this is you and me, Babe. It's okay."

"Oh, mmm...we shouldn't. What if I get pregnant?"

"Shh...come on..." I pulled out and thrusted deep inside her again, feeling the pleasure building as she wrapped her sexy legs around my hips, still purring no, as we began a mutual rhythm of satisfaction. Soon we were both covered with sweat and moaning like crazy. I felt as though my ears were ringing and that all the feelings in my whole body were concentrated into one as I held and squeezed her to me, feeling her squeeze me as though she was doing her Kegel exercises. I could tell when Tamara started coming, feeling her contracting around me, triggering my own climax, both of us screaming out when the moment hit.

"I love you, Tee..." I moaned. Opening my eyes to look into hers, hmm...I could see the doubt in her eyes, even through the passion.

"You know you really didn't have to say that," Tamara said quietly as I moved off her. She got up to head for the bathroom, leaving me with my thoughts. When she returned, I looked up at her, breathing deeply. I was nervous, but I realized I couldn't just let the subject die, that my feelings for this woman were real.

"I know I didn't have to say it, Tee, but you know I really mean it right? Every time I tell you I love you, you always say I don't have to say it, but I say it because it's the truth." I turned her face toward mine, trying to read her eyes. What was it about I love you that turned her off so much?

"I know Chris, and I love you, too," she said, biting her bottom lip. "I need to shower, and you do too. Me first." She smiled, getting up abruptly and heading out of the room.

Tamara . . .

With the bathroom door firmly closed behind me, I leaned against it, trying to catch my breath. In short steps, I padded over to the medicine cabinet and stared at my reflection. I was *beaming*. Who wouldn't after being wrapped up in sexual motions with their man? My smooth cinnamon-brown face had a glow to it, and my brown eyes were shiny and bright. Mindlessly fingering through the wild, wavy locks of my hair, I tried to pay no mind to the tears that were leaving tracks down my round cheeks.

"Tee," I whispered to myself, "it's okay. He *loves* you, Girl. You. He doesn't want anybody else." It was like my mind and my heart were playing two different games. Logically, I knew Chris loved me, but in regards to my heart, it had been stepped on one too many times for me to just give him ME: lock, stock and barrel.

"Leaving me already?" Chris asked, as I waltzed out of the bathroom with a towel wrapped around me, headed to the bedroom. In fluid motions, I stripped off the towel, and slipped on a pair of panties and a bra, along with a pair of jeans and tee shirt, all of which were located in the bottom drawer of Chris' dresser. Now tell me we weren't a couple?

Hopping into my Adidas while I dropped my dirty clothes in my backpack, I made my way back into the computer room, where Chris was sitting at his computer, waiting for a response to his question. His face read worried, and I didn't want him to doubt me, doubt us. Not after this morning.

I walked up to Chris, situating myself between his legs to bend over and kiss his mouth. "Well, Baby," I whispered, dropping another kiss on his lips, "I have some things to do today before we have our dinner tonight with the mothers. Sorry for the swiftness."

Looking down at Chris, I noticed the uncertainty in his eyes. "Are you okay, Tee?" he asked, reaching to take my hands in his. Blinking back the tears that wanted to fall, I smiled, kissing his hands. "I'm *very* fine, Baby," I reassured him. "Now lemme get outta here, and try to do some thangs before the dinner with our *mothers*."

Blowing kisses, I picked up my backpack and quickly walked through Chris' apartment to the front door. Before I had the chance to open it, Chris was behind me, spinning me into his arms to kiss me deeply, making me remember in all the heat the affect he had on me. "Mmm," I moaned, my eyes fluttering open. "Boo," Chris said, looking deeply into my eyes, making me shake inside of my bones.

"Yes, Baby."

"You know I meant what I said…right?" He continued to stare at me, and I was torn. I could feel the truth in his voice, see it in his eyes, but my heart was telling me not to swoon, to be smart.

"I know you meant it, Baby," I said, smiling, kissing him again. "I know, and I love you, too, Christopher." With that, I gave him one last kiss as he opened the door for me and I made moves to my ride. "See you tonight!" I yelled as I quickly left and headed home.

I have to backtrack a minute…I can't believe I let Chris sex me up without a condom. No matter how heated I've been in the past, I have always stopped for the jimmy hat. This time, I just let him. I said no, but a part of me didn't care because of how I feel about him and knowing that we're only with each other. But, damn, that was stupid of me. I'll have to hope and pray that nothing comes from this. The last thing I want to do is have a Baby's Daddy or get married or stay with a man because of a baby. I have a plan for all this. I prefer to go marriage THEN family and not vice versa.

I was so caught up in how Chris was making me feel. How good it was to be connected to him totally and feeling his love for me. I forgot all about my insecurities, or the fact that he didn't have a condom on, and just let myself fall into the lovemaking that we were experiencing. Baby was working me just the way I love being worked and then he said he loved me and I could feel myself stiffen. I know he felt it, too, but I couldn't help it. It scared the shit out of me.

Women are always talking about how men don't open up and say how they feel, but I admit women do this, too. I've been in love with Chris for a minute, but I have never told him. I couldn't. I was too afraid of getting rejected, of having my heart smacked and drop kicked.

I wonder how many of his FBs he told *I love you* to. See, *this* is the kind of mess my mind goes to when it's scared, thinking about his *other* women. I know there was the one girl he said he was gon' marry back a while ago, but he screwed it up.

I wonder if he loved her more than me. I wonder if he still has feelings for her. People say don't ask questions if you don't wanna know the answers. I don't know if I really want to hear the answers to those questions, but I can't help but think them.

Damn, I really love that boy and I don't want this to mess up. Okay, okay, there are more pressing matters right now, like trying to smile in front of our mothers tonight for Mother's Day. I know they have been waiting for some bells, but they ain't happening yet. I read somewhere that people who say they need months and years before they can decide to marry someone are just making excuses. They're just waiting to fall "in love" with that person. But in actuality, a person can know within weeks, months, of being with someone if they can mesh together, if they have what it takes in all aspects — personality, attraction, loyalty, etc.. — to make a relationship last forever.

I do feel that way for Chris. I love him, and I am *in* love with him. But, at the same time, I have this trust issue to resolve, and I have to *feel* beyond a reasonable doubt, that Chris honestly and truly feels that way for me. I won't settle for anything less.

Chris . . .

I spent the rest of the day lost, enveloped in a world that was not my own. I was flowing like you wouldn't believe. I became Julian Harris, my main character, fighting tooth and nail for his life in a courtroom tailored against black males in the early sixties. I had done a lot of research for this one. I had wanted to make sure that everything was true to life and that my writing had believability and literary merit behind it. Besides, it hadn't hurt to have Joop, a good friend of mine, in my corner. Being a History teacher and all, he had schooled me on any of the civil rights history that I had forgotten.

I ran my hands over my face. I was sweating and could almost feel Julian's hurt and righteous anger because of the unfairness of the times. I even shedded a few tears of my own as I wrote about his mother's feelings and the hardships she had to go through, raising a young black boy in the sixties. Okay, okay, I'm the one writing this joint, but can't a man have his sensitive moments? I feel the way one of my English professors used to say we should feel when we write. If I can't feel it, if it doesn't effect MY emotions, then nobody else is going to feel it either.

Just as I was wrapping up a draining courthouse scene, the phone rang.

"Hello?"

"Chris, Chris! Wassup brotha?" I immediately recognized Step, my college roommate, and one of my best friends.

"Not much, man. What trouble are you getting into?" Looking down at my watch, I was amazed at how quickly time had flown by. I had exactly an hour before I was supposed to be meeting Tee and our mothers at Red Lobster for dinner. I was literally tasting buttery lobster, or maybe it was my subconscious desire for fresh human seafood, or puntang to be exact. Yep, my mind is ALWAYS in the gutter, but my fantasies never take me far from my baby Tamara.

"I'm at work, Red, still in my office, but I wanted to see if you were playing ball with me and Joop later. I haven't called him yet, but I feel like shooting some baskets."

"I can't. This is Mother's Day. Don't tell me you aren't doing dinner with your moms, boy?" I asked.

"Naw, we did lunch earlier. Her, my dad, and Peaches. I swear he pisses me off like you wouldn't believe. This was for my mom and he still spent the whole lunch going at it about me." I could hear Step sighing through the phone lines. He and his old man never got along. Something that I never really had to worry about. My mom had raised my sisters and me solo. I had never known my dad and, like they say, you can't miss something that you have never really had.

"Well, Tamara and I are taking our moms out for dinner together. I need to start getting ready for that right now, as a matter of fact."

"Aww, man, you're whipped! Shorty got you doing the couple thing all the way, doesn't she?" Step snickered, laughing heartily.

"Shut up, aight?" I laughed back. "This is Mother's Day. I need to get ready to show mine some love, and with that thought, I'm out. Later, dawg."

After hanging up with Stephen, I quickly made my way into my bedroom, pulling out something to wear and jumping in the shower for a quick freshening up. Step was right in a way. This was a big time couples thing and, oddly enough, it had been Tamara's idea in the first place. I had tried hard not to think about her a lot during the day, trying to keep from disturbing my writing flow, and had pretty much succeeded. Her attitude this morning bothered me. I couldn't help but wonder if she had thought that my *I love you* was just passion talk, or a heat of the moment revelation.

Hell, I've had plenty of those. I'm no angel, but I know that this was not one of those times. It just seemed so right, she just

14

felt so good, and I loved her. I was deeply, truly, and madly in love with Ms. Tamara Styles. But the fact that she seemed hesitant to say it back or that she booted out of here so fast, didn't escape my notice. Not that I'm all cocky or conceited, (I'm not) but I'm also not used to women not saying it first, and especially not saying it back. *Could it be that she wasn't feeling the same feels for me? Damn now I really was buggin'. Women always loved me, right? So why wouldn't Tamara, right? And why am I starting to talk to myself like this? And why didn't she look happy to hear me say it?*

Maybe she didn't trust me; maybe she wasn't in love with me like that yet. How could she not be? That's pretty cocky to think maybe but hell, she should be. I mean, I'm not a dog or anything like that. I'm a decent looking guy, MORE than decent from what other women have been telling me since I first hit the puberty years, and I treat her good, damn good. *Why am I still talking to myself like I've lost my mind or something? And why was it so hard for her to say it back?*

The same thoughts just continually washed through my mind as I got into my Oldsmobile, took a deep breath, and gave a final glance in my mirror before making my way to downtown Baltimore.

Tamara...

I love my mother...I really do, but sometimes, we just *clash*, for use of a better term. As long as my mom and dad have been married and still, deeply in love with one another, I'm often times sitting and pondering how that reunion happened. My father is a very quiet man, who enjoys the peaceful life. Having retired just this past year from his long journalistic life, he spends most of his time building things, like assisting in the added rooms to our home. His idea of fun is a quiet evening in, with a good meal and a good movie, whereas my mother is flamboyant, to say the least. An ex- model, my mother's main concern was looking good. I will admit, even at the age of sixty, my mother was all that. She didn't look a day over forty, even though she insisted a day over thirty-five. Growing up, I fell into my father's realm of life, loving the solitude, the quiet life. But being the only child, my mother vowed to make me as extravagant and outrageous as her. She failed.

And she lets me hear that every time we talk. Like now, as I tried to talk to her to confirm our dinner tonight. As soon as she heard my voice, she began questioning me about Chris. When were the wedding bells going to be ringing; when were we going to bestow her with a grandchild; when were we going to stop living in sin. My mind had been tuned out to most of her questions as I fell back into thinking about Chris. Ever since I left his place, my mind was spazzing over the feelings I had for him. I know…I know he thinks something is up, and it pains me to think I can't get my heart and head together fast enough to reassure him. Chris is too fine to deal with me for too long. Any number of women would be willing and able to jump up in a relationship with him if I failed.

I gave my mother some excuse to get off the phone with the quickness and vowed to get myself in a calm place before this dinner. I spent the afternoon just lounging around, taking a long hot bubble bath, playing some Jesse Powell as I took my time dressing — something nice, but conservative for the mothers — a pair of dark red Capri pants, a white short sleeve v-neck top, and matching dark red jacket. I strapped on my new black platform sandals and smiled at my matching toenails and fingernails and how coordinated I was trying to be. With my mother, perfection is a necessity. The outfit, the shoes, the accessories, ALL COORDINATED or death would prevail upon me. As I released my hair from the scrunchie atop of my head, cascades of dark brown curls just fell around my head, and I laughed, knowing that Mom would mention that I do something to tame my wild mane.

I smeared on a bit of my chocolate kiss lipstick and checked my watch. I had called Chris earlier to tell him that I was taking my own car and would meet him at the restaurant. I just hoped that we could keep this morning's activities to ourselves and get through this dinner without any casualties.

"So, when will we get to announce some big news?" This was Isabelle, my *loving* mother speaking. We had been at the restaurant all of ten minutes, hugging, kissing, saying our hellos, and had just been seated when my mom decided this was the perfect time for this question. I looked into her face, similar to mine, but slimmer, more elegant-looking. Her plucked eyebrow was raised up at me, questioningly, and I sat silent.

Chris was sitting opposite me beside his mother. I glanced over at him, hoping for some help in fielding this question. He gave me a lame smile and continued to chew on some lettuce from his salad. If it wasn't a faux pas in my mother's book, I would have swatted a piece of tomato at his behind, but I simply smiled up at the two mothers who were awaiting an answer.

"Well," I began, clearing my throat, "Chris and I haven't really discussed this yet."

"And why not?" Chris' mother asked. "I mean you two are at the perfect age to begin a family and give us some beautiful grandchildren."

"And you two love each other, right?" my mother asked. In unison, Chris and I glanced up at one another and smiled, almost shyly. I could feel my cheeks glowing under my skin. No matter what was going on with us, that "love" was still there and very strong.

"Most definitely," Chris answered, giving me a wink across the table.

"Then why wait?" my mother finished. "There is no *right* time for anything. If you feel it, and you want it, you DO it. Life is way too short for waiting and trying to find the right time."

"Oh, but Mother," I said, trying on my best *proper* English accent, "now you know that's not how you see this at all. What about the bridal registries, and the millions of people to invite, and the perfect dress, and the perfect matching shoes, and the..." Chris and I broke into laughter at my rambles, but the mothers quickly jumped in to break it up.

"I didn't say that wouldn't happen," my mother responded. "There would be a time for an engagement at which we will, Evelyn and I (said with a smile towards Chris' mother) help to make sure the wedding is as beautiful and as perfect as it should be."

"Well dag," I said, "When will..."

"Dag?" my mother inquired. "Is that a word, dear?"

I could hear Chris snickering across the table as I tried to slip my *correct speaking* dictionary back into place. "Sorry, Mother. I meant to say, well, with you two doing everything, there would be no need to have Chris and I there, would it?"

"Now, dear," Chris' mother said, "we wouldn't exclude you two. You babies will be the main attractions."

"Like the elephants at the circus?" Chris asked, in a whisper. It took everything in me to keep the water I was drinking down. I could feel our mothers' eyes just bore into him and I wasn't going to save his butt this time. I sat back and enjoyed him getting the third degree.

But, as usual, the wrath came right back at me, as my lovely mother turned to me and said, "No, there will be no elephants. However, Tam, you are getting a little heavy on that backside. Surely you don't expect that to fit into any *nice* dress. Oh, and something will *have* to be done with that hair." Two insults in one. And with that, dinner was served.

Thankfully, dinner went quickly and smoothly, without too much more painful swats at my ego. I wasn't fat. What Mom didn't realize because she's a little lacking in the posterior, as well as in the front, is that most black women have fuller figures, something their men can sink their teeth into. I was very athletic and loved my daily morning jogs, and I didn't eat sweets…too much. No matter how sophisticated and successful I am, I will always feel ten years old when in the presence of my mother. Love her as I do…that woman, my mother, makes me want to put her in a sleeper hold sometimes, and tonight was no exception. I quickly kissed her and Chris' mother good night, watched them get into their cars and drive away.

Standing side by side, Chris and I watched our mothers drive off, out of sight. I could sense Chris staring at me, with those soulful brownish-hazel eyes of his, and I slowly turned to face him, tilting my lips upward into a soft smile. "Hi," I said.

"Hi back," he responded. I could feel his eyes raking down my body, from the top of my curly mane to the tips of my dark red colored toes. He was giving me one of those "come home with me" looks, but he knew as well as I did that we both had hectic days tomorrow, and besides, we were still trying to deal with what had happened that morning. Even with all that, I was standing here, looking at this man that I loved more than anything, and guess what? I'm hearing those damn bells and a funny tune called the *Wedding March*.

Chris. . .

"The moms got their own little gig going, don't they?" I laughed weakly, trying to ease the tension in the air.

"Yeah they do, but you know I told you my mom has this thing about *when* women should be married. She acts like the mother of Whitney Houston's character in *Waiting to Exhale*," Tamara giggled back.

I felt myself staring into Tamara's eyes. Was there anything about this lady that didn't stir me to no end? I really wanted to spend the rest of the evening with her. My body had an immediate reaction to her the first moment I saw her all decked out in those red pants, showing the shape of that sexy behind, her and her onion ass, and like a true onion digging into it brought tears to my eyes every time. *Damn, here I go again! I need to shake myself!*

"What you thinking about, boy?" Tamara had a look on her face that told me she knew *exactly* what I was thinking about. She stood against her car, this lovely blush rising to her cheeks, getting more of a heated look as I continually locked my eyes with hers.

"Thinking about you…" I pulled her close, burying my face in the base of her neck, planting soft kisses down her shoulder. She sighed, moaning a little. "Tamara…"

"Baby, I would love to be with you tonight, but I really need to sleep. We both have a busy day tomorrow."

"I work at *home,* remember?" I winked at her, putting my hands down her backside, cupping her to me.

"So do I, but you still have your scheduled writing sessions and I know you've been goofing off so I am *not* gonna help you do that...YA HEARD?"

"Uh huh, what happened to all your *proper* English?" I laughed. "Frontin' for your mama, you know you ghetto on da real!"

"Forget you, man!" she spat at me, rolling her neck in a homegirl fashion. "I'll see you later, baby," she said, kissing me softly on the lips. I deepened it, slipping my tongue into her mouth, exploring its essence.

"Chris, no…" She laughed breathlessly again, letting me know she was not unmoved.

"Aww," I moaned. "Alright, I'll let you slide tonight. See you, babe." I gave her cheek a slow caress before she got into her car, whispering out a soft, "Bye."

I chuckled to myself as I walked over to my car, thinking about our night. Leave it to moms to bring up the *M* word. Not that I had anything against marriage, especially feeling as I did toward Tamara, the thought had definitely crossed my mind. *How would I feel about having Tamara Styles becoming Mrs. Christopher Grimes?* Hmm,, something to seriously think about. But remembering her reaction this morning...well, needless to say, I wasn't feeling totally confident about her feelings for me.

I laughed again, shaking my head as I unlocked my car door. *Would you listen to me? Me, Chris "the bachelor" Grimes seriously considering giving up bachelorhood, and with a sis- tah who doesn't even seem too eager to grab hold of me.* But the thought of marriage to Tamara didn't scare me the way I always thought it would. Made me feel kinda good inside, as a matter of fact. I had to somehow find a way to make Tamara under- stand that this was real for me, that I was dead serious.

Ignition turned, CD player pumped, Mase and Puff Daddy bouncing throughout the interior of my car as thoughts of Tamara ran through my head.

I got home and slipped on pajama pants and a robe, popped open a Pepsi, and opened up Word to get to typing. I had my next chapter all outlined out in my head, and wanted to put that outline on my processor before it slipped my mind. That had happened to me too many times to count. It was taking me a lit- tle bit longer to get through some of the chapters than others, but I was determined not to give up this venture. Writing was my life. I had more so been a short story writer ever since High School, having had many published in magazines and even a few in an anthology of short stories.

I had also done some contributing articles to magazines and zines. My zenith had been an article that I had written for BMW magazine, called *Black Men in the Computer Age.* Yeah, com- puters were my field, but writing was my love. Journalism had been my major, but I had gone to school a couple more years, grabbing a second in Computer Science. A brotha can't be too careful in these days and times, nor too sure. But after a while I decided that I wanted to finally do what I had always dreamed of doing. Write a novel.

I took a breath and was about to start typing my outline, but oddly enough, my fingers had a mind of their own, and started typing something else instead.

Tamara…
Tamara…
Tamara…
Tamara…

Tamara...

Mm mm mm. My mother is a trip, dissing my hair *and* my booty, and pretty much giving me away to the highest bidder. She was such in this NEED TO GET MARRIED AND HAVE SOME CHILDREN tip. I remember when she used to laugh at me because I would talk about wanting a career and wanting to take care of myself before I got married. Many times, I had to *remind* her that she herself gallivanted as a model, that she too was a very independent woman. Isabelle swears she's from that old old old school, the place where a woman was the housewife, while her man took care of the money matters. Every time she told me that mess, I would fall over laughing. She did, on occasion, don the apron and make a mean dinner, but that wasn't the woman I remembered...and that wasn't the type of woman I was either.

That woman...always distracting me from the more important issues, like Chris. It was weird. During dinner, I didn't feel too apprehensive or nervous around him, but once the mothers split, he seemed a little cautious with me…well that was before we started kissing and he had a sistah wanting to forget sleep and go home with him. It wasn't even about the sex, even though it was the bomb of bombs…it was just being in his presence. Chris made me feel like the only woman in a room, in the world, but ...I just hate how my mind thinks. But, there *were* small moments of inadequacies between us, and it has me thinking. Is he already prepared to make me last week's news? Am I still the girl he wants to be with? I mean, yea, he really wanted me to come home with him, and Lord knows I was aching to be with him, too. I can't lie. I love the man, even through all these insecurities.

One thing that always has me tripping about men is their inability to vocalize. If they want sex, they can ask for that real quick, but when it comes to expressing themselves about a relationship or commitment or love or marriage, they act like they've forgotten how to speak. After a woman goes through that enough, she becomes almost shell-shocked — refusing to let that emotional side out for fear of being rejected. I mean, how many times has a woman gone with the flow, only to eventually tell her man she loves him, wants to be with him forever, and then all of a sudden he wants to see you less, making up lame ass excuses, other than the real excuse — he doesn't want to get close like that!!

But I digress...it's just that I can talk a blue streak about all these topics that are interwoven through this black love thang. It's funny how something so good can make you go insane at the same time.

After I parted from Chris, I quickly drove home with visions of my baby all through my mind. But as soon as I stepped through my front door, it was like I had taken a bottle of Tylenol PM. I barely got my shoes and clothes off before I just *tripped* into my bed, clad in panties and bra. You know those kinds of sleep where you don't even dream, it's just complete and total darkness and you sleep hard and wake up with a screaming headache?

That's what happened to me. I guess all the mental strain of the day before wiped me completely out. I'm usually able to "direct" pleasant dreams, but not this night. I only felt a darkness and, when I opened my eyes the next morning, I cried out...the pain was killing me.

After a short shower and an abundance of aspirin, I sat at my computer with a towel wrapped around me and tried to put my mind on work. As the founder and sole designer of *Design in Styles*, my job allowed me to sit at my computer, donned in pajamas, and create electronic magic. That's what I had planned this morning. Plopping down at my desk, I booted up my PC and stared at the stack of proposals I was writing for various multimedia projects. While my girls Dee and Sha found their joy in sports and the mind, I was the techno geek, spending most of my time in front of a computer, totally enthralled by it…but today, guess what? I couldn't concentrate to save my life.

My head was still killing me and I just couldn't stop thinking about Chris. "Damn," I groaned, rubbing my hands over my face. "I have to go see him." In the couple of seconds per hour that my brain was allowed to think through my migraine, I grabbed up some files and threw them, along with some disks, into my backpack and went into my bedroom to retrieve my laptop, dropping it into its case. I'd even be nice and buy breakfast to take over there. It would be brunch now, but hey, it was the thought that counted. This way, I could chill with my baby, we could both get some work done, and perhaps, just maybe, we could talk about this love thang.

I didn't even think about being cute today. With this head throbbing, I was lucky to come out my house matching. I settled on a pair of fitting blue jeans, a white tank top, and my Adidas, with a blue and green Adidas hat for good measure. I made it to Chris' place in record time, happy not to have the cops out today to pull my butt over.

There was a car, a black Accord, parked out front of Chris' place, but I paid it no mind. People around there parked like they owned the whole street sometimes. I dug Chris' key from my back jean pocket and let myself in. Dropping my bags onto his couch, I opened my mouth to call for Chris, but stopped. I heard voices coming from the bedroom.

"What the hell?" I muttered under my breath. I heard Chris and a woman's voice coming from the room. I stepped quietly up to the side of the slightly ajar door and listened in.

"What do you want from me, Dana?" I heard Chris ask the girl, a pretty girl. She was thin and attractive and I immediately wanted to run in and smack this black Barbie doll upside her head, but I bit my lip and continued to listen.

"I just want you to let us have another chance," this Dana said. I saw her walk up to Chris and place her well-manicured hand against his chest. I cringed.

"You know I'm with Tamara," Chris said.

"You have only been with her a couple of months. Baby, come on. You know you and I had something really beautiful going on. Back then, I just couldn't forgive you for what you did to me. But I can now...and I want to. Let me make you happy."

"Dana," Chris responded, weakly. However, he didn't push the girl's hand away.

"I love you."

I pushed the door open. My eyes were glued to Dana. I kept all the anger I felt deep inside of me. I wasn't going to go off...not yet, anyway. Chris' eyes damn near popped out of his head and ol' girl looked scared, too. I felt like I was in the showdown at the OK Coral and whatnot. No one appeared willing to speak, so I began.

"Hello," I said, slipping on an award-winning smile as I took Dana's hand in mine and shook it. "I'm Tamara."

"Uh, he...hello," she said in her whispery soft voice. "I'm..."

"I know who you are." I could feel Chris staring at me. The room just became electrified with intensity.

"I'm gonna go," Dana blurted out, already out of the bedroom. She didn't even bother to glance Chris' way. When the front door slammed shut, I turned and looked at Chris. He looked so guilty. My heart plummeted.

"Hey," I said, in a voice I didn't recognize. "I brought you breakfast." I could hear Chris following me into the living room, as I dropped down on the floor and knelt at the coffee table, leaning to grab the breakfast bag off of the couch. "I got us some of those breakfast sandwiches we get at Kaplan's all the time. I figured you hadn't eaten yet."

I pulled out the sandwiches, the orange juice, bottled waters, and napkins, and began to eat. The food was bland, the orange juice was too acidic, and the water taste like tap from a dirty faucet. My stomach felt like lead, but I kept that stupid smile on my face. Chris wasn't saying a damn thing. I didn't want to start ranting and raving like a lunatic, but the pressure was just building up in me.

It came out...fast and hard. "What is going on, Chris!? Ol' girl wants to get back with you?" He began to talk, but I quickly jumped back into the conversation. "I knew this shit was going to happen. I heard you tell her that you were seeing me. Where was the 'I love Tamara, I'm IN love with Tamara'? Huh? Where was it at then?"

Chris was rambling something off, but I had tuned him out...I was on a totally different page, a page that didn't want to listen to his sorry excuses. When he said those famous words, my head clicked back into the conversation. "I'm sorry." He sighed. "Nothing happened, we didn't kiss or anything."

Whoa, wait a minute, I said inside my pulsating, pained head. "Did I even SAY anything about you doing something? Only guilty Negroes come out their mouths with some mess like THAT!" My mind was gone. All I could see was every image of every bad relationship roll past my eyes. It didn't matter that I loved Chris or that I had vowed to try and not let my emotional baggage follow me into this relationship. It didn't matter that I was kicking myself inside for getting so riled up, or that I wanted to beat that girl's ass or that I wanted to beat CHRIS' ass. I got up from the floor, stumbling back into the TV. Chris tried to help me up, but I shook him from me.

"I thought this time would be different," I whispered, more to myself.

"What time?" Chris asked, knowing to keep his distance from me.

I spun around to face him, my eyes dark, my face hard. "This," I answered. "I tried to get rid of my baggage, to not think about how guys have continuously screwed me around. I tried to keep that from this relationship because you said you were different. Even when I found out about the barrage of women you have had, I told myself that was then and this is now. But, you're just like all the others..."

He kept saying words, words that I can't even hear right now. Something about love, and to please listen, wanting me not her, something, but I just couldn't, not right now. I snatched my bags from the couch and bounded for the door. When I turned to look at Chris, his eyes looked sad, his body defeated, and I wanted so bad to just take him in my arms, but I couldn't. ONE tear slid down my cheek, and I heard him say again, "I'm sorry, Baby" and I left. I needed air, needed to cry, needed to be alone, needed something. This relationship shit is for the birds.

I'm sorry. It's a nice sentence. Small and compact. It's used so much that it's more trite than *I love you.* Men use it so many times to make up for all the things they done did. I ain't saying women can't be trifling, but I'm a woman, so I'm all about being on the man-bashing wagon right now. As I sped home, the word SORRY continuously popped into my head, and I instantly remembered a poem I heard at a poetry club that Chris took me to once. The sistah was fierce and in obvious pain, and now, her words reflected how I felt:

27

Baby, you say in your most sweetest voice
I'm sorry

Just the hearing of that phrase
Has my vision blurry

Of the tears that fell
Dropping into my unwishing well
Of excuses you have given me
Clearly, you don't see

My well is full of your excuses
Your trifling words, those verbal abuses
To my intelligence

As my well overflows
Tears swell in my eyes
Eventually trickle down my nose
Though I suppose

You'd look at me with sincerity
To simply say you're sorry

Well I'm sorry too
For giving the sweetest thang I own
Me
To a SORRY excuse of a man like
You

They say actions speaks louder than words, so how does someone even think I'M SORRY is supposed to make everything better? It doesn't, but all I know is that right now, I am truly sorry, sorry for risking my heart.

Chris...

After Tee left I went into my living room, staring blankly at the TV screen. I couldn't even grasp what all the oohs and ahhs and laughter was about on the *Jerry Springer Show*. I couldn't believe what had just happened! Tamara had seemed like she was in her own world, and no matter how hard I tried, nothing I had been saying seemed to get through to her, or would make her listen...hell to get her even to *look* at me! And what was so bad was that she had me all wrong. I didn't even know what half of the things she was saying was even about. Damn! I felt like banging my head against a pole like one of those old Three Stooges' movies... I don't even know why I let Dana in. She had caught me right when I was about to take a shower. Fortunately, I was still dressed, so I was really surprised to see her at the door, and Dana being how Dana was she had just invited herself right on in, and even followed me to my bedroom when I went to get my Nikes.

That's when she made her move and started talking about we should get back together, and how I should dump Tamara. No matter how long I thought about it and tried to see it from a fair point of view, the only thing I could think was that Tee overreacted, big time! Yeah maybe I wasn't being forceful enough, but really Dana and I hadn't begun talking that long before Tamara showed up.

Dana and I had had this on again off again relationship for about a year, and I will admit, I wasn't mature enough to handle a real relationship back then and made a lot of stupid mistakes. Eventually, Dana and I were able to be cordial to each other. But I just couldn't figure Tee out, I mean I loved her, I was more mature, I hadn't made those mistakes with her, so she should know how sincere I am! But she wouldn't listen to me, didn't hear a word I was saying. What more does a man have to do to prove his self to a woman? I guess what made it look so bad is that Tamara found us actually *in* the bedroom. Everything inside me melted when I saw her standing there. And Dana had been *all up on me* and all up in my face at that very moment, which made it look even worse.

Finding myself searching wildly through my PC desk, I breathed a sigh of relief when I spotted what I was looking for, an unopened box of Newport lights. Yeah, okay, it was a filthy unhealthy vice that I had all but given up months ago, don't know why I always keep a pack around, but at a time like this, something is needed to calm the inner ache. All kinds of thoughts swam through my head as I lit my cigarette with shaky hands. The cancer sticks didn't ease the churning in the pit of my stomach, nor the feeling I had inside that told me I had just lost the best thing that ever happened to me.

The last two weeks were the hardest I'd had to deal with in a long time. The days seemed to drag by. Tamara was keeping herself on severe lockdown. I had been constantly calling and leaving messages for her hoping we would get a chance to talk, thinking that time would lessen the intensity. The thing is I'd much prefer her blowing up at me, than the deafening silence I was getting now. I spent a lot of time writing, trying to get my mind off of what was happening. Somehow it seemed like my best plots were hatched when I was stressing, as if somehow my own feelings and pain were transported into my character and best expressed through him. At least something productive seemed to be coming out of all this. I even canceled a speaking engagement with a writers forum group in PG County, too afraid that I would miss a phone call from her, a phone call that never came that is...

"Come on, Tamara, pick up," I said aloud to myself while I listened to the exasperating sound of her phone ringing. I *knew* she was there, hadn't even seen her at the park lately for her daily run, and that was one thing Tamara never missed out on.

Just as I was about to place the receiver down, I was suddenly alerted with a dry, expressionless, "Hello…"

At the sound of her voice, my heart started beating wildly in my throat. "Hey, Babe…" I breathed nervously to her. "I've been really worried about you, been trying to get you on the phone and wasn't getting an answer. I was about to put out an APB on you." I laughed jokingly. I knew I was rambling, but still it was so hard to believe I had finally gotten her on the phone, and she was so damn quiet.

"Uh huh," she said weakly.

"Are you okay, Tamara?"

"Yes, I'm fine thank you," came her chilly, proper response.

"Okay, um…listen, I hate how things are, and I…I really feel we need to get together and talk, you know? You know I love you, right?" Complete silence on her end. " I mean, I really didn't think that you would get so upset about me having an old friend here. Tamara, it was nothing. Nothing, I swear. I don't know what to say to that. I guess I just got confused for a minute." I paused briefly, hoping she would have a little mercy or something, anything to get me off the hook.

After realizing I wouldn't be so lucky, I continued on, "Dana and me, we were together for a long time, but I don't want to get back with her or anything. She was talking a lot of shit to me and I guess I'm still a bit confused. But one thing I'm not confused about is how much I love you, baby, and how much I miss you and how much I need you in my life, and how miserable I've been these last couple of weeks. I know you're scared. I am, too. I know you must be doubting my feelings for you a lot right now, but really, Tamara, you don't have anything to doubt, or any reason to think I don't love you with everything inside me. Can I please just come over and we can talk, and…and… *Please,* Tamara…."

There seemed to be complete silence on the other end of the line, until I recognized the soft choking sobs emulating from her.

"Babe? Babe, please don't cry..."

Total silence screamed back at me and then a click, telling me she had hung up.

"Tamara?...Tamara?...Tamara?..."

Tamara. . .

I'm gonna hate myself for saying this, but I'm really mad at myself. Pride always seems to get in the way of what a person should do. I can't even begin to explain all the emotions that were flowing through me just before I left Chris' place. All I know is that all this pride came into the picture and I just blew up. Pride for not wanting to be some sistah who just let things ride and forgave her man because she *loved* him. Love ain't all that. Ain't even *some* of that. If there is no friendship, no *trust, why are we together?* Or am I stupid for thinking like that?

The more I yelled at Chris, the more I yelled at myself for going off. I had never done that to a man. When things happened, I would just pull my tail between my legs and lick my wounds in peace. But this was different...*so* different. I was just starting to get into a groove of realizing that I would never have a man the way I wanted to have one. The idea of being single had worn on me, *became* me. I was cool with being with my girls and being by myself...or as my girl Iyanla would say, "*With* myself." But no, God felt the need to drop a man into my life, to make me think that happily ever after could happen to me...and I played a sucker. Played a sucker and got sucker-punched in the process.

Anyway, as soon as I left Chris' house, I jumped into the car and peeled off. I sped right to my apartment, and there I holed myself in for the last two weeks. I had my phone automatically take messages and I turned my pager and cell phone off. I didn't want to talk to Chris, I didn't want to talk to my girls, and I really didn't want to talk to my mother. I made a couple of trips out to the store, picking me up snack foods — popcorn, ice cream, cookies, chips — and bought some new movies I had been meaning to purchase, and just vegged out.

I worked myself like a slave with projects and finished many before their due dates. I just needed to keep myself busy because, if I didn't, I would stop and think and realize that just maybe I went a little overboard with the hysteria. Maybe I should have *listened* to Chris and heard what he had to say. But right now...UNH UNH...didn't want to.

After cabin fever began to settle in, I turned all communication back on — my e-mail, cell phone, pager, home phone, everything, and it all just went OFF. My pager had like 50 messages, my answering machine was full, my e-mail blew up, my cell phone had fifteen messages, and most of those were from Chris with variant themes — "Baby, please talk to me," "Baby I love you, we need to talk," "Baby, are you okay? Call me," "Baby, your mother called here worrying about you," and so on.

There were a couple of messages from my girl Shameika. I quickly called her back and let her know that a sistah was tripping for a minute, but she was about to come back up for air. Shameika decided that we just HAD to go out shopping and that was cool. Shopping always perked a girl up. I reluctantly called my mother because she was about to call the Coast Guard on me. After about five minutes of her giving me the third degree, I hung up on her. She had a way of pissing me off, at the times when I just needed someone to be there for me.

The phone rang. I knew who it was. "I'm sorry for hanging up on you, Mom, but you have to know that I don't need your constant lectures."

"I was worried about you, Tamara," Mom said, calming her voice.

"Okay, worried about me, got it. I'm alive, so moving on."

"What are you doing tomorrow?" Mom asked, her voice perking up.

"Mall with Shameika."

"Mind if an old lady tags along?"

I laughed. I wanted to say no because it had been a minute since I talked to my girl and Shameika was always good for cheering a sistah up. Besides, I couldn't dish dirt with Mom right there, but I decided to say yea. I could invite Shameika over for a pow wow afterwards.

"Sure, Mom," I said. "But you better be on your best behavior."

"Promise."

"Alright, well, I'll see you tomorrow...say noon at Security Square Mall. Give Dad...and yourself a big kiss for me."

"Love you."

"Me, too." I hung up and took a deep breath. I thought I might be okay, but then the phone rang again. I glanced at the caller ID and my small bit of cheer evaporated.

"Hello?" I said, expressionless.

Chris nervously said, "Hey, babe..., I've been really worried about you.. I've been trying to get you on the phone and wasn't getting an answer so I was about to put an APB out on you." I heard him laugh. He was nervous. So was I. I wanted to yell out that we needed to talk, that maybe, just maybe we could work this out, but right now, I was still feeling too vulnerable to listen to him speak.

"Uh huh," I said weakly. "Had my stuff turned off."

"Are you okay, Tamara?"

Was I *okay*? Was he serious?

"Yes, I'm fine thank you," I came back, with a very chilled tone.

"It's been two weeks since I've heard from you." My silence gave him the leeway to speak further. "Okay, umm..listen. I hate how things are, and I...I really feel we need to get together and talk you know? You know I love you, right? I mean I admit, I shouldn't have allowed Dana to even come into my bedroom, and I should have been more firm with her. I don't know what to say to that. I guess I just got confused for a minute, me and her were together for a long time, and it's not like I hate her or anything, but I don't want to get back with her or anything, she was talking a lot of shit to me...and I guess I'm still a bit confused, but one thing I'm not confused about is how much I love you, baby, and how much I miss you and how much I need you in my life, and how miserable I've been these last couple of weeks...., uh week. I know you're scared. I am, too, I know you must be doubting my feelings for you a lot right now, but really, Tamara, you don't have anything to doubt, or any reason to think I don't love you with everything inside me. Can I please just come over and we can talk...and..and... *Please,* Tamara...."

I fell hard on the couch. My heart was pumping wildly and I wanted so bad to tell him to come, to talk to me, to convince me that he was mine, and I was his. For a moment, there was nothing but silence on the phone...as if he was waiting for me to say something. I wanted to say something, but all I could get out were tears and sobs. My heart was heavy, my head was aching, and all I could do was choke out sobs...the kinda sobs where you don't even wipe your eyes, and your nose starts running and you look really unattractive. That's what I was going through.

"Babe?" Chris said, almost pleading. "Babe, please don't cry..."

I got scared, I got nervous, I got wanting, I got prideful, I got confused, I got off the phone. I didn't trust myself to speak, and I couldn't bear to hear Chris' breathing or his voice on the phone...it made me ache for him.

I mentally kicked myself. In the back of my mind, I knew…I felt, that I should let this die, that I should just chalk this up to a small hurdle and forget it even happened, but I couldn't, and it scared me. Scared me because I knew that my actions could come back to smack me right across the face…and I would just have to hope they didn't.

Chris...

"Chris, I just need a ride and if you aren't doing anything, what's the big deal, huh?" Dana quizzed.

"I know it's no big deal, but you being at my place really caused mad problems between me and Tamara. I don't want to intensify them."

"So, um, she's THAT insecure?" came the sarcastic reply on the other end of the phone. "I'm asking for your help. We're supposed to be friends, right? *Forever always?*" she whispered.

Forever always... We used to say that all the time to each other when we were together. Dana seemed to be pulling out all the punches to remind me of that time, too. Eventually, I allowed Dana to persuade me to take her to the mall. My feel was that I would drop her off and let her page me when she was ready to be picked up. As I pulled up to Security Square Mall, Dana gave me this look that told me what she was saying without her breathing a word.

"I just know you're coming in," she said, matter of factly. "You said you didn't have anything to do."

"How long you gonna be?" I asked with a sigh.

Dana threw her hands up in aggravation. "Look, why don't you just take me home if this is so hard for you, Christopher."

I sighed. Dana was pushy as hell, one of the things that I couldn't deal with when we were together. I should have just said *okay, I'll take you home then,* but as stressed out as I had been lately, I didn't feel like hearing her bitch, and just wanted this to be over and done with. "Okay, okay, geez..."

Not wanting to have any further stress with her, I pulled up into a parking space thinking that the quicker we went in and came out the better off it would be. Besides, there were a few things I could pick up at the CVS while I was here.

After about an hour in the mall, I started to understand why Dana wanted me to come in with her so bad. She needed a bag boy, I thought with a private laugh. We decided after a heated debate to grab some Chinese from the food court. I almost choked on a shrimp from my house lo-mein when I heard a familiar voice behind me. *Oh God don't let that be who I think it is!* I thought to myself, but wouldn't it be my fuckin' luck to feel Mrs. Styles' hand on my shoulder. *Lawd why me?*

"Chris!" she exclaimed warmly. "Tamara, Chris is here!"

Forming a fake smile, I turned around to address Tamara's mother. "Hey there." I smiled. "What y'all doing up here?"

I right away recognized one of Tamara's girlfriends who had gone to a Jazz bar with us one night, a short tiny chick named Shameika, with these odd looking hazel eyes. Standing behind her was Tamara. It felt like ages since I had last seen her.

Our eyes met and I felt this hot rush come all over me. Somehow, I just couldn't look away. It seemed like she couldn't either. She started walking toward me when suddenly she stopped. Her face seemed to fall, which I couldn't quite figure out why at first, until I followed the direction of her eyes and noticed she was staring at someone behind me. *DANA!* Damn... I had forgotten about her! Hurt and disbelief coated Tamara's eyes. I didn't even have to guess what she was thinking.

"Well, I don't believe I've met this young lady here," said Tamara's mom, as she glanced over at Dana.

"No, we haven't met. How do you do? I'm Dana. Me and Chris are *old* friends." Dana shook Mrs. Styles' hand, looking at me cautiously.

"*Lawdy....*umm," hummed Shameika, looking from Tamara to Dana with a twisted face and her glittering cat eyes. "Men are a trip, Gurl," she whispered loudly to Tamara.

The nosey bitch, I thought to myself. Leave it up to her pigeon girlfriend to stir shit up further.

"Tamara, can I talk to you for a minute?" I asked, trying to find something in her eyes to let me know that we could work this out.

"No...really, we *have* to be going. Come on, Mom. I need to get out of here, *now*," she said, avoiding my eyes. I really wasn't surprised that she was running. This was getting kinda old.

Mrs. Styles gave me a YOU KIDS REALLY NEED TO GET IT TOGETHER type of look. "Well, I'll see you later, sweetie. Tell your mother to call me, please." She gave me a kiss on the cheek, whispering to me, "Don't give up on her okay, and uh...get rid of the pretty hoe?" Throwing me a wink, she was ushered out of the food court by an anxious Tamara and the ever ghetto Shameika.

"Well...what a *friendly* bunch they are," commented Dana.

"Let's just go. We can take our food with us..."

My mind became as mixed up as a Pizza Hut super supreme pizza. I was stressed. All I wanted to do was get home, jerk my Johnson, or maybe have a stiff gin on the rocks to calm me down.

Tamara...

After I hung up on Chris, I stopped crying. It was as if talking to him just made me so angry. I could do nothing but cry, and now that I had hung up, the connection — no pun intended — had been broken. I busied myself the rest of the day with washing clothes, cleaning my place, writing some letters, even FedExed a couple of my projects out. I slipped on a pair of soccer shorts and a tee shirt, then brought out my old pair of Adidas that I used to run in and left the house. I figured a nice jog would do me good right about now, especially since it had been a while since I last went out.

Can I say a sistah was wheezing? It was my fault, though. I started out running way too fast and kept up that pace for five miles, 10 if you count the fact that I had to run back to my place. My shirt was drenched, clinging to my breasts, my back, my stomach, and my soccer shorts now felt like some spandex, all attached to my thighs. But my mind was clear and I was calm. That's all that really mattered.

I took a quick shower, threw on some more shorts and a tee shirt, and called me up Domino's. A sistah was in the mood for a deep dish extra cheese, mushroom, and sausage pizza, with a Coke. I remember back in college, Shameika and I would each buy a medium pizza and just gorge ourselves. Sha always managed to finish hers and maintain that very slim, bootified body of hers, whereas I never could finish, but what I had ate, fell somewhere on my fuller, curvy frame. There was just no justice, and there wouldn't be any tonight, cuz I was eating my pizza — all of it — and was gon' go to bed and get ready for tomorrow.

I woke up early. The pains were calling me out of the bed. My calves were sore and I couldn't pinpoint where the other pain was, but I knew it hurt when I walked. But pain be damned, I was going to look cute today at the mall, pain and all. And I did. I was in the bathroom, checking myself out. I had my hair pulled tight atop my head in a clip with cascades of wild curls falling down. My make-up was minimal, but I had to add the Chocolate Kiss lipstick. It just made my lips that much more inviting for men to want to kiss. I had on a black silk, button down shirt — letting the two top buttons open, showing smooth brown cleavage — and a knee length, clingy black and white striped skirt with slits up the sides that revealed my thick, solid thighs when I walked. I was just about to strap on a pair of my black platform sandals when I heard Shameika's mouth outside my door.

"Gurl!" she yelled. "Open this damn door!"

I laughed, strapping into my shoes — which gave me an extra three inches of height, and jaunted to the door. Shameika gave me a big hug and came in. "Damn, who you tryna fuck at the mall, Gurl?" she asked. People always wondered how Sha and I ever got together. I had my ghetto-sistahness about me, but for the most part, I only let it out during *appropriate* times. Sha, on the other hand, was just plain ghetto. From the extremely long braids she wore in her hair, hanging down the middle of her back, to the long manicured nails with crazy designs on them, her attitude, her voice, her language — which went *beyond* Ebonics, she was just the epitome of the Ghetto Princess, but she was my GURL, and I loved her.

"Shut up now!" I laughed. "I'm not sexing anybody, just wanted to look good for the mall."

"Well ya ass looks like it's 'bout to drop out that damn skirt! Work it, gurl!"

"Let's go," I said, trying hard to stop laughing. "You ain't right for nothing. Come on."

"Huh, you think I ain't right, wait til yo Mom sees you." Dang, that was true. Mom was used to seeing me in less...um, uh *hoochified* gear. Well, whatever. I looked over at my girl, who was wearing something I *think* she might have stolen from Foxy Brown, and thought to myself, *Mom will be too busy talking about what YOU'RE wearing to bother with me.*

The mall was where I needed to be. Sha, Mom, and I went in just about every shop in the mall. I had bags laden with Bath and Body products, some sexy bra and panty sets, a cute pair of *must have* sandals, and some sundresses that were on sale. Mom didn't mention my outfit once, even though she did a triple...or was it quadruple take when she saw Sha and me looking like we wanted to dance in a Luke video. I couldn't help but to laugh.

I was actually, genuinely smiling, with happy thoughts in my head. It was like Mom and Sha wanted to make sure this day went smoothly, and so far, they had succeeded. After all the shopping, Mom suggested going to Applebee's for a late lunch, her treat, and we were headed out to do just that, when I heard Mom squeal, "Chris! Tamara, Chris is here!"

I didn't want to turn around and see him, but I did. For an instant, this stupid smile jumped up across my lips. He looked good. He looked tired, but he still looked good. I could see his eyes staring back at me, *all over me* to be exact. I had noticed how other men were staring and drooling all day, but this was the first time I *felt* the stare. It was almost as if he ripped my clothes off, sexed me, and went to sleep in those brief glances.

I was broken from the trance when I heard my mom talking about some girl she didn't know. I looked up to see her shaking hands with DANA! Wow, I thought, feeling the smile from my face quickly dissipate. I had never felt so embarrassed, so hurt. I couldn't even hide my pain. I didn't cry, but on the inside, I could feel the tides of emotions just ready for me to be alone, so I could do just that.

"*Lawdy*....umm," hummed Shameika, looking from me to Dana with a twisted face. "Men are a trip, Gurl," she whispered loudly.

"You ain't *neva* lied, Gurl....*neva*." I responded. Dana looked up at me, a smug smile on her face, as she sat down beside my *ex-man*. "Hey, Tammy," she crooned, leaning into Chris. "How you doing?" I could see the discomfort in Chris' face, like he wanted to shed his skin and raise up outta there. I guess that's what it looks like when you get busted out in public.

"It's TaMAra," I said, slowly, phonetically. "Use your vowels, and add another consonant up in there, puhlease."

Shameika giggled. If I knew her like I KNEW I knew her, I know she was wanting a good ol' down and dirty fight, but Tamara don't swing like that. If she wanted him, and he wanted her...cool.

"You look good," I heard Chris say, his eyes staring right at my blouse and the stiffness of my nipples pointing against the thin silk fabric. Dana huffed, sitting back in her chair, and began eating.

"That's funny," Shameika said, looking around, "cuz there was some fine men back there who just said the same thing to her."

Any other time, I would have been mad at Shameika's instigating, but I laughed on the inside at my girl having my back. "In fact, one of them slipped me his number to give to her." I looked at Shameika, as she handed me a folded piece of paper. A damn *receipt*!!!! I knew I would be laughing at that for a while later, but for now I had to play it off. Chris' eyes glared at the paper, like he was trying to catch it on fire, but I slipped it into my purse. "I'll check it out later," I whispered, loud enough for him to hear.

It was odd. Even though I was mad at him, I was feeling so sexually charged right now. I was standing there, with my mom staring at Dana wondering why Chris was with her, I had Shameika throwing barbs at a silenced Chris, and I was standing here, wishing I could just get my groove on. No matter what was going down, Chris was still the best sexing partner I have ever had. And with his eyes still tightly glued to my nipples, I just wished I could pull him up and go to a nice dark corner, and relieve some of this tension.

"Tamara, can I talk to you for a minute?" Chris asked, staring at me like he was trying to find something in my eyes to let him know that we could work this out. I stepped out of my moment of *in heatness* to get back to the issues at hand. I didn't want to talk to him right now. Especially with that girl up around him.

"No...really, we *have* to be going. Come on, Mom. I need to get out of here, *now...*" I said, avoiding his eyes.

Mom gave Chris a hug and a kiss, and whispered something into his ear. He gave her a brittle smile, and I took her hand, quickly ushering us out of there. I took a deep breath, pushed down my sadness, and forced a smile up to my lips. "Come on," I said. "Still hungry, and waiting to get my Kiwi Lemonade from Applebee's."

Chris...

"See, it's just not worth it, baby. She dissed you like that, right in front of her mama and girlfriend, and you been sitting around feenin over her. Why don't you just think about some of what I've said, okay?" Dana was nonstop all the way to her house. I pulled into her driveway, waiting patiently for her to make her exit, my mind totally filled with Tamara, and becoming more and more depressed about our situation. *Why was I even bothering? It was pretty obvious that she didn't want to work it out, that she didn't care like I did.*

Lost in my thoughts, I didn't even notice that Dana had moved closer toward me and was planting soft kisses against my neck.

"She doesn't deserve you, Boo," she whispered in my ear. "Just let me make you feel good, okay? Remember how I used to make you feel *so* good?"

"Dana, no…" I crooned weakly.

"Shhh…that's not a word, forget that word and just *feel.."* Just as I was about to push her away, she covered my mouth with hers, slipping her tongue inside. I could feel her hand rubbing me up and down slowly at the front of my jeans, giving me an instant erection. I couldn't figure out in my own mind just why I was letting this happen. Maybe it was just the desire for some type of pleasure after feeling like shit the last two weeks, and all confused like mental succotash. I was even reasoning with myself, *why the hell not? Tamara didn't want me, she believed I was doing this shit so why not just do it and enjoy it? Hell I'm a man, right?*

Dana had loosened the buckle of my jeans and unzipped me. I could feel her lips tracing my belly button, dipping her tongue in again and again. "Mmmm…you still got that six-pack too witcha sexy…sexy ass," she moaned. "Mmmmm…"

I closed my eyes and just let her take control. Cleared my mind of all the garbage that had been invading it and just let myself *feel,* caressing Dana's hair, her face buried in my lap, feeling her licking around and around the head, feeling the sensation of her moaning as she took me in her mouth all the way to the base. I could feel her swallowing and releasing deep down in her throat. It felt SO damn good, and I just...well I just let it happen. I was gasping in short, jerky breaths, slowly thrusting up against her mouth feeding myself to her, when somewhere in the deep regions of my mind I could hear a Dru Hill cut coming from the car radio, and suddenly I wasn't focusing on the wet pleasures of Dana's mouth, but the familiar lyrics of this song, that had me and Tamara etched all through it...

What do I do with the nights, without you by my side...
They used to be yours and mine.
Without you, what do I do with the love...

"Stop okay? I don't wanna do this," I said to Dana suddenly, pushing her head away.

"You have GOT to be kidding me?" came her incredulous reply. "Just like that? You're gonna tell me you weren't enjoying that?"

I zipped my jeans up with shaky hands, closing the buckle, not even believing myself that I pushed that back, right in the middle of it. Dana was always da bomb at oral pleasures, and this time was no different.

"Yeah I was, but it's not all about that anymore, Dana. Yeah, you were able to pull me in for a minute there. Hell, I'm only human. But I love Tamara. Maybe she won't take me back. I don't know, but all this is doing is making her right, and making me the dog she feels I am, that she feels all men are. I could sit here and let you make me nut and not worry about shit. Hell yeah, I would enjoy it! But I want to somehow prove to her that I'm different, that my love is real, and I won't do that by sitting here fuckin' around with you!" I exclaimed.

"See, you ladies always say you want to find a good man that's gonna be true and treat you right, yet you know I love her and you're using everything you've got to make me what y'all complain that you don't want, a cheat... How would you feel if you and her were in the reverse?"

Dana stared into my eyes for several long seconds and finally said, "You really love her, don't you? She is *so* lucky...and too stupid to know it." She began gathering her bags, shaking her head in the negative when I offered to help her take them in the house. "I don't love her like you do, Baby. Still want your ass," she said in a low voice, laughing. "Really, good luck okay?"

"Night, Dana, and thanks," I said, kissing her lightly on the forehead.

"Yeah, anytime..." she said. The watery look in her eyes didn't escape my notice as she got out of the car, and made her way up to her door.

After about my third gin and tonic at Tully's Bar and Grill, and what seemed like a half a pack of Newports, I picked up my keys and dizzily made my way to my car, not even thinking about the drinking and driving statistics, my mind fixed solely on confronting Tamara. *She was gonna talk to me tonight, Goddammit!*

Here I was turning down blowjobs and shit over her, my head was spinning like crazy, I was miserable as hell, and on this night, she was gonna talk to me! She owed me that much...

I pulled up to her apartment complex and noticed her living room light was on. I wobbled up to her front door, banging loudly. "Tamara, open this damn door! I gotta talk to you!"

"What the..." Tamara jerked her front door open suddenly, both of us staring at each other, eye to eye.

Tamara. . .

Mm Mm Mm. Men are a trip and a half of a half. And I can't *believe* I was getting all hot and heavy thinking about him while he busted himself out. Looking all sexy in just jeans and a Nike tee shirt. I glanced down to spot the Nikes he was wearing, the ones I bought him for his birthday. Wearing *my* shoes with that trick.

I couldn't get out that mall fast enough. I felt like Mom and Shameika were flags the way they were blowing in the wind as I dragged them out of the mall and into our cars — Mom's and mine. I followed Mom to Applebee's and Shameika didn't even speak. She just kept mouthing *mm mm mm* and shaking her head. There really wasn't anything to say. And even if there was, I didn't feel like saying it.

We ate in silence, and left in silence, and as I pulled into my parking spot out front of my place, I told Shameika that I needed to be alone. The sisterly bonding session I had planned for us would have to wait. Hugging me tight, Shameika whispered, "Just call me if you need me, Boo."

Not five seconds into my apartment, I changed, threw on my Adidas, and went out jogging another 10 miles. If this kept up, I would be doing a marathon a day and be down to beanpole size. I didn't care, running and jogging always kept my mind free of garbage, and all these emotions were rating as garbage right about now.

After my jog, I popped some burritos into the microwave and pulled me out a bottle of Corona. I wasn't in the mood to throw out my Julia Childs' impersonation, so "bachelor" food it would be. I kicked off my shoes, down... for a second. "Lemme go show... ...uu, smelling the sweat on my body.

I dressed scandalou... ...ut I figured I would be alone, so who would know? I ...apped my hair, tying a blue bandana around my head, ...ore slipping into my new white bra and panties set — ...an a ribbed tank top bra and thong — and a pair of black sil... boxers, rode low on my full hips. I wasn't a thong wearer ...out Shameika insisted I buy a pair and wear them ...ound my man. Now I had the thongs and no man. I pulled on a pair of thick white slouch socks and padded my way back into the kitchen, grabbing another Corona and a bag of Doritos.

I flipped on my entertainment system and remoted to

Marvin Gaye's *Vulnerable* CD. Sitting back in my black leather chair, I closed my eyes, sipping my Corona and listened to the tunes. I remembered when my girl Deandra had peeped me on this CD. I was going through mad drama and she told me that this would just put me in such ease that I wouldn't be worrying about anything. And she was right. This CD made you take in long, deep, slow breaths and let them out just as slow.

My mind and body were just getting at a place where they could "rest" when I heard all this loud banging at my front door. I jumped, almost dropping my Corona.

"Tamara!" I heard Chris yelling on the other side of my door. "Open this damn door. I gotta talk to you!"

I knew my neighbors would be calling the police soon, so I didn't even sass him back. After picking up the Corona, I ran to the door and swung it open. "What the...," I managed to yell out before noticing the drunken anger on Chris' face. "What are you doing here?" I asked, my voice lowered.

"I need to talk to you," he said. "We need to talk....*now*."

I shook my head, but allowed him to come in. Slamming the door, I turned to face him, and found him taking off what little I had on with his eyes. There was this look Chris had. I called it the SEX look. His eyes would get this sexy, oozy appeal to them and his whole aura radiated sex when he looked at me that way, like he was now. I could feel his lips touch every part of me, without touching me.

"You're in," I said, whispering, my voice caught in my throat. "What do you want?"

I knew Chris liked to have a drink every now and then. Hell, so did I. It was like he sobered up as soon as he walked through my door. The outfit I was wearing didn't help.

"Don't you think this has gone on long enough?" he started. "There is nothing going on between Dana and me, and you should believe that."

"Why should I believe that?" I asked, throwing my hands up on my bare hips. "Because you say so?"

"Yea, as a matter of fact. I've never lied to you before, so why would I do it now?"

"I don't know why you men lie, I really don't."

"Tamara," Chris sighed, walking over to me. I started to step away, but didn't. I needed to talk about this. Chris stepped up close to me, close enough for me to smell the faint odor of gin and the cologne that I loved.

His fingers lightly traced my jaw and over my lips. "I love you, Baby," he started again. "I love you so much that this time apart has been killing me. I haven't gotten any work done, I haven't slept, barely ate, nothing. All I've been doing is calling you and making sure you were okay."

I began to speak but he cut me off. "Today, with Dana, she begged and begged and begged me to drop her off at the mall, and I told her that what she did the day we had the falling out was wrong, and that I loved you, wanted you. It was purely friend-wise that I took her to the mall, and once we got there, she begged me to go in with her."

"Do you always do what women want you to do when they beg?" I asked. I was swooning hard with every word he said, but there was just something inside me that didn't want this dead...not just yet, anyway.

"No," he said. "I don't. I just didn't feel like arguing, not even with her. I'm sick of fighting and I just want to love you, Tamara. Just you. Only you."

"I really want to believe you, Baby." I sighed, my lips in a pout. "I really do."

I felt his eyes rake over my body and I shivered. No man had ever been able to make me feel so electric. "You are so beautiful," he whispered. "So beautiful, and so sexy." His fingers lightly slid from my face, along my neck, and over my breasts, lightly pinching my already stiff nipples. I let out a slow moan, as he began to massage my breasts and pinch my nipples. "I want you so much, Tamara," Chris groaned in my ear. "Let me show you how much I love you, Baby."

I lost the fight. There wasn't even a need for me to try. I remember watching movies, seeing a man do wrong, and then come to the girl, tell her how much he loved her, wanted only her, and before the whole necessary conversation was over, he had her butt naked, crying out his name. I didn't like those women. To me, they were weak because they should have said no and finished the damn conversation, but I couldn't. My body was aching for Chris and I was tired of raising my voice and yelling. I was tired of arguing and being confused. Making love to Chris didn't consist of any of those things — maybe yelling, but it's the *good* kind of yelling.

His warm lips kissed up my neck and connected with my awaiting mouth and I groaned, remembering and loving how it felt to have his mouth on mine, his tongue playfully dodging and playing tag with mine. Chris pushed me up against the door and his hands roamed all over my body, over my breasts, down my stomach, and around to my butt, his hands slipping beneath the boxers, each hand squeezing a handful of the roundness. He groaned.

In one swift movement, Chris had me out of my boxers, and began to slide my thong down over my butt, my thighs, and my legs. When I stepped out of them, he quickly lowered his mouth down to my already wet hotspot. He kissed me all over as I cried out. Two weeks were nearly too long to not have him on some part of my body.

I felt my knees buckle, but his strong hands kept me up, up against the door, while his tongue kept me whimpering as he took long licks up and down, licking and sucking, finding my already hard button, needing him. I was lost, his tongue circling my clit, licking it, sucking it, flicking it, had me in a tailspin. His hands were kneading my butt and his mouth and tongue were kneading my throbbing button.

I bucked, I moaned, I cried, I whimpered, I shook, I came, hard and long, my body tingling all over, from the inside out. When I began to calm down, Chris began lazily kissing up my body. As he got to my stomach, I looked down, my hands running along his cheeks, but my eyes caught a glimpse of something on the back of his tee-shirt. Around the collar, on the back there was a reddish-brown blotch.

My body ran cold, and I pushed Chris away. "What's that on your shirt?" I asked, my voice extremely loud. Chris stumbled back, looking confused, wondering where our connection had gone. "What are you talking about?" he asked. "Where?" He looked over the front of his shirt, and didn't see anything.

"Look on the back of the *collar*," I said, again loudly.

He still looked confused, but I could see the moment he saw what I did. He didn't look as confident, as sure of himself. He looked, defeated. Here I was, ass all hanging out and he just came from seeing *her*? I snatched up my boxers and slipped them on.

"Chris!" I screamed. "You came over here to screw me after being with her?"

"Baby, listen, it wasn't like..."

"Shut up! Whose lipstick is that on your shirt, Chris? Whose? Dana? That ho Dana?"

As if on cue, the phone rang. I let it ring, Chris and I in a standoff. My answering machine went off, and a familiar voice came on. "Uh, Tammy...Tamara, this is Dana."

I jumped across the room and picked up the phone. My eyes shot knives at Chris who just stared at me, then the phone, and back to me. I clicked on speakerphone, and put down the receiver.

"I see we have a party here," I said, my voice cold and even. "Let's get it started."

Chris...

When it rains, it pours. Okay, let me say that more forcefully, don't want any misunderstanding here. When it rains, it fucking pours! I couldn't believe the type of day I was having. Just a couple of hours before I was sitting in my car, with a wet warm mouth working me like you wouldn't believe, and I pushed it back yep, why? Because I felt the guilt and wanted to do the right thing, and knew damn well I was wrong, and had no business with her. Now here I am, listening to this same so-called understanding chick dog me out. Nobody could ever tell me women can't be some sneaky bitches. Yea, she understood all right, understood that she couldn't wait to let Tamara on to what had went down, what she herself had instigated.

I could slowly feel the effects of my drinking binge wearing off as I listened to Dana on the speaker phone, giving Tamara her *woman-to-woman* talk, and by looking at Tamara, if looks could kill, let's just say I'd be a corpse.

"So I just felt you needed to know what the real deal was with me and Chris. I know you and he have been having problems, and uh, this evening something sort of happened," came Dana's fake cry of concern.

I looked silently at Tamara, shaking my head with a sigh. I decided to just give up and let them play their game.

"So just what are you trying to say, Dana?" asked Tamara.

"Well, we were talking, and then we sort-of...well, sorta started kissing, and touching. I feel real bad about it now."

A look of bitter rage came over Tamara's face. "You have got to be kidding me, right? You feel bad about it? Ha! You're a slut, Dana! I would expect nothing more from a ho!"

"You calling *me* a ho? Well Suga, if I am, I'm a damn good one, and Chris must of thought so, too, the way he was moaning and groaning when I sucked...his...dick," she crooned viciously.

Tamara caught her breath, her face flinching in shock, and me, I felt like praying, praying to whatever spirit being on call tonight to PLEASE take me, take me anywhere, but here.

Suddenly Tamara gave a strangled screech, lunging at me

swinging wildly. "You let her do you? You're a dog, Chris, a DOG!! I can't believe you! You let that skank ho blow you!" she cried.

"Stop it Tee, babe…it's not like you're thinking. Don't let her do this to us."

"I'm not your babe! I'm not yours!" Tamara cried hysterically.

"It's *nothing* like you're thinking," I pleaded, holding her arms down to stop her angry blows, although it was in vain, as she pulled loose, slapping me hard across the face. "Ouch! Stop it, goddamit! Stop hitting me in my damn face!"

"Chris? Chris, are you there?"

Both Tamara and I stopped at the sound of Dana's voice over the phone, both of us breathing hard, and looking at each other with mutual pain in our eyes. We suddenly remembered her presence on the phone.

"Will somebody please tell me what's going on over there?" Dana screamed.

"Let me up, Chris…" came Tamara's tired, hurt reply.

"Listen to me, Tamara…please?"

Tamara wiggled her way out of my arms, walked over to her phone, and disconnected Dana's call. Looking at her eyes from across the room, they appeared as deep pools, every emotion buried in their depths. If only I could read them, see inside her and know what her thoughts were.

"Leave now, Chris. It's over," she said, her cold expressionless eyes never leaving mine, never even blinking.
A sharp ache rumbled in my stomach. I felt as though I had been punched, and thought back to all the times when I had really been hanging out with my boy, Stephen, betting on who could run the better game, frontin' with women, really throwing them a line. Was this pay back? Was this the reaping of what was sown in my fuckalldababes days?

Shit. Why the hell was I putting myself through this torment, letting some double X chromosome diss me as if I had done something wrong, when I know I hadn't. I'm a man, goddamit! A grown ass man! And I stopped Dana, I really did. I didn't do anything wrong...

Grabbing my keys, I made my way to her apartment door and out into the night air, where I finally felt like I could breathe again, minus the sharp pains that was striking my belly with record speed. I was okay, I really was, I was.

So much for I love yous...

Tamara...

What do you do when your heart has been ripped from your chest, thrown on the floor, and stomped on? You die. You stop breathing. You cease to exist. That's what has happened to me. Hearing Dana cooing about how Chris let her go down on him, how he moaned and groaned from Dana giving him pleasure. I wanted to throw up and die at the same time. But instead, I got violent, going at Chris, hitting him with my fists, slapping him, with him wrestling me onto the couch to keep me from hurting him.

I only half-heard Dana on the speakerphone, yelling to know what was going on, but I hung up on her ass. She wasn't my man. I shouldn't worry about her...she wasn't the one who continued to tell me he loved me, and only me!

In a dead voice, I told Chris to let me up, that we were through, over, finished. I could see these emotions flashing over his face. He looked pleadingly, like he wanted to try and talk me into loving him, forgiving him. Then he switched to dismal, like he could tell from my expressionless face that I was serious. The final looked pissed me off. It was more like a FORGET THIS stare. Like he was transferring his guilt to me, like I made him let Dana go down on him. He looked angry like he couldn't get out of my apartment fast enough.

As soon as the door slammed shut, I began running around my apartment like a mad woman, ripping up pictures of Chris, trying to cleanse myself of him. I was on autopilot, something else was guiding me through my male removal session, but the phone ringing partially ripped me from my irate status.

I grabbed the phone and yelled, "Don't fucking call here any more, Dana!"

"Gurl!" It was Shameika. "What is going on? Dana? Is this Chris' girl?"

Hearing my girl's voice, I just broke down, babbling and crying into the phone. Even when Shameika hung up to come here, I laid on the couch, hugging the phone to my ear, letting the dial tone calm me.

"No, he did not let that girl get him off!" Shameika yelled. She was spread out on the floor with me, a gallon of Chocolate Chip Cookie Dough between us. You know your girl got your back when she comes out her house with a striped pajama set and a pair of Nikes on...with a baseball cap on...looking rough, but concerned. That was Shameika.

"Yea, he did, Girl," I said, my voice a lot calmer than earlier. "And had the nerve to look mad at me when he left, like I made him do that shit."

"Well you know how men are, Gurl," Shameika began, eating a big spoon of ice cream. "They feel that not giving them 100% or by doubting them, feeling insecure gives them an IN to have sex with whomever they choose...free of charge."

"Wait a min," I said, trying to clear my head. "Because I needed a minute to regroup, get my head straight, he took that as a sign to freak around?"

"Yup," Shameika answered, like every woman was supposed to know that. "Gurl, you know I deal with men like it's a job, okay...for pleasure and for friendship. I should have a Ph.D. in them, for real!" We laughed. "But seriously," she continued, "they be getting mad when their girls don't trust them, especially when their asses being legit and true to them. I be trying to tell them that some women have trust issues, that unfortunately infiltrated into their current relationships, and when something happens…even if it's not as bad as they think, the woman immediately goes to the most negative thing. It's what we do."

"True dat. What did they say?"

"They said that's not their concern. They be faithful, stay faithful, but there's only so much hanging around they can do, before they start to feel like they not loved or trusted and start hollering elsewhere."

"Sha, truthfully, do you think I'm in the wrong here? I mean yea, I have my trust issues, too, but I mean dang, I think about my past relationships, that Chris used to have several fuck buddies and be all about just getting his, then his ex, the one who left him, he didn't leave her, is in his bedroom, wanting to get back with him. Lawd only knows what would have happened if I didn't walk in. Then he gon' let her suck him off, and that's my fault? Girl, do you really think that?"

"Hell naw!" Shameika jumped up, walking into my kitchen to retrieve a soda out the fridge. "It ain't your fault, Gurl. To me, it's like men and women are different. DUH." We laughed. "I mean we both got our dogs and our straight people, but it's like men think so much with their dicks. If him and his woman have a fight, his first thought is to go screw somebody, forget the girl. We go, cry, talk to our girls, and begin to build our male hating wall. I'm not saying either is right, but I know that we at least don't use ourselves and others by just fucking our problems away."

"Amen to that, Girl," I said, suddenly falling silent, my head pounding. We sat there, on the floor in silence, both thinking. Men had a way of bringing women together, unfortunately, normally in pain, to commensurate their hurts and losses and to validate the pain, the frustration.

I was mad. I was angry. I was hurt. I felt betrayed. I was a lot of things that I couldn't even talk about. Not even to my girl, Sha. There were things that words just weren't strong enough to express, and so I chose to keep them inside, to discuss with myself, by myself. I was so angry, so blinded by my anger, at myself for getting hurt, and at Chris for making me feel this way. A part of me wanted to be manly and go get my freak on, to hurt Chris, but I knew it would hurt me more. A part of me wanted to go hide in a cave, and never deal with the male species again. A small part of me felt that I could have avoided this situation by forgiving and forgetting earlier...or by just letting is slide. I had a lot of parts, that wanted to do a lot of things, but I did nothing.

I continued to sit, on my living room floor, with my best friend, eating ice scream — hmmm, was that what I really wanted to do? — SCREAM, drinking soda, silently crying, head throbbing, and wishing that someone could tell me something to make me understand all this damn drama.

Chris . . .

"Now the first mistake you made, was letting her get your mind, the second, was letting her KNOW she had your mind."

"She didn't have my mind," I said. I was getting a little tired of Joop's tirades, even though he was one of my best friends. He was one of the most irritating type of brothas, the type of brotha who swore he knew everything there was to know about women, about everything to be honest, and was always giving unwanted and unneeded advice. We had long labeled him the dread locked, chocolate-skinned version of the Stokely Carmichael, save the black man, kill YT type. As far as I was concerned, he spent far too much time talking to those black Israelite peeps he hung around with.

Everything about Joop spoke black pride, from his well groomed, shoulder-length dreads, to the orange and brown Kente' shirt he was wearing. BLACK JESUS we used to call him on the courts. Nigga could slam dunk like you wouldn't believe, and he had been a militant giant at Howard, planning rallies and sit ins, and he gave the most powerful speeches you could imagine, and was an ace host and representative for our school when the Reverends Al Sharpton and Jesse Jackson had visited for homecoming that last year. Now he was a History teacher and the junior varsity basketball coach at Baltimore High, and loving every minute of it, despite the low pay and lack of respect teachers got from the inner city school system.

"I gotta agree with Joop on that one, Chris. You done had your heart out on your sleeve, man, and if we can see it, you know she has to have known she got you in the bag."

I looked over at Stephen, sighing mainly because I knew he was right in that speculation. Stephen was what one would call a BALLER. Step was a 6 foot 4, shaved head, Grant Hill, eat your heart out type of brotha, and usually had one thing on his mind, okay maybe two, sex and women, or women and sex, one or the other was his constant companion. He was always in good spirits, and never allowed anything to get him down. The last time I had really seen Step upset about something on the serious tip was when he was passed up for the NBA draft.

He had serious game, had won most valuable player three years in a row, and everyone, especially Stephen himself, thought that he out of all of us would be the one to make it. It took months of cheering up from me and Joop to get him out of that mental slump, but one thing we always had promised was to always be there for one another, helping each other to be the best men we could be, and Step, well he ended up giving up his life long dream of being the next Michael Jordan, and owned and operated his own Private Investigation firm. That is, when he didn't have his eye on the ladies.

We had decided to have a chill with the brothas night. We had checked out this new flick called *In Too Deep*, featuring LL Cool J, and that Omar dude who played in *The Wood*. And from there ensued a battle of words about the image that black men have in the media, and the struggle black men were having period. While having pizza at a restaurant a few blocks down from the theater, I had made the mistake of telling Stephen about Tamara in front of Joop, which ended up with Joop talking about how black women don't trust their black men, nor have their backs the way they should.

"See that's the big problem here, we have the white man in one corner dissin' us out, and in the other corner, where we should have our women supporting us, they be thinking the way YT be thinking, that we all dogs, that all we think about is sexin', or that we are the way LL portrayed *God* in *In Too Deep,* just a bunch of hungry thugs trying to get the cash the easy way. You got to be smart my brotha, don't let the sistahs be thinking you weak. See, a lot of 'em already think that. Now your lady, she probably running her mouth with her girls talking bad about you right now," Joop said, taking a swig of his Molson Ice beer.

"Maybe, but frankly, that's on her. I've dissected this situation through and through, and I really don't see what I could of done differently," I said, breathing deeply.

Stephen's eyes were planted in the direction over my head, causing me to look around to see what had caught his interest so much. The only thing I saw were three women sitting in a booth, one black, maybe mixed from her high yellow complexion and light eyes, and the other two where white cheerleader looking broads, one blond with the blue eyes deal, and the other, a brunette, with dark chocolate eyes.

"Look at that," Stephen announced, sucking his teeth. "They want me."

"They want you?" I laughed. "Nigga, get outta here!"

Stephen threw a kiss and a slow wink at them, smiling broadly and slicking his hand across his baldhead. Turning to look behind me again, I caught sight of the little waves and giggles of the three ladies in question. They were definitely reacting to Stephen's flirtation.

"Actually he's probably right Chris, I mean think about it, and just look at them. They got that *fuck us hard* look on their faces, and you do know that we are the most coveted, the most desired, the most sought after men on the PLANET right? I mean all the women want the king, the BLACK man, that's why the YT man hates us so much. And that's why our own women need to appreciate us more, instead of giving us a hard time about petty shit like Tomorrow did to you, and now you sitting around all sad over her, when you can have your pick of the litter. Look at you; big tear stains all down your face, acting all sensitive and shit. I'm embarrassed for you man, have a tissue," Joop lectured, handing me a used napkin covered with tomato sauce. Both Joop and Stephen burst out laughing giving each other a high-five.

"It's TAMARA, man, and you know damn well I'm not crying over no woman," I said, standing up after one last sip of my beer. "Look fuck y'all, I need to get home. I have things to do, and I haven't written a line in days."

"Hey, don't be mad, we just messing with you, boyee," Stephen said laughing. "I'll catch you lata. I'm going over here to get some digits, think I wanna eat me a slice of vanilla-flavored puntang pie tonight."

"Yeah, you better stay away from them white broads, you been done ate the wrong thing and end up with rickets," drawled Joop, picking up his keys to take his leave. "And if you riding with me bruh, let's go!"

Stephen had already started making his way over to the table of ladies, oblivious to Joop's words. I had driven myself instead of riding with them, and couldn't help but laugh at thinking about the conversation that would probably go down later between the two about Stephen getting white girls' phone numbers.

"Peace, man," I said to him, giving quick daps. "You take it easy."

"Shalom, my brotha, and remember now, don't let that woman control your mind. Be the king you are. You got the power!" Joop screamed after me, as I exited the pizza parlor, laughing and shaking my head at him. Joop was always the same, totally intellectual and a total trip.

Driving home, I stopped briefly to pick up some cigarettes from the 7-Eleven, noticing the Slurpee machine. It made me think of one person, a special lady who had stolen and then tore the hell out of my heart, and who just so happened to love cherry-flavored Slurpees.

Would there ever be a place or thing, that didn't remind me of HER?

Tamara...

I didn't get any sleep last night. Shameika stayed with me, and we managed to make it to my bed, where we laid and talked til the sun began to come up. When I looked over at the clock and saw that it read six a.m., I jumped from the bed and proclaimed that we should go for a jog. Shameika stared at me for about five seconds, but she jumped up too, and we threw on some shorts and tee shirts and headed out.

It was BRRRRRISK to say the least. But we sprinted for a long distance to warm ourselves up before pacing ourselves to a nice jog. After about an hour, we headed to this little coffeehouse that we frequented. We were nice and sweaty, and probably a tad bit stinky too, but we didn't care as we ordered two big cups of cappuccino and two huge chocolate chip muffins.

As soon as our butts were in seats, Shameika asked, "Gurl, do you feel BETTA? I mean dayum! You run all that everyday?"

I laughed. "At least every other day. It usually keeps my mind in a nice *stable* place."

"Are you in a stable place now?"

I bit off my muffin. "Men...are...fuck ups!" We laughed. "Yea, I feel a *little* bit betta!" Customers glanced our way as we fell over ourselves, laughing.

"Gurl," Shameika said in a conspiratorial voice, leaning into me, "men may be fuck ups, but one at 7 o'clock is eyeing you something fierce."

"Even though I look like I've been pimp slapped with an iron?" We laughed.

"Yea, and he hella fine. I'm talking GOOD LAWD fine."

Slowly, I played off dropping my napkin so I could bend over and pick it up. When I did, and my glance fell to Mr. Fine, I almost dropped it again. He smiled at me; a perfect smile encased in a face that looked like it was dipped in some sweet chocolate. I gave him my "hi" smiled and turned back around.

"Oh...my...dayum," I whispered to my girl. "If I was a guy, I would screw him." Shameika's eyes almost popped out of her head as she choked on her cappuccino.

"What in the *hell*?" she exclaimed.

I snickered. "You know how guys will just screw to screw? Like, *Oh, the sky is blue, I need to screw?*"

Laughing, Shameika replied, "Yea."

"I'm just saying, if I had that man mentality to screw when I'm mad, when I'm happy, when I just fought with my man, that pretty baby ova there would be lighting up a cigarette right...about...now."

"Well, don't look now...here he comes."

Dang, I thought to myself. I'm still sweating, I know I'm funky, and my hair is lying limp in my ponytail atop of my head. I have nothing going for me, so how this dude gon' even approach me?

I felt his presence when he stood beside me and looked down. "Hi," came this oozingly deep voice. I looked up, and smiled into a pair of piercing black eyes that seemed to just draw you in to him. "Hi," I said back, feeling Shameika memorize every syllable and word of this conversation.

"My name is Chaz Houston, and I just wanted to say hi, let you know that I was noticing you." I gave a quick glance to Shameika and smiled at Chaz.

"Noticed me looking a mess?" I asked.

"Your beauty far surpasses sweat." *Hmmm*, I'm thinking, *keep talking*. We offered him a seat, but he declined.

"I have to get going, already late for work," he explained. "But take this." He handed me his business card. *Chaz Houston, Houston Architects, Inc.* Impressive, I think.

"I can't leave here till you tell me that you're going to use that card," he said, giving me that million-dollar smile. I let my gaze fall from his gorgeous face...to how he was wearing his khakis, his shirt and tie, how he had one of those thick, stocky bodies, and how — even though I was used to tall, lean brothas — he was looking quite yummy.

"Okay," I responded, smiling. "But I should tell you that I have a boyfriend...OUCH!" I glared over at Shameika, who had kicked me under the table.

Chaz smiled. "That's not a problem," he said. "Nothing wrong with dinner, is there?"

"Not at all," Shameika jumped in. "Hi, my friend didn't give you her name, but it's Tamara, and I'm Shameika." They shook hands. "I'll make sure that my friend uses this number, cuz someone as cute as you should have someone as beautiful as my girl here for a dinner companion."

I couldn't *believe* Shameika sometimes. I could see why Chris got annoyed with her from time to time. Chris. Dang, we really did mess that up. I was really trying to keep the pain down inside so that I could keep going with the things that I needed to keep going with, but just that one thought of Shameika being annoying made me think of him. It seemed like I was probably gon' have a LOT of these episodes.

I sighed, outwardly, receiving attention from Shameika and Chaz. I glanced at my watch. "It was nice meeting you, Chaz, but me and my girl have to jet, get showered and off to work. But I will use this card...promise."

His eyes were questioning, but he smiled and shook my hand. "You do that," he responded, leaving out the coffeehouse.

"What the hell was that all about?" Shameika asked, obviously upset.

"Look," I began, rising from my chair, grabbing my trash.

"I just had a fight with Chris. How am I gon' be on my next adventure already?"

"Shit, Tamara, Chris probably don' already fucked somebody! He probably got Dana to finish what she started. What you gon' do, cry and pine and whine about you and Chris, or are you gon' jump into something that could be better?"

People were staring, but I didn't care. Shameika could really piss me off sometimes. Already had Chris screwing everybody and me a crybaby, saving my virtue for when Chris came back, that was if he came back.

"You know, Sha," I said, lowering my voice. "I love you, and you my girl, but this type of situation you have *no* right to be giving me advice for."

"And *why* is that?" Shameika bit out.

"Well, for one, you always proclaim yourself as the fuck buddy extraordinaire, and so what do you know about committed relationships?" I knew I had gone too far, I knew Sha's reasons for her actions...and had sympathized and empathized with her, but my mouth just wasn't feeling compassionate.

"Have you ever seen me crying and boohooing about some Negro, though? No, cuz I hit it and run...fuck the bullshit."

"Okay, yea, fuck the bullshit. I'm sorry, but for me, my body is the most *precious* thing I own, and I don't give it out just because I got an itch, or because there's a hot body around me. Back in high school, you and I had names for girls like that. Those names haven't changed, Girl." With that, I left out the coffeehouse. I didn't look to see if Sha had followed me, I didn't care. I was just tired of all the drama, and needed to get away. That's what I really wanted to do...pack up and go away.

Chris...

My life took on a life of its own, with me feeling as if I had no control whatsoever, like I was in slow motion where I could see what was going on but wasn't a part of it, like I could see myself acting out a scene. I hadn't truly realized how much a part of me Tamara had become. In the mornings when I would get up and fix banana nut coffee, I thought of her, the flavor of it on her lips with her morning kiss. Or while having that afternoon run, the one we used to always do together, I'd find myself looking for her, feenin' for just a peep of her and feeling like a fool. It was just so not cool to let oneself get in this type of mentality over a woman. I would see her, the cute tilt of her head smiling at me as though she had some grand secret.

I would hear her, calling me, telling me the things she used to say, moaning softly against my ear while I would be moving inside of her, gripping my back as the fireworks hit. I'd hear Joop, telling me, reminding me that I should never let a woman have control or get my mind like I was letting her. I'd hear my own voice, asking myself how I could have allowed a woman to actually do this, to actually work me over this way, me, Chris Grimes. Ego? Maybe a little, but an ego trip was what I had felt the other couple of times when a relationship hadn't worked out. This was different, this was aching, and this was physical, mental, emotional, real.

I slowly turned off the faucet, putting an end to a hot shower that had long turned cold. Hadn't even noticed the chill of it. I took my time dressing, slipping on a cool silk beige shirt that went tight with the new Stacy Adams shoes I had picked up earlier that evening at Security Square Mall and chocolate-cuffed slacks. I was fighting to get rid of some of the lotion I had poured in my hands to the point of overflow, wiping the excess on the dark blue comforter covering my bed. With a dose of the Gray Flannel after shave Tamara had given me and a last look in the mirror, I quickly made my way out the door to pick Stephen and Joop up. We were heading for Nubian Whispers, a private club on the Eastside of town that we would hit up every blue moon. Tonight they were having a Poetry-Slam. Joop bragged all the way there about the latest poem he had written and how he was gonna blow up the joint with his talent and style.

By the time we got there the place was already flooded with

beautiful women and brothas sitting around doing the *check you out* thang.

"Now this is what I'm talking 'bout, this is BLACK culture, Mon," Joop announced in a forced island boy accent, flinging his hand around at the booths and tables of African Americans sitting around getting their drink and flirts on. The place was humming with the sounds of *The Fugees* and their remake of *No woman No cry*, the Bob Marley classic.

"It's beautiful in here tonight," Stephen said.

"What's beautiful? Oh don't tell us you done got tired of your bland vanilla ice-cream already and have decided to dip into some mocha tonight?"

"Man, what you talking about? Don't start your prejudice shit, I love my black queens, never said I didn't," Stephen threw back.

"Love your BLACK QUEENS? You love your stringy-haired, narrow-assed white girls, ahhhh!" Joop snorted.

Although I had been listening to their exchange half-heartedly, I was sipping my whiskey sour, and trying to figure out why I was having the feeling that someone was watching me. Turning slightly to the left, I saw where the feeling was coming from: a light-brown complexioned, brown-eyed sistah was standing by the open bar and looking right at me. She had poured herself into this sexy black number that she looked smooth as silk in. She was nothing but legs from the edge of her thigh-length dress to the end of her ankles. As I examined her, she smiled slightly as if she just knew she had it going on.

"You're a racist, Joop, pure and simple, and you need help. The Emancipation Proclamation has long been signed and sealed. Get over it already." Stephen's voice brought my mind back to my own table where it belonged. The last thing I needed was another problem, another female in my life.

"Black people can't be racist, in order to be a racist you have to have power, that's a fable concocted by YT, and get over it? Boy, you ain't black talking that bullshit. For real, you're pissing me off now. I hate when a black man starts talking stupid listening to those devils you been screwing. You should be just telling them to shut up and stop letting them poison your mind like a lily white Delilah. See that's what happened to the black man Samson. He should have listened to his common sense rather than that oblong brain between his legs and he wouldn't have been deceived by her ass. I learned that at this new temple I visited last Sunday. Praise Jah."

"Lawd have mercy," I breathed in frustration.

Stephen took a couple finishing gulps of his Heineken. "Crazy nigga, look," he sniffed, "just because I like a little milk in my coffee once in a while.."

"In Eric Jerome Dickey's words," I cut in.

"Whateva," he laughed back at me. "I'm quoting from that dude's book you gave me."

"See there you go again," Joop cut in, "nigga. Now why do we have to call each other nigga? I don't know about you, but this here?" Joop put his hand across his heart in a militant fashion. "I'm a prince, the descendent of the founding fathers of the earth, the MANDINGOS of Africa. Ain't no nigga here."

"I'm cracking up! Man, I can tell when you've been to church coz you get in rare form!" I laughed.

"Ain't he, though?" Stephen smiled back, shaking his head.

"Brothas and sistahs, welcome to *Nubian Whispers*. We are happy to bring to you tonight one of the most talented poets in Baltimore, but before we introduce to you Brotha Kahlil Raasha, we have an open mike poetry-slam for your listening pleasure. Now who would like to start us off tonight?" The MC's intro pulled us out of our militant chatter. Joop quickly stood up, slipped on his glasses, scratched his neck, and walked over to the stage to recite his piece.

"Ahh, hell, here we go," Stephen said.

I laughed quietly, whispering, "Cut that out, bruh. Give him a chance."

"This is a little sumpin' sumpin' I wrote," Joop said, reaching the microphone. "Just thought I would share it with you all tonight. It's called *Can you hear the children's echo?* It's my dedication to the motherland, a salute to the people, and it goes something like this..."

Do you hear the children's echo?
Do you see their salty tears?
Can you sense their pain, their sorrow?
Do your feel their hurt, their fear?
As they walk there through the meadow...through the heat on mother's ground
there they clasp their hands together...listening for the drumbeat sound
Land that once was rich and green...home of the elephant and the Zulu queen
Burnt by the blazing of hatred's sun...led by strange sound of Dutch warrior ones
Though apartheid now has ended...does that freedom bell ring true?
Is there truly spirit in it...that spark of life... that pride we knew?
Questions form and yet we wonder...just what does the future hold?
Can we now bring back the thunder...or is it just a story we were told?
Were the drums and fires burning...did we march Mabaso's march?
Were King Shaka's nostrils flaring?...soldiers proud, fear- less and starch
Now we see our once blue rivers...crying with a bitter moan..
and the spirit that once glittered...has a quiet distinctive tone...
Do you hear the children's echo?

Do you see their salty tears?
Can you sense their pain, their sorrow?
Do your feel their hurt, their fear?

A thunderous applause filled the crowded club. I, myself, was in total awe of just how talented Joop really was. Brotherman dabbled with the poetry thing at HU, too, but he appeared to be getting better and better. Stephen totally agreed with me that Joop's poem was da bomb. When Joop came back over, we spent the rest of the evening giving him props and listening to the other poets. The sistah who was standing by the bar had apparently disappeared, which is why I was a bit surprised at the soft voice in my ear saying, "Good evening, I'm Cheri, and I wanted to slip you this before I left."

She handed me a small slip of paper. She leaned ever closer to my ear and said, "Use it, Boo," before walking quietly away. I turned to look at her and caught a parting glimpse of her shapely behind.

"Ouch! You lucky mofo!" Stephen exclaimed. "She's fine man! You gonna tap that?"

I looked down at the paper she had slipped me... *410-719-4593.* Hmm, I thought to myself, a Baltimore County number. Would I call her? Why was I feeling so guilty, as if even thinking about it was being untrue to Tamara. It was obvious that she had long moved on. She hadn't even called me or thought about me, probably. It had been weeks since I had been with a woman, even for something as innocent as a dinner, or done anything besides write, mope, and run.

Maybe it was time I moved on, too.

Tamara...

You know what's good about true friendship? Even when you go off with one another, eventually everything will fall into place.

I admit, I was really hot with Shameika. I love her like a sister, but we just have different tastes in life and love. I want that forever thang, even though that seems to be out of my reach, and Shameika believes in that wam, bam, thank you ma'am mess. I just refuse to be used like that. Even if the woman thinks she's running the show, in reality, she's not. Men want sex, and when a woman gives it up so freely like it's a FREE SAMPLE OF SHAMPOO IN THE MAIL, then she's not in control of anything, except fulfilling the man's needs, wants, and desires.

(deep breath) Sorry, got off on a tangent, but I meant what I said nonetheless. Anyway, Shameika and I are cool now. She dropped by my place, and as soon as we laid eyes on each other, we cried and hugged. As soon as I walked out of the coffeehouse, I regretted the words that fell from my lips. My girl…Shameika, well let's just say she has had a hard life, and the things she does today…in terms of love and sex and relationships, they *definitely* come from pains and struggles she's been through.

After profusely apologizing to each other, we fell into our normal *sistah girl* mode where we just chilled and enjoyed being in each other's company.

For the past several weeks, she's been doing whatever she can to get me out of my pending depression. I can't seem to do anything without thinking of Chris. That's probably why I haven't used Chaz's number yet. I still have it, but I tucked it under my panties in my lingerie drawer. WHY? I figured if I got an *itch* down there, Chaz would already be all up in my panties!! (laughing at self) Okay, okay. Stupid time over.

To curb my depression, I've been working like a S.L.A.V.E. or a Sistah Losing All Viable Emotion. I have turned off all emotions that deal with love and pain, and have been focusing solely on work, and getting my projects out. My clients have been loving me to the point where I think one of them wants to marry me. How about for the past three weeks, I have been putting in 14 hours a day, even on the weekends? I am NOW officially part of the self-proclaimed S.L.A.V.E. club, and for the next two weeks, I am vacationing due to finishing up all my projects for the month. My next project doesn't start for two whole weeks, so now I'm sitting around, and can't help but think of Chris.

I swear, I can still smell him on my clothes, and everywhere I turn I find something to remind me of him — gifts that he bought me, a couple of tee-shirts, some jeans, a pair of his Nikes — it was like he and I were slowly embedding ourselves into each other's life, and I really loved that. NOW, it's like what do I do with all this?

To think of it, I had some valuable stuff over his place, too. A pair of my soopadoopa, funky fresh, platform sandals, a couple panty/bra sets, and a couple of things that were just left behind from visits. But was I going to go over there? I mean during this past month neither one of us had called or even seen each other.

And if I knew his *friends*, Joop and Step, I was pretty sure they already told him that he was a weak punk, giving his heart to a woman who couldn't appreciate him. They probably told him, especially that damn Step, that we ain't good for nothing but sex. Hell, after only two weeks Chris was letting ol' girl suck his thang, so I know he probably don' got a couple of *new* notches up on that bedpost by now.

But that didn't matter now, because Chris and I were *over*. I just wanted my stuff. There was nothing wrong with that, was there? He only lived a 10-minute drive from my place, and it was a beautiful sunny day out. I could grab my backpack and rollerblade over there, grab up my stuff, and split. And so what if I decided to wear my hair out in luscious wavy curls, apply a little bit of makeup, and change into my red halter top, the one that pushes the breasts up, together, and out and have the men drooling and a pair of cut-off shorts that clung to my booty and snugged up against my kitty ever so invitingly? I wasn't trying to make a statement. It was hot outside, and I could always call Shameika afterwards and we could go rollerblading in our "sexy-sistah girl" gear and collect digits. Dressing like this had nothing to do with Chris, not in the least.

Now that I'm standing here outside of Chris' front door, looking like a Soul Train reject in my hoochie gear, I feel like maybe I went slightly over the top, but there's no turning back, so I knocked on his door. I checked, and there were no other cars near his place, but that doesn't mean he doesn't have a sistah up in here. It is Saturday morning, and I'm sure him and his boyz hit the clubs last night.

It took him a while to open the door, but when he did, my kitty actually *purred*. He had on a pair of black silk boxers that left *nothing* to the imagination, not that I hadn't seen all his luxurious goodies before, but it was a sight to behold...always.

His facial expression was nonchalant, like he didn't care one way or another if I was there or not, and I have to admit, that hurt like a mutha, but to compensate, his eyes did roam over my body appreciatively. *The outfit was a good choice.*

"Hi," I said, nervously, "can I come in?" Chris held the door open and I felt my booty get hot from his stare as I walked in.

"Wassup?" he asked, his eyebrow raised and a *why is she here* expression on his face. My heart plummeted, not like it had far to go anyway.

"Ummm," I began, stopping to tug off my rollerblades so that I could walk around the apartment without busting my butt. As I talked, my eyes made checks around the place to see if there were traces of another woman up in here.

"Nobody's here, Tee," Chris said, a sly smirk on his face, happy that he caught me checking.

I blushed, mad. "I came by to get my things," I said, raising a hand up to my hip, watching Chris' stare follow the curve. "I left a couple of things here that I may need, and I thought it would be a good idea to come get them. If that's okay."

Chris looked at me like he was disgusted, but he shrugged

and let out a groan. "Go do what you gotta do," he answered. He sat on the couch, his back towards me, and I wanted to go over there and throw myself into his strong arms and kiss him, but my pride wouldn't allow me to let what he did just disappear. *What did he do again?* Sometimes I had to rack my brain to remember that.

I sighed and went into the bedroom, where I found my brown platform sandals, as well as a SWATCH watch, some earrings, my handcuffs (wasn't going to let him use these on ANYBODY else), and some panties and bras. When I bent down to pull my panties and bras from the drawer, I heard a strangled groan. I looked up to find Chris staring at me at the doorway, with an obvious hard on struggling to be released from his boxers.

Immediately, I felt a dampness between my legs, and my nipples protruding against the thin fabric of my halter-top. I didn't say anything, I couldn't. All I could do was stand there and stare at this intensity that was in Chris' eyes. He walked over to me and stood, staring at me for what felt like eons, until he finally bent down and kissed me hard, knocking the breath out of me.

My knees instantly went out and I stumbled into Chris' arms. I heard myself moan his name, but it was like I was staring down at my own body being ravaged by Chris. He pressed me up against the dresser, his fingers finding my hard nipples and giving them a tweak. I squealed. He slipped one of his hands between my legs and rubbed it along the crotch of my shorts. Feeling the wetness there, he grunted.

I don't know how it happened, but before I knew it, Chris had stripped me of my top, and my shorts, tugging them down my hips, before dropping his boxers. I couldn't even protest because my entire body was wet and in need for him. We kissed, hungrily, I felt him push me onto the bed, pulling me up onto my hands and knees and I cried out when I felt him pressing himself against me. "Damn," he moaned. "You are soooo wet, Baby."

I purred and cooed and whimpered as Chris teased me, making me cry out, "Please...please...please."

In one hard movement, Chris filled me with his throbbing member and I screamed, falling from my hands to my elbows. His hands moved down my back, pressing me down, my booty raising up, as he pumped into me hard and forcefully. I couldn't do anything but scream. It felt so good. He kept whispering to me how wet I was, how good I felt, but I couldn't speak. I let my kitty tell him exactly how I felt as I milked his hardness.

I felt him swiveling his hips, slipping out to the tip, and slamming back into me. He alternated spanking my cheeks and I moaned and groaned. He slipped fully out of me and I cried, missing the feel of him inside of me. But I felt his hot tongue lick a warm wet line down my butt, trailing down to my wetness and I instantly came. "Damn, Baby," he grunted. "Taste so good."

My hips were thrashing like crazy and he got up and finished what he started, hitting my inner core so hard, I briefly wondered if this was because he was mad...he wanted to hurt me, but those thoughts quickly left my mind. I sat up, my hands on his bedposts as he snugged up behind me.

I cried out, yelling to him that I was going to come again, and I did, shaking and shivering and falling limp onto the bed. Chris held my hips up and continued to move harder, faster, and deeper into me, until I heard him cry out, and release himself deep inside of me, eventually falling onto my back.

Neither one of us said anything. We laid, breathing heavily, our bodies sweaty, sticky, and clinging to the other. Body parts tangled, bed messy. It was as if my coming released all this euphoria, and now I laid in the bed and thought to myself, "What did I just do?"

Chris...

It was so quiet in the room you could hear a pin drop, and

the only sound was that of my breathing and Tamara's. It was unbelievable what had just happened, but it was so damn good, and for some reason, I didn't want to look at Tamara, afraid of the expression I would see on her face. I mean, she had all but made it clear that she wanted nothing more to do with me, and why she had come here. Why she had allowed me to sex her was something I just couldn't comprehend. But I could see it on her face when I opened the door that she wanted me, and that knowledge made me want to fulfill my desire and dreams of her one more time. I couldn't seem to stop my heart from throbbing in my chest, throat, and head, and still couldn't look at her. She was still lying beneath me, face tucked against the pillow, me still inside of her with a semi hard-on.

"Get up. I have to go pee."

Her dry tone all but told me what she thought about what had just happened. She was sorry, and she didn't want me. I jumped up quickly as if I had just been burned, using the covers to wipe the mixture of our juices off myself, and slipped back into my black boxers in one step. I could hear Tamara flushing the toilet and running water, and knew she was putting her clothes back on, too.

"So how did you get here, Tee? I don't see your car. Did you roller blade over?"

"Yeah, I did," she said, slipping her things into her backpack. It was pretty obvious that she didn't want or plan to talk about what had just happened, and to be honest with you, I didn't know if I really wanted to either.

"I'll be outta your hair in a minute," she said cautiously.

"Look, why don't you let me run you home. That's a lot of stuff you have there, and it's gonna weigh you down." I grabbed my keys, determined not to take no for a answer, not wanting to see her exit from my life just yet, but not wanting to admit it to her or myself either. "Come on."

The ride to her place could be described in one word. TENSE. It's so odd how we used to be able to talk about everything, had more to say than there was time to say it, and now we couldn't even think of a single word to say to each other. Tamara kept acting like she was fiddling with something in her bag, rearranging things in it. Couldn't figure out what the hell she could be rearranging, but then again maybe it was her way of making sure she didn't talk to me. It was odd, too, that this had happened today, because I had just got to my crib and off the phone with Cheri, having made dinner plans with her for this evening.

No, I wasn't looking for a replacement for Tamara. *Could anyone replace her in my heart? Ever?* But I had decided after last weekend, after meeting Cheri at Whispers, that maybe I needed to move on a bit. At least start dating again. Whatever you wanna call it. And here was Tamara again, just in the nick of time, to fuck with my head and heart again, and I was determined not to let her do it, not this time. I cannot and will not deal with her insecurities. I tried as best as I could to make my facial expression as hard and emotionless as possible when I felt her staring at me at the stop light and turning onto Route 40. *What was she looking at? Why is she looking at me that way? She betta not be wanting to talk about our sexin'. Hell I KNEW she was sorry, but she best not say shit coz I can't take that.*

"You're going mighty fast, Christopher. You're gonna past my turn."

"I got this," I said sarcastically.

"Yeah, I KNOW you got it." She sighed.

"Then sit tight, and stop trying to run this."

"Whateva."

"Yeah, you're right. WHATEVA," I said, looking quickly at her. Her face was a mask of hurt and pain and anger all rolled into one. "Fuck this shit," I whispered under my breath, turning into her driveway. Tamara sat quietly in the passenger seat, as if waiting for something to happen. "I've got to go, Tee," I hinted, trying to escape this painful situation. Just to think that 30 minutes ago we were moaning in each other's arms.

"Oh yeah? Why? Heavy date?"

"Yeah, as a matter of fact, I DO have a date," I admitted, looking into her eyes.

"Negro, why am I not surprised?" she asked.

"Well, maybe you shouldn't be. You wanted this, right? You dumped *me,* Tee. Let's not forget that."

Tamara opened the passenger side door with hurried, jerky movements, as if she couldn't get out of my car fast enough. Grabbing her backpack and rollerblades all at once, she stopped suddenly, her back still to me. "What happened to us, Chris?" she asked, turning toward me, her eyes filled with tears. My eyes met hers, and it seemed like the moment was frozen in time.

"You didn't trust our love. You didn't trust *my* love. And you threw it all away."

Without another word, the love of my life disappeared from it, once again.

Tamara...

I dumped him...not the other way around? I didn't trust his love and IIII threw it all away?

All I could do was stare at Chris. It's like he was taking no responsibility for what had happened between us. Like *I* got weak after only two weeks apart and had slept with someone.

No...it was HIM who had done that. I felt as if someone was cutting off my air supply and I couldn't be around Chris, not now. My heart was about to die. I felt the tears clinging to my eyelashes, and I just didn't want to be around him when that happened. Chris' stare, his face was unwavering, like he truly believed every word that he uttered and that nothing else could be said. Without saying another word, I turned and slowly walked into my apartment. Dropping my backpack and rollerblades, I peeked out my front window, watching Chris in the car. It took him 10 minutes of talking to himself and beating the steering wheel before he finally peeled out of my driveway.

Watching his Oldsmobile peel off from my driveway, I continued staring out the window, trying to replay what had just happened between Chris and me. I *really* wasn't expecting us to fall into his bed and have sex…I honestly thought I would go, make him sweat seeing me in my outfit, get my things, and leave. But seeing him…I couldn't deny how much I had wanted him, physically and romantically. But as soon as it was over, I knew…*I knew*, that he regretted it. I could feel it and it tore me up inside…having him above me, our bodies clinging to one another and yet feeling so far apart.

I looked around my apartment. All of my rich, vibrant colors seemed dull gray. I couldn't breathe. I was taking long, hard, labored breaths. There was nothing I could do, short of just having a heart attack and finally putting an end to all this drama, pain, and heartache.

I went to my phone and noticed I had two messages. One was from Sha, asking me what I was up to tonight, and the other was from my ever-loving mother, wanting to know what was going on between Chris and me. "Evidently," I muttered, "nothing."

Chris had a date! The revelation of that rocked me, making me fall onto my sofa in a weeping fit. When the phone rang, I quickly picked it up, hoping that Chris some how wanted to apologize, to try and make this right between us.

"Chris?" I asked, exasperated.

"Girl, what is going on? You sound absolutely horrible!" With a huge sigh, I cried into the phone, hearing the voice of my sister-girl, Deandra, the third chick to my female Three Musketeers. With her jet setting as a sports writer slash business consultant slash every woman, it was rare to hear from Dee, but when I did, it seemed that it was at those times when I *really* needed a caring person to listen to me…and this time was no different.

"Dee, Girl," I choked out, "my life is so messed up. You would not believe."

"I'm figuring this has to do with a man…Christopher, so spill it, tell me what's wrong." For the next thirty minutes, my mouth was on *flow*, spilling out every sad and confusing instance of the final weeks of me and Chris' relationship. Finally taking a breath from my rambles, Dee suggested, "If he has a *date* tonight, why don't you call him and leave a voice mail message?

"It's *really* important that you get *everything* you need to get out…out, because it sounds to me like y'all are just stuck on pause, no one saying anything about what they feel, just a lot of sexual tension and blaming. You will never be able to go on, with or without him, unless you openly express yourself. Besides, you do it on his voice mail, you don't have to worry about him jumping in and keeping you from saying *exactly* what's on your mind.

"And you really should listen to me…after all, I have *no* man, and my prospects are mighty low, so I'm perfect to give advice over affairs of the heart." Dee and I shared a laugh, but I knew she was right. I had to get my feelings off of my chest.

There's something about drama mixed with tears mixed with lack of sleep that must drug a person. As soon as I whispered my good-byes to Deandra, my eyes fell shut, and I took a much-needed nap. Slowly, I opened my eyes, noticing the darkness that had enveloped outside and my living room. Rubbing the back of my neck, trying to rub out the pain that was growing there, I glanced over at my entertainment system, checking the time on the VCR. "Chris is on his date, no doubt," I mumbled.

Sitting up on my sofa, I let out a loud, exasperated sigh, as my eyes made contact with the cordless phone, on the floor beside my feet. Picking it up, I stared at it, debating with myself on what to do. "Dee's right," I whispered. "Even if Chris and I don't get back together, I need to get all of this off my chest."

Dialing Chris' number, I waited four rings for Chris' smooth voice to inform me that he wasn't in, and to please leave a message, he would get back later. When the beep sounded, I collected a long, hard breath, and said, "Chris, it's me. I don't even know what to say. Wait a minute, wait a minute, I do. Today, at your house, I don't regret what you and I did. I *wanted* to be with you, so please, don't get it in your head that I just wanted to screw you and leave, cuz I didn't.

"Secondly, you're right, I did want to end it, but I really didn't want to end it. I wish I could make you see what I'm going through. It's not all about what other men have done to me, Chris. It really isn't. Lemme flip the script on you. Let's say you came into my place and found me in my bedroom with an ex who had their hands all up on me, wanting to get back with me, and I wasn't giving 100% to tell him to go away, I'm taken. I know you, Chris, and I know you would have been pissed and mad, so don't say you wouldn't.

"Next, let's say you wanted some time to just think, and after just barely half a month, I come to you, wanting you and I pleasure you, but then BOOM, you find out that that same day, I let some other brotha go down on me. What would you have done? I mean really? What?"

The phone beeped, and I cursed it. "Fuck!" I groaned. Redialing, I hoped to be able to continue without Chris happening to waltz up in his place. The answering machine picked up, I was safe for a little while longer.

"Chris, Baby, I hope you got all of that message, as I was saying, okay, I know my pride had a lot to do with all of this, but I did what I know a majority of people, not men or women, just people would have done. I understand how you felt, you felt I didn't want you, so you let Dana do what she did, but does that make you right, and make me wrong, because you have been making ME feel like I did everything, when I did nothing, but try to love you, something that came so easily." I sighed.

"I know you have a date tonight. That's cool. I mean if you can't love me, you should be happy. But I just want to let you know that I love you, Baby. More than I can say on this damn machine, but I had no other outlet, you probably wouldn't have let me speak any of this out without fighting with me." I sniffed. "I guess it wasn't meant to be in this life." I began to openly sob. "I love you, Baby, guess I'll see you next lifetime."

I hung up the phone. I felt so incredibly dead inside, and this feeling made my next decision that much easier.

Chris . . .

Black. That's what I wore for my evening with Cheri, funny how it also seemed to match my mood. I tapped softly at Cheri's door, to be greeted by smiles and loveliness, she obviously having no idea of the screwed up brotha she was about to have dinner with. She looked as lovely as she had that night at Whispers, almost making me forget a bit of my gloom, but not quite. That scene with Tamara had completely floored me, and no matter how much I tried, I couldn't get it off my mind or the sight of her tears. I couldn't help but wonder if maybe she still cared a little. I mean why else would she have been crying like that. I wanted her, still wanted her, and would always want her, the afternoon in her arms proved that to me without a shadow of a doubt.

"Well, don't you look smooth." Cheri smiled, taking in my all my blackness. "All that black on a butter pecan brotha, nice combination."

"Well, you're looking rather succulent yourself," I complimented her, giving her the full effect of the famous Grimes' smile and charm. "Are you ready for dinner now or did you want to go for cocktails first?"

"Dinner please... You're looking at one hungry sistah right now."

Dinner went really well, or so I thought. The whole night I felt as if I was acting out a scene for the Oscars or something, smiling when I was supposed to, laughing right on cue. Cheri was no hoochie. She was beautiful yet smart, held good conversation and was just an all around fun person to be with, and if she had caught me at another place and time I know I would've been a lot more into this, and into her, but I just couldn't shake Tamara. The activities of today were too fresh and new, too potent.

"Ahem," Cheri coughed, vying for my attention. "Are you still with me, Chris?"

"Yeah, sorry, don't know where my mind was," I said with an uncomfortable laugh.

"Hmm, well I know this much, it definitely wasn't with me. You aren't available, are you?"

I looked up at her, my brow coming together in puzzlement. "What do you mean?"

"What I mean is…you aren't available, not on the market for getting to know me, for an attraction, or any kind of relationship." Cheri sipped slowly at her Kahlua and Crème. "Which is okay, but I must admit I'm a bit disappointed. I find you to be a very attractive, very positive brotha," she smiled, "but unfortunately, very unavailable."

"Hey, believe me, I'm not married. You think I'm lying?"

"No, no, that's not what I'm saying. But are you prepared to tell me there is no lady in your life, or at least in your heart right now?" she asked, looking at me intently.

"I have a situation that I'm dealing with, yes," I sighed, "but I'm dealing with it, and I really did want to spend the evening with you."

"I see, and yes, I could tell. It's kinda written all over your face," she said, resting her chin on her palm. "She's special, huh?"

I took a moment before I answered truthfully. "Very…"

"Hmm, well I tell you what, baby boy. When and if you ever become available or open to explore what could be between us, you let me know. In the mean time, I make a good friend," she said, smiling warmly.

I smiled back at Cheri, yet frowning inside. She was really a cool lady, and one day I may just have to take her up on her offer, but for now a friend in her sounded real good.

When I got home, the light on my answering machine was lit. It had been blinking as I walked out of the house earlier, but

I had ignored it seeing that I was running late. I was floored to find a couple of messages from Tamara, and even more so at what she had to say in them.

"Chris, it's me. I don't even know what to say. Wait a minute, wait a minute, I do. Today... at your house... I don't regret what you and I did. I wanted to be with you, so please, don't get it in your head that I just wanted to screw you and leave... cuz I didn't.

Secondly, you're right... I did want to end it..., but I really didn't want to end it. I wish I could make you see what I'm going through. It's not all about what other men have done to me, Chris. It really isn't. Lemme flip the script on you. Let's say you came into my place and found me in my bedroom with an ex who had their hands all up on me, wanting to get back with me, and I wasn't giving 100% to tell him go away, I'm taken. I know you, Chris, and I know you would be pissed and mad, so don't say you wouldn't. Next, let's say you wanted some time to just think, and after just barely a month, I come to you, wanting you and I pleasure you... but then BOOM, you find out that that same day, I let some other brotha go down on me. What would you have done? I mean really? What?"

The answering machine clicked off, ending whatever else Tamara was about to say. Then came a second message, Tamara again.

"Chris, Baby." She was calling me baby? My heart started beating wildly. Tee hadn't called me baby in so long, I had forgotten what it felt like to hear it. The message continued on...

I hope you got all of that message, as I was saying... okay, I know my pride had a lot to do with all of this, but I did what I know a majority of people...not men or women, just people would have done. I understand how you felt that I didn't want you, so you let Dana do what she did, but does that make you right and make me wrong, because you have been making ME feel like I did everything, when I did nothing, but try to love you, something that came so easily. I know you have a date tonight. That's cool. I mean if you can't love me, you should be happy. But I just want to let you know that I love you, Baby. More than I can say on this damn machine, but I had no other outlet, you probably wouldn't have let me speak any of this out without fighting with me."

Tamara began to sob, and I wanted to reach through the machine and hold her something fierce to keep her from crying like that. *"I guess it wasn't meant to be in this life. I love you, Baby, guess I'll see you next lifetime."*

"I love you, Baby." Her words echoed again and again in my ears, making me feel almost unmanly in the intensity of my feelings for her. GOD, I LOVE HER...and she was right about a lot of things. In the reverse, I would have been pissed, too. Yet there were so many things she couldn't see, she couldn't understand. We really needed to talk, and to clear all this bullshit up, because that's all it was, a bunch of bullshit, tearing up a love that's extremely hard to find.

I grabbed my keys, wasting no time as I headed for my car.

Tamara. . .

"I guess it wasn't meant to be in this life. I love you, Baby, guess I'll see you next lifetime."

I looked at the phone like I had forgotten what it was. My eyes were huge, tears were streaming down my face, and I really wasn't thinking about anything...except for ending the pain that I was feeling inside my heart.

It was right there that I *knew* the love between me and Chris was true, because I had never felt this kinda pain with any other man. The ulcer — which was curbed by a good diet and daily jogs — was blowing up big time, and it was painful to walk upright.

I dropped the phone on its base and walked around in circles in my living room. I knew what I had to do, but I didn't know how to go about doing it. "Okay, Tee," I coaxed myself.

"Sit and think a minute." But as soon as I sat down, I had bounced back up, the nervous energy in me not allowing me time to rest. I picked up the phone.

"Sha," I whispered, dialing her number. I knew she wasn't home, and so I thought I could leave her a message, tell her my plan, say good-bye, and that I loved her. On the second ring, Shameika's voice boomed on the other end. "Girl, wassup!" she yelled, obviously checking the Caller ID before answering. "What are you doing, Miss Thang?"

I quickly hung up the phone. This wasn't something I could do with a "real" person on the other end. I didn't want her to stop me from doing what I had to do. I walked into the kitchen, my hands grazing over the cutlery I had on my countertop. Believe me, I wasn't the suicide type, but I *did* need an out of this life.

I ran to my room, pulling out a suitcase and my roll-on bag and began packing quickly. If I knew Sha, and I did, she would be here any minute, wanting to know why I hung up on her. The fact that she didn't call back let me know that she had probably already left. I grabbed a handful of panties and bras, some sundresses, some pants, tennis shoes, sandals, whatever, and tossed everything into the two pieces of luggage. Lugging them into my living room, I snatched up the phone and quickly dialed a number.

"Delta Airlines," the voice on the other end chirped. For a brief second, I thought about kicking her, cause she sounded just too damn happy, but I responded with, "Uh, yeah, I'm in Baltimore...wanting to fly out of BWI...could you tell me of any flights you have departing within the next hour or two?"

There was silence on the other end, and then, "Um, Ma'am, you want ALL the flights?"

"If you don't mind," I said, exasperated. "This is an emergency, and I really need to know...puhleeeeassse."

After about two minutes, the Delta CHIPPER helper rattled off a list of flights that were bouncing from BWI, and I selected one.

"You sure you don't want to wait?" the operator stated. "It's going to be extremely expensive."

"Ma'am, how are you going to take money away from your own company?" I asked, controlling my temper. "I have the money, and if you would be so polite as to take down my credit card information and have my tickets printed for me when I get there, I would be ever so grateful."

"Okay."

After five minutes, I hung up the phone, snatched up my bags, and quickly made tracks out of my apartment. I can't even remember if I had locked my front door or not, the only thing on my mind was getting away...I knew when I wasn't wanted and I was going to take this time to try, try and forget the love of my life.

On The FLIP Side...

"No, she did not hang up on me," Shameika said, foot heavy on the gas pedal as she raced to Tamara's place. "She probably thought my ass wasn't going to be there."

Shameika cranked up the tunes that were rafting through her CD player — Eve — and bobbed her head to the music. She had been worried about Tamara for a while now, but she didn't want to baby Tamara. Shameika knew all about Tamara's past, and also knew that she was taking this break-up with Chris harder than with anyone else she had ever dated.

It steamed Shameika to no end that Chris could do Tamara wrong like he did, and she only prayed that she didn't have to deal with him, because she had a couple of choice words for his no good, shysty ass!

"I need to get over there and check on my girl!" Shameika loudly spoke, as if trying to convince herself. "She don't *need* that Negro Chris in her life making her depressed, and I'm gon' make sure I'm right there to help her through this shit."

Shameika weaved through the traffic on the beltway. She

lived in Woodlawn and was only three exits away from her girl in Catonsville, but there was an accident a couple of exits up and it slowed traffic to a snail pace.

By the time she reached Tamara's apartment, she noticed that Tamara's car was gone, and upon walking up to the door, she noticed it ajar. "Oh my Gosh," she whispered, fearing the worst as she went in, leaving the door open, just in case.

The apartment looked normal, tidy just as Tamara usually kept it. "Tee!" she yelled. "Are you here? Is anybody here?" She waited a minute and proceeded to the bedroom, where she saw everything in disarray, hangers on the bed, clothes on the floor, just a mess. "What in the hell happened here?"

In that instant, Shameika heard the creaking of the front door being opened further. "Oh shit," she whispered, her heart beating crazy in her chest. She tipped over to the other side of the Tamara's bed and knelt down on the floor, the footsteps coming closer.

"This is what I get for loving that girl," she muttered, praying that whoever it was would leave, and leave her *intact*.

Chris...

Hmm, I thought as I stepped up to Tee's apartment. Something didn't seem right. For one, the front door was unlocked and opened, and for two it was way too quiet. Tamara always kept something on, whether it was the radio or the TV. She was one paranoid woman when it came to living alone, which is one reason why she had always spent a lot of time at my place when we were together.

As I walked into her bedroom, the feeling that something was not quite right intensified. I made my way over to the right side of her bed about to look out of her window, when suddenly a feminine scream caused my own scream to fly outta my mouth.

"Ahhh! Damn! What the hell?" I exclaimed, raising my hands in a kick ass position.

"Chris! Oh my God you scared me to death!"

I found myself looking in the eyes of the ghetto queen herself, Shameika. "What you doing here, girl? And where is Tee?"

"Aha," Shameika looked at me with this incredulous look on her face, attitude so thick you could spread it like Jiffy peanut butter. "What am *I* doing here? The question should be, my brotha, what are you doing here. You're the last thing in the world Tamara needs right now and, as you can see, her car is gone, and so is she." Her neck seemed to keep rolling even after she finished her smart-alecky remark.

I worked hard to calm the *slap her ass* voice that kept hollering at me. I swear I am not a woman beater or the type of man who would get physical. I consider myself the *walk away from it* type, but whenever Shameika was in my company, I started feeling like Chris Rock, in that I don't condone hitting a female, but sometimes for those brothas who do, hell, if the woman they knocking the hell out of is like this trick, I UNDERSTAND.

"Look, can you just save all that and tell me if you know where she is? I really need to talk to her. Are you house sitting or something?"

"No, I am not house sitting," Shameika groaned, like it was a big bother to even breathe in my direction. "I came here to see her because she called me and then hung up suddenly. It didn't seem right, and I knew she was going through a lot because of how bad *you* dogged her, so I came to see what was up, and like I said before, Chris, Tamara doesn't need you here. You have done enough hurt and damage to that girl to last her a lifetime. You need to go on with your little hoochie mama and leave Tamara alone!"

I gave a heavy sigh, flopping down on the end of Tamara's bed, praying a quick prayer for strength and tolerance. "Look, for one thing you don't know anything about the situation. I don't have any other woman nor do I want another woman.

And, as for you, you need to go on and look for your own man. If any brotha would be crazy enough to want you with your big ass mouth, and stop dipping your nose in shit that doesn't concern you..."

"She's my girl so YES it does concern me, coz when your ass is gone, I will still be here for her. It's always the same ol' thing with all you triflin' no good, sorry ass brothas! I don't know what she even saw in your yella ass anyhow!" Shameika was almost breathless after her tirade, fighting hard to get control of her emotions. With her nostrils flaring she looked like a damn bull. I sat watching her for a minute, determined not to let myself get in the same spell as her. My main concern was Tamara, and I was slowly starting to feel that even Shameika didn't know where Tamara had gone off to.

"So, are you finished?" I asked her sarcastically. Suddenly the closet caught my attention, the EMPTY closet! I jumped up and, in two leg strides, I stood in front of it. "All of her stuff is gone! Sha, enough of all this. Do you have *any* idea where she has gone off to?" I asked, looking around her room noticing for the first time the hangers tossed around, which was way out of character for Tamara, her being somewhat of a neat freak.

"No, I don't," she said, "I got here about two minutes before you pulled up and was wondering the same thing myself. It's obvious that she's gone out of town. *Maybe to get away from you?"*

"Damn!" Suddenly, I wasn't hearing Shameika anymore as I rushed out of the room heading for the front door. I don't know why, but I knew I had to get to BWI, because something inside me said that she was getting onto a plane, and if she did, I would never see her again.

"Where you going? Where you going, Chris!" I ignored Shameika's question, jumped into my car, and with tires squealing, made my way as quickly as possible to the airport. My nerves were jumping, so rattled that I could barely make out the traffic in front of me. I stopped before making a right turn onto the interstate, but I didn't notice the Ford Windstar racing down the road, didn't notice or think about anything but getting to that airport. Suddenly, I felt something slam into the back of me, and felt myself rolling, flipping around and around till I came to a crash upside down stop, my airbag slapping me hard in the face and chest, as pain flashed through my body. The last thing that went through my mind before I slipped into unconsciousness was that I wasn't going to make it to BWI to stop Tamara.

Tamara . . .

I think the clerk at the ticket counter thought I was crazy. I came into BWI with my eyes wide, like I had seen something horrific. And on top of their wideness, they were just as swollen from the tears. I could barely speak to her, but I managed to whisper my name, show her the necessary ID, check my big piece of luggage, and snatch up my tickets.

Once at the terminal, I allowed myself a second of rest. I plopped down into a chair and let out a long, deep, shaky breath. I felt like I had just been TKO'd, and for real, I was *so* tired of fighting back. Tiredly, I raised my right wrist to check the time. I still had about an hour before take off, so I rose back to my feet, grabbed my roller and back pack and headed upstairs to get me a drink.

I'm not a drinker, but I'm not the biggest lover of flying either. I've only flown once before, actually, only left Catonsville once before, and that was to Chicago with Chris. We went there a couple of months back, spending a couple of days chilling on Michigan Avenue, shopping, hanging at the beach, and just enjoying all that Chi-Town had to offer. The flight was the scariest experience I had ever had. There wasn't any turbulence, but I swore we were going to crash, end in a fiery blaze, and for the whole flight I had my hands glued tight to my arm rests and my eyes closed as I prayed to God for us to land safely in Chicago.

And we had...THANK GOD. I told myself if I ever went flying again, I would get me a drink beforehand to calm my nerves. With my nerves *doubly* shot, I was thinking I might need a double. I ordered me an Amaretto Sour and sat at one of the small round tables that looked out into one of the strips the planes landed onto.

I sipped the Sour, trying hard to calm my fastly beating heart. I felt like America's Most Wanted, running from the law and whatnot. My mind was going a mile a minute, thinking about how irate my mother, and my father, would be that I just left and didn't tell them anything, thinking about Shameika calling everybody and their mother to find my behind, but mostly, mostly I thought about how I wished I could moonwalk back two months, back to before all this had happened, back to when Chris and I were feeling each other the *exact* way, and all was good, better than good. I felt the tears steadily stream down my cheeks, as I sat, wishing I could drown myself in them.

Just from the initial sips of my Sour, I could feel my insides grow warm and tingly and liquidy, just like I would get when Chris looked into my eyes or told me he loved me. Quietly, I wept. My body, still, my heart, amazingly calm, the only evidence of the breakdown being the tears that streamed down my cheeks. I was so tired, so unbelievably tired.

Truth be told, I don't even *remember* what we initially were fighting and arguing for. I really don't. Now, it's like, all I want is a calm...a deep breath...a quiet release of this pain...and the chance to start over. I wanted to start over with Chris...not even start over. I just wanted to forget that the last two months ever existed in my life. I wanted to love Chris and have him love me and feel *safe* in our love. I really didn't think that was too much to ask for. My tears came harder when my brain clicked to the fact that Chris had already been out on a date.

I had never called *what's his face* from the cafe. I wasn't interested. In my heart, and in my mind, if I couldn't have Chris, I really wasn't interested in venturing out into the dating scene again. And Chris said, he told me that it was my fault for all this. I couldn't trust him, love him enough. He was moving on. Oh well. Another one bites the dust in my life. Not surprised, not surprised at all.

Steadily sipping my Sour, I heard the sounds of my straw sucking nothing, and I snapped from my thoughts. My watch read that it was 20 minutes til the plane loaded, and I picked my things up and made it back to the terminal. I watched the plane land and the people who had flown in leave off the plane, running up to family, to lovers and hugging and kissing. I wished I had someone happily awaiting my arrival...return...whatever. A little too late for wishes.

When the last person left the plane, I looked up at the board behind the terminal, which labeled the arrivals and departures. My flight was on time, and beginning to board. Flight 1225 to Chicago. I figured if I couldn't be happy in my present, then a special blast from my past was in order.

Chris. . .

"Do you think he can hear us?" a voice said.

"I'm not sure, but damn he looks bad!" whispered another voice.

It felt weird being able to hear clear conversations, but not being able to respond. Felt like everything was in whispers though, and the pain in my head was bad enough to make me wish myself back to sleep. I let out an involuntary groan, moving slightly and moaning deeper still at the pain in my left arm.

"Christopher, can you hear me baby?" I recognized the

sound of my mom's voice right away. Opening my eyes, I could feel a patch or bandages partly over one of them. Felt as though every muscle in my body was crying out in pain.

"Yeah, I can hear you," I whispered between parched lips. "Dang, what happened?"

"You had an accident, dawg!" exclaimed Joop. "How many fingers do you see?" he said, holding up his hand, trying to smile a little. "You gave us quite a scare there, my brotha. How you feeling?"

My mom bent down and kissed me on the lips, tears evident in her eyes.

"Sore."

"But of course you are, dear. Here, have some water," she said, as she poured water from the pitcher beside my bed. Everything was focusing in a little bit more clearly now, including the pain. I was also starting to remember a bit more about what had happened. The lights, hitting my head against the window, and then all going black. Suddenly a thought came into my head, one that was most vital in my book.

"What about my car? Is it messed up bad?" I asked.

"Totaled, man. I mean, they said you rolled about four times so you can't expect anything else. You're lucky you got out in as good a shape as you did," said Joop, my mom caressing the side of my cheek.

Turned out that I was indeed lucky, a bad concussion, broken arm, and one hell of a case of whiplash. Of course I was at fault, got a citation and this of course would seriously fuck up my driving record and raise the cost of my insurance. All kinds of thoughts flew through my banged up head.

I cringed as a sharp pain went through my head. "What about the other driver? What was it, a van right?" I asked.

"Do you think you need something for the pain?" my mom asked, concerned.

I gestured weakly in the affirmative as she rang the nurse to bring me some Demerol. Joop went on to explain, "It was this

Hispanic woman. She was a bit banged up, but they treated and released her the day before yesterday I believe."

"The day before yesterday? What day is it? How long have I been out?" Just then, the sound of my room door opening caused me and Joop and my mom to look toward it, my heart stopping at the sight of Tamara standing there with concern and fear written all over her face.

Tamara...

I flew into O'Hare, grabbed up my bags, went straight to Avis and got me a nice car to drive around in while I was here. My mind was on "float," meaning I wasn't really thinking anything. It seemed that the higher the plane flew, the further away from Baltimore I got, the lighter my head felt.

I managed to get me a suite at Doubletree, which was one of my *favorite* hotels. It was the spot for me to be. The John Hancock building was right across the street and the lake and beach were just a stone throw away as well. As soon as I stepped into the lobby, I could smell the Doubletree chocolate chip cookies waiting to melt into my mouth. As always, they were decadent. Once in my suite, I gave the bellman a tip and fell onto the soft queen-sized bed. Before I knew it, I was out...dead to the world. Who knew that deadly stress and running away from my problems would make me so tired?

When I awoke, the clock on the dresser read 10 p.m., so I got up, showered, dressed in an all black linen pantsuit and sandals, grabbed my backpack purse, and headed out the door. My stomach was demanding to be heard and refusing to eat in, so I headed across the street to The Cheesecake Factory, which was on the lower level of the Hancock Building.

After gorging on dinner and a nice slice of strawberry cheesecake, I walked the Magnificent Mile, checking out the expensive shops on the strip, like Ralph Lauren and Gucci, gawked at prices from the windows and wound up walking past Oak Street to Lake Michigan. I remembered the first time coming here with Chris and laughing at the thought of a beach right beside skyscrapers and the busiest strip in Chicago, but hey, if anyone would do it, it would be Chi-Town.

I sat on a cement bench, letting the cool air from the lake chill me. The onyx water was rippling and lightly lapping against the sand, and I sat there for the longest time, my mind a blank. Eventually, my body told me it was too cold to be out here, even in late June, so I made my way back down to Doubletree and up to my room where I proceeded to drop my bag, slip my shoes off, and pass out in my bed, letting the numbness of my brain give away to a peaceful sleep.

I don't know how it was possible, but I managed to sleep the next day away, only getting up to call room service to bring me up my three meals. I laid in bed, surfed through the television, and welcomed the sleep that continuously took over me. Two days later, after spending most of those in bed, too, I was awakened by the shrill sound of the telephone. Groggily, I reached out, grabbing the receiver and pulling it under the blanket tent I created. "Hello," I grumbled into the receiver.

"Bitch! How you just gon' leave like that and not tell anybody?" I shook my head. It *sounded* like Shameika, but how she find out where I was here? "You need to get yo ass home right now, Girl!" Shameika continued.

I rolled over in the bed, groaning. "Girl, leave me alone!" I yelled. "I just want to be left alone. And don't be telling my mother OR Chris where I..."

"Chris is in the hospital!"

I choked on my words and fought with the blanket to get free of it. It took me at least five minutes to release myself and, by then, my breath was coming fast and hard. "Hospital?" I sputtered. "What?"

"He had a car accident a couple of days ago," Shameika explained, her voice quivering. "I racked my brain trying to think of where you could be and stupid me forgot about how you went on and on about loving Chicago, so..."

"Is Chris okay?" I asked, cutting in. Shameika was bordering on hysterical and I wanted to stop the high pitch of her voice.

"He's banged up *really* bad, Girl. *Please* just come home."

I don't even remember hanging up the phone, but I did. I quickly called the airlines, having kept my return date open. I wanted to see how soon I could get up outta here. When they said two hours, I hopped up, showered, dressed, and hobbled out the room with my bags, hoping I wasn't too late to see Chris.

I drove straight from BWI to the hospital, hoping that I would find Chris in one piece. I wrangled a nurse into telling me his room number and when I finally reached it, I peered into the door's window, noticing that Chris' mother and Joop were in there with him. I choked back a sob, seeing my baby's head bandaged, as well as his left eye. I steeled myself and walked in. I felt all eyes on me, but mine were rested on Chris. Slowly, I walked up to the foot of the bed, feeling Chris' mother hug me, tell me how glad she was to see me. I felt Joop smile at me, giving me the Negro nod of acknowledgment.

As if I demanded them, Joop and Chris' mother quietly left the room. I quickly ran up beside Chris and looked down at his arm, obviously broken, his face a little cut up, his bandaged eye and head and like an open dam, I broke. The tears came hard as I bent my head down to Chris, kissing his lips lightly.

"Don't cry, Babe," Chris murmured to me. "It's not as bad as it looks." I couldn't speak, all I could do was cry and lean into Chris without hurting him. After several minutes, I cried, "I love you." I kissed Chris' lips again, tasting my tears on them.

"I love you so much, and if anything had happened and I couldn't tell you that again, I don't know..."

"Shhhh," Chris whispered. "It's okay, Baby. You know I love you, too. More than anything." Hearing Chris say that, I instantly felt a calming surge through my body, making me feel warm and loved. As quick as those feelings came, another followed. Anger. I rose up, throwing my hands up on my hips as I stared down at the bruised man that I loved.

"Where the hell were you going in such a hurry that you had a damn accident!?" I asked, my voice slightly raised and shaky.

Chris . . .

Aches, pains all mashed together, it still felt good as hell to see Tamara come through that door. And now here she was, telling me she loved me, had always loved me, and giving me every reason to feel that God was shining down on us and giving us one more chance at our love.

"Where the hell were you going in such a hurry that you had a damn accident?" she asked, looking like she didn't know whether to hug or hit me.

"To you," was my shaky reply.

"To me?"

"Tamara, I was not going to let you get away from me without a fight," I began. "I got your messages on the answering machine but, by the time I got to your place, you had left. I talked to Shameika and realized that you must have decided to leave Baltimore and the only thing I could think of was that there was no way I would let the love of my life get away from me that easily." I grabbed hold of Tamara's hand, looking deeply into her eyes. "Baby, do you have any idea how much I love you? You're everything to me, everything I've hoped for, and wanted in a woman in a relationship, and if I had lost you, nothing would of mattered to me, it wouldn't of mattered to me if my eyes never opened up again...if I had lost you."

"Oh God, Chris," Tamara cried, shaking with emotion. "I love you, too...I was leaving because I couldn't stand being this close to you and yet so far apart. All I could think of was that I had to leave, go anywhere, just run away from the pain, and now it just kills me to think that my rash behavior could of gotten you killed!"

"Shhhh, It wasn't your fault; it was mine for driving so recklessly and not paying attention to where I was going. I'm just glad you're here, so very glad that you're here." The sound of my room door opening caused both of us to look up, exhaling deeply as my nurse came in to give me the Demerol caplets.

"How are you, sweetie?" The nurse asked, placing a thermometer between my parched lips. I tried unsuccessfully to answer her, her stern look causing me to shut my mouth quickly. I looked over at Tee; wanting to touch her somehow, keep her close to me so that she never ever got away again.

The nurse quietly shut the door after she finished giving me my painkillers and taking all my vitals, leaving Tamara and me alone. Tamara walked over to me; bringing herself close to me again. The love I felt for her was so real and rich, there was no room for trying to be cool or fronting or feeling whipped, like Joop would always say. If this was whipped, bring it on.

"I'm sorry about the Dana thing," I whispered. "I know I was wrong, Tamara. I guess that was part of the reason I was so defensive about it. I forgot myself for a moment because of everything that we were dealing with, and I felt that you didn't love me or want me like I wanted and loved you.

"But the things she told you, the way she insinuated it to you, it never happened that way. It was my love for you that brought me to my senses, and made me put a stop to it. See, she didn't bother to tell you that, but it's the truth I swear. And I know that doesn't change what I did, or make it okay, but I love you, Tamara," I said pleadingly, catching my breath as another sharp pain hit me. "I wish these damn pain killers would hurry up and start working."

Pain covered Tamara's face as she sensed mine. "Don't, baby, it's okay. Let's put all of that behind us. Like you said, nothing matters but our love. We both made mistakes. I should-n't have jumped to conclusions like I did, shouldn't have allowed past drama to cause me to doubt you. This thing is so crazy, the different ways men and women see things, he says she says, the opposite sex and relationships. Hell, we could write a book on it and *still* not completely understand one another. But when we both stop looking at our differences and just accept the fact that the one thing we can always agree on is to never let anything get in the way of our love, that's when we will finally be okay."

We looked at each other, our eyes damp. "Luvalwayz," I whispered to Tamara, lightly kissing her lips.

"Luvalwayz," Tamara mouthed back at me.

PART TWO ☆
Joop & Shameika

Joop . . .

"I can't believe this. Still cannot believe our boy is getting hooked, jumping the damn broom, taking the..."

"Nestea plunge!" Stephen threw in.

"Um..nay, that's goofy Step," I replied with a smirk. "Back in Africa and slavery times it was called JUMPING THE BROOM."

"Man, I know that," said Stephen as he wrestled with his cummerbund, fighting with a broken hook. "I mean, damn, I saw ROOTS. Everybody did. Maybe not a zillion times like you did, getting all worked up and ready to kill all caucazoids." He laughed.

"Naw, you'd rather screw all the caucazoids," I swung back.

"That's all good. I want ALL the ladies: black ladies, white ladies, Chinese mamas, Hong Kong honeys!"

I made a mock sound of regurgitation, looking at Stephen and shaking my head. "Man, that's nasty. Just plain nasty. I've been trying to teach you all these years how to be a black man and you ain't caught on yet."

"Well?" Stephen and I paused our ritual sparring, turning suddenly toward the sound of our soon to be wed partner. I couldn't help but smile. Chris, well that was one happy brotha. All decked out in his white. Better him than me, I laughed to myself, but maybe he was ready. Some brothas just get to the point where they feel they have found the ONE, where there is no doubt or hesitation. No matter how hard Step and I tried to get Chris to rethink things, he had been hell bent on this marriage. I had to admit to myself though, that Tamara changed Chris for the better.

Chris had been almost as wild as Stephen when it came to the ladies, IF THAT WAS POSSIBLE, and it was almost like a second job for me to try and keep my two boys in line. Oddly enough, both of them were older than me by a year, me just tasting my 28th birthday a month prior. All three of us had played basketball together at Howard U, them in their senior and me in my junior year. We had been inseparable every since, the three black Musketeers. And now here was Chris, breaking up the trio, jumping the damn broom.

"Well?" Chris said again. "Am I not one smooth, clean cut, handsome muthafucka or what?" Chris was styling in a white Zootsuit style Tux with tails to boot, and matching black and white wingtips. Step and I were equally styling in the same exact Tux, except for the red rose that peeked out of Chris' left pocket, whereas Step and I wore a black rose.

"My super clean brotha," Stephen smiled. "Chris, okay, I got to say this, for the hundredth and final time..."

"ARE YOU SURE YOU WANT TO DO THIS?" both Stephen and I sung out in unison.

"Yes I'm sure." Chris laughed, pure happiness written all over his face. Yeah, he was sure. That much I could see. I felt this tiny feeling of jealousy wash over me, *very* tiny though. Fingering the slight dimple in my freshly shaven chin, I looked at Chris and suddenly felt happy for him. I knew from the half grin on Stephen's face, he was thinking and feeling the same thing, too.

"Then let's roll!" Stephen exclaimed, giving Chris a bear hug. I looked at both of them and smiled, all three of us grabbing our Al Capone matching hats, and heading out to the church hall.

Shameika...

Look up 'shit' in the dictionary and a picture of my girl, Tamara, is there. Why you ask? Because today she is looking DA SHIT on the real! For the past ten months, I've been helping my homegirl plan the biggest day of her life, her wedding, and now the big day was finally here. You could have pimp slapped me with a wet noodle if you had told me this was how she and Chris were going to turn out. Their relationship was what I called, "What the Hell?" and after she ran off and he got in a car accident trying to get to her, I was pretty sure that the final curtain had fallen on this dynamic duo, but no. I guess God was like, "Somebody needs to be happy. Enter Tamara and Chris."

Now here we were, minutes away from my girl's "I do," and she looked like a vision on top of a wedding cake. She didn't want to go with the traditional white frilly gown. Instead, she chose a white silk, ankle-length gown. It was sleeveless, with a scoop neckline and a deep V in the back, with silk strings crisscrossing up her back. The gown melded tightly around her waist and slightly flared out as it reached her hips, draping down her legs, but the most exquisite part of the gown were the hand sewn red roses that were stitched throughout the gown. She really did look like a beautiful garden with that gown on, and when I helped her place the silk wreath of red and black roses — only a man would want black roses — into her curly upswept 'do, I looked into the mirror to see matching tears on our faces.

"Girl," I cried. "Come on now. You're going to mess up that makeup. Let's get to stepping, I'm sure your dad is outside this door pacing a ditch." We laughed. Tamara grabbed a tissue from the box on the desk and dabbed at her eyes.

"You're right." She smiled, her face glowing like a halogen bulb. Tamara rose up from her chair and glanced my way. "Aren't we looking stunning?" she asked, smiling. I have to admit, I was *extremely* glad that my girl had some taste, because I did not want to be stuck wearing a big lime green, foo foo dress. Instead, I wore a long, sleeveless black gown with a slit up to mid-thigh. Draped around my neck was a black and red sheer scarf that fell around my neck and down my back. My micro mini braids were placed in a chignon. All the bridesmaids, four in all, were dressed in knee-length red sleeveless dresses with the same scarf. I smiled, knowing that the pictures of this here black wedding were gonna be all of that.

"Girl," I laughed, "nobody's gonna be looking at me. YOU'RE the bride. I'm just the trusty sidekick!"

Laughing, Tamara's expression was wistful. "I wish our other sidekick was here today."

"I know, Girl," I responded, gently hugging Tamara. "You know Deandra would have given anything to be here with you today...the first of the Three Musketeers taking it down the aisle. I talked to her this morning and she was boohooing, crying over breaking her foot last week and having to get it operated on. But she told me that when you get back from your honeymoon, give her a call, send pictures, all of that."

Smiling, Tamara said, "You know I will." She stood quietly for a moment, her eyes tearing up. "You know, I really do love you two...very much."

Feeling myself choke up, I hugged Tamara fiercely, "And we both love you, too, Girl. Forever." I lowered the veil from Tamara's wreath and placed it over her face. "Showtime, Girl," I whispered.

Instead of the normal Wedding March, Tamara's aunt sang Brian McKnight's "Still in Love." It was da BOMB. I carried my bouquet of red and white roses and, with a demure smile, I stepped down the aisle. I noticed Chris, wide-eye and beaming and I gave him a wink. Believe it or not, he and I had become 'somewhat' friendly to each other, so I could at *least* smile at him on his big day. I almost missed a stepped when I saw his fine ass best man. Boy looked just like some Eric Benet. Was halfway expecting to come down the aisle and see him wearing no shoes like my boy Benet be doing, but luckily Chris schooled him on proper wedding attire.

Once my girl made her perfect entrance down the aisle and handed me her bouquet to hold, my eyes kept moving back to the best man. He was cute...damn cute. I hadn't spent a lot of time with Chris' boys, but I knew they called this one Joop. Where the hell that came from I had no idea. I could feel him staring at me, and I smiled. He looked like somebody I could get a nice ride out of and get my wheels oiled quite nicely. It had been a hot minute since I had any bodywork done, and hey, why not him...if he was interested.

Tamara leaned in to kiss her now hubby and the church erupted with cheers and claps. She turned to me and I kissed her, handing her the bouquet. Tee and Chris happily marched up the aisle and I was face to face with Joop, who raised his hand for me to take. I smiled at him and took his hand, the two of us walking hand in hand out of the church.

The wedding was the black event of the year, in my opinion, but the reception was out of this world. Tee and Chris danced to 'Spend My Life with You' and 'Come as You Are' by Eric Benet and then the DJ announced that the maid of honor and best man had to come up and get their dance on. Mary J. Blige's 'Beautiful Ones' boomed through the speakers as Joop guided me onto the floor. The cut was slightly fast-paced, so there was no heavy holding, caressing and swaying in each other's arms.

But, I did learn from that dance that Mr. Joop had moves way beyond a dance floor. Throughout the entire dance, Joop didn't take his eyes off of me. They were so deep and penetrating and, momentarily, I was lost in them. His hands barely touched my hips, but I tingled feeling them on me. Without thinking, my hands rose up and grabbed hold of some of his shoulder-length dreads. My eyes were closed and I began singing along with Mary. This *was* my jam. "Can't you hear the bells ringing, doves flying in the air...with this ring I promise to always be right there..."

"You have a beautiful voice," said Joop, breaking me from my singing. I looked up into his face and smiled. He really was attractive. Dayum. "Thank you," I whispered back, twirling around so that my back was against him. By now, everybody was up and jamming to Mary, which then glided into 'Back to One' by Brian McKnight. Dang, they were playing and singing all of my cuts today. Maybe it had *something* to do with the fact that I had picked out the DJ...suggested some tunes for him to play. Slowly, I began circling my tiny hips against Joop and I heard him groan softly. Ding Ding. I smiled inwardly, thinking I was going to have me something sweet to go with my piece of wedding cake tonight.

"Ms. Jones," Joop whispered in my ear, "you don't need to be starting anything up in here. This *is* a wedding reception." With long sways, I rubbed myself against him a couple more times, emitting the same groans from him. *Yea*, I said, laughing inside, *you sound soooooo worried about this being a wedding reception.* I turned back to face him, my smile pure and sweet.

"I'm sorry," I said, still smiling. "Would you *prefer* we do this some place else?"

Joop...

I was too black to blush, yet my cheeks were stinging, and I felt like every thought in my head must be on my face. This Shameika, damn she was a beautiful black queen. I loved her look, loved her petiteness, had always dug tiny petite sistahs, but what shook me the most about her were her eyes, how they tilted up at the ends, almost oriental looking, and had the color of cat eyes. I had asked Chris about her right after the ceremony. He laughed and informed me that she was an educated hoochie and to watch out for her. An educated hoochie, now that was a new one. That very description of her had me curious, and watch out for her? Hell, if that wasn't a challenge, I didn't know what was.

Now, toward the end of the reception, Ms. Shameika Jones and I were having another dance. She was definitely a flirt, deliberately standing on her tiptoes and pressing her tiny hips up against my 6' foot frame, causing a strangled groan to spring from my lips. Shameika smiled up at me, her head tilted up so that her lips touched the end of my chin. "I'm sorry," she said, smiling coy like. "Would you prefer we do this some place else?"

"Excuse me?" I replied back, looking at her a bit in shock.

She answered back with a smile, not saying a word. Just that smile. *Lawd!*

"Hey, everybody, they about to leave and Tee is going to throw her bouquet. Ladies, get over here!" I heard someone scream. Shameika gave me one last look before bolting over to the group of ladies, ready to catch Tamara's bouquet. "Okay, let's do this!" Tamara shouted, laughing at the bundle of sistahs vying to be the next bride on tour.

"Man, look at them. Women are a trip," Stephen said, smiling. "And I noticed you and meow grinding to the music all night. What's up with that, huh?" he laughed slyly.

"Ain't nothing up. She's just a lovely sistah, is all. Unlike you, my brotha, I respect our queens."

"Well, she didn't look like she wanted respect. She's looking at you right now like she wants some..."

"Step, for real, you need to shut up." I laughed, both of us looking over at Shameika, finding her looking right at me, tracing her lips slowly.

"Uh huh, just don't cut your lip on that KAT!" Stephen hooted, slapping me hard on the back before walking off. "Ladies, never fear, Stephen Lewis is here!" he sung, evaporating in the crowd of single ladies. I smiled and shook my head at him, turning to look up as Shameika approached me again.

"So," she said, "somebody over there just informed me that you rode a motorcycle. So when are you gonna take me for a ride, hmm?"

"You don't want to try and catch the bouquet?" I asked her.

"Naw, I don't believe in superstition, and this is all winding down now. Chris and Tee are leaving and I'm getting a little restless."

I could kinda understand what she meant. After the vows, my boy Chris only had eyes for his bride. Things were already changing, it seemed, and there were so many people here. I, along with Shameika, was feeling a bit restless. "So when are you going to gimme a ride, Boo? Does a sistah have to BEG you?"

"No, no, actually I rode it over here today. I could, umm…take you for a spin now if you want," I replied hesitantly. I kinda didn't know how to take Ms. Jones and didn't want her to think I was expecting anything.

"Sounds simply divine," she cooed. "Let me get my bag and we can roll." She pranced off and, pretty soon, we were saying our goodbyes. I gave Chris and Tamara a parting hug, hearing Tamara whisper out loudly to Shameika, "You work it, gurl!"

"Remember what I told you," Chris said to me with a warning glance. Within ten minutes, Shameika and I were climbing on my spanking new green Yamaha YZF. "So, where are we going?" I asked her.

"Where do you live, Boo?" she replied back.

"Park Avenue."

"Then Park Avenue it is," she said, kissing me lightly on the back of my neck, sending instant chills down my spine.

"So, can I get you something? A beer, wine?" I asked, watching Shameika as she removed her jacket. *Oh lawd…but she had a cute little behind…*

She shocked me, though, when she bounced back with, "Vodka, straight on da rocks, sweetie."

Well damn, I thought to myself, removing my Tux coat before throwing her a soft smile and quickly making myself busy with drinks.

"Power to the people!" I heard her shout. "I see you're into the black thang." I walked back into my living area to see her looking at my framed pictures of past Black Panther leaders with appreciation. Fingering with her long tipped nails my velvet picture of Rev. Martin Luther King, and brotha Malcolm.

"Definitely, I feel that a brotha aware is a brotha prepared." I winked at her as I reached out to hand her the Vodka. She, to my surprise, placed it on the coffee table, and placed both her hands around my waist in one step. I moaned as her warm lips met mine, her lips sucking my tongue as if it were a Popsicle, slowly, sensuously. "You're intoxicating," I whispered, after I could catch my breath.

"Uh huh, and I LOVE a brotha with dreads...show me your bedroom."

A brotha aware is a brotha prepared, I had said. Well, I was left to eat my words because one thing I was not aware of, nor prepared for, was the way this sistah was turning me out. She was wild, she was hot, she was sexy, SHE BLEW MY MIND! The last thing I remembered before passing out from sexual exhaustion was her moaning in my ear, "Damn, baby, I ain't never come like that!"

Hell. I never had either...

Shameika...

I think I saw Joop choke when we got to his motorcycle and I hiked my dress up around my thighs, allowing the slit to ride up beneath my panties so that I could straddle the bike. I made sure to hold him tight, my arms secure around him, my hands pressed against his chest.

When we got to his place, I was pretty impressed. I had a girlfriend who used to live on Park Avenue and the brownstones were nice with the gleaming hardwood floors. They were *classy* if you will. I chuckled when Joop gave me a raised eyebrow when I ordered Vodka, straight on the rocks, but hey... I can roll with the big dogs from time to time when it came to tilting back the 'hair on your chest' drinks, so I just shrugged and surveyed his place.

He was definitely militant, no ifs, ands, or buts about that, for real. "Power to the people!" I shouted, half jokingly, half serious. "I see you're into the Black thang." He said something about a brotha being prepared and aware, but I was busy glancing at his pictures, my eyes resting on Martin Luther King, Jr., but only for a brief moment.

Joop handed me my drink and gave me a wink and a smile. He was damn fine, with a capital, OOOOOH. This drink in my hand meant nothing to me, especially when I had the thoughts that were running through my mind. I placed the drink on the coffee table and slid my hands around his waist. On tiptoes, I took a kiss from him, letting my tongue slip into his warm mouth. When I found his, my lips softly clenched it, sucking it, and I heard Joop moan, as he whispered how intoxicating I was.

I ain't *neva* had a man tell me I was intoxicating, and hearing those words and hearing his moans and feeling the wetness between my legs and feeling my body light up, I knew that it was about to be on. "Uh huh, and I LOVE a brotha with dreads," I moaned. "Show me to your bedroom."

His eyes widened, but Joop quickly took me by the hand and led me into his bedroom. As soon as we made it into his room, I shut his bedroom door and pressed my small frame against him, bending his mouth down to meet mine. "I'm going to make you feel *so* good," I whispered to Joop in between our deep kisses, as his fingers quickly moved along my back and unzipped my dress. I stepped away from him, my eyes never leaving his face, as I dropped my dress to the floor and stepped from it. I was clad in a black lace bra and matching thong and the sounds coming from his mouth had a sistah ready to cry.

"Come here, boo," I moaned, and he came with the swiftness, molding his lean, hard body up against me. Quickly, I took off every piece of clothing from his body, wanting to see every part of his dark body and what I saw would have made me pass out if I didn't want him with such urgency. When I had him stripped of all his clothing, I pushed him down onto his bed and climbed atop him. I could feel him growing hard against my inner thighs and I groaned. I bent down, kissing his mouth, his chin, his chest, nipping at his nipples, licking my way down to his throbbing manhood. I heard him whisper, "Oh...yes!" and I smiled, taking him into my mouth, licking and sucking him til I heard a guttural cry come from him. "Shameika! Ride me, baby!"

I quickly slipped out of my panties and bra and crawled back up to him...straddling him. "You want me to ride you, huh?" I asked, licking his lips as his hands ran up and down my spine, causing me to shiver. "Yes," he answered. "Protection, Boo?" I asked, in a sexy tone, not wanting to break the mood. I may like to get mine, but I ain't stupid. His head motioned towards his nightstand. I opened the drawer, pulling out a condom. Smiling at him, I lowered down between his legs, giving him one final suck, causing him to groan and shiver beneath me. With the protection in place, I crawled back up to him, and slowly guided him inside of me. We both groaned. My hands dropped to either side of his head, my fingers against his dreads and I looked him dead in his sexy eyes. There's something about just watching a man during sex. It made my ego expand to see his eyes widened, the pupils almost dilate, his vision get blurry, the heat rise in them. I wanted Joop to feel everything that this little sistah had and I wanted to make sure he cried out *my* name by the time we were through.

I swiveled and grinded and pumped and bounced myself up and down Joop and never lost contact with his face, his eyes. I swallowed a lump of something...don't know what it was, maybe longing, but I pushed that deep, deep, deep down in me. That was Tamara's territory, not mine. I heard Joop grunt and thrust his hips up to me and I cried out. I had to admit Boo was giving it to me as hard as I was giving it to him. Sweat dripped from between my small breasts to his chest as we sexed like it was going out of style.

I leaned back, letting my hands hold me up as Joop squeezed my ass and brought me harder against him. "Oh shit," I cried out, feeling Joop get closer and closer to the place that had a sistah speaking in tongues, at least *this* sistah. "Damn, Sha...you feel so good.... I'm gonna come," Joop groaned.

"Come for me, Boo," I whispered, milking him profoundly, feeling my own explosion near. "Come for me."

With my words, Joop tightly gripped my hips and pulled me to him. I screamed as he tapped my core three hard times, making me spasm above him. I could see his face contorting, his breath coming hard as his build up led to a loud groan, my name uttered over and over again, and his own explosive climax.

I fell limp against his sweat-drenched chest, my heart racing and my breath caught in the back of my throat. "Damn, Baby," I moaned, "I ain't never come like that!" Joop moaned some unintelligible words to me, but I knew he was feeling it, too.

Just as my body began to feel comfortable lying atop of Joop, feeling his hands on my back, his warm breath on my neck, I felt the old regime kick in. I had to admit, I may like to get my wham, bam, thank you misters in, but I ain't neva kicked it with someone I just met, even though Joop and I had "known" of each other for a hot little minute. I dunno, something about Joop attracted me to him and I had to have him. Now that I had him, my storyline read it was time to get up and go home. Can't break the script. Spent too many years writing it, perfecting it.

I sighed, pushing myself up from the warmth of Joop's sex-satisfied and oh so fine body.

"What's up?" he asked, opening his eyes to look at me. Dayum, had to quickly look away. I swear that boy had some soul-searching, I know your whole life kinda eyes and I didn't need him to be my mind reader.

"Gotta go," I said, slipping from the bed.

Joop . . .

"Huh?" I shook the sleepy cobwebs from my head, thinking that I must have been dreaming when I felt the weight of Shameika's body moving off my waterbed. I jumped up quickly.

"Hey, Sha, baby, you ain't gotta go nowhere. Stay," I said, caressing her cheek and giving her a tender smile.

She looked at me with an odd look in her eyes for a moment, glancing down to finger the Ankh tattoo on my right bicep. Sighing deeply, she slipped her gown back on, picking up her bra and panties and heading for the living room. "Listen I'm sorry, Joop. What's your real name, by the way?" she hollered through the door, me quickly slipping on my black terrycloth robe.

"Um, Jamal. Jamal Evans." Something about this picture just didn't seem right. *Why the hell was she leaving?* I stood at the entranceway, watching her as she put her underclothes in her bag, taking a quick drink of her melted down Vodka, the one she had never gotten to. She walked over to my phone and asked for a cab. A CAB!

"I could take you home, you know."

"No need, baby. No worries. I'm an independent woman," she said breezily.

I was speechless for a second.

"Did I do something wrong? I mean, I know we hardly know each other. Believe me when I say that I really didn't bring you here for this. I'm not the playa type or a bootie caller. I've had an interest in you ever since I saw you at rehearsals and I really just wanted to get to know you better. Please don't leave. Stay and let's, I don't know, just talk for a while?" I could hear my old southern slur slipping in for a moment, me forgetting for a minute to pronounce each word just so. One thing I didn't want her thinking, was that I was some country bumpkin.

"Joop...Jamal, you did nothing wrong, I'm just a person who likes sleeping in her own bed, and I'm tired. It's sweet of you to say you wanted to get to know me, and believe me, you was all dat baby," she smiled sweetly.

"So can I get your number?" I asked, still for some odd reason pulling for straws.

"Naw, I don't give out my numba, but I'll call you. You in the book?" I nodded faintly. "Cool, then. I'll call you soon, babyboy." She smirked.

I honestly didn't know what to say. This had never ever happened to me before. Like I had told her, I wasn't really a one-nighter type of brotha. I had a lady friend that I used to kick it with for a minute and that was purely sexual. But, as a rule, that wasn't my thing. I have always felt too deep about things, even sex, to roll like that. I was always preaching to my boys about our people showing more respect for each other, and they, more respect for our black sistahs, and now here I was... *DID SHE JUST USE ME?* I scratched the back of my neck self-consciously, a nervous habit of mine whenever I was feeling uncomfortable. I was DEFINITELY feeling damn uncomfortable!

"Shameika...I have to ask, what was that?" Gesturing toward my bedroom, I looked at her solemnly.

She walked to the door, turning her back to me. Opening the door to leave, she suddenly turned around and said, "That was fun Joop, okay? Let's not make it more than it was and ruin things. Goodnight."

I spent all of my spare time for the next couple of weeks bottled up in my makeshift office, which was actually the extra bedroom that I had conformed into a computer/office room. It was early September, and I felt loaded down with reports to grade, besides all the homework I usually put off until later. I was taking some night classes at Towson U. I had finally gotten into the program part-time and was working towards my Masters in Interdisciplinary Studies with a concentration in African American Studies. My ultimate goal was still to eventually teach it at the university level.

Although I enjoyed working with high school students, sometimes the bad asses could get to you a bit too much. Yeah, it would take me a long time only going at it part-time like this, but on a teacher's salary I definitely was not a rich man and I still needed to support myself. Besides, I don't know if I am ready to give up my goal of converting and reaching some of the Baltimore City bad asses and self-proclaimed hoochie mamas that I was teaching. Somebody had to reach out to these little brothas and sistahs, and I had always felt it was my duty to do all that I could, always trying to get my students to see me as more a friend and confidant, rather than just Mr. Evans, their U.S. and Ancient Civilization History teacher.

I was kinda excited about my Tuesday night class. I had finally, after numerous letters to the Dean and the professor of the class, been able to talk my way into a Psych class that I needed.

I slipped on a pair of black jeans and a brown, orange and green striped shirt, Kente' colors, one of my favorites that I had picked up a couple of years back while touring South Africa on a vacation. I knew I was running late, despite how hard I had worked to get into this class. *Great* first day.

After running a few red lights to get to the campus, I raced into class, totally out of breath, clearing my throat as all eyes moved to me. I slipped into a chair at an empty table, scratching the back of my neck and slipping on my gold rimmed glasses before looking up to see a pair of cat eyes looking right into mine. Little Miss Shameika, the lady who had whipped it on me and then pranced out of my apartment, leaving me thoroughly confused, embarrassed, and totally dissed.

Shameika...

Let me state to you all one thing...I'm a playette. It's what I *do*. Don't really know why I do it. Okay, I do, but it's not important right now. Thing is I *can't* be tied down to any one man... that is unless he's really good at what he does, and I want to come back and *check out* his goodies more than once.

With this.....'independent'...mentality. NO, not a hoochie or ho...INDEPENDENT mentality. It flipped me out when I left Joop's place and was actually in the cab crying. Yes, CRYING, as in the cabbie was speaking all fast, asking me what was wrong, did my boyfriend hurt me, the whole nine. He was *really* being sweet, and I ain't neva met a dude who was quick to be like, no stay and let's talk...you don't have to leave. Always told myself it was better to hit it and leave the scene before they brought the body bag in to remove me. Joop really flipped the script on a sistah and you best believe it shook me up.

By the time I got home, I looked down right pitiful. I kicked my shoes off, threw my bag on my black leather sofa, and stripped out of my dress, walking around butt naked. Hey, it was my place. I could do what I wanted. I saw the light on my answering machine flashing like a Christmas light and, reluctantly, I hit the button. Nothing important. Three messages from three different guys wanting to know if they could see me tonight. Yet none of their asses wanted to go with me to my girl's wedding. Too afraid the gown and church would rub off on me and I would change my 'independent' ways. They didn't have to worry about that...I guess.

Slowly, I crept into the shower and loofahed myself, my mind going to what transpired more than an hour ago. Joop lit my ass up. "Dayum." I moaned, the shower spraying water on my face. "Boing, boing, boing." If I didn't know myself better, I would have sworn the word SPRUNG was close to becoming a part of me, but Miss Shameika Jones didn't play the sprung card...she left that to the men in her wake. After my shower, I toweled off and proceeded to lay my nude body upon my thick comforter. I let out a huge sigh as sleep quickly took over me, the last image in my mind being of the 'moment' that that sexy ass Eric Benet lookalike and I connected in spastic ecstasy on his waterbed.

I am BORED out of my freaking mind. Tee and Chris decided they wanted to be special, so they departed for like three weeks to different islands and whatnot. The last two weeks I had kept myself busy with school. My second semester at Towson U was kicking in and already there was work to be done. I was working on my masters in psychology. A sistah wanted to tap into people's minds. Tamara used to joke me, saying I already had the men down pat with the way I would leave them all like carcasses in my dust. Maybe she was right, but that wasn't what I wanted to do. I wanted to help counsel kids...kids who unfortunately didn't have it so great growing, for whatever reason, abuse — verbal or physical or mental — depression, school-related, whatever. I knew I could connect with them, and that's where my dream laid.

Anyway, all I've been doing is getting my school situation together and staying in. Could you believe a sistah ain't been with someone for two weeks? Last time....mm mm mm. Last time was with that fine ass Joop. I know by now he probably hates me. He probably has a right to but, hey, I can't change who I am. I saw Joop talking to Chris at the reception and Chris shot me this glance. I know he was telling homeboy to stay away from me...not to let me put my claws into him, have my taste, and then spit him out to wonder what the hell happened.

I'm sure Chris schooled him quite properly, so Joop knew what the deal was. HA! He even told me that he didn't bring me to his place to kick it. What type of shit is that? Men don't know anything about talking unless it's getting digits, macking, or asking when he could get a piece of her sweetness. I'm sure good ol' Joop was no exception, even if briefly, I thought he might be.

It was Tuesday night, six days and counting til my girl came back from her blissful honeymoon. I was sure I wouldn't get to talk to her for a good week or two after she got back. The high of her honeymoon would have her on cloud nine for a minute or two. I was getting dressed for my first session of Counseling Techniques, a course in Psychology that allowed us to learn counseling skills through role-playing and demonstrations. I just hoped I didn't have to role-play a crazy sistah, cuz I had that down. I checked myself in my full-length mirror. I was wearing a loose pair of jeans, which damn near hung off my bony butt, a Towson U sweatshirt and my black and gold Adidas. I pulled my micro braids into a ponytail, looped my L. L. Bean braided leather belt through my jeans, picked up my backpack and keys, and headed out the door.

Luckily, I only lived a good ten minutes away from Towson, having rented a place on North Charles Street. People would come to my place and automatically assume I was rich. These were the ritzy houses for sure. Right down the street from three big colleges — Loyola, College of Notre Dame, and Johns Hopkins. I was oh so lucky to have met little Jon. He was one of the kids I took care of at the daycare center where I worked. When he told me that his parents were getting a divorce — one reason why I gave him extra attention — he told me his mom got the house and that she was looking for someone to rent the small cottage outside her huge house. Enter moi.

Jon's mother and I had talked previously and had a nice rap-port, so it only took me 15 minutes of smiling and chit chat and a check for two month's rent before I was moving my things out of my mom's house and into my own place. It was most defi-nitely my haven. Large bedroom and living room, a kitchen with all the latest appliances, and a small dining room that overlooked the rose garden Jon's mother tended to. The bathroom had a whirlpool tub and I had two extra rooms. I converted one into a study/office and the other into a guest room. Never had a guest, but one never knew. I was *definitely* living large in my digs.

I opened the driver's side door of my hunter green Explorer and tossed my backpack in, then myself. I had exactly 15 minutes to get to campus, find a parking spot, and run to class.

I made it there in seven minutes, thanking God that I didn't see a cop on the way. God blessed me with a parking spot right next to my class's building. I quickly hopped out my ride and sprinted my way to class. When I reached the classroom, I wasn't breathing hard, but I had slight perspiration on my forehead. I wiped at it and smiled at some of the students I met in previous classes. Professor Stanford taught the Human Learning course I'd taken last semester and I smiled as she approached me. "Hi there, Sha," Professor Stanford said, smiling. "Glad to have you in my class again."

"Same here, Professor," I smiled.

"Getting an A this semester, too?"

"You know it!" I gave her my award-winning smile as I spun around to find me a seat. My eyes ran right into a sight I didn't think I would see again. Sitting over at a corner table, looking too cute in his gold-rimmed glasses, was Joop. I swallowed hard, never before feeling this insecure and *stupid* in front of a man. I looked at him, giving him a brief smile, and sat across from him at his table. This was going to be a long class for sure.

Joop . . .

There was no way I was going to be able to focus, concentrate, or anything else with Shameika sitting across the table from me. I mean, damn! Why did she have to pick this table, my table to sit at? I was having a hard time keeping the slight tremble from my hand as I scribbled notes while Professor Stanford spoke. I barely looked at Sha. I just could not meet her eyes. Just the brief smile she had given me when she entered had left me rattled.

Towards the end of the class, Sha reached out and touched my hand lightly. "It's good seeing you again, Joop," she whispered.

"Yeah, you too." I glanced up at her, but did not quite make it to her eyes. I stopped at her full lips, which was a mistake. Her lips took me back to another place where I had seen them, felt them, on me, working me, kissing me, licking, sucking all over my body. I was dying. I exhaled, willing myself to look away from her lips. I knew she could tell I was staring at them, big time. She licked them, as though subconsciously. *Yeah right, Ms. Mack, not this time...* I looked away quickly.

"So what have you been up to? I didn't know you were a student."

"Sha and what's your name?" Professor Stanford asked. "Jamal Evans," I answered back.

"Thank you, Jamal...could you just keep it down a tiny bit or wait a short while. I'm about to dismiss the class, okay?" She smiled.

Needless to say, I felt a little humiliated. Here I was a teacher myself, being reprimanded for talking, nicely as though it was, by another teacher. How come, I thought to myself, I always ended up feeling some kind of humiliation whenever Sha was around?

I jumped up abruptly after the class was dismissed, quietly stuffing my tablet and Psych book into my Eastpak. I walked straight out of the class feeling Sha's eyes behind me the whole time. "Wait, Joop!" she said, rushing to catch up with the long strides my legs were making. "Listen...hold up now. I'm not as fast as you. Do you have another class?"

"No, I don't," I said, turning to her and finally looking her in the eyes. I was starting to feel a bit childish running from a woman. Why it would bother me that she hadn't wanted to stay past the sex that night nor give me a call afterwards was beyond me. Most brothas would have felt like they got lucky that night.

She had the sweetest moves and the tightest grip I had ever known. She gave it up happily, freely, and didn't want a commitment, or anything for that matter. It had been fun just like she had said, so I should feel lucky, right?

"So if you don't have anything to do right now, why don't you let me buy you a cappy, espresso, a hot chocolate, or something," Shameika said, a hopeful look on her face. "Starbucks is right around the corner."

I thought for a moment. This semester was gonna be a long haul, and I really had no desire to hold a ridiculous grudge over something like this. "Yeah, that sounds real good." I smiled. "Lead the way."

Shameika actually was an amazing woman. Intelligence was an understatement. The sistah was into the mind. Like me, she was seeking her masters, she in Psychology wanting to help, now get this, help kids. She was just as devoted mentally into them as I was, even working in a daycare center while completing her masters. I was shell-shocked. We had so much in common. I lived to be a guide, educate our youth, and she had the same goals, with a different curve.

"I cannot believe you're a History teacher." She laughed.

"What, I don't look like a teach?" I asked her, smiling at her incredulous expression. I jokingly combed at my mustache with my fingers as she laughed.

"Hmm…not any teacher I ever had." Sha was giving me an up and down look of appreciation. I felt myself growing warm under her inspection.

"Well, I want to really delve into my studies," I said. "I want to teach at the university level, eventually, and really make a difference." I took a gulp of my double espresso, my hands swinging wildly as I tried to express myself. Shameika rested her chin on her hand, listening to me intently. "I think one of the biggest crimes we as a people have done to ourselves, is denied ourselves and our children knowledge of self, and of how rich our black heritage is. To me it's not about hating white folks or anything like that. It's about loving ourselves, you know?"

"Mistah MILITANT!" She laughed. "I knew it with your dreadlocks and your kente' self."

I did a mock clearing of my throat. "Not necessarily militant, but AWARE."

We were both quiet for a while, drinking our coffee and smiling at each other all goofy like.

"Listen, Joop," Shameika interjected. "I'm sorry about that night, the way I left. I enjoyed...REALLY enjoyed being with you, just as I have tonight, but of course in a different way."

I could feel myself tensing up. Cutting in quickly, I said, "Sha, it's cool. Really. Maybe we started the wrong way. Hell, I had no idea we had so much in common, school and also our both working with kids you know? I guess you're more mentally free, sexually speaking, and I took it or made it out to be more than what it was. I'm always told that I'm too serious and intense about everything and that doesn't make too good of a combination relationship wise. But, with as much in common as we have, we could be some hell of a friendship combo!" I smiled, wondering why my words sounded so hollow to my own ears. Sha gave me a surprised, odd look, that for a moment I would had thought was a hurt look, but she shot me a big grin after a moment and said, "You got that right, homeboy! Giving me daps and a shake."

We parted with a hug, me finally getting her phone number from her. I guess my saying friends to her made it far more comfortable. I slipped the tiny paper she had wrote her number on in my pocket with a sigh, jumped on my bike, put on my helmet, and sped off into the night.

Shameika...

Joop wasn't interested in me...well not how guys *normally*

are interested in me. The whole time during class he fidgeted, looked away from me, never once looking me in the eye, until I 'disrupted' the class by reaching my hand out to him, telling him how nice it was to see him again. It sounded trite as hell, but it was the truth. He had managed to creep into my head at least a couple dozen times during the last two weeks, and even though I didn't call him — and I know he was smarting about that shit — that didn't erase that night from my mind.

When a sistah finally caught his butt after class, obviously trying to get away from me, he was evasive, really just wanting to put space between us. But like storm clouds, when I asked him to hang at Starbucks with me, his evasiveness passed and he smiled and whoa, a sistah almost stumbled from the heat that oozed from his pearly smile. He accepted my invitation, and we had a really great conversation.

We both loved the kids, which was a big thang to me, and that made Joop much more impressive to me. The guys I usually chill with, you even just fix your lips to say kids and all you will see is burnt rubber in your driveway as they peel away. Joop was *definitely* not my normal kinda guy. But maybe, I thought, while I listened intently to him so expressively talk about what we as a people needed to do, I thought...maybe my normal kinda guy ain't exactly the type of man I should be checking out.

I will tell you this, I wanted to smack my own damn self for looking as dopey while he talked, but I was just so fascinated by Joop. He was beyond fine, he was intelligent, articulate, a nice dresser and undresser, and he seemed so genuine. Not the kind to tell you what you want to hear when you want to hear it so he can snatch the panties and make his getaway. I could sense that Joop was definitely one of the good guys.

I made a joke about him being mister militant and he came back with a mocking, "No not necessarily militant, but AWARE." Instantly, we both went quiet, thinking about how his *awareness* last time we were together left us soaked and spent in his bed. I quickly began to apologize for leaving his place the way I did and making him feel that I didn't enjoy what we had done, but he shushed me, saying that it was okay, that obviously my mentally free sexual spirit and his serious, intense personality weren't good for a relationship, but could be great for a friendship.

OUCH. Actually, damn and a big ass double OUCH. I was hurt, and my face probably showed it, cuz Joop was staring at me questionably. I threw on my best smile and came back with an affirmative and shakes and daps for my new *friend*. We parted, with me giving him my phone number. When I jumped into my Explorer, I sighed and rubbed my temples, feeling a headache coming on. *That's what I get for liking someone outta my league,* I thought, starting my ride, pumping up my Ruff Riders Compilation CD, and speeding out of Starbucks' parking lot.

When I got home, I immediately put on a pot of coffee to brew and found my *Amadeus* Soundtrack to pop into my stereo system. When the strands of Mozart permeated through my abode, I smiled, hugging my middle. Only Tee and my other sistergirl, Deandra knew that I was a lover of classical music, with this CD being my all-time favorite piece. Loved me some Moz. I slipped out of my sweatshirt, having a black DALINKWENT long-sleeved tee shirt under it. I whipped my belt from its loops and let my jeans ride low on my hips and kicked off my Adidas, padding around my place in thick slouch socks. I don't know what possessed me to do what I did next, but I jumped over on my leather couch and picked up my cordless phone.

I figured Joop had another five minutes before he would arrive at his place, and being the sleuth that I am, I had his digits before him and I even hooked up at the wedding. I dialed his pad up and when his answering machine came on, I held a breath, listening to his voice tell me he wasn't home. Okay, sistah needs help, falling and drooling over a Negro's voice and shit. Shameika didn't play that. Okay, beep. "Hey there," I said, my voice way too happy for my ears. "It's me, Sha. Don't worry about how I got your number." I laughed. "Just wanted to say hey. Thanks for having coffee with me and maybe you could call me up later when you get in. That's if you've got the time. Peace."

No sooner had I hung up the phone than I heard someone knocking on my front door. Upon opening it, I saw Jon crying at my doorstep, dressed in his pajamas, sneakers, and jacket. I fell to my knees, collecting his 5-year-old body in my arms. "What's wrong, Honey?" I asked, wiping the tears from his face. His blue eyes were brimming with tears as I smoothed his blond hair down.

"Mommy crying," Jon whimpered. "She won't tell me why, but she said to see if you could watch me for a bit. Can you, Sha?"

"Of course, Baby." I picked Jon up into my arms and closed my front door. Once I got him settled on my couch, with a glass of milk and some cookies and a coloring book, I picked up the phone and called his mother. She answered on the third ring, her voice strained.

"Hello?" Lara asked.

"Lara, are you okay? It's me, Sha."

"Oh hi, Sha," she answered, exasperated. "I'm sorry I sent Jon down without calling you first, but I didn't want him to see me like this."

"What's wrong?"

"My oh so loving ex-husband. Well, soon to be. It seems that he's about to get remarried."

"What!" I yelled, noticing Jon's curious eyes following me. I headed to my kitchen to pour a mug of coffee. Whispering, I asked, "What the hell is *that* about? He's not even divorced from you yet!"

"I know, I know. He called tonight, telling me about *Debbie*. He's been with her for over a year now! Can you believe it? While we were married at that! Hell, I left him because of *Susan*, so Lord knows how many other women there were."

"Damn," I muttered. A damn soap opera, for real. "Well, are you sure you're okay, Lara? I can watch Jon, no problem, but I wanted to make sure that you were fine."

"I'm not suicidal." She laughed. "I'm okay. Just shaken up a bit. And thanks for being okay about Jon. He loves you to death."

"And I love him, too. If you need me, call me, okay?"

"Thanks, Sha." Lara sighed. "I'll pick Jon up tomorrow morning to get him ready for school."

"No problem. Buh bye." Hanging up the phone, I moseyed into the living room, placing my coffee mug on my coffee table before plopping down on the sofa beside Jon, stealing one of his cookies.

"Hey!" He laughed.

"Hey back at you, Buddy!" I laughed back. "You're gonna be staying here with me tonight, okay?"

"Is Mommy okay?" he asked, his eyes sad. I hugged him to me.

"Yea, Honey." I smiled. "Just a little sad. Hey, how about we watch a Disney movie?"

Jon jumped from the sofa, barreling over to my TV stand, which housed too many videotapes, mostly Disney. "Yea!" he exclaimed, you got the best collection."

"Thanks, Buddy." I laughed, clicking off my stereo. The phone rang and I quickly picked it up. "Sha here," I answered.

"Hey." Inwardly I smiled, hearing the voice of Mr. Militant.

Jeep . . .

"Thanks for calling me back so soon," Sha breathlessly said over the phone line.

"Hey, I was gonna test your number to make sure it was the

right one anyhow," I joked. "Thanks for the coffee earlier, too. I enjoyed that. So what's up?"

"Nothing. I just wanted to touch base with you…okay so we just left each other, but anyhow…I'm just here babysitting."

I listened to the sound of Shameika's soft feminine voice. I know I may have sounded all cool and confident about the friends thing, but I was still extremely attracted to everything about her. I popped an old Bob Marley cut on my turntable. *That's right. I was still into the vinyl sound.* Sha went into how she was watching this little white kid Jon, his mom being in some 'my man had secret women' relationship and all, the whole deal sounding like a script for one of those daytime shows, *All my Children,* or *The Young and the Restless,* that type of thing. "White folks have some screwed up personal lives," I told her.

"True," she responded back, "but then again so do plenty of black folks. Besides, Jon is not white. He's *Jon.*"

"Ahh…okay." I laughed. "Listen. I better go. I have papers to grade, and I want to prepare my assignments for tomorrow. You talk about babysitting. My students range from 15 to 16 years old, and you would think some of them were the age of your little Jonnie there."

"Okay then, but listen. I wanted to ask if you wanted to get together tomorrow night and work on some of that Psych home-work together. She'd popped this thesis on us already. So, what do you think?"

I thought quickly for a minute. My tomorrow was packed. Plus, I needed to make a run to D.C. to visit my ailing grand-mother. "How about we do it Thursday? My next couple of days are kinda full."

With her affirmative answer, we were on. Thus began a month long getting to know you campaign. We met up a few times a week to study, becoming homework partners. We visited museums, spent time at the Harbor, and even rode to D.C.

to check out the museums and historical spots. I had never really chilled with a sistah so much and still kept it friendly, especially someone I had already kicked it with before. Oddly enough, I ended up spending so much time with Sha that I rarely saw Stephen or Chris. But Chris was so wrapped up in his new wife and all the sweet trimmings that came with it that he hardly noticed. That nosey playa Stephen had called a couple of times to find out what was up. The problem was, I didn't know myself. All I knew was that I had never enjoyed the company of a lady the way I was enjoying Ms. Shameika Jones'.

Halloween night we were chillin', listening to 'The Roots' CD, eating almost as much of the candy that we were dishing out to the kids who came a knocking at my door, and sipping on Verdi. I started instigating a fight with Sha about who killed Malcolm X, something I enjoyed doing because this lady, who for as tiny as she was, had a big mouth, there was no other way you could put it, but I loved battling with her. There were very few people, male or female, who could and would go toe to toe with me when it came to certain subjects like politics, religion, or racial issues, but Sha, she never backed down. Her eyes would get all big and start sparkling like the sun. They fascinated me, she fascinated me, and we fell asleep fussing, right on my black fur rug.

I woke up with a start, feeling a chill and realizing that I wasn't in my waterbed. Looking around, I noticed the fire was almost out in my fireplace. Sha was lying beside me on the rug, curled up as if she were freezing. I got up, put a couple pieces of QUICK START LOGS in the fireplace, and got a blanket to throw over Shameika. I sat there watching her while all of these emotions washed over me. I touched one of her braids. *She was so damn beautiful.* Made me think of how the ancient black King Solomon must have felt when he first laid eyes on the Shulammite beauty, that ancient black queen of old.

"Your cheeks are comely among the hair braids,
your neck in a string of beads.
Circlets of gold we shall make for you,
along with studs of silver.
Look! You are beautiful, O girl companion of mine.
Look! You are beautiful.
Your eyes are those of doves, behind your veil,
Your hair is like a drove of goats that have hopped down
from the mountainous region of Gilead.
Look! You are beautiful.
And there is no defect, in you..."

Sha gasped, her eyes opening, glittering up at me. "That was beautiful, Joop," she whispered.

I hadn't even realized that I had quoted the Song of Solomon out loud, couldn't look away from her eyes...all I could think about was how I wanted to worship this black queen tonight.

She was quiet, so very quiet as I kissed her eyelids, tracing her lashes with my tongue, kissing down her cheek, her jawline, behind her ears, tracing her earlobes, blowing softly... Quiet as I found her lips, kissing her deeply and feeling so profound like my own heart was bursting out of my chest. I looked deep into her eyes as I removed her clothing, kissing every part of her as it was slowly revealed. She was so quiet that I got nervous for a moment and hesitated, wondering what she was thinking, what she was feeling, about me.

I went down to her feet. She sat up slightly and moaned as I licked and sucked each toe on each foot, kissing up her ankle, her calf, behind her knees...skipping her center core to kiss and nurse at her breasts, nipples. I spent a little extra time here, she was tiny, just a mouthful and so sweet. She moaned again. *"Jamal....ohhhh..."* I went down, kissing her belly, her hips, parting her legs and kissing her inner thighs, kissing lightly between her legs... *"Yes Boo, right there pleasssssse..."* I opened my mouth and just *moaned* on her, sending deep vibrations, moaned and licked and sucked till she pushed me away, gasping, shaking as though she were covered with ice. *"Please, please now Joop."*

Covering her mouth with mine, I gave one single thrust of my hips, her screaming out against my mouth, gripping me, wrapping her legs around my waist and squeezing her muscles until I was trembling and moaning as loudly she was. I don't even know when the moment hit. All I know is that it hit us both at the same time. I felt like I was being pulled inside out, dying the sweetest death, but Sha, surprisingly instead of moaning she cried, earth wrenching sobs that left me totally confused as I held her.

Shameika...

Hearing from Joop the night I babysat Jon was like the beginning of something. Of what, I had no idea. My week seemed to fly back, with me anxiously waiting for Thursday to come. It turned out that I ended up watching Jon through the week, for Lara had some 'meetings' with her shady ass, need-to-be-smacked, ex-husband. I took him to school, went to work at the daycare center, picked him up, cooked us dinner, did homework with him and my own for the rest of the week. When I finally saw Joop, which was only like two days later, but felt like two weeks, he didn't even mind that Jon was hooked to my hip most of the night.

After that night, Joop and I were like sewn at the hip. At least twice a week, he and I were hooking up to do school work and we actually did *school work*. I don't know about him, but I felt other things up in the mix, but neither of us acted out on it. I have to say; it was damn hard to be up next to him, reading to each other, writing, laughing, joking, and not sharing a hug, a kiss, something. But oh well...like I said many times before...he wasn't my type...and I knew I wasn't his anyway, so moving on.

I was so focused with school and my new job as surrogate mother to Jon that I hadn't thought about a 'body fix' for going on a month now. When I finally saw Tamara, a good week after she got home, her ass told me I was glowing and that something good must have been going on with me. I didn't tell her about what happened between Joop and I...it was the first time I didn't go blabbing to her or Deandra about my life and it had felt odd, but I couldn't open my mouth to say I slept with Joop. Not that I felt ashamed...just that I enjoyed it so much, and I didn't want others to know how it made me feel to enjoy sex like that...the way it should be. Look at me, going goo goo ga ga, like I belong on some cover of a black romance novel. ANYway.

Three weeks into whatever Joop and I were doing with each other, I went to see my mother. Look up the word 'tight' in the dictionary, and there's a picture of my mother and me. She was the Apple to my Jacks, but believe me when I say it wasn't always that way. There was a dark period in our relationship that lasted...well, most of my life. It took a lot of therapy, a lot of counseling, a lot of self-reflection, and a lot of forgiveness to reach the place that we were at now. At times we had falling outs...usually when one of us wasn't feeling as good about life, so we decided to dredge up the past. Wouldn't you know it, the last time I saw her, she wasn't feeling too happy, and so I guess she figured we both needed to be unhappy.

As soon as I walked through the door of her house, kissed her, and handed her the roses I bought for her just out of the blue, she commented, "What's wrong with you?" I stood in the doorway, totally dumbfounded and taken off guard.

"What do you mean, Ma?" I asked, my eyebrow rising slowly. "What's wrong?"

"You're out there hoeing around." I stumbled into the house, shutting the front door.

"What?"

"Every other day you're out there, screwing God knows who, and at night you get your degree. Do you think being smart balances out being a ho?"

"Whoa!" I yelled, dropping my backpack on the floor and circling around my mother. "What did I do to deserve this, Ma? What's going on? Dad?"

"You think you can use him as an excuse for your life, don't you?" my mother spat at me. I had no idea where all this was coming from. She had never spoken to me with such anger and bitterness. I swallowed the tears and the memories that wanted desperately to fly out.

"Oh, so what he did to me wasn't wrong, Momma?" I cried, the tears refusing to stay in. "It changed my *life.*"

"Excuse!" she yelled. "Just a damn excuse. You know, he called today." I snapped my neck to stare at my mother's face, my face. It was amazing how similar we looked, and how right now we couldn't be so different.

"Called? Here?" I asked. "What did he want?"

"He was apologizing...like he always does. Asking for your forgiveness, for you to come see him." I snatched my backpack from the floor and opened the front door. I couldn't be here. Not with *his* presence in the house, not with my mother sounding so weak and pathetic, like she actually bought his words.

"NO!" I yelled, my voice high, scaring even me. "I will *never* forgive him for what he did to me. And with the way you're acting now...I may not be able to forgive you again for allowing it to happen!" I slammed out her door, thus beginning the week of darkness in my life.

And that's exactly what it was...darkness. Except for school and daycare, I didn't even try to keep myself up, to see anyone, to be bothered with anyone. I fooled everyone into believing everything was everything, even though I was dying inside. My whole life had basically been a show, a show starring a girl I really knew nothing about. This new episode with my mother just made me act harder, to show everyone that I was still the life of the party...even when I was *actually* the party pooper.

Party pooping to the point that I hadn't even called or talked to any of my male 'friends' since that night with Joop. And here I was, preparing to see Joop tonight and I had the urge to call him and say I'd check him later...I *knew* he would be able to see that I was going through some things, and the last thing I wanted to do was cry...to him.

HALLOWEEN! Joop wanted me to hang, dishing out candy together to the little rugrats he said, so I glued on my best smile, slipped on a pair of black jeans and a black DADA sweatshirt and headed over to Joop's place for some wine and trick or treat. I'm glad I didn't stay home. The entire night I spent in battle with Joop over this and that and I smiled the whole time, sincere, genuine smiles. I was *really* happy to be there, and I wasn't having sex. It just didn't add up. Before I even knew what hit me, I had passed out, falling asleep in front of the fireplace in Joop's living room. Instinctively, I curled up into the protective fetal position and slept.

I was awakened when I heard Joop reciting the sweetest words to me. He was so into what he was saying, he didn't notice me looking up at him through sleepy eyes. I told him how beautiful what he spoke was, and I saw all these feelings move across his face and within a split second, he was on me, so slowly, so smoothly that I couldn't move. The way he kissed me, gently removed my clothing, and made love to every inch of my body, I felt like holy water, clear and pure.

When he openly kissed me between my legs, I became speechless, only moans and groans and cries escaping my mouth. I wanted Joop so badly. I had never wanted anyone before, and that recognition brought on a building of sadness in my heart, a sadness that soared with the euphoria I felt from having Joop loving me like this. I begged him to take me and when he slipped inside of me, my hard walls momentarily crumbled and I cried out in pleasure, meeting Joop with equal heat and need. Joop groaned my name as his explosion came, and I met his explosion with equal ferocity.

His breath was hot and sweet on my neck and with the releasing of my pent-up passion, the dam of tears broke as well, and I blubbered all over myself and Joop. To put it mildly, he was stunned. He held me, rocked me, asked me what was wrong, but I couldn't speak. What was I going to say?

"What's wrong, babe?" Joop asked, wiping the tears from my face. I looked into his eyes, so deep, so sweet, so caring. I didn't know how to react.

"This..." I whispered.

"This what?" he asked, searching my face for answers.

"I don't ..don't deserve you to be so nice to me."

"What?" Joop's eyes widened and he really looked amazed at my words. I moved from the warmth of his arms and quickly got up, slipping on my clothes. It pained me to have to do this a second time, and I knew he may never forgive me, but I couldn't open this bag...not to a man.

With clothes on and distance between Joop and me, I felt some power reentering my body. I wiped the tears from my face and looked down at Joop. God, I wanted to lay back down there with him, love him, hold him and have him hold me and say those beautiful words to me again, but I couldn't do it. I smiled wistfully, seeing the pain, the confusion, the hurt, and the need to comfort in Joop's eyes.

"Jamal," I began, clearing my throat. "Jamal...I am *so* sorry. So sorry. I love this...more than you will *ever* know." He opened his mouth to speak, but I continued. "This...this romantic, sweet, loving thang? It's not me. I don't get this. I don't know how to react to this. Hell, I don't deserve this. I don't." Before Joop got a chance to respond, I ran from his place, jumping in my Explorer and sped away. The distance made my tears flow faster and harder.

Joop...

"Black Jesus! Wassup, babee!"

"Get over here, man! You're all late and we're ready to roll!" Chris screamed, as I strolled up to the brand new court in Chris's backyard, dribbling the ball as I walked.

"How long y'all been out here?" I asked.

"Longer than you, nigga," Stephen said, meeting me for a hard brotha to brotha chest bump.

"What's shaking, brotha?" Chris asked, giving me daps. "Missed you man, been trying to get you out here all week. What news you got, huh?"

I looked at both of my brothas, noticing Stephen's raised eyebrow, waiting for my response. I knew that he had been worried about me. Hell, I was worried about me, too. At least, I had been. The night that Shameika walked out on me for the second time after making love. Well, it shocked me, blew my ego so badly I went into recluse, didn't even go to class at Towson that following Tuesday. Maybe I just didn't understand women, or what they wanted, because I had been sincere in everything I had thrown to Sha that night, with every kiss, touch and caress I was trying to tell her how I felt about her, and she had walked away. I know she was feeling me, I KNOW she was, and this whole thing just didn't add up, which made it even more of a puzzle. *"The first mistake you made was letting her get your mind, the second was letting her KNOW she had your mind."* Wasn't I the egotistical fool who said that once?

"Well I'm here now, so let's see what you girls got," I said, quickly changing the subject from me. I dribbled a circle around the hoop before issuing a slam-dunk. "That's right, the savior is here!" I sung, referring back to the court nickname I was called back in our HU days. Stephen grabbed the ball, dribbling around for a minute before gracing us with one of his famous 3 pointers, which officially got our game rolling.

After class Tuesday night I spent a little time in the library. Sha and I had spent the whole class period in silence, none of the normal note passing and smiles and whispers we had been up to before. She looked hard, frozen like she didn't want her facial expressions read, and she succeeded. I couldn't figure her out for the life of me. We would always do a bit of research in the library after class, and I don't know why but I just had to be there even if she wasn't with me. It had our air, our essence. I had just opened my book, when looking up I saw Sha walking into the library. I gestured to her to join me.

"Hey," she said with a small smile.

"I didn't think you were coming in today."

"I'm just here to drop off some books. I'm about to head over to Tee and Chris' to check out their new house."

I started packing up my knapsack, feeling exuberated by her presence, and the fact that she was actually talking to me normally. What the hell was wrong with me after she had made herself so clear that she wasn't interested in a romantic relationship with me? I have no idea, but it had been a long couple of weeks since I had actually spent time with her, and I missed her like crazy.

"Well, I'm just about done here myself. Maybe I'll go hang with you over there," I said, trying to gain back some of our old camaraderie.

"Oh, okay."

"Um…do you mind Shameika?" I asked her quietly, searching her eyes.

"No, Joop. Come on, let's go," she said, hooking her arm through mine, smiling as we walked out of the library to our vehicles before riding over separately.

My mind was racing as fast as my bike as I spun over to Chris and Tamara's behind Sha. I don't know why I couldn't let her go, couldn't let this thing between us go. I had been able to front it off for a while, saying we were just friends and pretending that was okay, but it wasn't. That night in her arms proved that there was something really special here, that special type of forever thing. I just needed to find a way to make her see that.

Shameika...

Tell me how stupid I am. Go ahead, tell me dammit. After I left Joop's place in shambles, I had sworn to myself that I was gonna put myself in chill mode. Put up the emotional blockers, shut down my smiles, wear my heavy armor and keep from having contact with Joop. Except for class, I had done just that. I stopped going to the library with him, making up excuse after excuse. I stopped passing notes and smiling and joking with him in class. I went so far as to ask Professor Stanford to switch my class partner — in private, of course — but she said no, that Joop and I made a great pair. Little did she know.

I was doing well with this 'cold' thang...hadn't messed around with any dudes, didn't even talk to my girl Tee. Just vegged and spent more time with little Jon, who was becoming a regular slumber partner. Got to the point where he actually had a drawer in my dresser full of some of his clothes and a pair of pajamas and such. Lara was in a tizzy over all the shit her soon to be ex was pulling and, with all her trips to her lawyer, she needed someone dependable to watch Jon. Enter me.

Anyway, why am I stupid, you ask? How about after class, I went to the library? I knew Joop was going to be there, and I used my lame excuse of returning books to really see him. The damn books weren't due for another week and a half! As soon as I saw him, I felt my walls and armor begin to slip from me...only a little though. Like he had a remote control to me, but I stole the batteries. I told him that I was headed over the newlyweds' new digs and when he decided to join me, I felt myself tear in two, one side wanting to be like, oh hell naw, I need to be away from you, and the other side smiling, telling him sure. Guess what side won out?

Needless to say, we both ended up at our friends' new place and it was the out and out bomb. They decided to stay in Catonsville, and they lucked out when they found a house near the local high school and colleges. It was one of those old big houses, with the wraparound porch, swing, and all. Had at least four bedrooms, huge living room and dining room, gourmet kitchen, den, a library, a sunroom, club basement, and a huge backyard. I fell in love with it instantly. Growing up, I had *always* wanted to have a house like this to raise children in. I smiled wistfully, thinking of how I clung at that dream, even through the misfortune of my life.

Chris and Tee damn near fell out when they opened the door to Joop and me. I simply smiled and ran up to my girl, hugging her. "Hey, Baby!" I squealed. "Missed your ass." Tee laughed, dragging me into the living room where she sat down beside me on their loveseat. "Girl, I got pictures," Tee rambled, "and so much stuff to tell you." We both glanced towards the men, who continued to stand at the open door. "Only later," Tee whispered, laughing.

"Gotcha, girl." I laughed back. Tee pulled me in to her and whispered in my ear, "You here with Joop?" I gave her a withered smile, whispering back, "No, we had class tonight, Girl. I told him I was coming over and he thought he would join. Nothing else."

"Are you sure?" she asked, glancing into my eyes. Tee was the only person who could read me like a book, and with her knowing my whole life history, I just couldn't allow her to look at me any longer.

"So," I said to all in the room. "Can a sistah get something to drink up in here? I'm quite parched." Everyone laughed.

"What would you like, Shameika?" Chris asked, closing the door as he and Joop sat on the sofa across from us.

"Umm, a light soda, like Sprite or 7Up if you got it."

"No vodka, straight?" Joop asked, staring at me with intensity.

Smiling through my slight embarrassment, I laughed. "Naw, I think I'll go for the clear non-alcoholic drinks. That other stuff goes to the head, makes you do some crazy thangs."

"I'll take the same, man," Joop called behind Chris. I threw Joop my *don't play* look and turned back to my girl.

"So what's new?" I asked. "What's going on?"

"Nothing but happiness, Girl," Tamara beamed. "I got another week till I have to go back to work, so I'm just chilling with Chris, getting the rooms situated, and all that fun stuff. Oh, guess who I got a call from?"

"Who?"

"Deandra!"

My eyes flew wide open. "What the hell!" I yelled, smiling. "What's she doing now?"

"Girl is moving up in the world," Tamara beamed. "Girlfriend is coming back home soon. Got a job with the Orioles."

"No shit?"

"Nope. She's up in New York writing, and someone peeped her on the newly vacant PR director position in the O's organization and boom. She got it!"

"Who's Deandra?" Joop asked, his eyes glued on me.

Chris walked in, handing glasses of Sprite to Joop and me. "Deandra rounds out *our* Three Musketeers," Tamara said. "Like Step rounds out y'all."

"What's she like?" Chris asked. "Think she might be interested in Step?"

I laughed. "Not in the least," I mentioned. "The only running around Dee does is for jobs. She ain't interested in being the latest flava of Step's ice cream shop."

Tamara laughed. "Step ain't that bad!"

Chris and Joop stared at one another. "Yes he is," they laughed in unison.

"Well, anyway," Tamara cut in, still laughing, "Dee gave me her New York number, told you to call so she could see how your hot ass was doing before she came down."

I blushed, secretly cutting my eyes to Joop, who was looking as if he could testify to that hot ass remark. "Cool," I said. Tamara hopped up from the loveseat, grabbing Chris' arm.

"Come on, Boo," she said. "Help me get the food to the dining room table. Guys, I just know y'all staying. We're having fried chicken, macaroni and cheese, corn, and broccoli."

I clapped my hands, smiling. "Damn," I said, laughing. "Y'all having red Kool-Aid, too?"

Chris laughed. "For you, Sha...yea!"

"Screw you!" I yelled at Chris' fleeting back, laughing. As soon as Chris and Tee went into the kitchen, Joop hopped from the sofa to the loveseat. Inching himself close to me, I felt his eyes stare at me, demanding I look back, and I did.

"Hi," he said, almost in a whisper.

"Hi," I whispered back. I told myself not to, but I smiled.

"I've missed you." Joop lightly placed his hand on my knee, gently squeezing it. I closed my eyes to all the good feelings that came rushing to me.

"You have?" I asked, my voice slightly elevated.

"Yea. Don't you think we need to talk? Chris is asking me what's up between you and I, I can see Tamara is dying to know what's up, and I know you haven't told her anything. Is it *me*? Are you just not interested?"

Looking into the pools of his soul, what could I say? Could I lie, and be like yea, I don't like you, I just needed a quickie and you were da bomb, baby? I was really getting tired of secrets, of lies, but they were crying to me, begging me to keep them in, and I obeyed.

I shook my head slowly to the negative, letting him know

silently that it wasn't him. "Then what is it, Boo?" he asked, his voice so lulling, so sincere. I wanted so bad to just crawl up in his arms and go to sleep...to just feel his warmth.

"I....I can't," I began, cutting myself off.

"Boo," Joop said, running his fingertips alongside my left cheek, causing me to swallow a moan. "I really do care for you..." With that, he dropped an achingly soft kiss on my lips and retreated back to the sofa, leaving me staring at him, my mouth slightly open. When Tee and Chris appeared from the kitchen with food in tow, I still couldn't move. Joop had put me in a tailspin.

"You okay, Girl?" Tee asked, tugging at my arm to follow her into the dining room. I snapped out of my thoughts, noticing Joop looking deeply and lovingly at me. "What do *you* think, Tee?" I responded, jumping up, faking a smile. "Let's get our grub on." Raising from the sofa, Joop followed behind Tee and I as we headed off to dinner.

Joop...

I just couldn't stop, and frankly, I didn't give a damn who saw nor did I give a damn who knew that I wanted this lady, wanted her in my life. We chilled the rest of the evening with Chris and Tee, eating plenty of Tamara's country cooking. That sistah could throw down in the kitchen like my grandma used to do. I knew I needed to get to rolling, with me having to work in the morning, but I hung around as long as Sha did, hoping to get another moment to talk with her alone before the evening was out.

"Did I tell you that my agent told me that Doubleday didn't want my book? Feels my characters aren't black enough. I mean what kind of shit is that?" Chris was saying. "I mean I was like what the fuck is not black enough?"

"You know what they meant, man. They want books by

black men to portray black men in society's light, YT light. You remember that flick 'Belly'? All of us are supposed to be a couple of DMXs and NASs, not educated, not loving family, God or self, and we're supposed to, of course, be disrespectful to the women, calling 'em bitches and hoes. You know what I'm talking 'bout," I lectured. "It's the systematic destruction of the mentality of the black man, and they want us to keep on pioneering ourselves in that destruction."

"I hear you brotha. You got it right, too, but see I don't plan on changing my manuscript to please them. Even if I have to self-publish, I'm gonna stay true to Chris Grimes."

"That's right. Stay true to you. Racist muthafuckas," I grumbled. "Ain't a damn thing wrong with your book. I liked it." Nothing pissed me off more than racial disrespect. I knew that I got too wired about it sometimes. Okay, a lot of more than sometimes, but I had seen a lot, felt the sting of racism from a young age, and it had left a permanent mark which molded me into the man I was. I was raised an only child in the Deep South by my grandmother.

My parents? What I remember of them I honor to this day. My dad and my mom hooked up in the late 60's, got married, and bussed outta SC, going where they could better serve the people, the *Black Panther Party*. I was born in '71. By then, they were deeply entrenched and committed to the family. They rolled with Bobby Seale, Huey P, Assata Shakur, Ericka Huggins, having dealings with some of the top brothas and sistahs in the movement. Both were murdered, and yes, I say murdered, by the Feds in a shoot out in an abandoned warehouse. The most we got was an apology my grandmother had said, an apology for what they called an accident, a mistake, case closed.

When I was older, my grandmother gave me my father's journals; journals that he had written specifically for me, to aid me later in life. These journals helped raise me, trained me not to hate, but to be an AWARE and proud black man, and to watch the direction of my feet. And in the resurrection, I will thank my father for his gift, his journals.

In the meantime, the white southern hospitality towards blacks helped raised me, too, and gave me a lesson in justice, or rather injustice. After college, I got a teaching job in D.C. and moved my grandmother there with me where she eventually got a comfortable apartment in an elderly community, where she still resides to this day. She's a beautiful woman, that lady, and I love her to death.

"You're right Joop. On da real, they are some racist bitches. If I didn't have to worry about my moms whipping my ass, I'd say let's go blow up the damn building, don't want to publish my book!" Chris said, getting just as heated as me.

"Um..um..um..you two are gonna start a revolution up in here over a book!" Tamara laughed.

"Y'all so crazy," Sha said, laughing and shaking her head. "Tee, I need to go chile. I have to be at the center at 6am."

"Yeah I need to roll, too. Thanks for that tasty fried chicken, Tamara." I stood up beside Sha, kissing Tamara lightly on the cheek and giving Chris a hug. "Keep your head up, black man."

Chris and Tamara saw us off, Chris giving me daps and a brotherly hug before they closed the door behind us. I walked Shameika to her Explorer. I couldn't help smiling a bit. Babygirl was trying so hard not to look at me.

"Let me help you," I said from behind her, reaching for her car door to open after her unlocking it.

"Thanks," she said quickly, moving to get in her car before I stopped her by pulling her back against me, slipping my hands around her tiny waist. We stood there for several moments, listening to each other's harsh breathing, me tracing my lips against her neck and along her ear, moving my hands up and down her hips, rubbing and caressing her belly, and pressing her back against me. "I'm falling, baby," I whispered in her ear, "I'm falling." Then I walked away, got on my bike, leaving her still standing with her back to me, at the opened door of her Explorer.

"This Deandra is gonna wonder who we are," Stephen complained. "She didn't have anybody else to pick her up?"

Deandra was a friend of Tamara's that Chris was supposed to pick up from BWI. Unbeknownst to Tamara, Chris got held up with an agent and couldn't make it, so enter Stephen and me. Chris gave us Tee's description of her, and all we could do was hope for the best, but hey, anything for your boys.

"I don't know, but I guess we can just wait and see. Ain't but so many tall black women coming off this flight, I'm sure," I said.

We sat at the airport, waiting for her flight to come in. Stephen was telling me about this client of his who had him doing some peeping on her cheating husband. She wanted a more extensive investigation in order to get it all in case of a divorce and had run out of funds. That being the case, she offered Step herself as payment. We both cracked up about that.

"Man, it was too funny." Step laughed. "Thing is, her husband ain't even cheating from what I've seen, and I've been on his tracks for a month. She's just one of those greedy broads, you know? She knows damn well she just wanted some of dez chocolate nuts!" Stephen said smugly.

"Damn, you just foul, Step, you know that?" I couldn't stop laughing at that fool.

"Naw seriously, man. Some females think their shit has gold fur on it or something. I mean, why should I pay for something I can get free anywhere?"

"So what did you say to her?" I laughed. "You take her offer?"

"Hell, yeah. She had those Lauren Hill lips, man. *SLUR-RRP!*"

"No character, man. You just ain't got any character what-

soever Why should you have to pay for it? I bet you didn't hes-
itate." I looked at Step, shaking my head and cracking up. Step
was good at getting your mind off of whatever illed you, and
one thing that was illing me was that Shameika hadn't returned
my calls in days. I didn't want to think about that.

In the midst of our joking around, Flight 475 came in, and
soon we were peering through the crowd of passengers. Before
long, we saw a tall, model thin sistah walking toward us, clad
in sunglasses, a leather jacket, a matching thigh-length leather
mini skirt and legs that wenn on and on and on. The sistah was almost as tall as me which is a rare thing in a woman,
and had even challenged our tall Stephen, who usually had
women meeting him at the hest, height wise. Stephen and I
looked at each other and mohed in silent unison, "*OH SHIT!*"
Deciding that this just *had* to be Miss Deandra Winters, we
walked up to her smiling.

"Hmm, neither of you lok like Chris," she asked, eyeing
us. The sistah was beautiful with a capital B, sporting this 'back
in da day' Halle Berry hair cut, and flawless, sun-kissed golden
skin.

"No," Stephen jumped in. "Chris couldn't make it so he sent
us to pick you up. I'm Stephen, and this here is Jamal." Stephen
had a smile that was as wide as the Grand Canyon.

"Well," she said, clearing her throat as she removed her
shades. "I'm Deandra Winters."

Shameika. . .

I was greasy as hell by the time I finally left Chris and Tee's
place. Tee always could throw down, and having my mouth full
made me less likely to strike up a conversation with Joop, who
stared at me like I was his dinner. Tamara was just a smiling,
like she knew something was up, but Chris...Chris wasn't looking happy at all. He played it off pretty well, but I knew he

wanted to pull Joop aside and shun him away from me...to let him know I was no good. Might not to do it tonight, but he *was* gonna do that. Hell, I would have *loved* him to do it. At least I wouldn't have to continue feeling all these feelings. Chris would lecture, Joop would listen, and all would be well with the world, I hoped.

I wasn't surprised in the *least* when Joop got up to leave after I announced my departure. I ave Tee a hug, got Deandra's number, and parted. I tried to give Joop an air of *go away*, but he insisted on walking me to my Explorer. His smile made me want to smack him because he lied so damn smug, but I was just fixated on getting in my truc and getting home before any more drama ensued.

When Joop opened my door tried to say a quick goodnight and hop in, but he pulled me ainst him, holding me around my waist. Even through my jaclt, I could feel Joop's heat, his hands roaming along my hips ad over my belly. I could feel the wetness of his lips on my neck, my ear. When he whispered, "I'm falling," I felt like I had fallen also. I wanted so badly to let him know what I was feeling, but just as fast as the pleasure came, it left as Joop released me, hopped on his motorcycle, and sped off, leaving me hot and frustrated.

I ran into my place, having to pee like it wasn't funny. The phone rang as I washed my hands, and I quickly dried them off and sprinted to the phone, picking it up on the third ring. "Hello?" I answered, breathless.

"Am I disturbing you, Miss Thang?"

I dropped to the couch, laughing. "Shuddup Deandra!" I squealed into the phone. "I was running from the bathroom. Hey there, Baby! What's going on?"

"Girl." Deandra sighed. "Work, work and more work. I just got off the phone with Tee and she told me you'd be home by now."

"Yea, just rolled in. So, tell me about this jobby job you got with the O's."

"Well, I don't really start for a month, month and a half," Deandra said. "Like around the beginning of the new year. But I'm coming down next week to look into a place to *live*, Girl? I'll be there for a week, so I'll be able to have Thanksgiving with you guys."

"Oh shit," I whispered into the phone. "Thanksgiving *is* rolling in, isn't it?"

Deandra laughed. "See now! You're worse than me. How are you gonna forget the biggest grub day in America? What *you* been doing where you gonna forget that?"

I sighed into the phone, holding it close to my face. "Girl, life is hectic on a sistah."

"Too many men, huh?" Deandra chuckled.

"Actually, no. I haven't been with anyone in like over a month."

"*What!?* I'm not trying to diss you, Boo, but damn...that ain't like you. What's wrong? You okay?"

Was it *so* fucking hard to believe that I could be a normal woman, too? That I could want more than just sex? I shook my head, biting my tongue. "Yea, I'm cool," I whispered. "Just been working a lot at the daycare center and doing a lot of work for my classes. My landlady is having probs with her divorce, and I've been playing surrogate mother to her son."

"Girl, you better watch it!" Deandra exclaimed. "Boy be fluent in Ebonics in no time and his mother will be coming for you to deEbonicize him!"

I coughed from laughing too hard. "You're so stupid," I cried. "Too damn stupid. Anyway, where you plan on staying while you're here?"

"Well," Deandra cooed into the phone sweetly. "Tee offered me a room at her and Chris' house, but you know next week is their last week before she goes back to work, and I'm sure they have more rooms to *christen* before she goes back." We laughed. "I was hoping you had room for a sistah."

"Girl, hell yea!" I yelled. "Do you know I have a guestroom and *neva* had a guest? Bring yo ass on down here!"

Deandra laughed. "Cool, I was hoping you'd say that. I didn't want to spend a grip for a hotel room when I'm trying to get me a place to live."

"I heard that, Girl."

"Hey, are we having dinner at your mom's house this year?" Deandra asked. I shuddered. I hadn't thought of my mother since our fight over a week ago. Just having her pop back into my mind caused me to revel in sadness.

"Naw," I answered. "She and I aren't on speaking terms right now."

"Sha, why?" Deandra asked, concern in her voice.

"You *know*."

Deandra sighed. "I thought you two were able to move past that, Honey."

"I don't want to get brought down, so I won't go into details, but I will say this, my mother is *definitely* not past this...or loving me right now."

A moment of silence passed before Deandra spoke again. "So where? Tee's?" she asked.

"Yea, actually that would be a great idea," I said, thankful to have the understanding of my girl. "They got that big ol' house, and us girls can chef it out in the kitchen, while the men chill and watch football or whatever they do."

"HEY!" Deandra laughed. "You know I be loving football..so stop! Oh and who are these *men*? I only know of Chris."

Damn, I thought to myself...was acting like it was a *given* that Joop would be there with us. Wishful thinking. My silence made Deandra come back with, "Who you messing with, Girl? You bringing someone to Gobble Gobble dinner?"

"Naw, Chris has these two friends who might come...they're as tight as you, Tee, and me are, if you can believe that."

"Okay, Girl. Well look, I have to run. Got a ̄dline on a story and I need to make some tracks on that. I'll̄ lla at you later to let you know the exact day I'm heading ou̅ ̅kay?"

"Cool....love you, Dee."

"Love you back, Sha. Peace."

Hanging up the phone, I smiled, feeling that sist̄ ̄v love penetrate into me, almost making me feel invincible̅ ̅ain't *neva* met a man who made me feel so much love h̄ ̄my two girls...well..okay, one...but I'm not going to m̄ ̄ion him.

It was November 22, three days before Thanksgiving. ̄ ̄e week prior, I had worked diligently on my class assignments̅ well as putting in overtime at the daycare. It appeared to be̅ 'good' week for Lara, too, because I didn't have to keep Jor̅ once. Actually, this was a very good week. Except for class, I wasn't spending any time with Joop. I was quickly building my walls back up nice and sturdy. Even called one of my "friends" to check up on him. Had a date also, but when it came time to release some tension...my body just wouldn't respond. Appeared I had some more building to do.

My girl Deandra was going to be here any minute, and I was doing last minute preparation of my place, making sure everything was squeaky clean and that the guest room was spotless. I slipped into a black, ankle-length jersey dress that clung to my small curves. It was actually one of my Adidas gear dresses, with the three white stripes down the sides, and slits up both legs. I placed my micro braids into two ponytails, one on either side of my head and I had to laugh, cuz I looked no older than 12 or 13. I had my black mules and black leather jacket on the foot of my bed for whenever I would head out with Deandra, and I was set. The weather was pretty nice for November, so it was the perfect day for my girl to come down.

When the doorbell rang, I trotted barefoot to my door, expecting to see my girl and Chris, so you can imagine how my face looked when I found Dee, Stephen, and Joop on the other side. My eyes instantly connected with Joop as my girl ran into my arms, hugging me.

"SHA SHA!" Dee yelled, kissing my cheek. I hugged her back, tearing my eyes away from Joop.

"Hey, Boo!" I yelled back, equally happy. "Get yo ass on in here, Girl." Dee just about skipped into my place with her tall ass and Stephen almost seemed normal, with his polite hello and smile, his eyes fixated on Dee. When Joop approached me, he leaned in, kissing me to my surprise. Thank goodness Dee and Stephen hadn't noticed the exchange. I checked my emotions and whispered out a, "Hi."

"Damn, how'd you manage to look cute *and* sexy, Girl?" he whispered as he brushed past me and into the living room. Closing the door, I sighed, hoping I had the strength to withstand this man named Joop.

Joop . . .

It was mid evening Thanksgiving Day. I had spent the morning and afternoon with my grandmother in D.C. She had always been a person who cooked early, ate early, and went to bed early. I was back in Baltimore by 7pm ringing the bell at Chris and Tee's.

"Joop, it's about time you got here, boy!" Chris said as he opened the door.

"Wassup, Chris," I said, smiling as I stepped into their turkey-decored home.

"Well, check you out! Boyfriend is smooth. Sha, Deandra, come and check out this outfit!" Tamara exclaimed. Shameika and Deandra walked in out of the kitchen to check me out, all clad in black and red African attire. "Dang, you're looking good. What do you call that?" Deandra asked.

"This is a Mudcloth Grand Boubou," I announced proudly, sporting it along with a matching black and red headscarf.

"Now, see, I like that. That is really nice, Jamal," Deandra said. I looked over at Stephen and Chris to see them grinning like two madmen.

"What y'all laughing at, mon!" I laughed.

"Dude, we were just saying that you were born on the wrong continent on da real, Kunta'," Stephen joked.

I stroked the soft fabric of my Boubou, smirking up at my boys as I said, "Y'all just wish you had an ounce of my spirit and style. This was a gift from Sister Shavon Depré."

"Ahh ol' brother Jamal macking the sistahs over at the temple now, and GETTING PAID!" Chris laughed.

"Wrong again. I don't even go to the temple anymore. I'm on a spiritual quest, I told you. I go EVERYWHERE."

"You guys keep us rolling whenever we get together." Tamara smiled. "In fact, this is the first time ALL of us have been together like this. All of my girlfriends and you three boy scouts, that is. Y'all realize that?"

I noticed that Sha was very quiet and, in the midst of the friendly chatter, she had disappeared into the kitchen.

"Hey, Chris, what y'all got to drink?" I asked. "I'm gonna bounce in the kitchen and get something, okay?" I walked toward the kitchen door to seek out Sha.

"Hmph," Tamara huffed. "I'm sorry, Joop, but you know where the kitchen is. I am officially off duty, and everybody who walks through this door is family, so that's right, get on in there and help yourself!" Tamara declared. I laughed, leaving her laxing on the couch beside her husband, and Stephen and Deandra in their own little convo on the loveseat.

I walked into the kitchen to find Shameika fiddling with

something in the sink. I cleared my throat, trying to grab her attention, walking up behind her and placing my hands over her eyes.

"Guess who?"

"Hey, Joop," she said quietly.

"So what's up?" I asked, leaning against the sink to look at her.

"Nuttin'."

"Nuttin' huh?" I smiled, mocking her Ebonics. I reached out and wiped a soap bubble off her chin. She seemed to be constantly washing the same cup over and over again.

"So, are you seeing someone else now?" she asked to my surprise, lifting her lovely eyes up to me.

"Would it really matter to you if I were, Sha?"

Sha seemed to hold her breath for a moment before speaking. "We were never together, Joop. You don't belong to me and it's none of my business and I'm sorry. I was just asking, that's all. My bad."

I looked at Shameika and sighed. "Shameika, we were really getting tight. At least, I thought we were. I loved being with you, doing things with you, and the loving, baby, the loving was good, and you know it was." I stopped for a minute, trying to read her expression. "Sha, you never once explained what happened that night, never once explained why you keep running. Don't you think it's time you did? Cause, see, I know you're feeling me. It's all in your face. I see it in your face right now. Deny it…"

"No, Joop. I told you I can't..I..I just can't…" She closed her eyes tightly.

Voices coming toward the kitchen told me that our convo was about to have an ending, and as hard as it was to get a word out of Shameika, I couldn't see me getting another chance that night.

I leaned in close to her, quickly whispering, "After you drop Deandra off later tonight, come to me, to my place. I'll be waiting up for you. If I don't see you by 2am, I won't bother you again." Kissing her cheek softly, I said, "Be there, baby."

Shameika...

I made it through having to see Joop the day he and Stephen brought my girl, Deandra to my place. Stephen had to leave for *some* reason, so Joop had to go also. All I had to do was fake smile a couple of times and keep my distance from him and wham, bam, boom, he was gone.

Immediately after the door shut, Deandra and I fell on my sofa and began gabbing for two hours straight, trying to catch up on all the drama in our lives. The only thing that stopped us was my phone ringing. It was Tamara. She had just officially given herself the rest of the day off from work and was calling to let us know that we needed to look cute. The girls were hanging tonight. And BOY, did we ever hang!

We headed to Silver Shadows and got our dance on until three in the morning. I even managed to pick up three phone numbers from some major babes while I shook my groove thang on the dance floor. This was really our only day before Thanksgiving to chill and hang, so we made the most of it. Even goody two shoes Tee was a little tipsy after we finally left Silver, heading back to my place. There, we all slipped out of our shoes and fell across my bed.

"Whooooo!" Tamara yelled, giggling. "I think I'm drunk!"

We all fell over ourselves, laughing. "Girl, yo ass is more than drunk!" I exclaimed back. "Don't make me go tell your husband how you were dancing with that dude!"

"I wasn't dancing with him. Negro was trying to get a free ride of my caboose!"

Deandra laughed. "Yea, well, *you* were the one getting all the digits tonight, Sha. What do you plan on doing with all of them?"

"Ohhhhhhh, I dunno," I said, sighing, laying on my back.

"Dang," Deandra responded, laying her head up against my left thigh. "By now, you would have left messages on all three answering machines and have three dates this week."

"Leave our girl alone," Tamara slurred. "She already *got* a man!"

"Ooooh," Deandra squealed. "Give up the dirt...who is it?"

I glanced over at Tamara, begging her with my eyes to let this drop, but with her drunk ass, I knew it was useless. "Joop!" Tamara chirped. Deandra's eyes fell to me, her lips moving into a smile.

"For real, Girl?" she asked. "That sexy dreaded brotha who came to pick me up?"

My eyes didn't give anything away, and after several seconds, I closed them, laying back onto my bed. "Must be nice," Deandra said, whispering. "You don't even want to talk about it."

"Nothing to talk about," I whispered back. "I'm in between men right now...you know I don't fall and do that one on one shit."

Tamara and Deandra shared what they *thought* was a secretive, knowing glance, while I stewed in my sad drunkenness, thinking about how I was in fact falling for the one on one thang...wondering if I could ever be normal enough to actually *have* that kind of stability in my life.

The girls and me spent the next day sobering up and doing last minute Turkey Day shopping. It was obvious that us girls would have to be working it out in the kitchen because the guys were already talking about what games they would watch on the tube. Thanksgiving day, Deandra and I were at Chris and Tee's house early, helping Tee prepare the dishes: turkey, mashed potatoes, sweet potatoes, macaroni and cheese, sauerkraut, greens, green beans, sweet potato pie, and pumpkin pie. You would have thought we were cooking for the Army and not just a few friends.

Tee spent time laughing and giggling with her man. I noticed that Stephen appeared to be peeping Deandra out. I secretly laughed, knowing that my girl would not be giving *that* playa any kind of play. He really needed to save those smooth lines and cute smiles...he was now talking to a woman, not one of his airhead white girls...or whatever flava of the second he was into.

I was just getting the last of the rolls out of the oven as Deandra began transporting the food into serving bowls when Tee yelled for us from the living room, telling us about how sharp Joop looked. Deandra cut her eyes to me, and I kept in my flurry of feelings. Walking out into the living room, I stopped at the doorway. D...double DAYUM. He was looking so beautiful in his African garb. I never saw a *beautiful* man before, but Joop was definitely showing his beauty, his sexiness, his attractiveness, his machismo, all of it. I just leaned against the doorway, wistfully smiling his way, while he talked about some woman who gave him the outfit.

Instantly, my blood ran cold and I felt unbelievably sad, hurt, like I had been slapped in the face. He had another woman...while he was all up in my face, trying to get me to give him a chance? I dipped back into the kitchen, and began washing up the few dishes that lay in the sink. I swallowed all those feelings. I didn't have the right to feel them. Hell, men probably felt that way about *me*!

I shook my head, took a deep breath and let the uneasiness pass...only to return when I heard Joop clearing his throat, walking up to me and slipping his hands over my eyes. I quickly asked him if he was seeing someone else, silently kicking my own ass for being stupid enough to actually ask that. It was the wrong thing to do, because it just brought out all these questions from Joop. Wanting to know why I left him the last time we were together, what was I hiding, how did I feel about him. Things that I just didn't want to answer..couldn't answer right now.

As voices came louder toward the kitchen, I snapped my head to that direction. Joop leaned into me, driving me crazy with the scent of his body. He whispered into my ear, "After you drop Deandra off later tonight, come to me, to my place. I'll be waiting up for you. If I don't see you by 2am, I won't bother you again." With that, he kissed my cheek, leaving me with, "Be there, baby."

What do *you* think I did? While everyone ate heartily, I picked at my food, my eyes glancing over at Joop, who was doing the same to me. I felt this stirring inside of me. For Joop. Not just sexual either. I wanted to go on real dates with him. Check out movies, go to restaurants, go dancing, watch videos at our places, go for drives, talk, walk, and most importantly *love* one another. Never knew anyone to have a revelation at Thanksgiving dinner, but I had really felt that that was *exactly* what I was experiencing.

Tamara gave me enough food for a month when I left. I kissed everyone and after I saw Stephen slip my girl his digits, Deandra and I rolled out. I caught Joop staring at me, telling me with his eyes to come to him. It took a LOT of talking to Deandra for her to let me back out. She laughed, telling me to admit I was going to see Joop, and I lied, telling her that one of the guys I got digits from at the club wanted me to holla. Told her not to worry, I would be okay.

I quickly stripped out of my clothes and dressed in a pair of relaxed Levis and an old blue UNC Tarheels sweatshirt that Dee had sent to me years ago. Grabbing my jacket and keys, I headed out. As soon as I closed the door to my Explorer, I spent ten minutes fighting with myself, giving myself reasons for not going, reasons *for* going. I was scared...for real. The last time I spent with Joop was so magical, so da bomb, that I could almost feel myself wanting to tell about everything...something that I knew I couldn't do.

I sat there, my forehead resting on the steering wheel. Images of Joop and I making exquisite love flashed before my closed eyes, and I moaned deeply. I wiped at my eyes, surprised to find myself crying and started my ride. I didn't know what to expect...I would wait to stress myself out until I found out what

Joop's agenda was. All men had one...Joop would probably be no exception.

I quietly pulled my ride up in Joop's driveway and counted to fifty before hopping out. I felt like I had just had my last meal and was on my way to the gas chamber. I was shivering like it was fifty below, and my eyes were glistening from tears that had flowed on the way over. Finally at his doorstep, I took a deep breath, cleared my throat, and knocked on his front door...willing myself to stay until he at *least* opened the door...

Joop. . .

Talk about a ticking clock. My mind was so in tuned with the clock, that I could even hear it ticking through Kenny Lattimore's whining about losing his woman. I tidied up the place, washed some dishes from the morning, lit scented candles, showered, and changed into silk purple lounge pants and a tee shirt. Then I poured a brandy and waited.

To say I was worried would be an understatement. I mean I'm the one who gave the ultimatum, whether I would stick to it myself well...that remained to be seen. The soft tap at my door actually scared me. You know when you are waiting to hear something, HOPING to hear something, and then feel shocked when you do? I jumped up and took a deep breath, then opened the door. There stood Shameika, and me? I felt a smile shining on my face from the four corners: north, south, east, and west.

"Go on and say it," she said.

"Say what?"

"You knew I would come."

"Actually I didn't know, but I hoped. Come in, babe," I said, taking her by the hand and leading her inside. When we got to the couch, Sha immediately slipped her hands around my waist, pressing her forehead into my chest.

"Oh, Joop," she moaned. "I'm so scared, you just don't know."

"I want to know," I said, as I sat down, pulling her into my lap. "I want to know everything about you. I want to know what makes you happy. I want to know what makes you sad. I'm also scared, Sha, but when something feels right to me, when I can hear and feel the spirit telling me it's right, then I go for it. I hear and feel that spirit when it comes to you." Lifting her chin to look into her eyes, I continued, "When you deny it, you deny the forces of Jah, and you can never win like that." I touched her cheek. "Tell me what scares you."

She looked at me solemnly, her mouth opening as if she were about to reveal something, then closing it again. "Nothing scares me," she said, "I'm just glad I'm here with you." Shameika meshed her lips with mine, kissing me the way she did that first night, the night after Chris and Tee's wedding, sucking on my tongue. Her hands were all over me, touching me, caressing me through the thin fabric of my lounge pants.

I moaned against her neck. "You aren't gonna love me and leave me again, are ya? I mean a brotha has to think about his virtue," I joked, half-serious. Okay, more than half. Shameika smiled sweetly, shaking her head no and kissing me again.

"Do something for me, Sha," I said, feeling myself hardening from want of her but yet not wanting to rush things. Somehow I got the feeling that Sha thought that sex was all men ever really wanted from her. With me, she couldn't be more wrong. "Talk to me. Tell me about you. I want to know all about Shameika: your growing up, high school, college, everything."

Sha appeared surprised at my words, but we did talk. We talked all through the night, about everything. I told her about my parents, my grandmother, growing up in South Carolina, about my HU days and how me, Chris and Stephen hooked up, about some of my personal fears and confusions, hoping that she saw that I trusted her, hoping that she would trust me with hers also. And she told me about herself and her family. A little about her mother, but not much, and when I mentioned her father, she seemed to stiffen, then told me that they didn't really get along, and that was that. I could sense that was a totally forbidden subject with her, and with all the headway I had made, I didn't want to push, not just yet at least. We talked, and kissed and touched and even danced when a slow jam she liked came on the radio, and Shameika seemed completely surprised that I hadn't jumped her bones, making me wonder what the hell type of brothas she was used to seeing.

I fell asleep around the break of dawn after we had exhausted ourselves in conversation and kisses and laughs. I fell asleep with Sha curled up in my arms. In the midst of a warm dream, I could feel lips on me, kissing my stomach, lower, and waking me up in a flash. I looked down, gasping at the feeling and look in Sha's eyes.

"I love you, Joop," she said, just as she engulfed me, and showed me just how much.

Shameika...

Joop was so sweet to me...so unlike any man that I had ever been with. The way he held me, the way he talked to me, as if every word I said was pure gold. I had never remembered feeling so important and so loved in all my life. We talked ourselves to sleep...right in each other's arms just before the sun broke out. Actually Joop fell asleep, his warm breath tickling the back of my neck.

I could feel him against my body, so hard, so warm, and I knew that this, Joop was something that I wanted, that I needed. This rush of love just poured out of me, and I didn't know whether to cry from sheer joy or wake Joop up and share my euphoric feelings with him. I chose the latter. I turned around, facing Joop...placing feathery soft kisses along his face as I smiled at his beauty. My fingers lightly caressed his dreads as I thought about how I held onto them that night we created such heat and passion between us.

Lightly, I kissed his mouth, moving down slowly to pull up his shirt, kissing his stomach and lightly licking his navel. I felt him stir beneath me, and I slowly inched down his pants, my hands taking hold of his semi-hard erection. A groan escaped his mouth and I looked up, finding his eyes glued to mine, his mouth slightly parted.

Stroking him with my hands, I lightly kissed his tip and whispered to him, "I love you, Joop," before taking him deeply into my mouth. He moaned out my name as I continued loving him orally, wanting to let him know with each lick and suck and stroke how much I wanted him and wanted to please him. All my life, doing this was just to release some sexual tension, to make myself feel important, but this time…it all had to do with love and wanting to please, and be pleased.

Before Joop could release, he gripped my shoulders, bringing me up to him as we kissed. In one fluid motion, he had relieved me of my sweatshirt and bra and his mouth began it own exploration of my warm globes. I squirmed and purred as his teeth caught my nipples and grazed them. I rose up, slipping out of my jeans and panties, and shedding Joop of his pants and his tee shirt, wanting to see every inch of his beautiful body.

There wasn't a place on my body that Joop didn't touch with his mouth. He got me so riled up, so hot, so in need of him, that before I knew it, I was crying out for him to take me, make love to me. Joop pulled me up onto my hands and knees, maneuvering himself behind me. His hot mouth trailed kisses from the back of my neck, down my spine, finally kissing along my backside causing me to shudder. I pressed up against him, heated, begging him to take me, and when he did, my arms buckled from the sensations that sparked within my body.

I felt his hands press against the small of my back as he

moved deeply in and out of me, my center squeezing him, bringing him to me. "Damn, Boo," Joop cried, "you feel so damn good." With each thrust of him, I met him in equal fervor. I could feel him reaching my spot, the point that would have me releasing in orgasmic pleasure.

His movements quickened, and I cried out in sheer pleasure. His hands found my nipples as his pinched them, caressing my breasts. His body tight against my back, his thrusts coming short and deep inside of me. "Shameika," Joop crooned in my ear, attacking me with his thrusts. "Come with me, Baby."

Just his words ripped a loud cry from my mouth as I bucked against him, feeling myself release hard and fast, matching the cries and releases of Joop. After what felt like hours of cries and shakes and shudders, Joop laid me onto the floor and pressed his hot body tightly against me. He smoothed back my micro braids and kissed my forehead, the tip of my nose and my lips before staring me straight into my eyes and asking, "You know I love you Shameika, right?"

I felt tears spring into my eyes, but I kept them hidden. "You do?" I offered back, my voice low and soft.

"Yes, I do…I love you, Shameika."

My hands ran over his dreads, bringing him in for a deep, long kiss. "I love you too, Jamal. I *really* do."

Little girls often have dreams of falling in love with a knight in white armor and living happily ever after. They usually carry that dream until their first heart breaking relationship, when they realize that there really is no happily ever after, that it takes work to make a relationship work…but when you do work at it…it can be wonderful. Me, I never had the dream. They were stolen in my sleep at a very young age, and I thought I would never know what it felt like to have someone genuinely love me and who wanted me to be safe and happy.

Laying here, in the afterglow of the sweetest love I had ever experienced, I felt so beautiful, so wonderful, so special at that moment with having Joop love me, I felt my heart leaking, the ice that had housed it for so long beginning to drip. Slowly moving towards the door, my heart keeper looked outside of its peephole and saw Joop knocking, standing there, patiently waiting to be let in to the love I had to offer. For so long...most of my life in fact, I had kept anyone from getting in there...only allowing VIP access to Tee and Deandra. I was seriously considering creating a VIP pass for Joop.

Joop...

Love has a way of doing things to you, everyday has a new meaning, and you become more deeply aware of every light, every scent, and every sound. And no matter what you are busy doing, your mind always shifts to that special someone, wondering what they are doing, wondering if she's thinking about you the way you're thinking about her. That totally engulfing, consuming, explosive feeling that has you walking on cloud nine. I've never felt it before now.

Even while in class at times when I was supposed to be going over student projects and focusing on teaching, Shameika would float in front of my eyes. I would see her image or either I would hear her voice, something she had said or done. It reminded me of something a professor had told me once, when he said how you could live forever and never tire of the wonders of the universe. Well Sha was like my universe. I don't believe I could ever tire of new knowledge of her. I was in love for the first time in my life, and there was nothing that had ever compared to the feeling,

Weeks rolled by, weeks in which we were able to come to know one another even more. Shameika met my grandmother who loved her as much as I did. I was able to briefly meet her mom also, although Sha didn't seem to want to hang around there long. But we were building, learning, and finding new revelations about one another, and with these new revelations came one for me. I didn't just want her as my girlfriend. I wanted her to be forever my lady. I wanted her as my wife. That's right, Jamal Evans was seriously thinking about jumping the broom himself.

"Joop, I know you can't be serious? Man, if you get married, that leaves me all by myself. You niggas are wack!" Stephen had been bitching on and on from the moment we had hit the mall. I had talked him into going along with me to Lake Forest Mall to look for a ring for Sha, while continually trying to convince him that I was dead serious about this. I had it all planned out. On Christmas Eve, I would give her an on-bended-knee proposal. Now of course I would have preferred a Kwanzaa proposal, but I knew that Sha was into the Christmas thing, and so Christmas Eve it would be. I smiled to myself, thinking cockily how I could be one romantic brotha when the mood hit, and with Ms. Jones, the mood was hitting all the time.

"Look Step, this is it for me man," I said. "I have no doubt in my mind that Shameika is the one for me. I mean come on, bruh. We aren't getting any younger, and I sure would like a son before I get too old to kick it at the courts with him you know? Hell, you're older than I am. Aren't you tired of being alone all the time?"

"I'm not alone," Stephen argued. "I've got my business and I keep plenty of company and you know it. And I am used to have my boys too, till now. You and Chris are getting all mushy and wanting to do the family thing. Now your ass is sitting here talking about kids, too? Lawd! Whatever happened to that brotha that used to school us on not being whipped, weak, letting sistahs get your mind?"

"He grew up, man, and he found his queen, that's what. And those women you're around are not real company. You don't see that yet because the feeling has never ever hit you, but when it does then you will see what I'm talking about." We stopped at Kay Jewelers checking out a genuine pearl surrounded by a cluster of diamonds. I knew it didn't look like the traditional engagement ring, but I wanted something as unique and special and different as Sha was, and I was running out of time, with only two days away before Christmas Eve.

"So what do you think, man?" I asked Step, looking intently at the ring.

"I think it sux like a muthafucka, and you oughta forget about that shit and me and you just head up to D.C. on Christmas Eve and check out the honies at Republic Gardens."

"Step?" I gave him a warning look.

"Alright, alright I'm joking!" Stephen laughed.

"I'll take it," I told the cashier; a secret smile on my face, wondering what Sha would say when she saw her ring.

"Hurry up and open it, gurl! I shopped all week for this gift for you!" Shameika exclaimed. We were all chillin' at Chris and Tee's on Christmas Eve, me wired and hyper about the box sitting behind me, hardly being able to keep my mouth shut. I had warned Step to keep quiet about things when I got the ring. He was the only one I had told about my little gift, not even telling Chris for fear he would blabber to his wifey and she in turn to Sha, and I wanted her to be *completely* surprised.

"Oh Sha, this is so nice!" Tamara shouted, giggling with glee at the his and her matching black and gold trimmed robes, both monogrammed with her and Chris' initials.

"Well it's from both Joop and me," Sha said, looking at me smiling. "Look under the paper. There is something else there for y'all, too." Peeping under the soft tissue paper, Tee pulled out an envelope containing two tickets to the 93.9 Kissmas December 26th concert at Constitution Hall. Sha had said that Tamara was a hard-core Donnell Jones lover, and that the tickets would set their gift off perfectly. Well, she obviously knew her girl well from the hoots and hollers and screams that came from Tamara.

"I LOVE DONNELLLLLLLL!!! OH MY GOD, AND

GINUWINE, CHICO, CASE! "AHHHHH!!" Tamara screamed, giving Sha a big wet kiss.

"Dang man and here I was thinking it was ME she loved," Chris joked. "Thanks, really, this is cool!"

"Well I know I dig what y'all got me, too," I said, smiling down at the antique portrait of Mabasa at war. I knew Chris had gotten it because of the poem I had written talking about Mabasa in South Africa. Yeah brotherman knew my taste well! They had gotten Sha a couple of nice outfits, Tee laughing and saying that Sha LIVED for clothes. I couldn't help the naughty thoughts that flew through my head, thinking back to the warmth of her body underneath mine the night before. She definitely was more appealing to me without them!

I cleared my throat, more than ready to give my present to Sha. I couldn't wait to see her face when she saw it. Besides, I wanted to ask her before Stephen came over with his snarls about marriage. He was spending the early evening with his five-year-old daughter, telling us he would roll on over here later on.

"Okay, my turn. Sha, I got something for you. How about you open it now?" I smiled, pulling a big box from behind me.

"What is it?" she asked, grinning like a Cheshire cat.

"Open it."

She grabbed the box, shaking it lightly. "It's light, Joop!" she exclaimed, looking perplexed. "Oh, I hate the suspense. I really do!"

"Open it, girl!" Tamara laughed. "Shoot I'm curious my damn self."

Opening the box, Shameika found a smaller box. She laughed as she also opened that one, revealing a black porcelain hand, and nestled in the hand another tiny, tiny box. "A hand?" she asked, looking at me curiously.

"Open the other box," I told her, looking intently in her eyes.

Sha slowly removed the red satiny paper from the tiny ring box, revealing the pearl diamond cluster engagement ring. She gasped. I could hear Chris's "*Whoa*" as I waited for a response from her.

She looked up at me in question.

"The ring is for you. The hand is symbolic. You know I had to put the spirit in there somehow." I laughed nervously. "But the hand, it's what I want to ask your father for when I meet him, your hand. Will you marry me, Shameika?"

It was quiet for a moment, Sha just staring down at the porcelain hand. "Sha?" I lifted her head up to look at me. Her face was engulfed in tears, shocking me.

"What is it? I asked.

She looked down at the hand again. Her voice trembled as she said, "No, I'm sorry but I can't…" With that she got up and ran swiftly out the front door, leaving me with a hand, a ring, and the *we're so sorry* glances of our two friends, adding to my humiliation.

Shameika. . .

The moment I told Joop that I loved him, I felt my life change. There's really no other way to explain it. Lying in his arms, basking in the heat and love that we had just exchanged…it was *definitely* a miracle. Plain and simple. The sun was blazing brightly in the sky before we even got up from the carpet. I remembered the look on Joop's face when we finally arose and it was pure bliss. Brotha was happy…hell, so was I. Happier than a punk in Boy Town, as my mother would say.

We showered together, and Joop fixed me breakfast. Not much was said, but it was enough to know that our relationship was slowly raising above the friendship stage, past the hit it and leave it stage. I was nervous, but elated at the same time. We talked some more, making plans for dinner and a movie that night, and I quickly dressed, needing to run some errands before it got too dark.

As soon as I stepped into my place, Deandra was on my heels. "Where the hell were you?" she demanded, a scarf wrapped around her head, her body clad in black silk pajamas.

"Why are you still in your pajamas?" I asked, ignoring her. "It's after noon." I walked into my bedroom, Deandra in tow. She stood there, watching me remove my clothing and panties, standing buck naked in front of her. I grabbed an Adidas sweat suit from my closet and a fresh bra and panties before going into the bathroom, locking the door before Deandra could enter. I could hear her lean against the door as I turned on the faucets of my whirlpool tub, wanting a nice hot bubble bath.

After several minutes of silence, I slipped into the hot water, aahing as its velvety heat enveloped me. "Dee," I said, loud enough for her to hear me. "I know you're out there, and I'm sorry I left and didn't call or anything. I really am."

I heard Dee sigh. "I was just worried about you, Girl," she began. "I guess those motherly worries came to me, and I didn't know where you were."

"It's okay."

"Ummm, so, where were you, Shameika?" Deandra asked with a high pitch to her voice. I *had* to laugh. Girl was a stone cold trip, acting like she was just worried, when I know she wanted the scoop.

"You want the truth?" I asked, my voice containing the smile that was plastered on my face.

"You know I do," Deandra responded.

"I was with Joop."

The squeal that came out of Dee's mouth was one like in a horror movie. I shuddered in the tub from the sound causing havoc on my ears. "Girl, are you serious? You were really with Joop? So you guys are together or something?"

I laughed at the twenty questions, tickled. "Lemme see if I

can remember all dem damn questions," I joked. "Yes, I'm serious, Yes, I was really with Joop and ….Yea, Joop and I are together…or something."

"I knew it!" Dee squealed. "I asked Tee, but she said she didn't really know. She had her thoughts, but you didn't talk to her about it."

"Was nothing to say…still isn't. All I can truthfully say is I care about Joop a lot…a *whole* lot."

"I am so happy for you, Sha," Deandra cooed. "You deserve some happiness in your life."

I smiled. "We all do," I said. "What about you?" I asked, grabbing my loofah off my bathroom rack beside the tub. "Where's your *happy* man at?"

"Girl, puhlease," Dee said, sighing. "I have been so busy with work and been running from state to state so much with work, that I have no time for a man. Besides, ain't nothing but knuckleheads out there."

"Dee, if it wasn't for Joop…and maybe Chris," I said chuckling, "I would definitely agree with you. Men are *tired*."

"So, you gonna let me hold that black book of yours?" Dee laughed.

"TAKE IT!" I laughed back. "Even if I'm left alone, I don't want them muthafuckas!"

"Hey," Dee said, "Are the male Three Musketeers as great as the female Three Musketeers?" I knew that hint was in reference to Stephen, and I sighed.

"No," I answered, "I don't think so."

"You know, I was talking to Stephen, and for real, I swear he used at least twenty macking lines on me," Dee said. We both shared a long, hearty laugh. "I mean nothing real came out his mouth. I don't think he would know reality if it bit his sexy ass!"

"I will admit, Stephen *is* cute," I said, "but he's worse than me…and you know I ain't nothing but a devil, for real! Boy makes *my* black book look like a sheet of paper, no lie!"

"Damn, he rolling like that?" Dee asked.

"Most definitely, and not only are there a lot of women, but the brotha likes *flavoring*, looking like he got a spice rack full of women."

"So it's not even just sistahs he be rolling with?"

"No, Girl…he's an equal opportunity gigolo…goes where the action is."

Deandra sighed. "Why are all the men…all the good looking men so not ready for love and relationships? Why aren't they, Girl? Tell me that."

I smiled softly, sighing. "Girl, I wouldn't know," I responded, grinning to myself. *I had me a sexy, beautiful, loving man*, I thought to myself, giggling as I dipped my head under the bubbly water.

Joop and I were tied at the *hip*, ya heard? We did the movies, the restaurants, the art gallery, the black wax museum, the harbor, the clubs, every and anything. Even Chris appeared to have accepted the fact that Joop and I were trying to make a love jones happen.

Joop took me to meet his grandmother, and I instantly fell in love with her. She looked like the type of grandmother I would have loved to have had. She was small and appeared fragile, but she was a strong-minded woman, who lived to bring joy into people's lives, and just with the one visit, I was definitely smitten with her, calling her Grandmom as Joop and I left her after a day of spending it together with her.

With Joop having introduced me to his grandmother, I felt obligated to bring him into my world, but only a tad bit. I brought him to meet my mother, and every nerve in my body was on edge. I cringed as she opened the door, fearing that she was still in this warped/hatred mode against me. She appeared pleasant, and I thanked God for giving me that. Joop seemed to be very interested in the stories my mother told, the few that were pleasant anyway, like my loving to sing, the more "sweet" birthdays. I could see Joop devouring everything in my childhood home, the framed pictures of my mother and I. I *know* he noticed the absence of pictures with my dad and I, but he didn't question. I'm sure he was holding this info in until it was necessary to ask me.

Before I knew it, Christmas was upon us. I had been so busy with the daycare center, helping Lara pack up her ex-hubby's shit, seeing Deandra off as she told me she was coming back in time for New Year's, finishing up my projects for school, and hanging with my boo, that I didn't even bother to check out a mall or store to do any kind of Christmas shopping.

After calling up my girl, Tee to see if she had time for me, we both agreed to hit the mall in a shopping frenzy. After about four hours in the mall, I had gifts for Deandra, Joop, my mother, little Jon, and even good ol' Stephen. Tee whined and cried about my not buying her gift, but I had to politely inform her how tacky it would be to buy her or Chris' gift while she was present. She didn't care.

We eventually drove back to her house and were chilling in the kitchen drinking tea, when she *finally* mentioned Joop.

"Girl, why did you wait so long to ask me about him?" I laughed. "He and I have been one on one for several weeks now."

"I dunno." Tamara grinned. "I think I didn't want to jinx it. You two are just too cute together. You know, even Chris told me last night that you have been a positive in Joop's life."

I damn near spit my tea out. "Stop lying!" I exclaimed. "He *really* said that?"

"Yea, he did. Girl, you have to admit…you were a wild child from way back. Chris was worried that you would hurt his boy."

"I understand that," I muttered, staring into my brown-colored tea. "But *you* know the circumstances of a lot of my stupidity."

A silenced encased us before Tamara came back with, "Have you told Joop about your father?"

My eyes widened. "Hell no!" I cried out. "I don't even know how I would go about doing that. I don't even know if he would talk to me again."

"Why, Girl?" Tamara asked, placing her cup onto the table and reaching her hands out to take mine. "You know that what your father did wasn't your fault, right?"

"Yea, I guess."

"There is no guessing about it. You were a little *girl*. A *girl*. He abused you. He hurt *you*...for a really long time. That wasn't your fault."

I tried unsuccessfully to keep my tears inside. They tumbled out. "But how could any man, *knowing* about that want to be with me, Tee?" I asked, my voice tight. "I'm like tainted goods. More so now that I let all them damn negroes so freely have a piece of me."

Tamara came around the table and hugged me close to her chest. I let the tears turn into sobs. "You are not tainted, Sha," Tamara whispered. "You know, you really need to talk to Joop. Tell him everything, cry to him, let him be there for you, so you can finally start with a clean slate and feel like you *deserve* the happiness that is knocking on your heart."

I smiled wistfully, thinking about the night Joop changed my life. I had thought about the VIPs that resided in my heart. I had wanted to give Joop a VIP card, and maybe to make this possible happiness more real I needed to tell him everything, so that we could start this love jones with trust and pure happiness...and not doubts or painful pasts.

I had thought seriously about telling Joop about my father, had even planned to do it later on after we got back from having our Christmas Eve party at Chris and Tee's house. I had practiced it over and over again in my mind. How I would tell him what my father did to me, how my mother knew and never did anything, how I had managed to forgive her, and not my father and all the ugly complications that went along with this horrible secret. But something stopped me. My father.

No one knew this but Tee and Deandra, but by the age of sixteen, I had endured nine years of physical and sexual abuse at the hands of my father. As a kid, I didn't know it was wrong, just that it hurt. But when the sexual abuse turned to physical abuse, I immediately associated both with pain and pain with wrong, and went to my mother. I was eleven. She yelled at me and slapped my face, telling me that I was liar, that I would burn in Hell if I ever repeated this to anyone. And I never did. I went to school, excelled in it, and my singing. I was the stellar student and daughter. I was creative enough to make up stories for the bruises that I couldn't hide, and was creative enough to try and think of other things when my father came to my room at night.

After the first night, I began sleeping in the fetal position and sucking my thumb. Even now, I slept that way, minus the thumb, which I learned to give up at sixteen. The year that blew everything out of the water. I guess my perfect appearance was my way of keeping in the pain, because one night, before my 'scheduled' appearance by my father, I slipped into the bathroom, picked up his razor, and sliced my wrists. I didn't even feel the pain of the slices, for everything I had endured the last nine years exponentially surpassed it.

My attempted suicide led to my finally telling my story to people. After a quick trial, my father was sentenced to ten years for abusing me. At sixteen, I thought ten years was a lot, even though I *truly* had preferred that he stay in jail for the rest of my life. The "rest of my life" or the ten years were merely a dream. The good ol' justice system let my father out on good behavior after five years, two days shy of my 22nd birthday.

For the last five years I have kept as my main goal to keep him out of my life...and my mother's, but for my mother it's been nothing but drama. Every time my mother and I have gotten to a calm place in our relationship, my father has shown up to wreak havoc into her life…thus the hateful episode we had a while back.

I thought I was rid of him, thought I could be happy, for once in my life. My friends were happy and healthy, I had a real man loving me…it was Christmas, everything felt so good…so good that I didn't see pain as it rang my phone while I was packing up my Christmas gifts to head over Chris and Tee's. On the third ring, I picked it up.

"Hello, Sha speaking," I answered.

"Hi." I felt my body cringe and my stomach convulse, wanting to throw up, but I had nothing to give. I didn't speak. "I know you don't want to talk to me, but I had to call and wish you a Merry Christmas. I *really* want to let you know that I have changed, and I have, Shameika. I am so sorry for hurting you and I…"

"Noooo!" I screamed, my tears flying wildly. "Don't you *ever* call hear again. I hate you!" With that, I slammed the phone down, stumbling away from it, looking at it like it was possessed. Shaking, I grabbed my gifts and managed to make my way to my SUV, dumping the presents in. Once I had my seatbelt secured, I flipped my visor and reapplied my lipstick, wiping my tears, and taking deep breaths.

"It's okay. It's okay. It's okay," I told myself, starting my car and preparing myself to move into a more pleasant, loving atmosphere.

And it really was a loving atmosphere. Everyone was so happy, it was easy for me to fake that I was okay. I squealed when I opened my presents. Chris and Tee got me clothes, mostly Adidas gear, something that Tamara and I had loved since the beginning of time. Tamara practically took my head off in joy when she saw the gifts Joop and I bought her and Chris…matching monogrammed robes and tickets to the 93.9 Kissmas Concert.

I noticed how excited Joop was throughout the entire evening. He seemed to be preoccupied and refused to let me hold my gift or even look at it, until everyone had unwrapped theirs. Finally, he handed me my gift. It was a big box but it felt so light. Tamara yelled for me to opening, saying she was curious also. I opened the box to find a smaller box, and I smacked at Joop.

"Damn you." I laughed. I opened that box and saw a black porcelain hand that held an even smaller box. "A hand?" I asked, giggling. "You got me a hand?"

Joop continued to beam, telling me to open the small box. When I did, I froze. Inside was a pearl-diamond...what looked like an engagement ring. I gasped and felt my heart racing in my chest. I felt jittery, but a good jittery. I didn't want to start jumping to conclusions and screaming yes, so I raised my eyes to Joop, asking him with my eyes what this ring was for.

"The ring is for you. The hand is symbolic. You know I had to put the spirit in there somehow." Joop laughed. "But the hand, it's what I want to ask your father for when I meet him, your hand. Will you marry me, Shameika?"

My father, I thought, instantly allowing the phone call, the past to rush forward, causing me to cry. I couldn't look at him. I couldn't look at Chris or Tamara either. I just balled, the tears running too fast to do anything with.

"What is it?" Joop asked, reaching out for me, but I shook his hands away.

I glanced at the black hand...the beautiful ring and shook my head no, handing it back to him. "No," I whispered, choking back tears, "I'm sorry, but I can't..." Before I could finish my sentence, I grabbed my keys and coat and ran for the door, not looking back.

My heart literally fell from my chest, locking itself away. I knew that Joop would never want me again...I *knew* this. This was the ultimate hurt, the ultimate diss, and I totally blew it with a man who was good and wonderful and beautiful and loving. But then again, that kinda love wasn't meant for me anyway.

Joop...

Fuck it! Fuck forever, totally, no doubts, no disputes, fuck it! I spent the next few days building again, building up my good and solid *fuck it* attitude. I have never in twenty-eight years allowed a woman to make a complete, absolute fool of me the way Shameika did that Christmas Eve. I left immediately after she did, not paying any attention to Tamara's, *you don't understand Joop, there is so much you should know about Sha that you don't understand,* and to Chris' look of I told you so, I warned you. I didn't want to see anybody. I wanted to be the invisible man till the ache stopped dwelling in my heart. I returned that mockery of an engagement ring the day after Christmas, and broke the goddamn porcelain hand in a million pieces.

I tried to rid my apartment of all memorandum of Shameika, and reread to remind myself of what my father had wrote to me in one of his journals, *A real black man triumphs over adversities. A real black man learns to swallow hurt. A real black man never allows a slap from someone else to taint HIS essence.* Well I needed to start being a real black man, instead of the weak fool that I had been over love, over a woman.

I ignored the telephone all week, knowing that most of the calls were from Sha, her trying to apologize. I didn't want or need an apology. I wanted to be left alone. I had had enough. The fed up type of enough. Toward the end of the week while I was engulfed in studies, there was a knock at my door, I immediately ran to get it thinking it was UPS with a package that an old HU frat brother had told me he was mailing. There instead of the UPS man, stood Sha.

"Hey, Joop," she said.

I was silent, feeling my breath being taken away, as the

175

blow to my stomach renewed its hurt. I quickly swallowed the huge lump in my throat.

"Listen, Sha, I'm busy. I'm trying to get some studying in while I have a chance before school starts back up next Monday."

"I know but...but I just wanted to see how you were and to tell you that I'm sorry I embarrassed you in front of our friends, and I'm sorry that I didn't..," she stopped, looking up at me with her huge, hazel tear-filled eyes. She looked at my stone-cold face, me having devoid myself of any emotion, trying as hard as I could to feel nothing as she talked, and not giving in again or let me become weakened by her tears.

"You don't love me anymore, do you? I killed it?" she swallowed as I looked away, not wanting to look at her any-more, feeling myself weakening and wanting to give in and be a fool one more time, but saying a silent prayer to Jah not to let me.

"Oh God...I'm sorry! I'm so sorry Jamal!" she said. Then she was gone. I stood at the door in a daze for long minutes, just staring at nothing...

Shameika...

I ran so hard to my car that I thought I broke my knees with the hard, quick juts my feet made from the front door to my car. I jumped in, turning it on, and screeching out of Chris and Tamara's driveway. I can't even tell you how I got home with all the tears. By the time I reached my place, I almost ran over the sidewalk where my parking spot was, breaking hard and being banged up against my steering wheel, realizing that I had forgotten to hook my seat belt.

I shook my head, stumbling out of my ride and up to my door. More or less, I fell in, turning the doorknob and just hav-ing my body *push* the door open. Once my feet had secure grounding, I began stripping out of my clothes, a trail following me into my bedroom, where I finally stood, naked.

"Dammit!" I cried, picking up a framed picture of my mother and me from my dresser. We were smiling and happy. I had to be at least four. I gripped the picture, my tears falling against the glass of the frame. "If you had *helped* me! *Saved* me! Goddam you! I hate you! I hate you! Hate you!" I continued to cry, falling onto my bed, curling up into my normal fetal position. I tugged on my comforter, curling it up and over me. I continued crying, shaking, convulsing with dry heaves, until the shrill of the phone stopped me in mid-sob.

My heart literally jumped into my throat with hopes that maybe Joop was calling to talk to me. I swear, if it was, I would have told him everything and anything for him to love me. When I answered the phone and heard the "Hey, Baby," I gagged.

"What do you want?" I groaned into the phone.

"Damn, why you gotta be like that, Babygirl?" It was one of my 'friends'. Niggah didn't understand that if I ain't hit you in months to go on and find some other girl to fix you up. "I wanted to wish you a Merry Christmas, Boo…wanted to know what you were up to."

"Why? What do you want?"

"Thought maybe we could spread a little Christmas cheer to each other." The sound of his laughter made me sick, and I dropped the phone to rush to the bathroom, finally finding something to empty into the toilet bowl. When I returned, I picked the phone up from the floor and he was still there.

"What happened?" he asked.

"Got sick," came my cold reply.

"So, what's up?" he asked. "What, you don't *hang* anymore?"

"If you mean do I fuck anymore, the answer is no, I don't!"

"Look girl, what, you don' got you some nigga who pretends to like your ass or something? Any other time you give up the shit all too freely."

"You know what?" I yelled into the phone. "Lose my fucking number! For real, do that. I may have been too free to give up my shit before, but y'all men ain't worth the fucking drama. So have a merry fucking Christmas, and don't call my ass any more!" I slammed the phone down, my breath surging in and out of me.

I quickly picked up the phone, punching in a number. "Silhouette Salon," the older feminine voice piped through the phone.

"Miss Emily," I said, coughing back tears. "How did I know you would be there on Christmas Eve?" We both laughed.

"Girl, hush your mouth," Miss Emily said. "You know my butt will be here tomorrow, too. What's wrong, Baby? You don't sound too good."

"I'm not good, Miss Emily. I was wondering if I could come in tomorrow? Say around noon? You know how you do with the hair and talking. I need my healing fix."

Miss Emily laughed. "You know I always reserve a spot for you here. I'll see you at noon, okay?"

"Okay and thanks," I whispered, smiling for the first time since leaving Chris and Tee's. Hanging up the phone, I sighed, falling into my bed, pulling my comforter up around my neck and begging for sleep to take me away. An hour later, it did.

"So you and this Joop are over, huh?" Miss Emily asked, while she transformed me from Ghetto Queen, to just plain ol' Queen.

"Yea, that boy ain't even trying to talk to me." I sighed. "For real. It don't matter anyway, cuz I'm just no good to anybody."

Miss Emily smacked my hand with her comb. "Shut that mess up. You are a beautiful and loving woman. You are worth a lot. A lot more than you think."

I looked into the mirror, noticing my small face surrounding by all my *real* hair. No one except for my girls knew that most of this was mine on my head. "Thank you for your words, Miss Emily." I smiled to her through the mirror. "Now tell me, what are we gonna do with all this mess?"

"Girl, please. All this beautiful naturally curly hair!" Miss Emily exclaimed. "We could do magic!"

"Well then magicize me, Honey," I said, Miss Emily and I falling over ourselves laughing.

The days leading up to New Year's Eve were pretty quiet. Mainly because I kept to myself. I tried to call Joop, but the brotha had his phone on lock down, refusing to answer. I spent a lot of time staring at myself in the mirror. My head was already small and now with no hair, it looked magnified...but cute. I just told Em to get to cutting and she cut til I had a good two inches on my head and left it natural, with soft curls clinging against my scalp.

I had managed to see my girl Tee a time or two throughout the week, and she consoled me...for Joop and my hair, telling me I did look cute, but damn, could I had saved just a tad more hair for my head??? She told me how Joop left right after I did and they hadn't heard from him since. She mentioned talking to him on my behalf, but I chilled her on that. It was over. I had to face that and try to move on.

The day before New Year's, I got a phone call from Deandra. She was all frantic, telling me that delivery men were bringing her living and bedroom sets and could I please go and let them in. She had already called her landlord and the key was there for me to pick up. Deandra would be arriving tomorrow for good, but she would really owe me big if I could do this for her. I sighed, knowing that she knew Joop lived right across the damn street from her, but what was I going to say? No? I whispered a yes to her, hung up with her smiling and happy in my ear and took off my pajamas — today was chill day — and slipped on some jeans and a sweater. I pulled on my multi-colored winter hat and leather coat and made my way over to Dee's place.

I parked a block down and walked up, not wanting Joop to notice my Explorer. Thirty minutes later, the men had the furniture in the apartment and an hour after that, they had it all put together and arranged. I gave them all a tip and ushered them and myself out of Dee's place. Standing on her stoop, I looked across the street, noticing Joop's car parked in front of his brownstone. I knew he didn't want to see me, I knew he was ignoring me, but I couldn't help it. I marched across the street and without second-guessing; I knocked on his door.

As soon as he opened the door, I regretted it. The look in his eyes was colder than the weather. "Hey, Joop," I said, my heart pounding against my chest.

He just stared at me in disbelief, like I had some nerve showing up at his place after the shit I had pulled. He quickly looked away, his eyes busying themselves with a spot on his door. "Listen, Sha, I'm busy," he said. "I'm trying to get some studying in while I have a chance before school starts back up next Monday."

I looked over his face, seeing that soft skin, those dreads I loved to tug on, the man I loved, and I just couldn't walk away just yet. "I know," I came back with, "but...but I just wanted to see how you were and to tell you that I'm sorry I embarrassed you in front of our friends, and I'm sorry that I didn't..," I stopped, looking up at Joop, my eyes filled with tears. No emotions came to the surface of Joop's face. He remained cold, uncaring and choking back a sob, I whispered, "You don't love me anymore, do you? I killed it?" He still didn't look at me, that in itself telling me all I needed to know.

"Oh God!" I cried out, letting the tears flow. "I am *so* sorry, Jamal!" Once again, I was left fleeing a scene, but this time, I

180

wouldn't come back and apologize. This time...it was over. Joop was through with my defected ass, and I was just about through with me, too.

When I got home, I immediately called Tamara, balling before she got a chance to say hello. "What's wrong, Girl?" she whispered into the phone.

"It is...so...so...o..over between Joop and me, girl," I cried. "I looked so stupid going ova there today."

"You went over to his place?"

"Yea, Dee called me, asking to let the delivery men into her place, and...and I just couldn't help it!" I cried, the sobs making it hard to finish or even begin sentences.

"What did he say?" Tamara said in her calm, motherly way.

"Nothing, absofuckinglutely nothing! Just turned away when I asked him if we were over. And I swear...I swear Tee, if he had given me one moment that said we could work this out, I would have told him *everything...e.v.e.r.y.t.h.i.n.g*...but he didn't. It's over."

I closed my eyes, feeling the warm, salty tears run down my face, onto my lips. "Girl, I want you to calm down...okay?" Tamara said. "Take some breaths, go put on your Mozart, drink a cup of tea, take a long hot bath, and relax. It's not over till the fat lady sings."

"Girl, that bitch done hit the scale at a ton and just finished an aria, okay! It's *over*."

"We'll see about that."

"What are you going to do?"

"Don't worry about me, just go do what I said...call me if you need me...or I will see you tomorrow night at Stephen's place. Okay?"

I took a deep breath, whispering, "Okay...love you, girl."

"Always to you, too, Sha."

Placing the phone back on its base, I closed my eyes, praying to God to give me just *one* more chance with Joop…promising to do it right this damn time…to let him in to *all* of me.

Joop. . .

The phone kept ringing relentlessly. I tried to ignore it as I shaved, cursing as I nicked myself AGAIN. *"Damn! Who the hell could that be?"* I had decided against New Year's at Stephen's, where everyone was planning on meeting to see in the millennium. Y2K, finally! But I would be seeing in the Y2K without the people I was most close with. I couldn't be around them, knowing that Shameika was supposed to be there also.

So instead I planned on going to a party at James Akron's, he was the head varsity basketball coach at Baltimore City High School. We hung out sometimes; even if he did drink too much in my opinion on those hang out nights. I laughed when he mentioned his New Year's Eve party, thinking that the boys on the team would crack up if they saw how their coach could down a forty in ten minutes flat.

The phone rang again, with me quickly picking it up this time. "Hello?"

"Joop? This is Tee. About time you answered that damn phone. I knew you were there."

"Hey. What's up, Tee?" I asked, wiping shaving cream from my chin with a towel.

"I wanted to tell you to bring a bottle of Champagne with you tonight, and a couple bags of chips, too," she said.

"Um..Tamara I'm not coming over Stephen's tonight, I have other plans," I said quietly.

"You mean to tell me, you'd rather see the millennium in with somebody else than with your closest friends? Chris is gonna be so hurt, and so is Stephen. We've been going all out for this thing tonight, even Deandra is back in town for New Year's."

"Chris and Step won't mind. They understand and I will

give y'all a ring right after the ball drops. I just thought I would go to this other party I was invited to. You know it's not personal. I have mad love for you guys," I said evasively.

"Shameika will be there, too. That's the problem, isn't it? That Sha will be there?" I was silent, not wanting to answer her questions.

"Look Tee I need to put some clothes on. But, like I said, I'll ring you guys at midnight. Tell everyone hi, okay? And happy New Year's."

"Joop, we need to talk. You and I."

"We will. I'll talk to you soon." I quickly hung up the phone, scratching my neck nervously as I looked at my reflection in the mirror.

Twenty minutes later I was dressed, and opening the door to head out when there stood Tamara. She pushed her way past me, took off her coat, and took a seat.

"Like I said, Joop," she said, crossing her legs, straightening her collar and looking me dead in the eye, "we need to talk."

"Tamara…" I sighed. "You don't give up, do you?"

"Not when it comes to two people I care about, no. If you would just listen for a minute, maybe you will understand why Shameika rejected your proposal and why she behaves as she does."

I jiggled my keys subconsciously. The last thing I needed was to hear more excuses about Sha, and why/how a woman could be warm and loving one minute, and yet doing a helter skelter on you the next. I didn't want to hear anymore. I couldn't hear anymore for my own sanity. "No," I said, equally meeting her eyes with a determination of my own. "I don't want to work anything out, and I don't want to know why she gets this weird, sick kick out of playing her mind games and dicing over other people's emotions. She's played mine for the last time, okay? I really should thank her. She's taught me a valuable lesson, so let's not go there Tam…"

Tamara cut in. "He molested her, Joop. Her father, the man

you told her you wanted to meet so bad, and wanted to ask for her hand in marriage? Had been molesting her most of her childhood life."

I was stunned. Listening in quiet shock as Tamara poured Sha's painful story on to me. The abuse, and her mother's compounding on it by not protecting her. Her attempted suicide at age sixteen and her father's trial, and ultimate conviction. It all started to make more sense now. Her little odd ways and the shield of protection she masked with her toughness. And me, I simply added to her pain by trying to be all chivalrous and making a big deal about *asking* her father for her hand. No wonder she turned me down flat!

"She loves you, Joop. She can't take any more blows in her life and she's devastated and lost without you. I know she hurt you. I can only imagine how this all has affected you, but swallow it, be the strong man that I know you are, and go to her?"

Tamara couldn't mask the tears brimming in her eyes, and I didn't need to be told twice where I needed to be at this moment. I hugged Tee tightly, thanking her for being a nosey interloper, in which she laughed tearfully.

Both of us made our way out of my apartment. Tee to her destination, and me with one thing on my mind, finding Shameika, and wrapping myself around her pain, to help her heal it.

Shameika . . .

I managed to get a full eight hours of sleep, which surprised the hell out of me. Guess those Tylenol PM do work. It was New Year's Eve! After today, no matter what happened in my life, it would be different. We were hitting the MILLENNIUM and I just hoped that when it came, Armageddon wasn't following.

I spent the day pampering myself, taking a long hot bath, with my music filtering through my place, just like I fell asleep last night. I pulled out a black silk button down shirt, which tied around the waist and matching wide-legged slacks. I hit my lips with gloss, put on my gold hoop earrings and school ring, and slipped my feet into my leather boots.

Glancing at myself in my full-length mirror, I smiled. Even through the tears and heartache, girl looked good. I fluffed my short curly 'do and went into the kitchen to grab my two bottles of champagne, platter of crab cakes and other munchies I whipped up this morning for the party, and was about to head out the door when my doorbell rang.

"Damn," I muttered, placing the bottles and the platter on the kitchen table. I trotted to the door, opening it. My breath was taken away when I saw Joop standing on the other side, looking freaking irresistible in his all black attire, black slacks, black turtle neck and cloaked in a three-quarter leather coat.

"Damn," he whispered. "You look so beautiful...love the hair." My eyes questioned him, as he asked, "Can I come in?"

"What do you want, Joop?" a bitter tone caught up in my voice.

"Can I come in, please?" Unlike Joop did me, I stepped aside, allowing him to enter. When I shut the door I turned to face him, my arms crossed.

"What?" I asked. "I hope you aren't here to humiliate me further. Yesterday was *quite* enough, and right now I'm teetering on the edge of insanity."

"I talked to Tee." I stood there, my mouth gaped open, my tears silently falling from my eyes. I knew she was up to something, but I didn't know what. Now, knowing he knew, I should have felt happy, but I was embarrassed, embarrassed that he now knew I wasn't complete, wasn't whole.

I didn't say anything. I watched Joop take off his jacket and lay it on my couch. I watched his body, dressed in black like me, move closer to me, stopping a good foot away. Finally, he broke the silence. "Why didn't you tell me, Sha?" he asked, his voice sorrowful. "Did you think I would blame you? Think less of you?"

I bit my lower lip to keep it from trembling, to keep the sobs in. I was still speechless. When Joop reached out and touched my hands, I flinched, but he caressed them in his warm hands, bringing them up to his lips to kiss. "Shameika," he crooned, "I love you, girl. I won't even begin to tell you how pissed I am at your father for what he did to you. He took your shine away, made you hate yourself, made you not even know how to love being in love, how to trust it."

I crumbled, the tears gagging me. Joop pulled me into his body, wrapping his arms tight around me, caressing up and down my back. "Cry, angel. Let it all out," Joop whispered. His voice was tight, and I could tell he wanted to cry for me, and it touched me. I never knew what it felt like to have a man cry for me…because of my pain. The realization of that made me cry all the harder.

Joop took his hands and gently raised my face, my tearful eyes boring into his glassy ones. "I love you, Shameika," he said, strong and sure. "What your father did to you. It was sick, unforgivable, but it wasn't your fault, it was his, you were a child, a victim, and it doesn't change how I feel about you. If anything it makes me want to love and protect you even more, so that nobody can ever hurt you again."

"But I'm not like other girls, normal girls, I have felt so *dirty* for so long," I whispered, my eyes never leaving his. "After my dad…I did a lot of shit, became fast, easy, I just didn't care."

Joop kissed along my forehead, across my wet eyes, before whispering, "Baby, that's all in the past. Do you love me?"

"There are no words to describe how I feel about you, Jamal. For real."

"Promise me something?"

"Yea."

"Will you promise me that we can talk about this, all this? I want to hear from you about *everything*. I want to hold you…and let you cry and scream and yell or whatever you need to do to be able to move on and deal. Let me love you…and you me."

"I wanted to tell you everything *yesterday*. I was just looking for a sign that said you were open to talk…and you didn't give me one."

"I know…I just couldn't give it to you. I wanted so bad to just tell you I loved you, but I was afraid of you hurting me again."

I ran my hand along Joop's jaw, smoothing his lips with my thumb. "I don't ever want to hurt you again, Boo," I whispered, leaning in to kiss his warm lips, moaning at the feel of them.

"I don't ever want to hurt you either," Joop responded. "I love you, Shameika…more than anyone or anything. All this drama we've been dealing with in this cipher? It doesn't mean a damn thing. I'm ready for the world, as long as it's with you."

"You're my heart, Boo. My heart," I cried, slipping my hands up around Joop's neck to bring him to me, to feel his warmth. "From this day forth." We kissed for what felt like till the next millennium. When we finally broke away, I smiled, feeling an opening to my heart, feeling a bit of my pain ease quietly from my body. I wasn't healed…that was going to take more than I love yous to cure, but I was willing to allow someone to help me get to the point where I could finally smile, with pure happiness in my heart.

I felt the VIP doors opening to my heart, opening for someone else to partake in the warmth and pure love that only the ones I *truly* loved could experience. Enter my boo, Joop.

PART THREE:

Stephen & Deandra

Stephen...

"If you don't stop!"

"If you don't stop!" I mocked back, smiling at the irritated yet smiling face of Deandra Winters. I flicked more water in her direction, quickly looking back down to my sink full of dirty dishes as she looked up at me again, smarting.

"I swear you are so silly, one would never believe that you're a grown man!" Deandra huffed.

"Why would I want to be a grown man tonight? This is New Year's Eve, the Millennium; tonight is the night to party and be a kid at heart, I just need some sweet shawty to play with," I said, throwing her a wink.

"Well sorry, I am not your play toy nor your SHAWTY, tonight or any other night for that matter."

"Why you so mean, girl?" My face brightened as I picked up a paper party horn and blew it, startling her and giving her booty a little pinch at the same time, she jumped.

"GRRRRRRR! If you don't stop! Chris, call your friend!" Deandra screamed.

I couldn't help it. I was laughing so hard I had to stumble into the living room holding my stomach as Chris and Tamara came wandering toward the kitchen doorway to see what was wrong with Deandra.

"What y'all two doing in here?" Tamara smiled, kinda out of breath.

"Stephen is in here working my nerves," said Deandra, rolling her eyes at me. I smiled at her mischievously, as I heard Chris laughing, "Yeah, that sounds like Step."

"Naw I ain't doing nothing to Miss Lady." I laughed. "We're just chillin' and just doing all the work while you two love birds make whoopee on my couch. Don't be putting no cum stains on it now." I laughed. Tamara's cheeks blushed furiously. "Yeah, that's right. I saw y'all!"

"Oh my God!" Deandra exclaimed. She's obviously not used to my candor yet, I thought to myself, but she would be soon!

At the sound of the bell, I hurried toward my front door. Opening the door, there stood Joop and Sha, grinning all gooey like and staring at me with this sickeningly dreamy expression on their faces.

"HAPPY NEW YEAR!" they both shouted.

"Looks like it's a happy, happy New Year for you two," I replied, smiling at two people who obviously got it together. They had had a blow up from what Chris had told me on Christmas Eve, both of them having left before I could even arrive for the party, but from the looks of things everything was now looking chocolate and rosy. I couldn't help but look over at that sexy thing Deandra as she came smiling and running up to hug Sha, couldn't help wondering if I would ever get a taste of her *chocolate* bud. She was fine, *foine*! Tall, slender, had these big ol' almond joy eyes, and a nose that stuck straight up in the air, especially when she was looking at me. I smirked, looking at her sexy little proper ass. She really thought she was gonna be able to withstand the charms of one Mr. Stephen Lewis. Well, we would just have to see about that.

I smiled broadly at her, making sure she didn't miss the twinkle in my eyes, nor my killer smile as I said to all, "Okay people, let's bring in the millennium!"

Deandra...

New Year's Eve. I couldn't even *remember* the last time I was home in Baltimore when the clock struck a new year. And this one was a BIGGIE! I was starting the New Year, the big 2000 with a new job, back home, and with new friends...one of which was splaying me with water while I tried to help him wash up in the kitchen.

I had briefly met Joop and had known Chris through my girl

Tamara and I was splitting hairs trying to figure out how this Step character fit in with those two men. When I met him last month, he was throwing out some lines that had me rolling. I had to admit, he definitely had looks going for him, with his tall, brown, baldheaded self…and a smile I was guessing had many a females willing to give up the goods…not this sistah.

He was just chiding me with his water antics and his smiles and his winks, but when he pinched my butt, I almost jumped out of my skin. It was hard, but I kept the blush from rising in my cheeks, and yelled for Chris to get his friend. Step was working my *last* good nerve.

Luckily, Joop and Sha showed up and I had my attention diverted to them. I ran to my girl, hugging and kissing her and noticing how happy she was. My heart felt good to know that my girls were getting that love thang in order, but I also felt a pang in my heart, because I felt like the odd woman out, like *this* kind of happiness was beyond my reach. When I released Sha, my eyes roamed over to Step who was all smiles at me, winking. Inwardly I sighed, wondering if *that* was the type of man I was destined to be with…someone who'd use me for my body without getting to know the woman inside of the body. Oh well, this was the beginning of a new century…I needed to put on my happy face. Smile intact, happiness on, let's roll.

"Okay, everybody!" Shameika yelled, her tiny frame perched up on Joop's lap. "2000 countdown is upon us…I know y'all got some New Year's Resolutions, so let's give 'em up! I'll go first." Clearing her throat, Sha placed her champagne flute on the coffee table and ran her hand through her short-cropped curly mane. Smiling at Joop, she dropped a kiss on his lips, emitting oohs and aahs from us. She blushed. "Shuddup y'all," she laughed. "Okay, now my resolution is to express myself more."

Tamara laughed. "You're the most *expressive* girl I know."

"Hush, I mean to express myself…me…Shameika. Let the people I love know more about *me*, so they can understand me."

"That's a good one, babe." Joop smiled, softly rubbing Sha's back. "I'll do mine now," he said. "Now y'all know me and y'all know that for the most part, I am a very happy black man. That's all I want, to continue being as happy and blessed as I have been."

Sitting beside Joop and Sha on the sofa were Chris and Tamara, who looked equally blissful. There went the tugging of my heartstrings. "Well," they whispered at the same time, laughing.

"Well what?" Sha and I said in unison.

Chris and Tee glanced at one another and the glow on their faces was indescribable. "We uhh, kinda have something to tell you guys," Tamara whispered.

"Man, will you spill it," Stephen groaned. He was sitting beside me on the leather loveseat.

"Well, we will say this." Tamara smiled. "Our New Year's resolution is to have a healthy baby this summer."

Everyone went silent and then screams erupted. Sha and I quickly jumped over to Tamara, pushing Chris out of the way. "Oh my God," I cooed. "You're gonna be a mama?"

Tamara nodded and we squealed again, while the men gave Chris daps. "Congrats, Man," Joop said, patting Chris on the back.

"Thanks," Chris gushed, the happiness radiating from his body.

"Dang," I said, laughing, "Step and I might as well just shut on up now! How can we beat a baby being born?"

Step pulled me up from the floor and brought me back to the loveseat, having me sit upon his lap. "We could say we're having our own little one." He laughed, wrapping me in his arms. Everybody burst into laughter as I tried to wiggle my tallness from his arms. He was relentless, not letting me go. Eventually, I sighed and sat there, giving him the eye.

"Not in this lifetime," I whispered to him. "Anyway," I huffed, "my New Year's resolution is to get in touch with my wayward sister."

"When's the last time you talked to Roxy?" Tamara asked. I watched Chris place his hand against Tamara's belly, rubbing it protectively. I felt a *kick* in me, but swallowed it.

"Girl," I moaned, "it's been a while…at least a year. Wanna find her butt and make sure she's not up to no good. You know Roxy was always famous for wanting to leave the straight and narrow…wanted to be so different than me."

"That's just what little sisters do," Shameika chimed in. "Give her a couple of years and she'll mature up, get her bearings, be more responsible."

"That coming from a girl who belongs to the Three Musketeers?" Tamara laughed. "You know we all got a touch of *bad ass* in us!"

Stephen pulled me against his chest, whispering in my ear, "So, where's your *bad ass* at?" I tried unsuccessfully to get from his lap, only to moan back at him, "Don't worry about it."

"So what's your resolution, Step?" Chris asked.

"Well." Step smiled, eyeing me with his sparkling, mischievous brown eyes. "I would like to get this *one* lady I know to stop giving me the cold shoulder."

"Ha, ha, ha." I laughed. "Okay, you got any *other* resolutions?"

Step laughed. "Yea, for real…I want to spend a lot more time with my baby girl, Paris, and do like my man, Joop…get my happy on." Briefly, my eyes met with Step's and I smiled. Don't ask me why, because I have no idea. I knew his 'happy on' had nothing to do with me, but I smiled nonetheless.

Shameika squealed. "Okay, party people, ten seconds and counting!!" In unison, we all began counting down…"Five, four, three, two, one!! Happy Millennium!!!" We all picked up our champagne flutes, clinked them and gulped down our champagne. Joop and Sha…and Chris and Tee began couple smooching and wishing each other a happy new year, and before I could be down about not having someone, Step had swept me up into his arms, his hands pressing against my back as his lips descended upon mine in a long, warm, deep kiss. I can't even remember how long the kiss lasted, but I knew when it ended, because the coolness swept over me where his kiss had me warm and heated.

When his lips parted mine, I let my eyes stay closed just a beat longer, wanting to banish all emotion from my eyes when I looked into Step's. The look on Step's face startled me. I was expecting that cool, macking bravado that he carried around like a badge, but instead his eyes were warm, just like his lips were.

I pressed my hands firmly against his chest, allowing myself some space from the hardness of his chest. "Happy New Year's, Deandra," Step whispered to me, his lady-killer smile returning, with the mischievous glint in his eyes.

"Yea," I said, rolling my eyes. I should have known that decency didn't dwell in good ol' Stephen. "Happy New Year's to you, too."

Stephen. . .

Have you ever felt so high, that when you finally woke up from it you wanted to kick your *own* ass? That's how I felt as I laid in my bed Sunday morning. Me and my boys Joop and Chris had partied all night long with the ladies New Year's Eve, and New Year's day of course they wanted to spend with their ladies, and so that left me to find my own party, which I did of course. I ended up chillin' with a few of my lady friends, drinking and trippin'. Shit, it's fun being the only male at a party sometimes, *and actually having the ladies find you attractive.* Even amongst a bevy of beautiful babes, I thought about Deandra.

That lady was a *cold fish* if I ever saw one. Hmmm…except for them lips.

I laughed at that thought, dragging myself out the bed with a groan. Looking at the clock I was super shocked to see that it was noon ALREADY! Damn I had slept the whole day away, and still hadn't called my baby. I jumped in and out of the shower, brushed my teeth, dried off and wrapped a towel around my waist as I shaved, shaping my mustache, and carefully clipping the hairs from over my upper lip. I doused some after-shave on my face, and rubbed some vitamin E Kemi oil on my hands to rub on my shaved head and my face, before using a washcloth to wipe off the excessive shine. Didn't need to be looking like one of them shiny niggas like back in the day when mamas used to rub thick Vaseline over all the super dark brothas so they wouldn't get ashy. Finishing up by slipping on some Karl Kani blue jeans, Nikes, and an old sweatshirt with *KAP Fraternity* on the front of it, I was finally ready to settle down with a cup of hot black coffee and call my shawtygirl.

"Daddy!" she exclaimed with joy.

"Hey boo, what's Daddy's princess up to today?" I smiled, feeling the instant warmth that came over me whenever I talked to or was around Paris, my five-year-old daughter. She was the source of all the happiness in my life right now. I mean yeah, your work could bring you satisfaction, so could a hot woman, but happy? Well that was a different type of thing, and whenever I saw her shining eyes or heard her voice, so thrilled to hear me or see me, I felt my purpose for being alive renewed within myself.

"I wanted to throw some New Year kisses to my baby," I said, making kissing sounds to her through the phone. "What you been doing today?" I asked, after she kissed back at me.

"Well, playing with my toys and my Barbies, and I was about to ride my car you gave me but Mommy said I had to wait till after lunch. Can you make her let me ride it now?"

I smiled. Paris always tried that age-old trick of getting parents vying against one another, but me and Shelby, her mother, always got along, at least where Paris was concerned, which was a good thing. "Nope, if Mommy says wait, then you?"

"Wait," she pouted.

"Good girl," I said, smiling. "Now listen. I need to speak to Mama. Put her on, okay? And I love you, Paris."

"I love you, too, Daddy!"

"Stephen? You know she's trying to ride that daggone car from morning till night, don't you?"

"Well, she likes it. I knew it was a good choice."

"You spoil her, just spoil her to death, then I have to deal with her attitude, and she has really been a trip today," Shelby complained, her Spanish accent super strong like it always was when she was complaining or fussing about something. Shelby was Puerto-Rican, which always used to get Joop riled, although he did say that it was better than her being white, and that at least Rican women had some black ancestry in them.

"Well I told her to wait till after lunch like you said, and she agreed so see she ain't that bad." I smiled. "Anyhow, I'm gonna be by to get her tomorrow after work. I can just take her to school Tuesday morning, okay? Right now I need to run to the office, do a little work."

"You're working on a Sunday?"

"It's just another day to me," I said, as I slipped my gun-belt around my waist, and the tiny thirty-two caliber in the ankle hook I always wore. Being a former cop, I knew one could never be too careful, and even now with the type of work I did as a Private Investigator, I still couldn't. Oddly enough, although I had majored in Biology at HU, I never really wanted to do anything with it. I wanted to play ball, or at least that is what my father had convinced me was my calling, and I just followed along. From the moment I could pick up a ball he had been skooling me for the NBA, throughout Junior High, High School, and

SHONELL BACON & JDANIELS

Howard, that's all I have ever been made to think about, or to strive for, never even allowed myself to believe I wouldn't make it. So when I didn't? Shit, I was depressed for months, didn't know what to do with myself. It's like when you dream a dream for so long, that it becomes real to you. And my father, he was devastated, crushed, disappointed, felt I had DELIBRATELY failed just to spite him. I can still remember as a kid, being outside late into the night, him pushing me, harder and harder.

"Move boy! You run like a punk! Jump! Dunk it!" I still can remember being tired, sleepy at midnight, still on the courts with my dad, and that anxious feeling that would somehow show on my face, holding back tears and shit and hearing him say, *"So you gonna cry now huh? You a faggot or sumpin'? You gonna cry coz you can't measure up? Act like a man boy! Straighten up and fly right or you will ALWAYS be a punk!"*

And through all that I *still* didn't make the NBA, and to him, that was a slap, an unforgivable slap.

After a few months of my mourning period I got my ass up, dusted it off and decided to be a cop. That of course shocked everyone who knew me, but for the first time in my life I was doing something that was real, and not just part of a dream that was bred into me, doing something real, and being GOOD at it.

Of course, I eventually wanted to spread my wings past being a D.C. cop and then a State Trooper, so for the past two years I've been working my realistic dream job and running Lewis Investigations, and for the first time in my life, I feel successful and content at something else besides bouncing a ball or making a three-pointer.

So much for mental ancient history, today was Sunday, January 2, 2000, and I had shit to do. "I'll holla with you later Shelby. Kiss my boo, and I'll be there to get her at 5:30 tomorrow."

I hung up the phone, grabbed my hat and jacket and whipped out the door.

Deandra...

Two hours into my new job here with the Orioles, and I was *still* smiling. Maybe it was just the working in sports that had me so excited, I dón't know. I came in this morning to happy faces and kudos and handshakes...even a visit from two of the top players on the team. I was on CLOUD NINE. I was already compiling information for the internal and external magazines, as well as information for the Orioles media guide. Opening day was still months away, but the faster you got things done, the more you could do...that was my motto anyway. The most magnificent thing about my job...besides the job, was my office. GAWD, it was huge and beautiful, decorated in the wood, hunter green and burgundy colors I had requested. I was on the 10th floor, and my view was of the entire field of Oriole Park, which left me speechless. The first time I had ever came to Oriole Park, I cried when I left. It was just *so* beautiful, and the midnight sky and wonderfully lit architecture of OPACY had me wanting to live there. That was eight years ago, and I still felt the same way.

I stared at the field for the first fifteen minutes of my day, and my mind wandered to Step, wandering if he liked baseball. I shook my head, trying to get him out of my mind...which was so hard to do. Sitting on his lap on New Year's Eve, having him kiss me, I had never been so flustered. When I finally left the party at the break of dawn on New Year's Day, I didn't even sleep. I sat up, watching the bowl games and drinking my chilled bottle of champagne, my mind remaining solely focused on Stephen. I guess with me being the 'new girl on the block', he assumed I would give him a taste of something. He may be a good kisser and have looks going for him, but he had a lot to learn about getting a *real* woman.

I was in the middle of mindlessly scribbling Stephen's name on a notepad when my phone rang. "Deandra Winters," I answered professionally.

"Hey, Girlfriend!" It was Shameika and, from the sound of the shouting on the other end, Tamara also. "What you doing for lunch, you big time PR Director?"

I rocked back on my leather chair and laughed. "Well, Girl...and tell Tee wassup...I have no plans. What you girls got going?"

"Well, we're gonna hit Hooters."

"WHAT!" I laughed into the phone. "Hooters?"

"I know I know, but they got some bombing ass wings, and well...hey, our mommy-to-be wants wings...HOOTERS wings."

"Lawd." I chuckled, looking down at my paper and quickly scribbling over Stephen's repeated name. "Okay, if Mommy wants wings, then I will meet you guys in about half hour at Hooters. I know it's gonna be crowded...you know how men *love* themselves some hooters...oh, and the wings too!"

We shared a big laugh, and hung up with one another. My pager rang out just as I placed my phone on its base. I slipped it from my hip and glanced down at the number. It was my home number. I had transferred all answering machine messages to my pager. While I typed up some last minute things into my laptop, I dialed up my place using the speakerphone. Punching in my access code, I heard the voice of my sister wafting through the speakers. "Bonjour mon ami," Roxy crooned to me. The message was brief, but from what I gathered, she was in Paris and left me her number.

It had been a good year since I had heard from my sister, and needlessly to say, I was shocked to know that she was in Paris. "I hope she ain't in no mess," I muttered, shaking my head. I was still racking my brain when I grabbed up my cell phone and Coach bag and headed out for lunch.

"Can y'all believe it?" I asked, chewing on a spicy buffalo wing. "Out of the blue Roxy just *calls* me, and she doesn't say anything."

We had been at Hooters for over half an hour now. It took us fifteen minutes just to get a seat because Hooters is the place to be for businessmen during lunch hour. Where else can you be served hot steaming plates of food by a scantily clad, hot, steamy babe? Once we got to our table, we immediately began talking about three different topics at once, Sha about Joop, Tamara about being a mom, and me about my sister. After allowing Sha and Tamara their time to gush, I began rattling off about Roxy.

"She's in Paris?" Sha asked, picking up a curly fry from the big basket between the three of us. "What is she doing there?"

"Lawd only knows." I sighed. "She mentioned once wanting to be the female Picasso and running off to Paris and stuff...but I dunno. Guess I'll have to call her tonight and see what my *lovely* sister is doing with her life."

I picked another wing from my basket and ate it, reaching for my Corona to take a sip. Hey, I wasn't a drinker, but I couldn't do the wing thang without at least *one* Corona. In mid-sip, I looked up to find my friends spying me with devilish smirks.

"What?" I asked, wiping my chin. "Sauce on my face?" They shook their heads in negative. "Then what? Y'all know something about my sister?" No, they shook their heads again. "Okay, do I have to cause a scene up in here? What's going on?"

Tamara eyed Shameika and leaned across the table, smiling at me. "What's up with you and Step?" she asked.

I coughed and wiped my mouth with a napkin. "What are you talking about? Step and I are *nothing*."

"Oh, so what was that kiss about?" Shameika added. "You were all up on his lap, looking all into his eyes after that kiss. What gives?"

"*Nothing*," I repeated. "He pulled *me* into his lap. He kissed *me*."

"So, you felt *nothing* when he kissed you, *nothing* when you were sitting on that nice lap of his?" Shameika and Tamara squealed, receiving attention from some of the patrons.

"No," I whispered, half convinced myself. Tamara jumped from her chair, waving for someone to come and sit with us.

"Speak of the Devil." Shameika sighed. I turned my neck, looking behind me to see a smiling Step at the entrance, the hostess at the door allowing him to go through. I turned back in my seat and sighed, much to the pleasure of my two best friends.

"Shall we see what Step thinks about that kiss?" Shameika joked, her and Tamara laughing at the blush rising in my face. Step *would* have to show up...why in *my* life?

Stephen...

My stomach was talking some serious jive, grumbling and bitching at me like crazy, and there were two body parts that I always listened to when they wanted to be fed, my stomach and my vessel of love. Right now I was mostly concerned about my vessel of grub, and putting something in it. Instead of ordering take-out at my office, I decided to get some millennium air and go out instead. My secretary Bridget had brought in food from home, she was always cooking up something, and would always bring extra for me, but today she had some funny look-ing squash casserole shit that I wasn't feeling at all. I knew I had made a smart move with Bridget, her being an older lady I didn't have to worry about mixing business and pleasure. Instead she was more like a mother figure, loved me like a son, and was completely dedicated to the job. So that left me dining alone, which was cool by me. Sometimes a brotha can get to that desperate point where he doesn't give a damn if he has company or not, just FEED me!

I decided on Hooters. Don't ask me why, but I never could resist watching some big tits and thighs while munching on wings. I smiled at that thought. The hostess seemed to recog-nize me right away, greeting me with a smile in which I echoed back at her. "Are you dining alone?" she asked. Before I could answer I glanced across the restaurant and spotted Tamara, Shameika and whoo hoo, Deandra! Tamara was gesturing for me to join them, and I was all too happy to oblige.

"Wassup, ladies." I smiled, instantly taking a seat beside Deandra, who from the look on her face wasn't too pleased. Oh well, in that case...I sat closer to her, feeling her stiffen up as I draped my arm around her shoulders.

"You miss me, Boo?" I asked, smiling broadly at Tee and Sha's giggles and Deandra's blushing face.

"What reason would I have to miss you?" she responded back, her eyes opening wide as I swiped one of her hot wings. "Sure, Step. Go right ahead. Help yourself."

"Actually, I'm not normally so rude..."

I started saying, choking back a laugh when Tee and Shameika shouted, "YES YOU ARE!"

"Naw I'm just starving today, didn't even have BK, and," I continued, grabbing Deandra's hand suddenly and sucking hot wing juice slowly from each finger while eyeing her intently, "I'm a growing boy."

"Ohhhhhh, Dee, Dee." Shameika said.

Tamara giggled, pushing at Deandra's shoulder and winking at me. Deandra turned a lovely beet red! Snatching her hand away with a slight groan...I smiled at her before noticing a big-busted waitress.

"Yo! I need some more hot tits over here. I mean some more hot wings!" I turned attention again to my blushing Deandra, as she slid a bit down further on the booth seat.

"Um, Stephen, that reminds me." Tamara winked at Sha, smiling as she continued on. "Shameika and I were just asking Miss Winters here about that little smoochy smooch you two engaged in on New Year's Eve. Care to tell us what that was all about?"

Ah, Deandra was uncomfortable. I could see that as clearly as a shim with hooters. I had to laugh, smiling over at Tamara and Sha. I then looked innocently at Deandra. "Well y'all know a brotha has it going on like dat…"

The ladies' giggles drew the attention of the couple at the table beside ours. Deandra turned a couple more colors the shade of red, and seemingly slid down in the seat another inch or two. I leaned over to her. "Go down any further under that table and your head will be resting in my lap." I winked. "But, then again, that's not a bad idea at all."

"Can we finish up here, please?" Deandra spat out, glowering at her two grinning friends. She was all fire and ice. There had to be a little spice somewhere hidden within that ingredient, and I was gonna find it.

After lunch, I was all too happy to see that Deandra had parked near me in the parking garage, Tamara and Sha having rode together and having parked on the other side. She was quiet as we walked, but me? Hell I wasn't used to quiet women, especially any quiet sistahs, kinda unnerved me a little, something else I wasn't used to. Nothing unnerved Stephen Lewis.

"So…" I said as we got to her car, "why don't you let me buy you dinner one night?"

She laughed. "Um…I don't think so."

"And why don't you think so?" I asked her, smiling at her jittery expression.

"Because we, me and you, are very different, and…I'm pretty busy with my new job, too busy to get wrapped up in anything else."

"Well damn, Baby. I'm just asking for dinner, not marriage," I said, smiling softly as she reddened once again, "and as for us being different? Well we'll just have to see about that, won't we?" Giving her a military salute as I backed away toward my Ford truck, I said, "I will ask you again, so expect it."

Deandra...

Step is a stone cold TRIP! How is he just gonna waltz up into my lunch with the girls? Oh yeah, I forgot, they were in on it too! Having him all up on me, his arm around me, his smiles and niceties directed to me. I was as stiff as a rod in his 'friendly' embrace, and a part of me wanted to just peel out of my skin and flee the scene. Unfortunately, there was another side of me that wanted to actually *smile* back and enjoy feeling his arm draped around my shoulder. Oh, I shuddered just to think about it. Step just riled me up, and I was beginning to feel like there was no way for me to get rid of him. We parked in the same garage, had to walk back to our cars together; he had the nerve to ask me out for dinner. I had a mind to ask him if he thought *I* would be his dinner, but I bit my tongue. Knowing Step, he would come back with some rude comment, like the 'hot tits/hot wings' one from Hooters, and I just might have to slap the taste out of his mouth.

Anyway, after I parted from the ever-graceless Stephen, I shot back up to work and put in another three hours of information entry and 'getting to know you' chats with various personnel. Once I set my calendar and organizer, placing every large and small 'thing to do' on and in them, I was ready to travel on home and have me a little ME time…pat my back for having a successful first day on the job.

On the way home, I took a cell phone call from one of my athletic clients, who shall remain nameless, except to say that he wanted to discuss a charity event he wanted to do that coincided with the release of his new line of 'Airs'. By the time I got off the phone with him, I was already planning his event and the business connections in my head, ready to get home and type it all into my laptop.

As soon as I stepped into my place, my pumps were off my feet and my laptop case was lightly dropped onto my sofa. I padded on stocking feet into my bedroom and quickly began to relieve my body of my fire engine-red, three-piece skirt set. I was a tomboy at heart, and never liked wearing "girly" clothing…still don't. I had more pantsuits than dresses or skirts, but I thought I would look the part of a powerful woman today, and so…donned the skirt. After I rolled off my stockings, I snatched on a pair of low-riding baggy blue jeans and one of my tummy-revealing sweaters, you know the kind people be like, 'that won't keep you warm', but it's cute so you buy it? That kind. It was dark brown with cream stripes and showed off the tight tummy I worked damn hard to keep.

Slipping on a pair of socks, I padded back towards my living room, making a right to the kitchen, where I put on a pot of coffee to brew. I flipped my TV on to ESPN, and plopped down on my couch, taking out my laptop and booting it up. Five minutes into my lightning speed typing, my pager went off. It was my home phone. I had forgotten to turn my answering machine back on, and in doing so, it went off, the red light blinking like crazy…all messages were from Roxy, who was in the process of leaving a message.

I quickly picked up my cordless. "Yo Sis!" I yelled. "What the hell are you doing in Paris?"

She laughed, one of her highly theatrical, girlish laughs. "Oh, and hello to you too, dear sister," Roxy crooned back. "What does a girl have to do to get her sister to call her, huh?"

"How did you get my number?" I asked, resting back onto the sofa.

"I called Mom and Dad."

"Whoa!" I laughed. "You called who? Okay, what's going on? You haven't talked to any of us in God knows how long, and out of the blue, you're calling Mom and Dad and leaving fifty million messages on my machine? What gives? Talk to me little sis!"

"Okay okay, stop with the twenty questions, will you?"

Roxy sighed. "I'm okay and yes, I'm in Paris, just as happy as can be."

"What are you doing out there? Painting?"

"Oh, I paint the *entire* world, my dear." Roxy laughed, the sound harsh, almost forced. "Everyone loves me over here."

"Hell, people love you *here* too, Girl. You really need to bring that narrow butt of yours home."

Several seconds ticked by, followed by a sigh from Roxy. "I know," was all she said. A beat later, a loud booming voice came from the other end of the phone, a man's voice. I couldn't figure out the French too well, but I *know* I heard him yell to Roxy to get off the fucking phone.

"What's going on over there?" I asked, my voice rising with fear. "Roxy, are you okay?"

"Sis," Roxy whispered, her voice trembling, "I'm at the Sheraton."

"Which Sheraton!" I yelled, my throat tight. "Talk to me." I heard Roxy scream and what sounded like a smack before the phone went dead. I was frantic, my Caller ID didn't show a number or anything, and all I had was *Sheraton*. I spun around in at least twenty circles before I gripped the cordless in my hands and dialed up Shameika's number. On the third ring, Joop answered.

"Hello?" he answered.

"Joop! Oh my God, where's Shameika?" I cried.

"Calm down, Dee, she's in the shower. What's wrong?"

"My sis…sis..sister, she's in trouble, and I don't know what to do!" I choked back my tears, gagging on them. "Got a call from her…she's in Paris, some man was cursing at her, I think he hit her."

"Oh damn! Do you know where in Paris she's at?"

"She could only tell me Sheraton before the man hit her. I don't know what to do, Joop! I really don't! Maybe I should call the police."

I fell onto my sofa in a crying heap, listening to Joop try to calm me. "The police? They can't do a thing with her way off in Paris, call Stephen," he said.

"What? What does Stephen have to do with this?"

"Dee, he's like one of the best private investigators on the East Coast and definitely the best in Maryland. Call him, go see him, tell him what's going on…He'll get on it ASAP, I promise."

I shook my head, trying to think. "You still there, Dee?" Joop asked.

"Yea…Yea…okay, I'll do that, thanks. Tell Sha I'll call her later, okay?"

Joop gave me the address for Stephen's office and whispered, "Okay, Boo…you take care of you."

"Later." I quickly hung up the phone, pacing my living room. The biggest thing in my life going on, finding my sister, and I needed *Step* to help me do that. The question of his attraction to me, and regretfully my secretive, growing one for him fluttered in my mind, but I pushed it back. This was about my sister right now, and I needed to help her. I slipped my feet into my brown Mountain Gear and put on my black swing coat. The only action I had was to go see Step.

Stephen . . .

I swear wild is too mild to describe some of the shit that comes across my desk. Sometimes I would get interesting, involving cases that I could really sink my teeth into, like missing persons, or children, but mostly I got lawyers looking for evidence to prosecute or acquit their clients. I really dug those types of cases because basically I was still Five-O at heart. But sometimes I would get wives or husbands looking to catch their mates in some type of compromising situation, those were more irritating, getting in the middle of a husband and wife situation always was, but I couldn't turn them down, they were my biggest money makers. Well today was no different, full of wild and wacko cases but right now all I could think about was how to get one Monica Jason out of my office. I made a big mistake with this blonde bimbo, that is, dating a client, or maybe I shouldn't call it dating, screwing is the word, but hey, I'm trying to be kind.

I was trying as best I could to ease her out of my office, it was already 4:30, and I had to pick up Paris at 5:30, and knowing my baby girl she would be waiting and tapping her feet.

"So why haven't you called me Stephen?" Monica asked.

"I was gonna get with you if I found out anything, remember I told you that?"

"No that's not what I'm talking about suga," she said in a dripping, sexy tone, her green eyes issuing an open invitation. She slid up close to me, slipping onto my lap. "It was good last time wasn't it baby?" she whispered. I had to smile, coz hell yeah the sex was good, and she was blessed to abundance with *other* talents as well, but THIS was my office, and she was too damn anxious and pushy. Just as I was about to purposely dump her ass out my lap, and of course pretend it was an accident, the door to my office opened, and there stood…Aw lawd, Deandra Winters.

"Oh, excuse me," Dee said, "your secretary said you were free and that I could come right in, but I'll come back later." She backed up as if to leave, with a look of disgust on her face as she eyed the blonde, green-eyed Monica. With Dee being a sistah, I pretty much could guess what her thoughts were.

"Wait!" I called out to her. "Come on in. Ms. Jason was just leaving."

"Yeah, I guess I was," Monica said, giving Dee an up and down look before parting. "Call me, baby," she cooed, shutting the door behind her.

I couldn't keep the smile off of my face as I looked at Deandra. She looked, well, she looked indescribably beautiful, and what made her even more so, was that she seemed so unaware of it.

"So did you reconsider my dinner invitation?" I asked.

"No, I'm here for business, and from the look of things," she said, looking toward the door that Monica had just walked out of, "from the look of things, you have more women than you can keep a hold of."

"Naw, you got that all wrong. That was a client. You, I wanted to see for personal reasons only," I moved my eyes toward her lips, then glanced back up at her large almond shaped eyes. She looked like that deer Bambi, I thought to myself, smiling slightly.

"Stephen, seriously, I'm here for business. Joop told me to come see you, and I really need to know if you can help me." Deandra had an almost desperate sound to her voice, which gave me immediate rise of concern.

"What's wrong?" I asked. She sighed deeply, rubbing her hands over her face before closing them in a praying stance.

"I got a disturbing phone call today, from Paris, France. That's where my baby sister is. Roxy. Remember I mentioned her at New Years?" she continued as I nodded, listening to her intently. "Well, she had been calling and leaving messages all day. I didn't even know she was in France, no one in my family has known her whereabouts for about a year now, I only knew she was okay from her postcards and little things like that, but still I've been worried sick. But today after I got home from work, I got another call. We talked for a minute, and to be honest Step, she didn't sound herself at all. She sounded, I don't know, weird, almost scared."

I listened as she talked her voice rising and falling with emotion. "Anyhow, all of a sudden this man's voice comes over the phone. He was French. I could tell by his accent, telling her to get off the f-ing phone! Then I heard, a..a slap, and, I don't even know where she is in Paris. All I know is that she said Sheraton, and I don't know Stephen, I mean I don't even know what I'm doing here, or what you could possibly do to help me

211

but if you can.." She stopped talking, her eyes filled with tears as she looked at me.

Damn. Talk about a bleeding heart, I could feel her fear and pain as she talked, and couldn't help taking her in my arms as she shook with silent tears, circling my hands around her waist as I sat on the edge of my desk. "Hey, it's gonna be okay," I whispered to her. "Maybe it wasn't as bad as it sounded, but whatever it was, I'll find out okay?" She lifted her head, looking up at me, her lips bumping into mine.

I tightened my hold around her a bit. I couldn't help it. She wasn't pulling away and I wanted to kiss her, and kiss her I did. I parted her lips slowly, slipping my tongue inside her mouth when I felt her responding, pressing her body against mine. Her response lit a hot flame in me. Hearing her moaning, I moaned back in return, caressing her back as she stroked my mouth with her tongue, her warm kisses turning into soft bites along my neck. Talk about seeing stars, all I could do was hear in the back of my mind my own voice crooning out, *"Oh my God...Oh my God...Oh my God."*

I must have been moaning those words out loud, because suddenly Dee gasped, looked at me and gave an "OH MY GOD" herself before spitting out, "I got to get outta here! Stephen um..," she put her hands over her kiss-bruised lips, "I'll call you, you can let me know if you think you can help, bye!"

In a flash she was ghost, and all I could do was sit on the edge of my desk, with one word coming to my mind. DAYUM...

Deandra . . .

Temporary insanity. That was the plea I would defend myself with when questioned about kissing Stephen. I still couldn't believe I had done that. One minute I was crying and distressed over my sister, and the next minute, I was moaning against Stephen's lips. And didn't I kiss his neck…bite it, too! All I know is that shame on me, I momentarily forgot about Roxy when I was pressed against Stephen's hard body and felt his tongue take a dip inside my mouth. I did feel like I was catching da fever for a minute there, but hearing Step moaning out *Oh my God* over and over doused the embers that were burning within me, and brought me back into reality.

When I ran out of his office, I continued running until I got to my ride, jumped in and made a mad dash back to my brownstone, wanting to cleanse myself of all thoughts of Stephen. At a stoplight, I flipped down my visor and glanced at my beet red face, noticing the brightness of my eyes, the flush on my cheeks, the slight puffiness of my lips. My fingers automatically rose to my lips, feeling them as my eyes closed and a "Mm mm mm," escaped from between my lips. The sounds of horns blaring snapped me out of my thoughts, and I continued home.

When I finally made it home, I quickly stripped out of my clothing and got into the shower. I needed to feel *totally* cleansed of Stephen, but all the shower managed to do was conjure up *more* thoughts. I gasped loudly when the image of Stephen sneaking into my shower crept into my mind. The thought, what if my hands were Stephen's, made my skin prickly, made my heart race under my skin. Stephen was a smooth brotha…his embraces, his kisses managed to slip into my mind and thoughts, but I was gonna work hard to keep them right there. Hell, he had some breasty white woman up on his lap when I stumbled into his office. She *looked* like she was feigning for what Step offered. Lord knew how many other women he had in his wake. I wasn't gonna be a chump like that. Never had, wasn't gonna start now.

Finally dressed in my blue and white striped cotton pajamas, I nestled up onto my couch and dialed Shameika's place. She answered on the first ring. "Girl!" she exclaimed. "I've been ringing you off the hook since I got out the shower earlier. What's going on?"

I glanced over at my machine, hitting the on button. "I don't even know." I sighed, rubbing my forehead. "I've just come back from seeing Stephen."

"Oh?"

"Don't even question it, Girl. This was about Roxy. I'm really scared for her. Joop thought I should get Stephen to help me, so I went over there to ask."

"And what did he say?" My thoughts floated straight to that heated moment when I felt the warm wetness of Step's tongue searching for mine.

"Uh…," I stuttered, "he said he would help. I'll call him tomorrow and give him more info about Roxy…hopefully it will lead to something."

"You know me and Tamara are here for you, right?" Shameika asked. "I called her when I couldn't get in contact with you, and of course she got upset."

"Which isn't good in her condition…"

"No, it's not, but listen to me. I know Step is a knucklehead and all, but he *is* good at what he does. *Very* good, so I hear." I stifled a moan, taking that double entendre for what it was *definitely* worth. Step was *very* good indeed.

Wrapping up my convo with Sha, my phone beeped, alerting me to another call. "Girl, lemme go," I said quickly. "Somebody on the other end."

"Okay, holla at a sistah later," Sha responded, "okay?"

"Cool. Love you."

"Back atcha Girl." Clicking over, I answered, "Hello?"

"Hey Deandra." I placed my hand over the phone, not wanting Stephen to hear me cursing under my breath.

"Hey, I thought I said I would call you tomorrow?"

"I know, but you left so fast, I didn't really hear you."

"Oh." I shook my head, running my fingers over my short

hair. "So, I assume you're calling about info on Roxy, right?" I didn't want to begin any talk about the kiss...I had no idea what to even say about that. "Hold up, I have her info in my office."

"Uh, yeah," Stephen said, with a slight chuckle. "Okay Boo." I frantically ran through my bedroom, into my office, where I pulled out a cabinet drawer, searching for my family files. Being the organizer of the family, I had information on any and everyone in our family. Running back to the phone, I said, out of breath, "Okay, I'm back."

"Mmm." Just hearing that moan, tickled my ear, causing me to shiver.

"Step, what is your problem over there?"

"You...sounding all outta breath, like you been..."

"Anyway," I quickly jumped in, not allowing him a chance to finish that statement, "Okay, here's the info I have." I ran off Roxy's full name, Roxy Lauren Winters, her social security number, date of birth, where she last lived, and some names of her friends. Step reassured me that we were going to get my sister back and that everything would be okay. I don't know why, but I believed him, and it relieved some of the tension that had build up inside of me.

"Gimme a couple of days, okay?" Stephen asked, his voice very warm, caring, with a professional tone.

"Okay," I answered. "But you call me as soon as you know something, okay?"

"You know I will."

"Thanks, Stephen," I offered, my voice falling into the warmth of Step's. "I really appreciate this."

"Don't even sweat it, Boo," he said. "Just wait till you get my bill." We both shared a laugh before hanging up. When I did, I fell back onto my sofa, pulling the throw from the back of the sofa over me. When I dozed off, I had reassurance in my heart and a thought of Step in my mind.

To keep my mind from thinking about Roxy, which was hard, I drowned myself in my work. I was always the type of person that was in bed by ten and up at five to hit the gym before work. Even when I was in school, I would be up at four in the morning, up and ready for my four-thirty soccer practice. I guess that habit never died with me, because all this week, I've been up at five, went for a run, came back, showered, dressed, and headed for work, where I stayed till at least 6pm, before coming home, fixing dinner, eating, showering, and pretty much going to bed. I was boring. I openly admit this. If it wasn't for Sha and Tee, I would have never known what a club was. Never had the time to be bothered, which was also probably why in my whole life, I've only been in *one* relationship, and that was over a year ago. He left me...said I was too ambitious, needed a more 'homey' woman, so I let him loose. Homey wasn't in my vocabulary, so neither was he.

It always struck me funny how different Roxy and I were...yet we looked exactly alike, minus her disadvantage in height. Whereas I kept to myself and strived to achieve in any and everything, Roxy only cared about 'the moment'. By the time she had graduated high school, she had been in love at least three times, and was no longer a virgin, whereas, I was a virgin till I met Jake, the man who thought I wasn't womanly enough. Roxy always called me the "*Ice Princess*", saying that I wouldn't let a man near me even if I was on fire and he was the only one who could put me out. That wasn't really true...just that I had to *feel* something...a something that let me know that this person was worth having me. *Why did I kiss Stephen then?* I shook my head, annoyed that I let him creep in...more annoyed that my thoughts went quickly to Roxy, even though I was attempting to relieve the tension inside until I heard from Stephen.

Funny…we were the typical American family. We had a mother and a father who loved each other more today than they did when they first met. Dad was a professor of English down in Florida, and Mom was a caterer, running her own small business. I thought of calling Mom and Dad and letting them know the drama their daughter had gotten herself into, but I decided to wait…maybe I wouldn't have to worry them, stress them. I was usually the one who kept the watchful eye on her…making sure she didn't stray too far from the norm. Mom and Dad had given Roxy and I everything we ever wanted, and I was grateful for everything…yet Roxy always wanted more. I shivered to think if her wanting *more* caused her to get into something over her head.

I guess I would have to wait to hear from Stephen…

Stephen…

I watched Rico Lorenzo gulp down his third quarter pounder. He slurped his Coke and let out a huge burp, drawing the disgusted glance of a petite brunette sitting near us. Rico smiled at her, crumbs all over his mouth. I swear I have never known a person who could eat like Rico. His Santa Claus belly attested to his gluttonous appetite.

I looked at him, shaking my head as I sipped on a Sprite. "So are you gonna slow down with the food for a minute and tell me what I need to know? I'm not paying to watch you eat."

"Um…" He stuffed a mouthful of ketchup-coated fries in his mouth. "She's a whore."

"Who's a whore? What are you talking about, Rico?"

"That bitch that you told me to check up on, Roxy Winters. She's a whore." He laughed at the pissed off look on my face. Now don't ask me why what he said pissed me off. I guess partially because I knew how Deandra would react if she heard Rico calling her sister a bitch and a whore.

"Why don't you just tell me everything, *okay*?"

"Okay, listen. She was up in L.A. for a long time turning tricks, but not just your regular type of hooker. Maybe hooker is the wrong word for her. She was a high-class chick, one of those grand a night, sophisticated ones." I guess the shocked look on my face must've said it all, Rico putting his hand to his heart and continuing with, "I swear to God, I was shocked too when I got all this. I mean this baby was into some real shit. She worked in a French joint, only the richest dicks could probe that salmon cake. Anyhow, she left Los Angeles four months ago, with a..." Rico stuffed the remaining half of his burger in his mouth, and pulled a tiny slip of paper out of his pocket, "...a Thomas Dugue', a regular of hers from what I was told."

I sighed in frustration. "That's it? I paid you a hundred fifty bucks for that shit? What about WHERE in Paris? What about more info on this Dugue' motherfucker?"

"Damn, Stephen, you tight. I mean, what more do you expect me to find out? With her being in another country the track is lost. Your client needs to get a PI in Paris, or either you should send somebody there to check things out."

"Hmm…" I thought for a moment. "That's not a bad idea," I said, standing up to take my leave. I flung a couple of dollars across the table at him. "Have another burger on me, witcha greedy ass."

"Thanks, man!" He laughed even harder as I shook my head at him, walking out the door.

Something didn't sound right with this whole situation. Forget the fact that Roxy was a call girl. That was the polite way to put it. A high-class call girl, which was unbelievable seeing how straight laced and proper Dee was. But what really didn't add up was the way Deandra said her sister sounded. Scared, not like herself, and that scream and slapping sound she mentioned. No, none of it sounded right. I could feel the rush coming over me like it always did when there was something that had me hyped or perplexed. I knew I wouldn't be able just send somebody else to Paris. When I had this feeling, I had to take care of this myself. And whether or not Roxy would want to come back to the states with me, I knew, remembering the scared look on her face, that I had to do this for Deandra.

I called Dee as soon as I got to my loft. It had been a few days since we had last spoken. Needless to say, I wasn't prepared for the soft sexy sound of her, "Hello?"

"Well hello, hello." I smiled.

"Stephen," she said, sounding happy to hear from me.

"How you been, lady?"

"Waiting for you, to hear what was up," she replied softly.

I smiled at her words, laying back on my bed thinking about her face. "Now see there are different ways I could take that, but I'm a gentleman so I won't do that."

"Yeah, I bet you are," she said coolly before laughing.

"You have a nice laugh, Miss Deandra Winters," I whispered over the phone. "You have a nice everything as a matter of fact, but that's another story." I could halfway hear her breathless '*thank you*' as I talked. "You know…I enjoyed that kiss the other day. It made me think about you half the night. I ended up having to take a cold shower." I waited for her response, and got none, just the sound of her breathing. "What are you doing?" I asked.

"Nothing," she said, still in her sweet soft tone, "just relaxing on the sofa."

I paused for a moment before my curiosity got the better of me. "What do you have on?"

She said nothing for a long while. I was expecting her to hang up and was about to change the subject real quick when she popped back with, "My PJs. I try to relax while I'm at home."

"I bet you're looking sexy in your PJs. You're beautiful. You know that? I've been thinking about you a lot and you know why I needed that cold shower so badly?"

"No," she whispered.

"Cause I was so 'hard' thinking about you, wondering what you would feel like, imagining me tasting you, *there*. It was so damn real I could almost hear you moaning, begging me not to stop, holding my head and pressing my mouth to you."

"Stephen..." she said with a moan.

"I'm serious. I'm not just talking, you know?" I breathed a shaky breath, feeling my heart beating out of control. "Listen," I said, clearing my throat suddenly, "I do have some information for you. I know you say you're in your nightclothes but it's really not too late, is it? Maybe you can meet me for a drink and we can talk about this info I have? I promise, business only." She didn't say anything. "Deandra?"

I could hear her coughing a little. "Yeah, um...give me twenty minutes to get dressed. Where should I meet you?" she asked, her voice breathy.

"How about Ruby Tuesdays? There's one near Security Mall. You know the place?"

"Yeah, I'll see you in thirty."

After hanging up the phone, I felt the need of a repeat of just what I had been talking to Deandra about, a cold shower.

Deandra. . .

WOW. That's all I could say. I was just minding my business, reading the latest *Sports Illustrated,* when the phone rang...it was Stephen. I don't even know what came over me, but I was actually happy to hear from him. Smiling all into the phone. I didn't even know where my voice was coming from. It was all soft and sweet and I just couldn't stop smiling or laughing.

While I jumped up from my sofa and ran into my bedroom to dress, my mind kept flashing back to Stephen's sensual words, how he had been thinking about me, what he wanted to do with me, and I had to admit, my body was responding to the deepness of his voice, the soft crooning of his words, just like he was actually touching me. Dressed in a pair of black fitting jeans, a dark red blouse and my black loafers, I tousled my hair and grabbed up my coat. "He got game," I muttered to myself, snatching up my pager, wallet and keys. "Gonna have to time his butt out," I continued, shaking my head, "not going to let him get into my head." Still muttering, I closed my door and headed out to Ruby Tuesdays.

At Ruby Tuesdays, I spotted Stephen in the back of the restaurant. Instantly, my face flushed and I coughed nervously. I slowly made my way up to the table, and he stood, coming close to me to pull out my chair.

"Hey," he said, his voice in a whisper. I turned my head, his face so close to mine I could smell the mint flavor of his toothpaste. My eyes peered at his lips, moving up to his dancing eyes. "Hey," I responded back, stifling a sigh.

Finally sitting down, Stephen maneuvered himself back into his seat across from me, his eyes glued to my face. For a while, we didn't speak. We just stared at one another like we had things to say, but didn't know how to say them. "So," I began, but halted when a waiter came to the table. Not hungry, I ordered an Amaretto Sour, and waited as Step ordered a Heineken. When the waiter was out of earshot, I whispered, "So, what was up with that phone convo earlier?"

Stephen blushed, and I laughed. "Whoa," I said, still laughing. "I didn't know you did that!"

"Did what?" Stephen asked, trying to play it off.

"Blush, Stephen…you're blushing. You didn't think I would bring up your little phone sex, did you?" When Stephen didn't respond, I got brazen, way too brazen for Deandra Winters. "Guess what?"

With dry mouth, Stephen responded, "What?"

I stared directly into Stephen's eyes, slowly licking my

glossed lips as I whispered, "I've thought about you too...I would swallow you up, Stephen." Inwardly, I was tickling myself in making Stephen so speechless, but it irked me that I actually had been thinking about him.

"Dayum," was all Stephen uttered from his mouth. He raised his glass of water with a shaky hand and took a swallow from it. "For real?" he asked, his eyes searing my lips, as if he had already positioned them on his place of pleasure.

"Most definitely," I whispered, blowing him a kiss across the table. I knew I was carrying this too far. Later on, I would apply my temporary insanity defense to this. I reached across the table, taking his left hand in mine, and bringing it to my lips. Parting my lips, I slowly sucked in his index finger, hearing Step groan. I let my tongue circle around his finger as my lips tightened around his finger. Stephen's dark brown eyes widened as I released his finger, flicking my tongue against the tip of it. I smiled at him, releasing his hand. "That," I whispered, "times infinity."

"Dayum." I giggled, watching Stephen lose his cool, his ability to be as suave as he normally was. The waiter arrived, placing our drinks on the table.

Raising my glass, I took a sip from the straw and glanced over at a shakened Stephen. "So," I said, my voice clear in its sultry, deep tone, "what's this information you have for me?"

In a flash, Stephen's shakiness faded and seriousness flooded his face. My playful mood dissipated, and a rush of uneasiness clouded me.

"Well," Stephen said, "I didn't find out much, but what I did find out, I think will surprise you."

"Okay." I sighed. "What? Is she alive?"

"As far as I know, yes."

"As far as you know? What *do* you know?" Grimly, I sat, listening to Step tell me about my sister's *high-class* life. I wanted to gag, but kept myself from doing it. My sister was selling her body. In my eyes, selling her soul. She was doing it in LA…and now, probably in France with that Thomas man, who was probably the man who was cussing her out on the phone. Words floated in and out of my mind: whore, slut, trick, call girl, escort…they all added up to the same thing. I didn't feel the first tear fall from my cheek. I didn't notice when Step took my hand and held it. I just couldn't understand why my sister would do this. We never needed for anything. Our parents made good money. If she needed it, they would gladly give it to her before allowing her to sell herself for it.

Reluctantly, I looked up into Stephen's eyes. I felt so embarrassed to even be in public right now. Our family was respectable, decent, and my sister had destroyed that with her sexual escapades. She was always fast, but this was ridiculous. I had half a mind to let her ass deal with whatever shit she had gotten herself into, but my loving, caring, sweet, sisterly side arose, and I knew I would help her no matter what she did.

Staring into Stephen's eyes, a thought fluttered into my mind. Step knew this when he called me, when he began his sexual banter with me. Did he assume the apple didn't fall from the tree? I quickly snatched my hand from Stephen's, glaring at him.

"So, is this why you tried to phone sex me?" I asked, the tears still falling.

"What?" Stephen responded, looking at me like I was crazy.

"My sister is a slut so I must be one, too? I'll be so quick to give of myself to you…for free, because my sister gets paid to give up herself?"

"You've got it all wrong, Deandra," Step said, rising from his seat. But I beat him to the punch, rising from mine first.

"I got it all wrong? Tell me, Stephen, how many women have you been with in the last month you? How many have you *ever* been with? I know your rep, man. It's all about getting *in* the panties; so don't play like you didn't want that from me. I guess knowing my sister fucks every Tom, Dick, and Harry gave you hope you could kick it with me. You're a pig!" I raised my drink and tossed it into Step's astonished face, as I rushed out of the restaurant.

I wasn't a slut, I thought to myself, tears cascading down my cheeks. The last thing I wanted any man to think was that he could have me just to say he had me…so he could *brag* about it. Step was fine, but he wasn't that fine for him to think that of me.

Stephen . . .

I got to admit, I've seen a lot of movies where the leading lady would toss a drink in a dude's face and then storm off, but I ain't never had that shit happen to me before. I was shocked and a little pissed, too. I mean, damn, she blows up at me because of her sister's business tactics? And then that crap about me thinking she must be that way, too? I don't know about other men, but dramatic women and me did not get along! After she left, I looked around me, everyone looking in my damn face. My wet, sticky face. I left a ten on the table and bounced.

I decided to let Deandra cool off before I called her to see if she wanted me to work on her sister's case or not. The more I thought about it, and her, the less angry I became and the more turned on I was, even with her dramatics. The sistah had spark, fire! Hmm...I couldn't help but remember the sexy move she made before she lost her temper, sucking on my finger and telling me how she would swallow me whole. I mean, damn, this lady had a Sybil complex! Fucking Doctor Jeckle and Mr. Hyde. She was sexy one minute, and then...whoa! For a minute there, when she was going off on me so bad, I thought her head might start spinning like that *The Exorcist* chick Linda Blair.

Thoughts of her still drifted in and out of my mind, even a couple of days later while at my parents' house playing ball with my old man. It was my Friday to have Paris and she had wanted to spend some time with Nana. Although the air was always thick when my dad and me got together, for my baby's sake, I gave in and took her to Nana and Papa's.

I missed several baskets. My mind was still somewhere else, on a specific lady, when I suddenly heard my old man going off. He was complaining like he used to when I was a kid. That I'm not focused; that I'm not with the game; that's why I always fail.

"What? What are you talking about?" I asked him.

"I don't know where your head is, boy, but you're better than this. I mean, you're missing unnecessary baskets."

I exhaled, trying my best to keep my temper down as I listened to his random bitching. "Listen, we're playing for fun, right? I'm not on the court. I'm here, playing a simple one of one with you. What difference does it make?"

"You're right," he said, throwing the ball hard against the backboard. "You're not on the court and why is that? It's because of the same things you are doing right now. No focus. No concentration. There is no reason for you to be wasting your life away playing cops and robbers when you could have been the star I raised. It's a damn waste!"

It never changes; nothing EVER changes where my father is concerned. A waste? A failure? I was a starting teamster even in 6th grade, played varsity as a High School freshman, varsity as a sophomore, MVP my Junior and Senior year there, played for the USA All Stars, was MVP my sophomore, junior and senior year at Howard, and he calls me a FAILURE? I heard my mom calling out from the patio door that dinner was ready, but ignored it. Turning to my namesake, Stephen Lewis Sr., I exploded, "You're never happy with anything I do, are you? Why the fuck do I keep coming around here!"

"Watch you mouth, boy!"

"WHY THE FUCK DO I KEEP COMING AROUND HERE!" I screamed again.

I heard a gasp. Paris' surprised eyes looked into mine and then she spilled a tray of cookies at the patio door. I felt sick, sick of her having heard me talk like that, and sick of the man whose name I carried, and who I resembled so closely standing in front of me. "You want perfect from me, because you couldn't be perfect yourself. You want me to be what you never were! You blame me for your own self-disappointment and I'm tired of it. What ever happened to I love you, son? What ever happened to you're doing a good job, Stephen? You're a success Stephen?"

"Stephen, don't honey," I heard my mom breathe. But I couldn't' help it. It was a ritual thing with my father and me and it was ALWAYS my fault.

"No," I said, putting my hand up as my father started to respond. "There is nothing more to say about it. I may not be your Michael Jordan, Dad, your STAR, but I'm a star at who I am. I'm sorry you can't see that...Let's go, Paris. Kiss Nana goodnight."

"Bye, bye, Nana," my crying daughter said, kissing my mom, tears running down her cheeks, making me feel even sicker at this whole scene. I didn't want to hurt my mother, but I had to get out. I had to breathe. I had to get away. I ignored my father's hurt expression, kissed my mom, grabbed Paris' hand, and left.

Later that evening, while tucking Paris in for the night, she asked, "Daddy?"

"Yeah, Boo?"

"Do you hate Papa?"

I felt stricken by her question. The last thing I wanted my daughter to believe was that the way I had went off at my father was okay, but I had been too embarrassed to bring it up after leaving my folks' house earlier. I stopped by Checkers and got burgers for her. I played Playstation games with her for the rest of the evening, but I knew Paris, and I should of known she was going to bring up the episode before the night had been over. I knelt beside her bed so I could really look at her. "No, Paris, I don't hate Papa. I was wrong for how I talked to him. It was disrespectful. I know you wanted to spend the night there and I'm sorry, baby. Okay?" I kissed her forehead as she nodded, her soft black curls falling against her cheeks. As I walked toward the door, she called out again.

"Then tomorrow you can call him and tell him sorry, right?"

I sighed, chuckling to myself. I guess it's true what they say, about out of the mouth of babes. I told her yes and shut the door, more than ready to chill with an ice cold Heineken.

Just as I was opening my Heineken, the phone rang. "Hello?"

"Hey, Step. It's Deandra."

Deandra. . .

It took me almost a week to get up the nerve to call Stephen. Not because I was mad at him, but because I was mad at myself. I didn't give him a chance to explain himself, and normally I was more understanding. When I finally decided that I *would* apologize, it was five days later. I was snuggled up in my bed, dressed in only my bra and panties, the room well heated and my comforter feeling like Heaven around me.

When Stephen answered the phone, I said hi…waiting for Stephen to say something else…he was so quiet. When he did speak, his voice was quiet, giving me a "Wassup?"

"Are you mad at me?"

"Not any more," Stephen answered, a soft groan emitting through my phone. "I want you to know that I didn't mean anything by the phone conversation we had last week."

I looked at the phone, my feelings kinda hurt. "You didn't?" I asked flatly.

227

Stephen chuckled. "Well, I meant for it to get you thinking about me...but not to make you think I thought you were fast, you know?"

"Yea, I do." A moment passed before I added, "So we're cool?"

"As ice, Boo," Stephen crooned through the phone. I instantly felt naked, Stephen's voice trickling through the fiber optics and dripping all over my body. I sighed, whispering back, "Cool."

A silence enveloped the conversation, until Stephen came back with, "What are you thinking, Deandra?"

What was *I* thinking? He *really* didn't want the answer to that. Laughing, I answered, "You don't need to know that."

"Tell me...please."

"Umm, well, I was thinking about *you*."

"What about me?" Stephen's voice had a softness to it, like he was being drawn into the warmth of my inner flame. I liked...but didn't like that.

"Just how I'm laying here...in bed...in my panties and bra...and talking to you is making me feel *so* warm."

I heard Stephen sit something down before responding with, "Want to come over...so I can make you warmer?"

"I shouldn't even be telling you this...feeling you like this."

"Why, am I so bad?"

"Mmm, no...I guess. I don't know. You make me fight with myself."

Stephen laughed. "Fight with yourself?"

"Nothing. Nevamind."

"I've been thinking about you all week..."

Just hearing that made my heart quicken. "You have?" I asked.

"Yea...that finger action...Dee, dayum, I wanted you *right there* in the restaurant..." My silence egged Stephen on. "Your mouth...the way your lips moved when you spoke, when you licked your lips…so damn sexy. I wanted to kiss you…wanted you to use your mouth on me…"

I sighed, loudly, feeling my body get too warm for my comforter. Kicking it off, I said, "Stephen, you need to stop talking like that."

"Why, Baby? Tell me you don't want it, too…"

"Stephen." I sighed, feeling a damp heat grow between my legs. I stifled a groan and shivered hard.

"What, Baby? Talk to me."

"Need to stop…so hot…" I stopped, hearing a soft girlish voice on the other end.

"Hold on, Deandra," Stephen spoke, his normal deep 'calm' voice back in check. After about five minutes, he came back, apologizing. "Sorry," he said, "my little girl wanted some water."

Hey, any diversion was a great diversion. I felt myself slipping, and this woke me up. "No problem," I said, straining to retrieve my voice. "You know, there was a real reason for my calling you."

"Besides talking dirty to me?" he asked, the smirk on his face obvious.

"Yes." I laughed. "I want us to go to Paris. Money is no problem, and I want *you* to help me find my sister."

"I can go…no problem, but what about your job…you just started."

"We can go at the end of the week…if you can work your schedule out…I just won't get any sleep from here till then, catching up and assigning my work to others before we jet. You're okay with me going, right?"

"I would *love* the company," he answered, making the hairs on the back of my neck stand on end.

"Okay, cool. I'll arrange the flight and hotel reservations, and I'll call you back in a day or so."

"Sounds good."

"Well," I whispered, wanting to break this connection

between Stephen and I, "I'll let you go to bed now…I'll talk to you later."

"Okay…sweet dreams, Deandra."

"You, too." Before hanging up, I heard Stephen whisper, "Of you." I fell asleep with a huge grin on my face, thinking of Stephen.

"You and Step…in Paris?" This was Shameika and her loud butt. It was the night before my trip to Paris with Stephen, and I had invited my girls over for dinner…my cheesy lasagna. When I told them about it, they both roared in laughter, already planning the wedding.

"It's just for *business*," I reassured them both, dishing out the lasagna and pouring each of us a glass of iced tea. "I worked my ass off this week, and after talking to management and personnel, I managed to get my work covered for at least two weeks. I want to see for myself that Roxy is okay."

"So, are you and Step gonna be sharing a room?" Tamara giggled, sipping on her tea.

"No! Now y'all stop. I don' already told you guys that Step wasn't my type. I'm not going to make this a love connection to round out our Three Musketeers merger!" I guess the girls figured that with Tamara and Chris happily married and with child and Shameika and Joop practically *living* together, that it would be only right that Stephen and I got together and made our *union* — that is, the union between our groups — complete. Step and I were *not* the missing piece to this puzzle.

"Okay." Shameika laughed. "The man is fine as hell and your body is so in need of an oil change, I can hear your ass squeaking when you walk. You're digging him. I *know* this and he obviously has some feelings for you."

"How would you know this?" I cut in…trying to chew down a string of cheese.

"Cuz, men be talking just like our asses do! He was talking

to Joop about you and, well, Joop told me, and thus...now you know."

I stopped in mid-chew. "Stephen talks about me?" I asked, not willing myself to believe it.

"Yea, girl. He told Joop that he's never met anyone like you before."

"I guess somebody's gonna be having some *romance* in Paris, huh?" Tamara smiled, as I continued to be stuck in mid-chew. Stephen was talking about me...to other people...*our* friends. Hiding the stirring within, I laughed it off, and quieted myself by eating.

The flight to Paris went pretty smooth. I met Stephen at BWI, and our conversation was quiet, yet pleasant. I went to sleep thinking about the fact that Stephen had talked about me to someone. Very flattering, but scary at the same time. What did that mean? Did it mean anything? I barely slept except to toss and turn and although I was with Stephen, I easily drifted off to sleep. I awakened to the feel of Stephen's arm draped around me and my head resting on his shoulder. I covered my mouth to yawn.

"Hey there, sleepy head." Stephen smiled. "You know you slept through most of the flight? Captain just announced that we would be arriving soon."

"Dang, I must have really been sleepy," I said, yawning again.

"So I guess you haven't been sleeping well lately?" I raised my eyes to Stephen's, noticing the mischief in them. I swallowed a smile, answering, "You can say that."

"*All* my nights have been that way this week." I looked away from Stephen, rising up to sit in my own seat. *Please Please Please*, I begged to myself, *don't fall.*

We landed at Roissy-Charles de Gaulle, where Stephen and I picked up our luggage and made our way to Avis to pick up the rental car I purchased for our time here. I had purchased separate rooms for us at the Hotel Sofitel, which was connected to Roissy-Charles. Other than very basic French, I was at a loss in terms of the language, so I figured the closer we stayed to the airport, the better chance I had of getting someone who could speak English.

Stephen was unbelievably quiet throughout all the exchanges, hitting me with smiles every time my eyes made their way over to him. Finally parking our car in the hotel's parking lot, hotel attendants quickly came out, slipping our luggage onto a cart and wheeling it into the hotel as if they just *knew* Stephen and I were a couple. Stephen laughed.

"You can remove that *I don't believe them* look, Deandra," he said.

"Huh…what?"

"I can see the wheels in your head rolling…they saw us get out the same car from the lot…that's all." I rubbed my forehead and walked past Stephen. "You think you know somebody," I said, tossing it over my shoulder.

"I know more than you want me to," he offered back, as I felt his gaze burn a hole in my back.

Stephen . . .

This brotha was seriously smiling in the inside. Hell, the outside, too. That was nothing unusual, but the inside. Hell, it was grinning like a muthafucka! Now don't ask me why, but I was feeling good, really good. Maybe it had something to do with being in one of the most beautiful and romantic cities in the world, and with one of the most beautiful women I had ever laid eyes on, but hey, I think I best keep that thought to myself.

I smiled secretly as I slipped the key card in my hotel door, glancing over at Deandra as she wrestled with her door. The doorman waited patiently with our bags. We had side-by-side rooms, and…I noticed as I walked in, adjoining rooms. I laughed and tapped on the door leading to Dee's room. After a minute she opened her door, with a shocked look on her face.

"No they didn't give us adjoining rooms," she said.

"Yeah, they did." I laughed, my nosiness getting the better of me as I peeped into her room. "But look, think of it this way, at least you've got me available as your BODYguard."

"I don't need a bodyguard, thank you. Now out! I need to unpack," she barked.

I laughed as I walked back into my own room, closing the door but not locking it as I settled down to make a few calls. I had done some early probing during the week on Dugué, writing down a few numbers that Rico had gotten for me.

"I need to speak to Monsieur Thomas Dugué. I'm a personal associate of his from Los Angeles and he has been expecting me." I made my voice sound feminine, gay like, feigning being a *very* personal male friend.

"I'm sorry, but he isn't available to take your call. Perhaps you can call back later, Monsieur," said the heavily accented voice over the phone.

"Okay look, chile. Give me his office address and I'll just come by to see him tomorrow, okay? I did have it but, lawd, I can't remember what I did with it for the life of me," still making my voice high and effeminate.

"What the hell?" I heard Dee say, looking at me as she covered her mouth to stop a giggle, her having taken advantage of our adjoining rooms.

"Shhhh…" I winked at her.

"Monsieur, I am terribly sorry. If you just leave your number I'll get him to call you, but I can't give you the information you are looking for," the French lady said, sounding almost frantic.

"Okay, fine. I'll just have to go to his house, and believe me I'm gonna raise holy hell about this STD he gave me! I've been trying to keep it quiet, but if you want me to take it to his home, fine!" I screamed, fighting hard to keep the smile out of my voice.

"Oh no! No, Sir, s'il vous plait! One moment! I'll give you the main address! One second!"

I covered the mouthpiece of the phone, cracking up along with Deandra, as she asked, "Stephen, what in the world are you up to?"

"Finding out where this mutha works. This number I called is just the answering service. Hello?" I said, as the voice operator came back on the phone. "Yes I got that, and mercí, mercí to you, too, shawty!" Hanging up, I looked up at Dee smiling.

"Dayum you're good!" She laughed. "Sounding all *sweet*."

I chuckled. "Hell, I needed more than just an answering service number, and that's all I had, but now…" I waved the little notebook with his office address on it. "Let's go have dinner. Then I'm gonna go visit his office and see what souvenirs I can pick up."

Deandra laughed again, looking at me with a surprising admiration. We showered and changed, then met outside our rooms, locked arms, and walked down to the fancy French dining room for dinner.

We had a good time. Let me repeat that a different way. *I* had a good time. I'm not so sure about Deandra, but she was smiling, listening as I told her about myself, and about Paris. And there was admiration still shining in her eyes as I talked about my years on the police force, and what made me change to Private Investigation work. She was easy to talk to, surprisingly so, and had an extremely warm persona. I listened likewise as she talked about herself, her work and her travels, how disappointed she was that she wasn't able to get home for Tamara and Chris' wedding, and how happy she was that Shameika had found happiness in Joop. From listening to her, I could tell that she felt the same tight connection with her friends that Joop, Chris, and I had. But what really surprised me was when she told me that she had played B-ball in high school and college. I mean she was tall yeah, but the sistah sounded like WNBA material from her statistics!

"Damn you got game, huh?" I smiled at her, amazed.

"Hell yea. What are you thinking, only men can have it going on at the courts?" She smirked.

"Naw." I laughed and winked. "But check this out. When we get back to Baltimore, I'm gonna have to test you out."

"No problem. I can go one on one with the best of them, whether they be female or male!" She poked her long manicured index nail into my cheek dimple. I smiled broadly at this incredible women sitting across from me.

Yeah, I thought to myself, *we WILL see...*

Deandra...

Can I openly say I was having a good time with Stephen, even though it *definitely* was not my intention? I was a little set back when I noticed that he and I had adjoining rooms. I had to remember to keep that door locked at *all* times. But so far...so good. I laughed my *butt* off while he feigned gay to some woman on the phone, was still chuckling about it when we made it to restaurant in the hotel for dinner.

We laughed and talked and I really did see a different side to Stephen...one that I didn't think existed. He *obviously* loved his daughter, Paris, and that touched my heart. He talked about his love for basketball, and of course, I had to school the boy on my talents. I was deeply feeling *something* for Stephen, but I didn't know what it was. I was never the one to lust for someone. Hell, only being with *one* man in my life attested to that! But I will tell you this, when I dipped my finger into one of the dimple pools on his face, I wanted to lightly drag that finger to his mouth...have him suck it, like I did his at Ruby Tuesdays.

But Deandra Winters could only be bold but *so* many times, so I simply smiled, reluctantly pulled my finger back and we quietly finished our dinner.

Back at our hotel room doors, Stephen informed me that he would come talk to me when he got back from Dugué's office.

"There will be no need for that," I said, leaning against my door. "I'm going with you."

"No, you're not."

"Yes, I am…Roxy is my sister and whatever information you get, I deserve to be there when you get it."

"Dee, did you or did you not hire me to do this job for you? Hell, I allowed you to come to Paris, against my better judgment." I gave Stephen a *what the hell* look as I swiveled my neck and threw my hands up on my hips.

"You didn't *let* or *allow* me to do anything, Stephen. Come on, you said you were my *body*guard…protect my body while I'm with you tonight."

The look on Stephen's face made me eat my words. He took one slow sweep of my tall frame encased in a black silk sleeveless dress and smiled. "Oh, so *now* I can protect your body?" He laughed. "But when *I* want to do it, you won't let me?"

"Precisely." I smiled. "So, knock for me in about ten minutes. I'm going to change." Stephen stared at me and shook his head, knowing there was no use in arguing with me. As I entered my room, I only hoped things went smoothly tonight, so I wouldn't regret having tagged along.

Stephen laughed as I came out of my room, decked in black jeans, black boots, a black sweater, and my black leather jacket. "So, did you bring a black mask, too, Ninja?" he howled at me.

"Shuddup," I said, "you're dressed in black, too." And he was, looking like a fine piece of ebony man in his attire, which replicated mine.

"Yea, but I don't *look* like I'm up to no good. Come on." I closed my mouth and followed Stephen out to the front of the hotel, where they offered a cab service. Sliding into the back of the car, I sat, quiet. I didn't know what train of thought a P.I. had when they went into a job, and I didn't want to destroy Stephen's concentration.

As Stephen gave the driver our destination, he glanced over at me, asking, "What are you thinking about over there, Boo?"

"Nothing. I was just giving you quiet time. Didn't know how you went about preparing your mind to do things, you know?"

Stephen smiled, taking one of his hands and moving it on top of mine. His hand was warm and I took it into mine, holding it atop my lap. "Thanks for the concern, but I don't need silence to focus. I've been focused since you told me about your sister."

I held his hand, palm up, tracing the lines with the tip of my index finger. When I heard him sigh, I looked over at him, smiling. "So you've been *very* focused the whole time?" I asked, wondering where all this bravado was coming from.

"Well," he said, clearing his throat, "I've had *one* distraction, but she's been oh…so…pleasant a one." I turned my head to look out of my darkened window, hoping Stephen or the driver couldn't see the blush that rose to my face. With one fluid motion, Stephen wiggled his hand from my hold and slipped it around my shoulder, his long fingers lightly moving along my opened jacket to lie against the thin fabric of my sweater. I held my breath as his finger followed the stiffness of my nipple.

Gulping down a moan, I whispered, "You know the driver can see us." Stephen's fingers seemed to take hold of my protruding nipple, pinching it. "Stephen," I moaned, "do you normally do this before a job…during a job…" My voice trailed off, as Stephen turned me to him, reaching out to fondle my breasts over my sweater, the feel of his fingers on my aching nipples making me shiver. My eyes were diverted to the driver, who had a knowing smirk in his eyes as he looked back to the frosted Plexiglas that separated us. I couldn't even tell Stephen to stop...I didn't want him to.

For the rest of the ride, Stephen was silent, minus the heavy breathing, and I couldn't get myself to look at him. His fingers were expertly feeling me up, while my hands moved up his thighs, lightly stroking the crotch of his pants, where I could feel him stiffening. Stephen jumped. "Dayum, Deandra," he talked into my neck. "You do that...and we might not get out this car."

Our moment was interrupted when the car stopped, and the driver in his heavy accent informed us that we were at our destination. We glanced up at one another and quickly Stephen pulled me closer to him, his mouth crashing down on mine, causing me to groan. The kiss ended abruptly and we both stared forward, trying to remove any hint of passion from our eyes.

Glancing at him, I noticed my gloss marking his lips and I leaned over, slowly wiping it off with my fingers. "You ready?" Stephen asked, his voice husky, his warm breath tickling my fingers that still rested on his lips. Taking a deep breath, I answered back, "Yea." I got out the car as Stephen told the driver to wait for us. We'd only be ten minutes at the most. Outside of the heat of the car, I welcomed the coolness of the night air. I closed my eyes, feeling this incredible avalanche of burning desire and wetness between my legs and I cursed myself for allowing these currents of heat and need to rush into me so quickly. But I knew the only way to stop them was to keep Stephen at bay...but I didn't think I wanted to do that anymore.

Stephen was *really* good at what he does...okay, from what I know, he's damn good at just about everything, including making a sistah flustered and in need, but that's another story. We managed to get to Dugué's office, and with the doors locked, I was ready to just go back to the car, but Stephen pulled out a small black case that held tools and within seconds, we were walking around Dugué's expansive office, rifling through his things. Within five minutes, we were out of the office, with Stephen having retrieved Dugué's personal phone book and some other things. The whole ride back to the hotel, Stephen laughed at me, joking on how wide my eyes were, how scared I was of getting caught.

Back at our hotel room doors, I nervously looked up at Stephen. Throughout the entire short-lived escapade, I was thinking about Stephen and his hands on me, making my entire body groan. He must have felt it also because Stephen glided his body toward me, smiling. His fingers lightly traipsed along my cheek as he whispered, "Tomorrow morning I'm going to see Dugué and pretend to be an investor…feel him up, see if he cracks."

I looked into his eyes, nodding. "Cool…I'll be here when you get back. Like I have any other place to go." We chuckled. An uneasy pause entered our conversation, and I replaced it with, "Thanks for doing this, Stephen. I'm glad I came to you to help me."

"Are you really?" he asked, his eyes on my lips.

"Yes." I sighed. I reached out to Stephen, pulling him in for a hug, which of course led to other things. Stephen's hands moved down the back of my jacket, softly cupping my butt, pulling me to him. Groaning, my hands tightened around his neck, bringing his lips to mine. I felt my back pressed up against my door and my body pressed tight against Stephen's.

"You know," Stephen whispered in my ear, "we could go into your room…and take off some of these clothes…" He licked my ear lobe. "…and I could make you feel *so* good, Baby."

"God," I moaned out, pressing my hands against Stephen's chest, softly pushing him away. I looked at Stephen, my eyes full of want for him. "Stephen, I'm not even going to front with you…it's obvious there's an attraction between us…and every time we kiss…in the car…right now…I can't even say anything but damn."

"Deandra, I want you too," Stephen whispered to me, his

right hand reaching out to roam the curve of my breast. I moaned. My nipples were already hardened as his long fingers moved across my breast, giving my nipple a soft squeeze.

My eyes widened and I squealed softly. Leaning in, I kissed Stephen, long and deep, hearing him groan *oh my God*, like he did the first time we kissed. With shaky hands, I unlocked my door, turning to him. "Let's go take cold showers…separately…see what tomorrow brings," I whispered, raising my eyes to his. He smiled at me, as if knowing I was trying to bide time…like he knew that eventually him and I were going to connect on *all* levels.

"Sweet dreams, Deandra," Stephen whispered, heading into his room.

I closed my door, leaning against it, whispering, "Of you."

Stephen . . .

I looked suspiciously into the piercing blue eyes of Thomas Dugué, he being a rather small man, but one who obviously was accustomed to having a lot of power over others.

"Have you been following me?" he asked. "Who are you?"

"I haven't been following you. I've been checking up on you. We have a mutual friend. Roxy Winters?" I asked, raising my eyebrows at his knowing gaze of recognition.

"Did she call you, ask you to come here? Who are you, goddamit!"

"I'm Stephen Lewis, P.I. from the states, and no she didn't ask me to come here, her family did, and you should also know Monsieur Dugué that Ms. Winters is noted as missing in the states, and that you are the chief suspect."

Dugué stood up suddenly, flinging his arms as he spoke, telling me that Roxy had come to Paris with him willingly and that she was a whore. "So then why did you lie and say you were an investor?" he yelled. "I've committed no crime. You

have no jurisdiction here. I've only been helping the little trol-
lop out, and she has been happily parading around like a filthy
courtesan. She can go back to the states anytime she wants. I
would be glad to be rid of her!"

"So where is she?" I asked. Something about Thomas
Dugué didn't seem right. He was being so eager to hand Roxy
over to us. If that was the case, why had he been so upset with
her for telling Dee of her whereabouts?

"Listen you, you Stephen Lewis, I don't know you and I
don't know if Roxy knows you either. She's off at my country
home, but give me your number, and she can call you if she
wants to be found, oui?

I stood up, scribbling the hotel number on a piece of paper
on his desk. I definitely wasn't going to give him my room
number. I had the advantage and planned on keeping it. "I'll
give you two days. If I don't hear from her, I'll be back with the
authorities…and don't think of doing anything stupid. I'm
watching you."

Back at my hotel room, I stretched, thinking about my conversation with Dugué. I hated being in unfamiliar territory, without the proper contacts, but I was determined to either go back to
the states with Roxy Winters, or with the knowledge that she was
happy and content here, and not in any real danger.

It was quiet in my room and with no sound coming from
Dee's room, I became curious as to what she was up to, that and
the fact that here lately she was never far from my mind. I slipped
off my black boots, and tried the adjoining doors to our rooms,
noticing hers was not locked. I walked inside, hearing music playing through the doors leading to the Jacuzzi. Yeah, Miss Winters
got the lucky room, a private Jacuzzi and sauna room connected
to hers. She had her eyes closed, her hair wet and slicked back
against her head while hot bubbles caressed her skin.

"Having fun," I asked her, smiling as she looked up at me.

"Yeah, this feels great. I've been trying to keep myself occupied while you were gone." She looked at me, almost shyly.

I started unbuttoning my shirt, not losing contact with her eyes. "Can I join you?" She was quiet, biting her lip and watching me as I stripped of all my clothing except for my boxers. I slipped into the hot bubbly water beside her.

"That's a French radio station?" I asked, looking toward the music box beside the Jacuzzi.

"No, I put a Celine Dion CD in. She's one of my favorites."

Have you ever completely lost your vocabulary? No words coming to your head or your mouth? Well, that was me. Deandra's eyes stayed closed. She licked her lips as the smoke from the Jacuzzi caused sweat to drip from her face. I moved toward her, her eyes still closed as I pulled her against me, her back pressed against my chest hairs. I moved my hands up her rib cage; she had a super tight figure, not an inch of access, evidence of the weight training she had told me she was into. She rested her head back against my shoulder as I explored her body, caressing the deep indention between her ribs, and bringing both my hands up to her breasts, cupping them and squeezing as she gave little breathy purrs of pleasure. I eased my hands back down her belly, Deandra still quiet as I touched her. Moving my hands down further, I slipped my right hand down the front of her thong panties, and brought my left up to circle and caress one of her nipples.

"Step..Stephen..." she moaned, opening her legs further as I found the swollen bud between them, nestled in soft wet curls.

"Shh..." I whispered, "let me take you there..." She moaned again, rolling her hips in a circle as I pressed and probed and rolled her bud, thrusting my hips slowly against her backside as I tried to stifle my own moans. I could sense her building, building as I fingered and caressed her, pulling her to a peak. Looking down at her face I saw mixed emotions, pleasure, shock, fear, and then finally ecstasy as I slipped two fingers inside of her, moving them in and out, pressing against her clitoris with my thumb and rubbing and squeezing till finally she spasmed and came, clenching my fingers and moaning as the pleasure shook her. Her head jerked forward and I brought it back against my chest, not wanting to miss a moment of watching her expression as she spasmed again into a second climax, screaming out this time and falling limp against me.

Both of our hearts were beating rapidly. I felt as if I was about to have my own eruption just from the knowledge of hers. I kissed her forehead as her breathing slowed, having come down a bit from her orgasmic high.

"I'm gonna go dress for dinner," I whispered, smiling softly at her as she looked up at me with an astonished expression. I grabbed my clothes, glancing at her one last time before disappearing into my own room.

Deandra...

I didn't even move when Stephen left the Jacuzzi. My body was still going through the motions of finishing the spasms that exploded inside of me. I lay against the side of the Jacuzzi, my breathing erratic, my body satisfied, but not satisfied. It took me a while to get out of the Jacuzzi on shaky legs and make my way to the bathroom to shower. Looking in the mirror on the medicine cabinet, I swore I noticed a change in my face...like a permanent blush that radiated in my cheeks, like I was happy.

Something in me was saying to be daring tonight, and so when I dressed, I selected my matching red lace bra and thong set, along with a red dress I brought along. It was as if I was having a premonition about all that would transpire here because there would be *no* reason to have anything this sexy, unless I *knew* I would want to impress and entice Stephen. The dress was a dark crimson red, with spaghetti straps, softly cupping my breasts, and then lightly caressing my body just above the knees. A slit was along my right thigh, and a matching scarf finished off the dress. I slipped on my sheer black hose and my black heels and primped into the full-length mirror that was on the back of the bathroom door. With minor make up, my eyes had a smoky, dreamy look to them, and my lips were sheathed with a dark red lipstick. I left my cropped hair slightly damp and curly atop my head.

Smiling into the mirror, I snatched up my black handbag and knocked on Stephen's adjoining door. "Come in," he said. I steeled myself from getting weak in his presence and strutted into his room, his jaw damn near hitting the floor as he gazed at me. Mine almost fell, too, as I stared at Stephen, his tall body clothed in black slacks and a red and black designed shirt. *Were great minds alike or what with the red and black thang going on?* His shirt was unbuttoned, revealing his firm brown chest, with hair sprinkled over it. Slowly, I crept up on him, my hands reaching out to touch his warm chest. Snapping myself out of my weakening state, I buttoned up his shirt, smiling at him. "Stop drooling and come on…I'm famished."

It was hard to get through dinner. I could tell by the look in Stephen's eyes that he was on the same wavelength as me…skip dinner and go do something more *educational*. But as I continued to stare deeply into his eyes, he was ever the professional. "I don't know about this Dugué," he said. "He was all too willing to give us Roxy."

I blinked the heat from my eyes and cleared my throat. "So, you think something bad is going down?" I asked.

"Not sure, but I gave him my phone number and gave him two days to get it to Roxy to call us. Told him that I would be coming with the authorities next time."

I took a sip of my white wine. "So for two days we're supposed to do what?" Stephen's eyes twinkled as he blew a kiss at me.

"The possibilities are endless, Deandra." He smiled. I felt a tingle flow through my body with the slowness of my name from his lips. Smiling back, I responded, "Okay, Casanova. Calm that libido down. You know, we could get a list of all the Sheratons in Paris and call them, see if they have a Roxy Winters there. I know that Dugué said that Roxy is at his country home, but maybe he's lying."

Stephen smiled, reaching for my hand across the table. "That's why I'm so crazy about you," he said. "We think alike." *He was crazy about me? Sooo crazy about me?*

I blushed. "Well, it's just a suggestion. Maybe tomorrow…"

"No, no, no," Stephen said, "Tomorrow is Valentine's Day." I smiled, totally forgetting that. "Don't tell me you forgot?" I nodded yes. "Well, I know we're here to find your sister, but hey, we're in the most romantic city in the world, on the most romantic day of the year…you know we're checking out this city."

I laughed and rubbed Stephen's hnd. "Okay, if you *insist*."

Stephen laughed. "But I promise we will do the Sheraton thing before we get back in contact with Dugué."

"Cool." I finished up my drink, giving Stephen the eye. "Well, how about we go upstairs? We have a long day tomorrow if we're going to be jet setting over the city." Stephen's eyes softened and a hint of wanting drifted over them. I felt a tightening in my lower belly.

"Anything you want," Stephen said, winking. Stephen took the bill folder from the waiter and placed bills for dinner and a tip into it. "Let's go."

Rising from my chair, Stephen settled his hand at the small of my back as we walked to the elevator and entered. As soon as the doors closed, Stephen pulled me into his arms and kissed me.

"Deandra," he sang into my ears, his hands moving along my thighs, up under my dress. For the ten-floor ride, Stephen and I continued groping and kissing and moaning our names out to each other. By the time the soft bell rang out, informing us of our floor arrival, Stephen was wearing my lipstick, and my scarf was lying on the floor of the elevator.

Stephen picked it up, placing it into my hands as we both slowly marched up to our doors. At my door, Stephen dropped a kiss onto my lips, whispering good night before entering his room. Inside of my own room, I fell against my door, my hands tightening against my belly. The burning that permeated my body made me ache inside. I slipped out of my heels and dropped my handbag onto my bed.

My head was total STEPHEN. I knew that compared to him, I was a virgin, only giving of myself once in my life to someone. I knew that he was a playa. Paris only highlighted his *better* sides, but those sides made me want him so badly. I knew I wouldn't be able to sleep through the night. After milling around my room, pacing and debating, I made my way over to the adjoining door, quietly opening it.

Stephen had dimmed his lights, and was sitting on the edge of his bed, facing me, as if expecting me. I was scared, could feel each nerve in my body shaking as I walked to him, his arms opening up and slipping around my waist, his head resting against me. I bent over, kissing his baldhead with tiny warm kisses. I felt his hands moving down my back, cupping my butt and squeezing it. Tilting his head up, I kissed his lips, parting them with my tongue. His fingers trailed up my spine, finding my zipper and moving it downward. With the movement of his fingers across my spaghetti straps, my dress fell to my hips, and with one quick shake, it slid to the floor.

Stephen's gaze trailed over my body, his hands making sure to familiarize themselves with every part of my body. I quickly unbuttoned Stephen's shirt, slipping it from him. "I want you so much, Step," I whispered, his body moving back against the bed, me following.

"I want you, too, Dee," he whispered back. Atop of him, I kissed his head, down across his forehead, over his eyelids, his nose, his cheeks, flicking my tongue across his lips, hearing his moans against my mouth. While I kissed the crook of his neck, Stephen's hands caressed by butt, softly grinding me against him. My lips continued their kissing exploration, kissing along his firm chest, gently licking and nipping his nipples, which caused my name to resonate from his mouth. He took in a breath when I kissed down his tight stomach, flicking my tongue out along his navel. As fast as I could, I removed his pants and boxers, my eyes getting a full view of the brown delight that was Stephen.

I whimpered softly, as my gaze fell upon the stiffening of his manhood and his apparent desire for me. In a blink of an eye, Stephen removed my bra and panties, kissing me hard and long, maneuvering my body beneath him. With one look at his eyes, I knew Stephen couldn't wait any longer to have me…and I felt the same way for him.

"You are so beautiful," he whispered, kissing my lips, down my neck, his lips connecting with one of my nipples, causing me to cry out. As his mouth nursed me, his left hand traveled down between my legs, lightly moving to find my hidden treasure. My cry alerted him that he found it, and he stroked it, making me bite his shoulder with each throb within my center.

"So wet," he moaned, his warm mouth trailing over to my other stiff nipple to give attention to it. My heart was beating so hard I couldn't think about anything but Stephen, my hands moving along his back, the roundness of his butt. I could feel his hardness pressing against my inner thigh, begging to be allowed entrance into my inner walls.

"Stephen," I cooed, "I want you…please…now." I slowly parted my legs and with one fluid motion, Stephen raised himself above me and moved his way inside of me. I immediately *grabbed* at his love muscle, almost forgetting how good it felt to be in synch with someone…but I had never felt *this* kind of connection with anyone. Ever.

Slowly, I wrapped my long golden legs around Stephen's waist, bringing him closer to me. His eyes bored into mine and I refused to look away. I wanted him to see all the pleasure that I was feeling at this moment. With each slow, deep thrust, I cried out, raising my hips to match the rhythm Stephen led with. "Dayum, Babe," Stephen grunted, "you are so tight." He swiveled his hips as he moved smoothly in and out of me.

My hands found a place at the hollow of his lower back. "Harder Stephen," I cried. "Harder."

"Shit," Stephen cried, as my inner walls beckoned him deeper inside of me, wanting him to find the most sensitive part of my being, the part that would have me lost in him. Stephen rose up onto his knees, his large hands moving down my neck, over my awakened breasts and nipples, down my stomach and to my hips, bringing me to him.

"Oh God," I moaned, his thrusts coming harder, faster, deeper. His hands were tight on my hips as he bucked against me hard. Quickening the pace, Stephen moved his hands over my heated passion, finding my love button peeking from its hood. "Oh…oh..oh.oh," I cried, the sensations overtaking me. I twitched and bucked with each rubbing of my button, with each powerful thrust of Stephen inside of me.

I watched Stephen's face, the intensity of it, the emotions hidden there. I could feel the building of what could only be described as *explosive* deep inside me. "Stephen," I cried, over and over, bucking against him. He leaned his hard body against mine tightly, grinding his hard, throbbing manhood in and out and in and out of me in rapid succession. My hands found his butt and assisted in his swift entrances and exits from my body.

"Deandra…" Stephen moaned in my ear, "I'm there. I'm there. Come with me." Looking into Stephen's eyes, I kissed him, our moans and groans escaping down our throats as our combined explosions wreaked havoc over us. I couldn't stop shaking as tidal waves of orgasms hit me, flowed from me.

When I finally quieted, Stephen kissed my forehead, pulling me tight against his hot body. We didn't speak. There were no words to say. We just held each other tightly, sleep and exhaustion finally taking over us.

The feel of light entering through the curtains coincided with the feel of Stephen raising my leg over his hips. Before I could open my eyes, the sweet feeling of him inside of me took me to another level. "God, Deandra," Stephen whispered, causing my eyes to flutter open, eyeing the peaceful look in his eyes. "I've never met *any*one like you before."

Lying on our sides, Stephen pulled me tight to him, the only movement being the pumping of his hips, the sounds of our morning love making the only noise in the room. On the tip of my lips were words I knew I couldn't say to Stephen…not right now. He had to say them first. I felt myself falling quick for him. Hell, I had *fallen* for him. The cries and moans that tumbled from my mouth proved that. I came harder and faster this time, my body still overly sensitive from our 'session' late last night. We laid there, Stephen stroking my hips, his hardness still residing within my throbbing wet center. Our breathing was labored, but I felt my heart catch in my throat when Stephen whispered to me how good I felt, how beautiful my body was, how much he wanted me, resulting in another eruption of explosive releasing to flow from me. Signed, sealed, and delivered were feelings that I had already known: I had fallen in love with Stephen Lewis.

Stephen. . .

I sat watching Deandra silently as she curled her hair with a curling iron, then applied lip-gloss and perfume. I was already dressed and ready for our Paris adventure and more than content just to sit and watch her get ready. Every once in a while she would look at me through the mirror, smiling softly and blowing me kisses. She was glowing, and I couldn't stop the high blush I felt come to my face with the look I saw in her eyes as she turned around and looked at me. Deandra was definitely a different type of lady than I was used to being with. She was a worldly, wise, successful businesswoman, and yet very innocent in other areas. Something warned me that for her the night we had spent together was not a little thing, and that unlike a lot of women I had been with, she was fragile, and not one to be toyed with.

"So, what's on the agenda for today, Mr. Tour Guide?" she asked, smiling sweetly.

"Mr. Tour Guide? I'm just as inept as you are in this city. You're gonna be showing me around." I laughed.

"Well," Deandra said, slipping her arms around my neck and examining my face intently, "then we will see it all with oneness of eyes, together..."

I laughed nervously. Her eyes were penetrating, her and her Bambi eyes, large and beautiful, and her feelings were written deep in their depths. Regardless of the fact that I was feeling her big time, the feelings I was having were actually a bit scary to me, and I didn't want to define them. I was feeling almost shy with the way she was looking at me, and shy was one word that could never be assigned to me. "You sound like a poet."

"Well, baby, you make my heart hum like a poet." She winked, me smiling broadly at her.

"Stephen..." she whispered, kissing me on the lips softly.

"Let's go," I said, sighing deeply.

Paris was beautiful. And with it being Valentine's Day, they had it lit for lovers. We saw everything we could squeeze into one day, all the famed hot spots of the 'City of Love'. We walked from the Arc de Triomphe, down the Champs Elysees, through the Tuileries. Deandra cooed and gasped when we visited the 'Louvre', she took a zillion pictures of The Mona Lisa, and pictures by this Musee d'Orsay, and all these other artists that I personally had never heard of. She was definitely Filet Mignon, whereas I was like a piece of Popeye's fried chicken I told her, we both got a laugh out of that one.

"Well, I like fried chicken. I especially like it brown, seasoned, and extra crispy like you," she said, licking my lips as we drank our after dinner cocktails. We had a late dinner at Jules Verne in the Eiffel Tower, after having done so much touring and shopping that we both felt like starving maniacs.

"So are you ready to call it an evening, Miss Chicken lover?" I asked her, caressing the small of her back. She smiled, as I paid the bill, grabbed our bags and called a driver to take us back to our hotel. On the ride back we were quiet. I felt like I was in another world as Dee kissed, licked, and sucked on my neck. I guess she had figured out that my neck was a weak spot for me, because I could barely get out of the car and carry the bags up by the time we got to the Sofitel.

After we got into our rooms, Deandra disappeared with a smile, saying she was gonna shower and be right back. My mouth felt dry as I waited for her. I was about to take my own shower when a better thought popped in my head. I undressed, and walked through our adjoining doors to Dee's bathroom. It was warm and steamy from her shower running. I tapped on the glass, not wanting to frighten her, slid it open, and slipped inside.

"Hi…" she breathed, her beautiful body covered with soap. I pressed her against the shower wall, exploring her mouth deeply as she kissed me back, moaning. Remembering what I had been dying to taste for months, I got on my knees in front of her and slipped each of her long legs over my shoulders.

Deandra...

I don't care if I'm addicted to Stephen. I really don't. I don't want rehab. I don't want an intervention. I just want to continue feeling him the way I have been. After our night…and morning of intense love making, Stephen and I slowly made our way out of bed, into the shower and on a Lover's Day tour of Gay Paris. It was *beautiful* to say the very least. We hit every landmark, not even stopping for food till nightfall. We gazed into each other's eyes, playfully kissed and hugged, held each other's hands. I felt like a black couple on one of those romance novels, like good girl/bad boy get together, clash, fall in love, and live happily ever after. I was oh so feeling this man.

On the way back to the hotel, I just couldn't keep my hands off of Stephen, sliding up ever close to him, kissing his lips; his neck and hearing those sexy moans come from him. By the time we got out the car at the hotel, we were both in need of a cold shower. Instead, I opted for a heated one, leaving Stephen with a kiss at his door, telling him that I would be right back after my shower. I slipped out of my clothing, and turned the shower on. It was beautifully designed, round, with frosted glass surrounding it and gold piping above the glass and faucets. Stepping in, the hot spray pelted against my skin.

I began cleansing myself when I heard a soft tap on the glass, followed by Stephen opening the door of the shower. "Hi," I whispered, as he entered, his long hard body pressing me against the glass of the shower as we kissed. Stephen's lips moved slowly down my wet body, as he knelt before me, lifting one, then my other leg up over his shoulders. My hands automatically went up, grabbing old of the gold railing above the enclosed glass. The first touch of Stephen's mouth against me caused me to squeal out in pleasure.

"Oh Stephen," I crooned, his hands hard against my backside as his hummed against me before lashing his hot tongue against my love, taking long licks up and down. I looked down, past his smooth bald head, strong shoulders, to his mouth, watching as he kissed every part of my sensitive area, before pressing the tip of his tongue between my lips, wiggling upward, finally hitting his destination, my swollen clitoris.

I purred, rocking my hips against his hungry mouth, which seemed to be on a mission of having me left sexually spent. His tongue made slow circular motions around my button. "You taste so good," Stephen whispered, over and over, in between tastes of my love.

"Oh, Boo," I cried, my voice high pitched, my breath caught in the back of my throat. "Oh God...Oooh."

"Yea, Baby," he said, beckoning me to give him what he wanted. And I was there, feeling the heat and the wetness build inside of me, causing me to shudder harshly. I was getting so sensitive that I tried swaying away from Stephen's mouth, but he whispered, "No," grabbing my hips and steadily feasting on my sweet treats.

The feeling of his tongue lapping against my aroused clitoris continuously caused me to release the bar, my hands gripping his slicked baldhead. "Don't move," I cried, "right there...there...oh, Stephen, I'm coming!" I bucked against his mouth, my sweet juices being quickly taken in by Stephen. I shuddered a second and third time, peaks of passion just taking over my body.

Slowly, Stephen rose, kissing my mouth, my taste against his lips. Before I could even catch my breath from the oral pleasures, Stephen gripped my hips, raising my long legs up around his waist, slipping his hardness deep inside of me. "Stephen!" I yelled, hearing his grunts of pleasure as he penetrated me deeply. I wrapped my arms tightly around his neck, kissing his mouth, whispering to him how good he felt, how I wanted him to come. And when he did, I heard my voice hitting notes I never thought possible. My name being whispered over and over again in my ears as Stephen began to come down from his sexual release.

For several minutes, we just gazed into each other's eyes. I swear, I could read *I love you* in Stephen's but his lips didn't move...and thus, neither did mine. In pure quiet, we cleansed one another and stepped out of the shower.

Clothed in hotel bathrobes, we both fell against my bed, holding one another, softly kissing. "I have never felt like that before," I whispered to Stephen.

"Neither have I, Baby," he whispered back, causing a smile to erupt from my lips. Dropping another kiss against his sweet mouth, I leaned over him, reaching for the phone.

"You know," I said, blushing, "all this *activity*, neither one of us has called home to tell people what's up. I'm gonna call, Shameika."

"You sure?" Stephen asked, lightly untying my robe belt. I giggled. "Behave for a minute," I said, laughing as I dialed. Shameika picked up on the second ring.

"Girl," Shameika yelled, "what's going on? All of us have been over here worried."

"Well," I began, but was distracted when Stephen slowly parted my robe and began to kiss along my left breast.

"Deandra," Shameika said, "you there?

"Uh, yeah," I said, my voice hushed. Clearing my throat, I spoke again, "I'm cool. As for Roxy, Stephen went and talked to the man who said he knew where Roxy was, gave him some b.s. about Roxy wanting to come with him." Stephen playfully bit at my nipple, causing me to yelp.

Shameika laughed. "Girl, what's Stephen doing to you?"

"Nothing!" I said, too loudly. "Hey, who's there? I hear voices." I tried to divert Shameika's attention, but it didn't work.

"That's the gang, Girl, but don't be trying to change the subject. Where Stephen's ass at?"

"In his *own* room," I countered with.

"Your nipples tastes like Hershey's Kisses," Stephen whispered to me, receiving a shiver in return as he went back to licking and kissing and sucking my erect nipples. It was hard, but I managed to hold a somewhat sane conversation with Shameika.

"Anyway, I just wanted to tell you guys that Stephen and I are okay, and hopefully in a couple of days, we all, including Miss Hot Ass Roxy, should be home."

"Okay, Girl." Shameika giggled. "You know I don't believe your ass, but Mom-to-be wants to holla for a minute."

I heard Joop and Chris yelling their daps for Stephen over the phone before Tamara spoke. "How are you, Girl?" she asked, her voice soft.

I sighed, more because of what Stephen was doing to me. I lightly smacked at his head and he tugged on my nipple in return. I laughed. "I'm okay, Girl," I responded. "I think everything's gonna be okay with the Roxy thang. At least I'm praying so."

In a conspiratorial tone, Tamara asked, "I meant between you and Stephen. Girl, have you…"

She let her question dangle in the air, as if I would automatically answer it, which I did. "No," I whispered, Stephen looking up at the serious look on my face.

"Just to let you know, Dee," Tamara said, "whispering, that one syllable, *no*, just confirmed to me that you're lying." My hands moved softly over Stephen's baldhead, as he crawled up on me, kissing my neck.

"Not lying," I whispered, "but I have to go…"

Tamara chuckled. "Yea, yea, yea, I'm sure you do. Happy Valentine's Day," she crooned.

Stephen's lips caressed my ear lobe, nipping it. "Same to you all," I whispered back, hanging up the phone. "You just couldn't stop touching me, could you?" I laughed, playfully wrestling with Stephen, before he pinned my arms above my head. His strength was too powerful to move and all I could do was coo and cry out as his tongue made wet circles around my stiff nipples. "Oooh," I moaned, "who are you, the energizer bunny?"

Stephen laughed. "Yea, Baby. With you, I just keep going

and going." He licked a line from between my breasts, up my neck, finally resting his full lips on mine.

"Stephen, you should call home," I whispered against his mouth.

"Right *now*?" he asked, lacing my lips with feathery kisses.

"Yessss, now. Round one is over, make a call...we can go for round two after."

"Promise?" Slipping my hands under his robe, they fell upon his semi-hard on, lightly stroking it, making Stephen shiver.

"Oh, most definitely," I said seductively. Stephen grabbed up the phone quickly, causing me to laugh.

Stephen . . .

I was so wrapped up in Dee, that I almost forgot who I was calling as the phone rang. "Yeah..." Shelby said. She always had a rude way of answering the phone, with "*yeah*".

"Wassup?"

"Step? Well, damn, it's about time you called. You forgot you had a daughter or something? Or, okay, let me see. You took a minute break to come out the pussy to remember your responsibility?"

It took a minute for Shelby's words to localize in my mind, at first me being more concentrated on Dee's kissing lips. Then when her words finally did register... "What the hell! Girl what are you trippin' on?" I sat up suddenly, Deandra looking at me with curious eyes.

"You, man! You go trailing behind some fancy trick, while your daughter is here with me sick! Don't worry, I don't give a damn who you're screwing, but Paris should be your number one priority over your dick!"

News flash! Shelby never failed to put a guilt trip on me whenever I had to go away for any reason. Not that she and I have even wanted to kick it for years, but still she always acted as if her having had my child gave her papers on my personal life.

"Shelby, you don't have to tell me what my priorities are. I know what they are, okay?" With her shitty attitude there was a lot more I wanted to say to her, but I wanted and had always tried to keep a peace with Shelby, mainly because of our daughter. "And what do you mean Paris is sick? What's wrong with her?"

"She's had a fever for the last day and a half, and a bad cold."

I rubbed my temples, feeling frustrated. "Well, did you take her to the doctor?"

"Oh course I did, Stephen. I know what to do with a sick child, and he said it was just a cold, that she would be fine, but that's not the point, she's been whiny and irritated and wanted to talk to her daddy, and I couldn't even get in touch with you to make that happen. AND, what is this she was telling me about you cursing around her?"

"That was a little argument between my dad and me, and she just happened to walk in on it. I explained all that to her, Shelby, and told her I was wrong...Look, just let me speak to her."

"She's asleep. She has a cold, remember? Call back lata!" Suddenly I was listening to the dial tone. Shelby was in rare form today, and me, I needed air, fast. I hung up the phone, and got up, wrapping my robe around myself.

"What's wrong, baby? That was your daughter's mother, I take it?" Deandra softly asked.

"Yeah...I'm sorry. I'll be back. I need some water or something," I said, squeezing her hand before heading through the doors leading to my own room. I hated, hated being made to feel like I was neglecting my daughter, and Shelby knew this. I hated it even more when she insinuated that I didn't know how to act around her, like asking why I cursed around her as if that was something I always did. The very fact that it surprised Paris to the point of her mentioning it to her mother should tell Shelby something. We had lived together long enough where she knew me through and through. But some women loved to go for the killer vein when they were pissed about something, and where Shelby and I basically did get along most of the time, when she was pissed, she was one of those killer vein ladies, one of the main reasons I had moved out in the first place.

I was a good father. I always took care of Paris financially, overly so, making sure she had the best, wore the best, always spending time with her, and mostly I made sure I did something my father never had. Told her I loved her. I was a good father.

"You okay?" Deandra asked, coming up behind me. She wrapped her arms around my waist and lightly kissed the back of my neck as I looked at the Parisian night-lights outside my picture window.

"Yeah, I'm cool," I said, turning to her and feigning a smile.

"Let's go back to bed and talk," she whispered, with me following her back to her room. It had been a long day, and suddenly I was feeling real tired.

So there we were, having a cuddle time. I had to smile a little, being that I hadn't had cuddle time with a lady in a long ass time. With Deandra, there were a lot of things I hadn't done in a long time, and a lot of feelings I hadn't felt.

"Do you and Paris' mom not get along?" she asked me.

I sighed. "Yeah, we do, most of the time. I'm a bit worried with me being here in Paris with my Paris being there sick, that's the biggest thing, but Shelby said it was just a cold."

Dee was quiet for a moment, her face buried against my neck with her playing with my chest hairs as we talked. I felt so at home. Is that the right way to put it? At home, with her, like she was where she belonged, in my arms, and I where I belonged, in hers. And to be honest, I have never felt like that with a woman before, not even Shelby. Our live-in relationship was mostly a fun time, a party thing, we dug each other sexually and decided to share a roof, but although we were friends, we didn't have a real spiritual connection.

"That's a beautiful name, Paris, it's funny how we are here

in Paris and your daughter's name is Paris." She laughed. "I like it, and I can't wait to meet her. Do you think she'll like me?"

I smiled. "Paris likes everyone. That's the kind of person she is. She's just five and has the persona of a twelve-year-old. She'd like you right away, because you're pretty like her Barbies." I traced Deandra's arched brow with my tongue, kissing her softly on her forehead and her nose. I could feel her smiling.

"Well I don't look like Barbie. Wrong color makeup!" She giggled. "What about your parents, you think they will like me? I want to meet everyone important in your life, Stephen. I want to know everything about you," she said, sitting up to look into my eyes. I could see hers sparkling at me in the night darkness.

"My father and I don't get along. He's never gotten over the fact that I didn't make the NBA."

"Oh…I guess that is a bit surprising to me. You seem so in place with what you do. You know, like it was your calling? And you do seem like a cop." She smiled, "At least, to me you do."

"I love what I do, and I loved being a cop, but HIS goal for me had always been pro ball. I made his goal my goal for a long time. That is the main reason I went to college. I mean, I'm glad I went, but I only did it to play ball so that I could have a shot at the draft picks. For a while there, basketball wasn't even fun for me anymore. I was too busy trying to be the image of a star, and had been for so long…in junior high, high school, and college, and it was fun in a way, but after a while? It became work, and that's when I lost my joy. So really, when I didn't make it, as he wanted me to, I was depressed about it, but mostly because he was, and I let him down. I've been my happiest since I started living for me, for Stephen." I gave a big sigh, feeling the mental weight that I had carried about my father for so long.

"You know, Step, working in the field I do, I've seen a lot of guys playing the game for someone else and not themselves. Especially with black guys, with society making it seem like their success is measured by statistics, and that's sad, because sports is a game, and should be fun, but it's not always like that. So really you're lucky things happened as they did, because listening to you now, I don't think you would have been happy playing pro ball."

I looked at Deandra, seeing the warmth and understanding in her eyes, once again I felt that 'at home' feeling. "I know now I wouldn't have been. I would have been still living for him. I like basketball, love it in fact, and I love to play even to this day, but I don't want the pressure. I want it to be fun and a game. I just want him to be happy that I'm a success in my way, and not have him keep thinking I'm a failure because I didn't live his dream."

"Well, you're a winner to me, and I feel like with you, I scored big," Deandra said seriously, an unspoken emotion shining in her eyes.

We both drifted into sleepville, and the last thought that danced through my head, was my feeling in total agreement with her last comment, but in the opposite. With her *I* was the one who had scored a winner, a slam-dunk…of the heart.

Deandra. . .

By the time Stephen stretched and yawned and tumbled out of my bed, I was at the desk on my laptop, using my hacking knowledge — most supplied by my girl Tamara — to get into the Sheraton hotels that were online. I quietly laughed to myself, thinking how these webmasters and Internet security thought they were so intelligent in how they made certain files private, for only internal uses…thinking no one would ever get a glance at them. I knew no one at the hotel would willingly give me information for my sister…so I thought I would *take* it. The list of Sheratons in Paris was exhaustingly long, and I was only on the 12th Sheraton when Stephen walked up behind me. He nuzzled my neck, whispering good morning as I turned to face him. I slipped my arms around his waist, my head falling against his hard stomach. Noticing the worry lines etched across my forehead, Stephen kissed me there, saying, "So, no luck yet?"

Sighing, I answered, "No, that was the 12th hotel and they had no Roxy Winters there." Stephen kissed the pout on my lips, pulling me up from my chair to hug me tight around my robe-clad body. "We'll find her, Baby," Stephen whispered in my ear. "Don't give up."

"Oh, I'm not," I responded, leaving the warmth of Stephen's arms to crawl up onto the bed, resting my back against the headboard as I pulled my legs to me. "If we don't find her this way, we'll have to get through by way of Dugué." Stephen crawled onto the bed, kissing both of my bare knees before sitting beside me.

"I don't trust Dugué as far as I can throw him. Like I said, he was just too willing to give up Roxy, and then says he'll have her call *us*? I don't buy it."

"Neither do I."

"The only recourse I see is for us to get the local authorities involved and handle Dugué that way. If we don't hear from Roxy by the end of the day, bright and early tomorrow morning we'll be going for Dugué."

"But you know," I said, leaning against Stephen, "he knows this. Don't you think he'll run by tomorrow?"

"If he does, he'll be followed. I have someone on him twenty-four seven. He won't go far."

"Well, lemme check some more hotels." Stephen jumped from the bed, removing his robe, allowing it to drop to the floor. Instantly, I felt a stirring rush through me as I stared at his lean body, that sweet brown skin, the hair on his chest, that line that led to that miraculous manhood of his that looked ready to take me on. My mouth went dry, no words could flow from me. I just stared as he smiled at me, so sexily that I wanted to drop my robe and take him right there, but I stayed put.

"I'm gonna go take a shower," Stephen mouthed, each word moving me that much closer to the end of the bed, hence, closer to him. "Wanna join me?"

I laughed. "I told you that I need to check more hotels. Stop trying to tempt me with your *body*."

"Okay, I'll shower alone. Let *this* go to waste."

Snickering, I said, "Stephen, I'm sure you won't let it go to waste." Stephen chuckled, turning to head to the bathroom, my eyes moving along his strong back and the firm roundness of his backside. Stifling a moan, I hopped from the bed, making a move to the desk to begin the tedious task of looking for my sister again.

It took reaching twenty-five Sheratons to actually make some kind of headway, to build up my hopes of finding my sister. There wasn't a Roxy Winters registered at the hotel, but there *was* a Roxy Lauren...Lauren being my sister's middle name. I picked up the phone and moved to the bed just as Stephen walked out from the bathroom, a towel wrapped around his waist.

"Stephen, I think I found my sister," I said, too excited. He quickly came to the bed, sitting beside me.

"Are you serious?" he asked.

Yea, one of the hotels has a Roxy Lauren there." Stephen's eyebrow shot up. "My thought exactly, using my sister's middle name might throw one or two *very* slow people off...but I think it's her, in fact, I'm definitely sure it's her."

"You want me to call?" Stephen asked, taking the paper that I scribbled Roxy's number on from my shaky hand.

"Would you, because I think my nerves are shot." I handed him the phone, my hands moving to my chest, rubbing softly. "Feels like I'm about to have a heart attack with all this drama. Call."

Stephen nodded, leaning in to kiss my forehead. I watched him dial the number, and the nod he gave me, alerting that someone had picked up the phone on the other end. "Yes," Stephen said, his voice very clipped and professional, "May I speak to

Roxy Lauren? This is room 612, correct? Well, the desk attendant told me that there *is* a Roxy Lauren in that room…" He paused for a moment, looking at the phone ringer oddly, "Hello!" Stephen yelled, before slamming down the receiver.

The look in Stephen's eyes told me my suspicions were right. "Baby, take a quick shower and get dressed," he said quickly. "I'm gonna call the hotel back and ask for directions and get dressed. I heard a girl in the background yelling, and I think it's Roxy."

My mind was on autopilot. My fear crept into my chest, paining me. All I could think about was the safety of my sister, praying that Dugué wasn't being told at this very moment about the previous phone call. Sensing my anxiety, Stephen leaned towards me, kissing me, whispering, "It's going to be okay, Baby…go get dressed."

I think I broke a record showering and dressing…but I was on a mission…

Stephen…

It was a tense ride over to the Sheraton hotel. Deandra was shaking like a leaf, and really there was nothing I could say or do, she had real reason for fear. "I don't know what's going on here, but Roxy definitely didn't sound like she wanted to be in that room," I said as I drove the rented vehicle we had acquired.

"Oh God! You think somebody is hurting her?"

"No Dee…she's okay. I can feel it," I said, squeezing her hand as we pulled into the parking lot.

Walking swiftly through the lobby, I stopped at the front desk, quickly telling the attendant that there was trouble in room 612 and to call the police. Deandra and I made our way to the elevator and the 6th floor, with us soon tapping on room 612. As far as I was concerned, Roxy either would want to go with us, or she would not, but just in case Dugué tried any funny business, I had my thirty-two caliber close at hand.

When the door opened, there stood Dugué, recognizing me immediately. "Monsieur Lewis, you are not welcomed here, now if you would kindly leave," he said angrily.

"Not without our first speaking with Miss Winters, now I know she's here. If she wants to stay with you in France, let her tell us herself." I looked over to Deandra, who was frantically looking over Dugué's shoulder for Roxy.

"She is not here, now if you don't leave, I will call the police!"

"We already have. They are on their way here now," I replied with a wintry smile. Suddenly I was feeling pretty fed up with Dugué's games and pushed my way past him, Dugué flying hard against the wall. My hand was firmly on Deandra's back, making sure she stayed close to me.

"Roxy! Are you here?" Deandra called out.

"Dee Dee!" Looking around, a shorter version of Deandra came running out of double connected doors, a dark bruise under her cheekbone. Deandra ran to meet her, both ladies crying, hugging and kissing.

"I was so worried about you! Oh God!" Deandra cried.

"I want you two to leave, now! Roxy belongs to me. I paid for her services. She is going NOWHERE!" Turning my attentions toward Dugué again, I was confronted with this little pale shithole of a man, pointing a revolver at me.

I laughed sarcastically. "Why don't you put your water gun down? You don't want to go there with me. If Miss Winters wants to leave with her sister and me, she can. Because I don't know if you are aware of this, but she is an American citizen, and where we come from, slavery has been abolished. Now I don't know what the fuck has been going on here, but we're walking out that door, with her, now." Looking over toward Deandra and Roxy, I gestured for them to go grab Roxy's bags while I kept a careful eye on Dugué.

Dugué was shaking, tears rolling down his face, obviously a sick case of obsession. "Don't go, Roxy! I love you!"

"No, I want to go home, please," Roxy cried, steadily packing her bag. I was trying to feel Dugué out. He was no longer pointing his revolver our way, but simply holding himself up against the wall, weeping like a sick man. I shook my head in disgust. He obviously had brought her to France, she being unaware that he had no intentions of ever letting her go back to the states. I kept a close hand on my pistol housed in my gun belt behind me, not wanting to frighten the ladies, but still not quite sure about this Dugué character either.

"Go on to the car," I told Deandra, as she and Roxy made their way to the door. Dugué appeared lost in his own world of grief. I proceeded to back my way out with them, not wanting to turn my back on him. While turning my head for one split second toward the ladies, I suddenly heard him cry out, "No!" He pointed his revolver to his own head. The ladies screamed, and the sounds of the police running down the hotel hallway could be heard. I rushed toward Dugué to stop him, when suddenly he instead pointed the gun in my direction and fired. I heard the loud pop sound, and fell to the floor, feeling the pressure and pain in my chest and the horrified screams of Roxy and Deandra.

"Stephen!!!"

Deandra . . .

Slow motion. That's the only way I could describe what happened in Dugué's hotel room. Seeing my sister Roxy with a bruised face, and Dugué, who looked like his whole world was leaving as I took Roxy's hand and hurried us both out the door…it was definitely something out of a novel…not in the *real* world, and yet here I was, afraid for my life, my sister's life, as well as for Stephen's life.

I was hopeful that we all would manage to get out unscathed when Dugué yelled, "No!" and put the revolver up to his head.

Roxy and I turned back into the room, as Dugué turned the gun in reverse and fired a shot at Stephen. As if being shown frame by frame, Stephen fell slowly to the ground, grabbing his chest, a loud yell coming from him. I could hear the police running down the hallway, but the only thing I could do was scream, this piercing scream that expressed the horrific pain I was in, seeing my baby, my heart, hurt.

Roxy and I totally ignored Dugué's cries and ramblings, as we both fell to our knees beside Stephen. I slowly raised his head to my lap, feeling his neck, checking his pulse, happy to feel one there. My tears were flowing too hard to see anything, and I chanted, "Everything's gonna be alright, Baby" to Stephen, kissing his forehead.

The police came barreling into the room, guns out. Before they could even tell Dugué to put his weapon down, he looked over at Roxy and told her in French — Roxy telling me later in English, "I love you…you are mine, if I can't have you, I don't want to live," and he snapped the revolver into his mouth and fired, causing screams to emit from my mouth. Roxy just knelt there, quiet, frozen, tears streaming down her bruised face.

My attention was given back to Stephen, who lay still in my arms. As officers contacted the hospital and went to inspect Dugué 's lifeless body, a detective came over us, speaking in French. I shook my head, crying, "Don't speak French."

"Sorry, Madame," the detective said, kneeling beside Stephen. "I called the paramedics. They will be here shortly. He's still breathing, yes?" I nodded. "This is Monsieur Lewis, yes?" I nodded. "He's been in contact with a detective in our force about the Dugué situation. We had hoped to resolve this matter without any bloodshed."

"I think we failed," I whispered, stroking Stephen's cheek. "Baby, if you can hear me, open your eyes," I said, staring down at Stephen's silent face. My hand moved along his chest, and I felt something hard under his shirt. With all the commotion, I never actually looked anywhere, *but* at Stephen's face. Now, I noticed there was no blood. Swiftly, I raised his shirt; there was a vest, a bulletproof vest. "Oh my God." I sighed, looking into Stephen's face just as his eyes opened slowly.

"Damn," he groaned, his hands moving where he was shot. "Bitch stung like a mutha."

"Stephen!" I cried, kissing his mouth, kissing his face all over. "You're okay." A new batch of tears fell, as the detective slowly helped Stephen up and into a chair. The paramedics rushed in to attend to a dead Dugué. After checking on Stephen, they informed us that he only had the wind knocked out of him...some bruises on his chest. Asked him if he wanted to go to the hospital to get checked out.

"Naw," he whispered, taking deep breaths, "I'm cool."

Roxy was still in shock, never leaving my side, but not saying anything either. I was in a blur, my eyes never blinking, just staring at Stephen as he talked to the Detective. He told us how he wore a vest in every case he investigated for protection. I still couldn't speak. I just waited. Half an hour later, when all was settled between the police and us, we began our journey back to the hotel. I drove, glancing over at Stephen who sat quiet in the passenger seat. We were all individually coming down from extreme horrific highs, but I barely remembered any of it. Only thing I *knew* was that I had almost lost Stephen. I thought I *had* lost him, and that hurt me more than anything...I was in love with this man...he was *mine*, and this...this horrible situation, confirmed that to me.

Back at the hotel, we all showered, dressed, and came together in my room. I ordered drinks to the room, because for one, I knew I needed one, if not a few to calm my rattled nerves. Stephen was lying back on the bed, and I sat beside him, my sister sitting in a chair, holding a drink to her lips. I felt like I was staring into a mirror as I looked at her, except she was smaller, more demure than I. She looked so tiny, I wanted to run up to her and hold her, but I needed to know what the hell happened.

"So, you wanted to come to France?" I asked, sipping the gin and tonic that laced my glass.

Roxy nodded, drinking. "I met Tom in California," she began, coughing, rubbing the warmth in her chest that came from her drink. "He was one of my regulars…" Her voice trailed off, her eyes moving to me, as I kept from flinching. "He was really nice to me, and I kinda fell for him. It's not something you're supposed to do in the biz, but it happened. I was working for myself, making great money, and when Tom popped into my life, I thought maybe I could finally stop *working* and try my hand at a normal life.

"He offered me $10,000 to come to France…" I gasped, but Roxy held her hands up to me. "No, not for *sex*, per se," she continued, "he knew I wanted to paint, wanted to help me with my education. He never told me this was going to be anything but him and me having fun, and him helping me out. I went because I cared for him. You know I always wanted to come here and paint." I nodded. "Well, he offered me that chance, and I took it. Three months in, I realized that painting wasn't it for me…or maybe I wasn't good enough to persevere, who knows, but I wanted to go back to the states, but Tom said no, I was here to stay."

"What, he had you locked up for the last five months?" I asked, glancing over at Stephen to make sure he was okay. He smiled at me, listening to every word that poured from my sister's lips.

"In a way. When I became adamant about wanting to leave, he hired bodyguards who never left my side, even when I had to use the bathroom. I couldn't do anything for myself, and it was implied that to escape would mean harm to me…I had no choice but to stay.

"The day I called you, the bodyguards had slipped. One

injured himself and so I only had one watching over me, but Tom had him doing other things. By then, I had become complacent; realizing I was going to be here forever, so Tom had began to trust me more. During the day, I managed to get time to call, but you never answered the phone...any of the times I called. Luckily, I got in contact with you. Stupidly, I left the number, and if you had called asking for me, I don't know what would have happened."

I sighed, walking towards my sister and kneeling before her. "I'm just glad you're okay, Sis," I leaned in, hugging her. She hugged back.

Kissing the top of my head, Roxy concluded with, "Tom walked in on our phone conversation and went off, actually hit me." She pointed to the bruise on her face for emphasis. "Been in seclusion that whole time, with two bodyguards watching me since then. Tom was brilliant, but missed simple things, like using my name for the room. Who wouldn't know it was me?"

"I guess he didn't think that anyone would come for you," I said. "It's been a while since you've even contacted any of us." A silence fell in the room. "Not now, but Roxy, for real, when we get home, you are going to tell me *everything*, from why you would leave us, never contact us, to why you decided to sell yourself...I don't have the foggiest idea why you would do this, and I want to understand."

"Of course you wouldn't understand, Deandra." Roxy sniffed, crying. "You're the perfect daughter. Intelligent, driven, athletic, beautiful, talented, admired, all of that. You knew since you kicked your first soccer ball, since you shot and made your first three-pointer, that you would work in sports. I never had a clue what I really wanted to be, never had guidance like you did."

"So you saying Mom and Dad didn't love you like they did me?" I asked, moving back from my sister to glare in her eyes. "If you are, don't even go there, because they *love* you."

"No, not saying that, but...it doesn't even matter, because

you wouldn't understand. You're the first born, the first to get all of Mom and Dad's love, and the leftovers were for me. I was never pushed into choir, into sports, into anything that could test me, give me some help as to what my interests were…so I never had any interests. I was smart… I think that's hereditary, but I never did anything *with* my intelligence…not like you."

Before I could respond to my sister, my hotel phone rang, causing me to jump up and snatch the phone from its base. "Hello," I said. "Uh, yeah, he is. Hold on, please." I turned to Stephen, handing him the phone. "It's a call from the states. They tried your room and you weren't there, so they checked here."

I watched Stephen's expressions on his face, and I grew frightened. "Calm down, Shelby," he said into the phone, as he raised from the bed. "Is she okay? The hospital?"

Roxy looked at me, questioningly, but I knew not what to tell her. I shrugged, my attention moving back to Stephen. I mouthed, "Paris?" and he nodded.

"Okay, Shelby," he rushed out his lips. "I'll take the next flight out, and will be there as soon as I can." Hanging up the phone, Stephen glanced at me, fear in his eyes.

"It's Paris," he whispered. "She's in the hospital."

"Oh my God," I responded. "What's wrong?" Stephen moved slowly off the bed, moving towards our adjoining door.

"Shelby didn't say, or if she did, she's way too frantic for me to actually hear what she was saying. Just that Paris got sicker…she had to take her to the hospital."

I walked to Stephen, wrapping him in my arms for a tight warm hug, before kissing his lips lightly. "She's going to be okay," I whispered. "I'll pack."

Stephen gave me a wistful smile and a "Thank you" before going into his room. I barely answered my sister's questions about who Paris was, who Shelby was, what was going on. All I knew was that this rollercoaster of a life I was living was once again hitting a down slope, first with my sister, then with Stephen being shot, and now this…All I could do was buckle in, and make sure that Stephen got back home ASAP to his baby girl.

Stephen...

My chest was sore, extremely so, but I didn't say anything about it, not wanting to worry Deandra. And I was worried myself, worried sick about my daughter. The flight back to the states was long and tiring and achy. I quietly sat beside this other brotha, who tried talking my head off about everything under the sun, while Deandra and her sister sat in front of us catching up and talking about our ordeal. When we finally got to the BWI airport, I was more than ready to get to John Hopkins and check up on Paris. After grabbing our bags from the terminal, I kissed Deandra briefly and took off, turning toward my truck.

"You've been so quiet, Stephen. Are you okay?" she asked, stopping me for a moment.

"Yeah, I am. I'll call you later, alright? I quickly kissed her goodbye, nodded to Roxy, and jumped in my truck, making my way to the hospital as quickly as possible.

"Paris?" I said, seeing her lying in the hospital bed, surrounded by a breathing tent of some sort. Shelby was sitting in the recliner next to her bed.

"Shh…she's asleep," Shelby whispered, walking toward me.

"How is she?" I whispered back. Shelby wrapped her arms around my waist in a tight hug. I tried hugging her back but gasped when she pressed her head in my chest, pulling back from her. If that bullet had of went through me I would have been one dead brotha.

"What's wrong?" she asked, concern written on her face.

"I had a minor confrontation, I'll tell you about it later. Right now I'm concerned about our baby. How is she?"

"She's better. She still has a high fever but the doctor says that's normal with double lung pneumonia. She's responding well to the antibiotics and he says she'll be better in no time."

"Pneumonia? Damn, how the hell did she get that?" I exclaimed, walking over to touch Paris' forehead. She was hot, very hot.

"It just happens. I didn't have her going out without a coat or anything, Stephen," Shelby said defensively.

"Shelby, I never said you did. I know you're a good mom. I'm just trying to find out how she is."

"I'm sorry. It's just this has been stressful for me, and we needed you here," she said, rubbing her temples. "I'm sorry I came off as I did on the phone, Stephen. I know you said you went to Paris on business, and even if it was personal, it was none of my business. I had no right to speak to you as I did."

Shelby and I had always had an amicable if not friendly relationship, even after our breakup, which we had, both eventually agreed, was the best thing for both of us. We sat talking for a while longer, me waiting for Paris to wake up, which she didn't seeing that she had fallen asleep just before I got there Shelby had told me. It was late, so eventually Shelby suggested that I go home and get some rest, and that she would call me when Paris woke up. I was hesitant, but eventually agreed, kissing Paris on the forehead, and taking off for home.

So much was clouding my mind. Relief that Paris would be okay, relief that all was well with Roxy, and that we had gotten her back in one piece, including getting me and Deandra back in one piece, too. But thoughts of Deandra flooded my mind, and of our days and nights together. She had been right before, about me wanting to get with her sexually. I had wanted that from the moment I first saw her. But it turned out to be so much more intense, emotional and not just sex, and I really hadn't betted on that.

And even though she hadn't said it, she had that look in her eyes, that LOVE look. And I felt it in the way she touched me, made love with me, as if she was giving me a treasure. I can sense when a lady is diggin' me, but the knowledge that she was feeling me had me spinning. On one hand I was glad, unable to keep the smile from my face. But on the other hand, it made me nervous, feeling that *run* feeling that I always felt whenever a lady was pushing for more, or getting too close.

I rode past her place on my way home, deciding to stop by and tell her how Paris was rather than call her. As I walked to her brownstone I felt anxious, very anxious to see her, almost desperately so, yet still feeling that odd feeling to run. "I'm not gonna let this lady get to my mind," I said out loud to myself, my feet moving faster even as I spoke. "If she tries, I'll just let her go. Nothing to it. I'm not ready for love. I'm not."

So tell me why my heart was beating so fast when she opened her door with her beautiful face shining up at me... Tell me why it was, that all I wanted to do was take her in my arms and never let go, as if the three hours that had passed since we had left the airport was three hours too long...

Deandra...

The last three hours I sat and listened to my sister try and explain to me why she chose to sell her body to men she didn't even know. I had to agree to disagree. I've *never* thought of sex as a means to an end, of doing it to *get* something. That's probably why I had only been with one man my whole life. And I had waited, waited till I felt secure in our relationship, waited till he told me that he loved me and only wanted to be with me.

Unfortunately, our relationship ended, but we managed to stay friends. I guess because we were such good friends before we moved into a sexual thing, we were able to salvage something after our mutual split. Knowing how I am, and how faithful and true I am to my beliefs, I found myself thinking why I slept with Stephen, why did I allow him to enter my body, my heart, without so much as *one* I love you being uttered to me, not even in our sexual trysts.

I felt a gnawing in my stomach as Roxy interrupted me from my thoughts. "Can we just start over?" she yelled to me from the living room. I had gone into the kitchen to retrieve two Coronas, one of which I handed to Roxy as I sat beside her on the sofa.

"We have no choice," I responded, sipping my beer. "But lemme tell you, from here on in, I don't *even* want to hear about you putting blame of your life on any of us, you hear me? You are *young*, go back to school, finish up your degree, *do* something."

"I know." Roxy sighed, nodding, her long hair moving across her face. "And I will, Sis. Gimme some time to regroup, okay?" I scooted over to Roxy, hugging her tight to me.

"And you can stay right here with me." I smiled, kissing Roxy's forehead. We were interrupted from our sisterly moment by the ringing of my doorbell.

"Hold the love." I laughed, jumping up to answer the door. Seeing Stephen there, I automatically leaned into him, gently hugging him, kissing his lips softly. Smiling, I whispered, "Come in, baby."

"How you feeling?" Roxy asked from the couch.

"I'm okay," Stephen answered, giving Roxy the Negro nod of acknowledgment. "Little stiff, but I'll be fine.

"How's Paris?" I asked, my eyes never leaving Stephen's.

He sighed. "Double pneumonia, but she'll be okay in a couple of days. She was asleep when I got there. Shelby said she'd call when Paris woke up."

I nodded, giving Stephen another hug. I couldn't pinpoint it, but he sounded, felt different. His eyes didn't even have the same glow I remembered. I felt the gnawing in my stomach intensify as I asked him if he wanted a beer.

"That'll be cool."

As we walked to the kitchen, I told him that the gang was on their way over.

"They wanted to make sure we all were in one piece," I offered as we hit the kitchen. Once the swinging entrance door closed, I turned to hug Stephen, looking at him. "Are you okay?" I asked, my voice a whisper.

"I'm cool, yeah," was his unemotional response. I turned from Stephen, going into the fridge to grab a beer, dropping it on my first attempt.

"Shit," I muttered as the beer broke. I knelt down, cleaning up the beer, the glass, my heart feeling heavy, the smile in my body quickly evaporating. "Ouch!" I yelped, slicing the tip of my finger with the glass.

"Are you okay, babe?" Stephen asked, bending down beside me. I got up the rest of the glass and placed it in the trashcan before moving to the sink to run cold water over the small cut on my finger.

"I'll live." I reached in the cupboard above the sink for a box of Band-Aids. Bandaging my finger up, I turned back to Stephen and blurted out, "So, what are we going to tell the gang?"

"What do you mean?" Stephen asked, reaching for a beer in the fridge.

"Like, well, about us." My left hand moved up to stroke Stephen's cheek, leaning in to kiss him. "Are we going to tell them that we're together? I mean, being with you in Paris, before we left for Paris…I really care about you Stephen…I love you." I saw Stephen's jaw twitch and an ice-cold streak ran up my spine, making me inwardly cringe.

I could feel tears fill in my eyes, but I kept them tight inside. "Do you love me?" I asked, my voice soft, with a hint of fear in it. After a pause, I asked. "Do you like me just a *little* bit?" To me, these were questions that were yes or no, and with Stephen standing there saying nothing, I had my answer.

I chewed the gloss off of my bottom lip, keeping myself

from crying. A humorless laugh came out of me as I patted Stephen on the shoulder. "You don't even have to answer," I said, my voice cracking, betraying me. "We don't have to tell them anything…there's nothing to tell. We kicked it…had some fun…meaningless sex…"

"Deandra," Stephen whispered, but I cut him off, my tears falling.

"It's cool, Stephen."

Roxy!" Shameika and Tamara squealed Roxy's name. I closed my eyes, silently counting down from ten before wiping the tears from my face.

"Ahh," I whispered. "Friends." I briefly glanced at Stephen before placing on my happy face and exiting the kitchen.

Stephen…

Deandra was chilly, like an ice-cold brew the whole night. With her coolness, the hugs and hellos from our friends, and Sha and Tamara greeting Roxy whom they had not seen in years they said, it was hard to get a word in edgewise, which was unusual for me. I usually went out of my way to be the life of the party.

Deandra said she loved me. Did I love her? She was wrong about one thing. My silence wasn't an instant no, it was an instant shock, realizations that just weren't coming out as fast as hers were. But her tears, and her words that it was cool, that we had just been kickin' it, had those feelings brimming on the edge and about to overflow when the doorbell had rung.

"So tell all, what did y'all see, DO!" Tamara asked laughingly.

I looked over at Deandra solemnly; she had this permanent fake smile on her face and wouldn't even look my way. Shameika and Tamara and Deandra talked on and on about Paris, avoiding the subject of Roxy's troubles of course, but wanted to know all the haps with me and Dee, with Deandra trying to listen and answer the best she could, without directly speaking to me. To say I felt uncomfortable would be an understatement.

"Wassup with you guys?" Shameika finally asked, "Damn y'all all quiet with each other, you know we want to know the SCOOP." I looked at Dee, the color rising high in her cheeks with her still avoiding my eyes. I cleared my throat.

"Paris was nice, we saw a lot of famous places, had dinner in The Eiffel Tower, saw famous art pieces, like The Mona Lisa, stuff like that," I said. Shameika and Tamara gave each other a look.

"Well that's *nice* but...what's wrong with you two?" Tamara asked, looking from Deandra to me.

I looked at Deandra again, her face tightening, as she blinked her eyes rapidly. The doorbell rang and she hopped up quickly to answer it, as if relieved. Joop and Chris walked in smiling, giving me daps and telling me about the good game I missed. I have to admit I was glad to see them, I missed our hang out times, and, I was starting to feel a little outnumbered with the ladies here.

"Well we need to get together this week, I need to get my game on." I smiled. Just then my cell phone started singing this little tune it does in my pocket. I quickly answered it, getting up to stand in a private corner of the room. It was Shelby.

"She's awake, and guess who she's asking for?" she asked over the phone.

"Great," I replied, "I'll be right over." I hung up, looking toward Deandra and everyone else in the room. "I need to go for a short. I'll be back though so don't talk about nothing till I get back." I laughed.

"Aight, man. We'll catch you in a shorty, then," Chris said. I walked toward the front door.

"Dee?" She got up slowly and followed me out the door. "We need to talk. I'll be back later. I promise, okay?" I reached out to caress her cheek, with her jerking back away from my touch.

"So did one of your other ladies call?" she asked sarcastically, her eyes glassy with concealed hurt.

"No, it wasn't. I mean yes, it was. I mean, it was Shel..."

Cutting off my nervous jabber, Deandra put her hand up saying, "Don't explain. It's cold out here and I'm going in the house. Bye."

And there she went, and there I stood, with the right words still left unsaid. So much for super smooth Stephen Lewis.

Deandra...

I stood there at the door, motionless, having shut it, closing Stephen out of my house...possibly even my heart. I stood straight, steeling myself from the tears that begged to be released. I could feel my back burning, knowing that the gang was all staring at me, wanting to know what was up between Stephen and me. The whole evening was a sham in my opinion, faking like I was happy when my heart was breaking. I knew I had two good seconds left before the dam would break.

I turned towards the gang, not looking at anyone in particular as I said, "The beers are in the fridge, help yourself to whatever," and quickly walked into my bedroom, shutting the door behind me. As the door shut, I began balling, crying almost uncontrollably as I fell onto my bed. Within seconds, a soft tapping was heard on my bedroom door, followed by Roxy, Shameika and Tamara walking in and sitting around me on the bed.

"Okay," Shameika said, in the calmest voice she could find, "what the hell is going on?"

Tamara wiped my tears, as Shameika reached onto my nightstand, handing me tissues. "Girls," I cried, "I am *so* stupid."

"You fell for him, didn't you?" Tamara asked. I nodded, crying harder. "What happened?"

I sat up, leaning against my girls as they each touched me,

with a hug, a kiss, sisterly love. "Minus drama, Paris was *so* nice y'all. Even before Paris, Stephen crept up in me. I kept fighting him off, but my defenses fell, I wanted him.

"We get to Paris, and things just ignited. I mean the way he looked at me said he was feeling me, just like I was feeling him. Everything about Stephen was just calling me to him and he did…not…disappoint me."

"Then why is he tripping?" Shameika asked.

"Why does he have you crying?" Roxy added.

"I dunno." I sighed, sniffing. "It's like after all the shit went down and Stephen was shot at, everything in me just doubled and tripled, my love just expanded upon itself and I knew I loved him, that I was *in* love with him, and I think he saw it. I think he could feel it, and it turned him off.

"I mistakenly said those three words just before you guys got here and he didn't respond."

"No, tell me you did *not* tell that niggah you love him?" Shameika cried out. "And his ass said nothing back?"

"Just stared at me, shocked, like a deer caught in some headlights."

"Girl, you should have known his ass was no good anyway," Shameika went on, "I told you his ass was like thirty-one flavors with varieties on top of those flavors. Niggah wouldn't know a good woman if she smacked the hell out of him."

"Now, Shameika, come on," Tamara countered, rubbing my shoulder, "you don't even know the whole story."

"Girl, from day one we knew Stephen was a dog…it's what he does, hell even *he* proclaimed himself Gigolo Number One."

"So, you saying someone like that can't change? I mean you don't know his life, you don't know what he's thinking, and I bet Deandra doesn't know either."

"I know a lot more than you guys do," I jumped in. "We talked about a *lot* things while in Paris. His parents, mainly his father, his daughter, his ex, his job, a lot. All I can go by is what he says and does, and up until a few hours ago, I thought I *knew* what he wanted...I thought it was me that he wanted. Y'all know I don't give myself to everybody...hardly even anybody. It meant something to me when I was with Stephen."

"All I'm saying is don't shut him out," Tamara said. "If anyone knows how you feel, I do. I know you remember all the times I called you in New York, crying my eyes out over Chris and all the time we lost together because we didn't listen and communicate with one another. Don't do that to you and Stephen. What did he say before he left?"

"That he was coming back tonight," I said, hiccupping. Crying always resulted in random hiccupping for me.

"Well, don't even stress over this, Boo," Tamara responded. "Talk to him, I mean really talk, ask him the questions that you want answers to. Find out where his head is before you make any rash decisions."

"I still say he's a ho...always will be one," Shameika snorted, "but if you want to take the reasonable way out, follow what Tamara's saying to you."

I leaned my head against Tamara's shoulder, closing my eyes to think. I did love Stephen, God knows I did, and I didn't want to regret not letting him have his full say. I whispered, "I'll talk to him," and was caught in the middle of a tight sisterly hug that warmed my heart and gave me hope.

I had managed to be a good hostess for another two hours, Roxy and I talking about our Parisian adventures before filing everybody out. Roxy wasn't in a very talkative mood, actually showered and dressed in a pair of my cotton pajamas before going to my bedroom to sleep. I had told her I was waiting up for Stephen, so I was going to chill in the living room.

I showered, dressing in a pair of red silk pajamas, leaving my cropped hair wet and curly atop my head. I turned on my stereo; *The Best Man* Soundtrack quietly playing Sygnature's cut, "Wherever You Go." I lay on the couch, singing along with the CD.

When my clock struck midnight, I felt a tear at my heart. Stephen hadn't shown up, and I wasn't about to call him, like I was begging to see him. Him not coming by told me all I needed to know. He didn't love me; I was purely a warm body to get up close and personal with. I had to chalk this up to one of the few *big* mistakes in my life, the first one being ever giving myself to Stephen in the first place.

I turned the lamp beside my sofa off, curled up and cried myself to sleep.

Stephen...

I felt so relieved after seeing Paris. She was still sick of course, but doing much better, and she appeared so happy to see her daddy. She even got me to go pick up her Playstation and TV from home and hook it up so that we could play games, which of course the nurses frowned on, including Shelby, but using my sweet talking technique, I was able to bring the nurses around. Shelby just smiled and shook her head at us. She had been with Paris night and day, and I knew she was tired, so I volunteered to stay with Paris for the night. Shelby was relieved, saying she would be back in the morning. I thought about Deandra, vowing to myself that I would have to call her and let her know I wouldn't be able to see her till tomorrow. I HAD to talk to her.

Around 7 a.m., I woke up, not knowing where I was at first, till I recognized Shelby. "Get up man, I want to give Paris a shower and you could use one yourself," she said, sniffing at me and laughing.

"Dang, I didn't know you were coming here this early." Yawning, I agreed that I really did need to go home and shower, and maybe grab some breakfast. I had fallen asleep playing games with Paris, not even getting a chance to call Dee I suddenly remembered. *Damn, Lord knows what she must be thinking.*

"I'll be back at lunch time, baby, okay?" I told Paris, kissing her soundly on the cheek. She shook her head no, and pointed to her lips. "*MWAH!*" I kissed her again, this time a wet one on the lips, she giggled weakly. "Lata, boo."

I made my way to Deandra's. Forget a shower and breakfast. I needed to get this thing straight with her and fast. After ringing her bell for a few minutes, I felt the nerves hitting. I knew she was there. Her car was right in front of her building. Just as that thought hit she opened the door, her eyes swollen and red, as if she had been crying for hours. I felt my heart drop to my stomach.

"Baby I'm sorry! I was gonna come back like I said, I swear…you've been crying?"

"Stephen, look. You have nothing to be sorry about. I'm the one who has been a fool, and who allowed myself to be taken away by a Paris illusion of love." She turned her back to me, walking back into her apartment as I followed her in.

"No, honest, it wasn't an illusion. It was real. I had gone to the hospital last night. That was Shelby on the phone. I tried to tell you before. Paris had woken up asking for me so I went, and she wanted me to stay with her last night, so I meant to call you during the night and let you know, but I fell asleep, honestly Deandra," I pleaded.

She breathed deeply, leaning against her wet bar with her eyes closed. "Alright then. I hope she's okay?

"She is, much better, I have to go back at lunchtime, but I felt we needed to talk, I don't like things this way between us."

I walked up to her at the wet bar, slipping my hands around her small waist, trying to pull her close. "*Don't Stephen…*" she cried, not pushing me away, but turning her face to the side so that I wouldn't be able to look into her eyes. "Don't use me for your play thing."

"I'm not," I whispered against her neck, "I love you..."

She laughed in jerky hiccups. "You're just saying that because you're what? Horny?"

Because I'm horny? No she didn't say that, dayum! "Dayum, Deandra, do you really think I'm that much of a dog? Did I say it before just to get in your panties? I wouldn't say it if I didn't feel it, dayum!" I walked away from her, flopping down on the couch and running my hands over my face. *A brotha is damned if he does and damned if he doesn't,* I thought to myself.

"So...you meant it?" she asked, touching my arm tentatively as she sat down beside me, "Baby..."

"Did you really think that time in France was any *less* meaningful to me than it was for you? That I wasn't feeling you just as much as you were feeling me? Yes, I meant it. I love you, with everything inside me." Her face changed, from hurt, to doubtful, to hopeful, to this beautiful glowing look that radiated from her to me. She moved closer, putting her hand to my cheek in which I promptly kissed.

"I love you too, Stephen, so much." Pulling my face close she explored my mouth, straining against me and moaning deeply. We both pulled away breathlessly after a moment. "Why didn't you say it back after I did last night? Shoot, you could have spared me a bucket of tears." She pouted. I licked at her bottom lip.

"If you recall, I didn't say I *didn't* love you, and in the middle of that conversation Sha and Tee showed up. Deandra I knew how I felt about you, but I didn't define it as love as quickly as you did, that's all. Yes I have been a womanizing type of man. I didn't come at you thinking I had found my one and only. I came at you thinking you were fine and I wanted to kick it with you. But that was before, before you put your magic on me."

"What magic?" she whispered, tears of joy rolling down her beautiful face.

I kissed her again, pulling her close into my arms. "Before you took my fears of commitment, and my fears of real love, you made them disappear like smoke." I touched her soft blushing cheek, admiring in wonderment again her beautiful eyes. "And you gave my heart a home."

"God, Stephen." Deandra sighed, kissing my lips lightly, "Thank you for coming into my life."

They say that all black women are waiting to exhale, but one thing black women may not be aware of about us so called playa brothas, is that we are roaming simply in search of a place of our own. And while wrapping my arms around Deandra Winters, hell I felt like Dorothy from *The Wizard of Oz*, and one pure thought came to my mind...I don't have to roam any longer, because there's no place like home.

EPILOGUE:

⭐ One Year Later

"I swear, this baby is too cute!" Shameika cooed, holding little Rosalind in her arms. At nine months old, Chris and Tamara's daughter was the darling of the gang. The next *ruff rider* Shameika joked.

"Yes she is," Tamara joined in, dressed in her overalls and a tank top. Pushing her wiry hair behind her ears, Tamara hopped over to Shameika, causing squeals to erupt from her daughter's mouth. "She's just a *bootiful* baby," she chimed, reaching to pick up Rosalind, holding her close and rocking her gently. "I think Chris and I did a good job." They laughed.

"The guys trying to hook it up out there." Deandra laughed, entering the sun porch of Chris and Tamara's house. Smells of barbecued spared ribs, hot dogs, and hamburgers wafted to the porch as they sizzled up on the grill. Last year, Tamara bequeathed her house as the spot to be for Memorial Day and this was their Second Annual Grimes' Memorial Day Cookout. "All three of those knuckleheads pushed me away from the grill, talking about *this a man thang*. You know, I'm not even gonna say I told you so when they burn stuff up."

Deandra sat her tall frame, clad in an Orioles shorts set, beside Shameika, giving her a squeeze. "Hey!" She smiled up at Rosalind's golden round face, Rosalind's gray eyes shining down at her smiling. "There's my girl, looking all cute in her red overalls." Rosalind cooed back, as if talking, resulting in laughter from the women.

"Roxy told me to tell y'all wassup," Deandra went on. "You

know she's up at school in New York and her finals are next week, so she decided to study for them."

"This is her last semester, right?" Tamara asked, sitting in a rocking chair opposite the porch swing Shameika and Deandra sat on.

"Yea, graduation is June 10th. We all got invites. Sis is getting her bachelors in interior designing. All her credits miraculously transferred and all she had to take was her interior design courses. Actually got her first paying gig."

"Dang!" Shameika yelled. "She betta just go on with her bad self. I'm afraid of her."

"You and me both." Deandra laughed. "I'm just happy she's happy. Mom, Dad and I helped her search schools all over the country, told her to take some career assessment tests, sit and think about what she wanted to do with her life. Took a minute, but homegirl got it together."

"Well, so do you." Tamara smiled, playing kissy face with Rosalind. "I mean dang, been with the Os for over a year now, I saw your face on the front of *Baltimore* magazine last week...they're calling you a rising star in the sports industry, Girl. Had that sexy Cal and Brady beside you while you struck that *power* pose." They laughed. "Have you smelled yourself lately?" Tamara covered Rosalind's ears. "Cause you the shit."

Deandra laughed, running her right hand over her short curls. "Yea," Shameika chimed in, "and what about that?" Shameika pointed to the two-carat, marquise-cut diamond that perched atop Deandra's slender finger.

"Well, what about *that*?" Deandra countered, pointing to the pearl and diamond ring that graced Shameika's finger. Shameika laughed, her shoulder-length micro braids brushing along the sides of her face.

"Well we *know* about Sha." Tamara laughed. "When we gonna be hearing them bells, Dee?"

"I've been asking this girl that for a month now," Stephen

said, as he, along with Chris and Joop came in from the backyard. Deandra got up, allowing Stephen to sit down before placing herself in his lap. His arms slithered around her waist as he
dropped a kiss on the back of her neck.

Deandra laughed. "Well, like I told my *fiancé*, I want to find
a house first, and get settled in…I also told him that I would
like a Christmas Eve wedding."

Stephen nodded. "Oh yea, you did say that."

Shameika laughed, kissing Joop's lips. "See, y'all sound
married already. He ain't even listening to you, Girl!" Everyone
laughed.

"Oh, Chris," Shameika added, reaching over into her backpack to slip a book out. "My psych professor wanted to know if
you would autograph this." Shameika handed Chris a copy of
his book, his first book, which was published earlier this year,
already a rousing success. "I think knowing you're gonna get
me my A!"

Chris chuckled. "Yea, I'll sign it. Want an A+? Tell her I'll
also give her a signed copy of my second book when it drops at
the end of the year."

"Shoot," Joop said, sidling up beside Shameika, "seems like
everything popping off at the end of the year. My babygirl and
I are getting married in September. Chris' second book drops in
November, more wedded bliss when Dee and Step make it
down that aisle in December…"

"Guess we need to start planning, huh?" Stephen whispered
in Dee's ear.

Turning her head, Dee smiled, kissing Stephen. "Oh, I know
you know that's right."

"Well, I have a little news, too," Tamara said, holding a
sleeping Rosalind.

"If you say you're pregnant, I might have to tackle you,"
Shameika joked. Tamara blushed.

Everyone's eyes went to Chris, who was beaming right

along with his wife. "Y'all just a damn baby machine!"
Shameika laughed. As if déjà vu, Chris took his sleeping daughter from Tamara as Shameika and Deandra ran to hug her.

Tamara laughed. "You know, the biggest day of my life is
when I found out. Last week, I was talking to the publishing
company that wants me to write a book about sisters on the
web, and while in the middle of contract negotiations, boom, I
got sick."

"Oh no!" Deandra laughed, along with everyone else.

"Yea, *oh no*. I managed to make it to the bathroom before
getting really sick, but afterwards I went straight to my doctor
and was like, I think I'm pregnant. She ran the test and con-
gratulated me. I'm only a little over a month along, but I'm a
mommy-to-be again!"

"And my mommy-to-be needs food," Chris said, kissing the
top of Tamara's head. "Come on, guys. Everything is ready and,
if I do say so myself, tasting damn good." Everybody rose to go
out into the backyard, Tamara snatching up the baby carrier.

"Hey," Tamara said, smiling. "I heard that the big house two
doors down is going on the market. The couple is retiring and
moving to Florida. What do you think?"

Deandra glanced at Stephen, who smiled back at her. "We
ain't never gonna get rid of each other, are we?" Deandra joked.

"Hell naw!" Shameika laughed. "We're stuck together like
glue! We're the Three Musketeers!"

"No," Joop said, "*we* are." Everybody laughed as they made
their way out onto the lawn, Shameika and Joop still battling
over which sex deserved the title of the Three Musketeers.

"Well while those two are fighting over who the REAL
Three Musketeers are, I'd like to make a toast." Christopher
said. He handed a Hi C juice box to each.

"Hi C! Damn brotha this is gonna make me throw up, I need
some liquor!" Stephen laughed.

"Shut up, Step!" the ladies said, laughing.

"My Boo likes Hi C," Chris winked at Tamara. "You can get your drink on in a minute." They laughed. "As I was saying, this is a toast, to the two best friends a brotha could ever have, and the three most beautiful sistahs in the world." He raised his juice box up. "Here's to brotherhood, sisterhood, and most of all, love."

"Always…" Tamara said softly as she looked at Chris, remembering fondly their words spoken together two years prior.

Shameika, Joop, Chris, Tamara, and Deandra and Stephen, all raised their juice boxes together, feeling like the six musketeers rather than the double set of threes they once were, singing out in unison, "LUVALWAYZ!"

Special Preview

Draw Me In With Your Love

By Shonell Bacon and JDaniels

Draw Me With Your Love is the second novel in the LUVAL-WAYZ trilogy. Set in the Big Apple, this exciting novel reintroduces Roxy Winters, the notorious baby sister of Deandra from Part Three of LUVALWAYZ. Roxy has picked up the pieces of her frail past and has moved on to New York where she is about to graduate college and look for a job in interior designing. She falls into a plum position at a hip art gallery, designing a bookstore and café for the gallery, and it's this job that propels Roxy into her first love: ART. Her boss and soon-to-be friend insists that Roxy goes on The Art of Life cruise to capture her love, but she captures more than art when she meets Antoine Billups, an up and rising Manhattan artist. Right away, the two are lost in mutual attraction, but as the cruise ends, so too does their road to a relationship. Roxy's past won't allow her to open her heart to love, but little does she know that her heart has its own plans, and it includes making a love connection with Antoine.

Antoine's best friend, Nicole has serious doubts about the mysterious Roxy, but as her own life becomes devastated by the affects of hatred and homophobia, she finds it hard to offer Antoine much advice.

Despite her plans to thwart a romance between herself and Antoine, Roxy finds herself immersed into a super romantic love story that seeks the final destination of luvalwayz.

Past lives, lies and outside interference threaten the young lovebirds in their quest for luvalwayz, and Roxy can't help but wonder: Will she ever get the love of her life and the artist of her dreams to help her cast away her demons? Will he be able to work his artistic magic on her soul, by drawing her with his love?

Chapter Six

Nicky

"**D**ammit!" I exclaimed to myself. I was fuming over the $200 food cost bill I had just gotten for the $500 luncheon I had catered the week before at Ingles Incorporated. Adding it up, I could see that I had basically been jipped. Had to pay that lazy bitch Jennie her seventy-five, and that left me…grrrr, it was too indecent even to think about!

"These little luncheon gigs are just NOT panning out."

"Girl are you in here talking to yourself again?" I turned around to see Mya's smiling face.

"Hey, baby girl," I crooned. "Damn, I've missed you!" I swiveled over, slipping my hands around Mya's slim waist, lifted her chin up to mine, and brought her thick juicy lips up for a kiss. Mya flickered her hot tongue against mine, causing me to give her tight little ass a squeeze.

"Mmmm…" she moaned. "Girl, you know you need to stop, making a sistah's body get to humming."

"Uh-huh, I'll make it hum alright." I smirked. "And what you doing here anyhow? Hubby finally let you out the house?"

"Hubby ain't got nothing to do with this," Mya said, smiling. I had been bumping with Mya for about six months now, regardless of the fact that Mya was married to a man, that was HER biz, frankly I didn't and still don't believe in relationships, not gay ones, not straight ones, notta. There were very few gay women or gay men, that I knew of, who actually were able to make a committed relationship work, and Mya's so-called MARRIAGE to her husband, yet her weekly coming by to hit it with me, also showed that he/she marriages weren't all the scream people try to make them to be either.

Mya wandered purposely into my bedroom, not even looking behind her. I smiled. Cocky bitch, she knew I'd follow her sexy ass. I stood at the door watching as Mya slipped off her thin, short summer dress, letting it slowly slip to her feet. She was looking good. Standing braless, with her perky high tits and black thong. I stood watching for a brief moment, seeing the heat in her eyes, walked into the room, pulling my DMX tee shirt over my head. I was about to take off my own bra and jean shorts before something in Mya's eyes got the better of me, causing me to swiftly walk up to her, fall to my knees where her hot, swollen love was sizzling before my lips. I pulled the crouch part of her thong aside, and planted my lips against her heat.

It was gonna be a hot afternoon.

I re-plaited my final braid, and had just showered and changed into my regs. This time my EVE tee shirt, boy boxers with baggie FUBU shorts, which hung loosely on my hips. I took a last look in the mirror and chuckled. I mean let's face it; I was not what one would call a girly

girl by any means. Maybe I wasn't the smoking cigars, flipping people the bird dyke type of chick, but I was definitely what was considered, soft butch.

I was headed down the cluttered hallway to grab my mail when the double doors to my apartment building came creaking open.

"Antoine!" I screamed. Antoine's face lit up, showing me that famous ear-to-ear smile of his. Now Antoine, that was my booboo, not my boo. See, I don't have boos, male nor female, but Antoine was my booboo, my baby. He had just spent a whole week cruising away in the Caribbean, and damn had I ever missed him!

"Baby, you're back!" I ran down the stairs, giving him a big squeeze.

"Yep!" He smiled, hugging me back. "My plane got in last night. I had to pop by and see you, sis, and grab my mail too, by the way." He laughed. Antoine had this cute laugh and voice that sounded and had always reminded me of Lorenz Tate's voice. Now Lorenz Tate, he was cute. I had always said that if I had ever been into dudes, I would have had to taste me something that looked like him. Now my booboo didn't look nothing like him, but he sure sounded like him. Antoine was chocolate and beautiful, but what made him unique was that his features, or most of them, weren't black at all, just that deep brown skin, and them fat ass lips.

"What you looking at, yo?" He laughed.

"Just breathing you in and thinking about how good you look, Suga. I've missed you…" I touched his cheek. Damn I loved this boy.

"Well I've missed you, too," he said, his eyes getting a soft look in them as he looked into mine. I was about to give him another tight hug when I sensed someone behind him. "And…" He continued, "I have someone I want you to meet. This is Roxy. Roxy, this is my sis and best friend in the whole world, Nicky."

The short, redbone creature smiled a toothpaste cheesy grin at me, and it hit me as soon as I saw her. She reminded me of those girls back in high school that used to make my life a living hell. The cheerleader types that would always call me names like dyke and lesbo.

"Hello, Nicky. It's so nice to meet you. Antoine has told me so much about you," she cooed.

Something was happening, I felt my fingertips tingling, as my invisible claws started making their way out.

Antoine and I, and his new friend, were sitting comfortably at my kitchen table. I stood up to get some glasses. "So, Roxy, do you drink? I know you don't, Antoine." I laughed.

"And you know it," he said, smiling. "Got milk?"

"Yeah, I got some milk for you." I gave my breast a lil squeeze. Miss Girl got pretty red in the face at that, and I just had to laugh.

"You're a mess, Nicky." Antoine laughed, shaking his head. "Didn't I tell you she was a trip, Roxy?"

"Yes, you did," she said. "Do you have any white wine?"

"Nope, got sum Thunderbird and grapefruit juice. That's whatcha call Ghetto-mixer. I take it that's not your speed right?" I raised my eyebrow at her.

"I've had Thunderbird before. I may surprise you. So, Nicky, Antoine says that you are a cook?"

Why was my face burning? A cook? "I'm no fuckin' cook, girl. I'm a caterer and pastry chef. A CHEF! You understand?"

"Ah, OK, my bad." She laughed. The lil skinny bitch was laughing at me. I hated when someone called me a cook. I had been to two different schools, one in Stanton Island and one in New Jersey, mastering the art of cuisine. The last thing I would call myself is a damn cook!

"Well, anyway, I'll take some of that Ghetto-mixer," she quirked, with this amused look on her face.

After we got settled with our drinks and Antoine's milk, Miss Thang proceeded to tell me more about herself. How she and Antoine had been working out and had met on the cruise and how they were friends, which bugged me the fuck out. How she could sit here and tell me she was all friendly with MY best friend, as if she were introducing him to me.

298

"So what, you two were kickin' it on the love boat, huh?"

Antoine looked at me with a cut it out stare. I shrugged and smiled innocently.

"The love boat. Now wouldn't that have been fun," Roxy said animatedly. "Really, we are just friends. I just looked him up when we got back here and wanted to know if he wanted to go work out."

"Well, you just got back yesterday. Didn't waste any time, did you?"

Antoine broke in, changing the subject. "So what have you been up to, Nick?"

"Well, working as always, and oh! You know you missed Nelly at Jays the other night, boy! He was off da heezy. If I was ever into dudes, I'd have to do him!"

"Ever into dudes. What do you mean, Nicky?" Roxy asked.

Damn, I had almost forgot that Miss Thang was sitting there.

"Nuttin, honey. Just a figure of speech." I cheesed a smile. The last thing I was going to do is tell some chick like her my business. I was just so used to being open and free with Antoine.

"Well, Antoine, I'm still feeling a lil jet lag. Still a bit off from the cruise. So I'm gonna go catch my train, OK?" Roxy announced.

"Listen, why don't you let me call you a cab?"

I finished off the last sip of my Thunderbird, watching their exchange. Antoine was digging this girl and there was something about her that I wasn't digging, at all...

About the Authors

Shonell Bacon's first passion and love is writing. A member of Blackwriters.org and Chief Editor of the online African American literary e-zine, **The Nubian Chronicles**, Shonell has written several short stories and poems, having pieces showcased at TimBooktu, Sisterfriends.com, Prolific Writers, Shades of Romance magazine, Merci magazine, and Daily Diva.

Currently, Shonell is at work on promoting **LUVALWAYZ** with co-author JDaniels as well as penning another novel with JDaniels while working on a screenplay.

Shonell is a 1996 graduate of the College of Notre Dame of Maryland (B. A. degree) and a 2001 graduate of Towson University (M. A. degree). She was born in Baltimore, Maryland and currently resides there.

JDaniels is a native Virginian, who is presently living and working in Frederick, Maryland. Having a multitude of interests, writing has always been a first love, including poetry and song/lyric writing. Right now, JDaniels is working on the completion of the third novel of the **LUVALWAYZ** trilogy, along with Shonell Bacon and has recently completed the romantic adventure, 'Serpent in My Corner.'

JDaniels is a staff writer, co-founder and an editor for the popular online e-zine **The Nubian Chronicles**, and is co-founder of **TNC Communications**, which is a portal on the web designed to assist new and established writers to create a web presence, along with providing promotional support.

Presently JDaniels is writing diligently and seeking a Bachelors degree in English.

Visit the authors online at www.luvalways.com.

ORDER FORM

Use this form to order additional copies of *Strebor Books International* Bestselling titles as they become available.

Name: _____

Company _____

Address: _____

_____

City: _____ State _____ Zip _____

Phone: (_____) _____ Fax: (_____) _____

E-mail: _____

Credit Card: ☐ Visa   ☐ MC   ☐ Amex   ☐ Discover

Number _____

Exp Date: _____ Signature: _____

	ITEM	PRICE	QTY
1.	*The Sex Chronicles by Zane*	$ 15.00	
2.	*Shame On It All by Zane*	$ 15.00	
3.	*Luvalways by Shonell Bacon & JDaniels*	$ 15.00	
4.	*Daughter by Spirit by V. Anthony Rivers*	$ 15.00	
6	*God's Bastards Sons by D. V. Bernard*	$ 15.00	
7.	*All That and A Bag of Chips by Darrien Lee*	$ 15.00	
8.			
9.			
10.			

Subtotal	
shipping	
5% tax (MD)	
Total	

SHIPPING INFORMATION	
Ground one book	$ 3.00
each additional book	$ 1.00

Make checks or money orders payable to
Strebor Books International
Post Office Box 10127
Silver Spring, Maryland 20914